**Also available from Rhenna Morgan
and Carina Press**

Men of Haven series

Rough & Tumble
Wild & Sweet
Claim & Protect
Tempted & Taken
Stand & Deliver
Down & Dirty

NOLA Knights series

His to Defend
Hers to Tame

Ancient Ink series

Guardian's Bond
Healer's Need

Also available from Rhenna Morgan

Unexpected Eden
Healing Eden
Waking Eden
Eden's Deliverance

TRUSTED & TRUE

RHENNA MORGAN

carina
press

**carina
press®**

Recycling programs
for this product may
not exist in your area.

ISBN-13: 978-1-335-63995-0

Trusted & True

Copyright © 2022 by Rhenna Morgan

Carina Press
22 Adelaide St. West, 41st Floor
Toronto, Ontario M5H 4E3, Canada
www.CarinaPress.com

Printed in U.S.A.

For my dad. I still miss you.

TRUSTED & TRUE

Chapter One

Callie

"Hi, my name's Callie, and I'm an alcoholic and drug addict." Off and on for over six years, those exact words had rolled off my tongue countless times. Today, the quaver in my voice made it sound like it was day one.

The people seated in the circle around me echoed back a strong and friendly, "Hi, Callie."

And then there was nothing but silence.

Silence and a host of patient expressions aimed my way while I clasped my sweat-slick, shaking hands a little tighter in my lap. For the first time in a long time, I didn't recognize a single face in the room. None, that is, except my sponsor who'd helped me move over the weekend and now sat on my right.

I cleared my throat before I spoke—not that it did much in the way of adding confidence. "So... I'm new to the Dallas area."

Nope, not really true. Try again, missy.

Shrugging, I let out an exhale on a self-deprecating chuckle. "Okay, *returned* is probably more like it. I left here a little over six years ago for Louisiana. It was either go to treatment there, or pay for my drinking and drugging with a bullet to the head."

I glanced at my sponsor, Maggie, beside me.

Damn, but that woman was an angel. Hard as hell when she needed to be and never let me off easy when I had my head up my ass, but seemed to have an unlimited supply of patience where I was concerned. She smiled and dipped her head in encouragement.

Letting out a slow breath, I wiped my hands on my jeans. "The thing is, that trip to rehab didn't work. I mean, it did for a bit. And it definitely screwed up my being able to stick my head in the sand about my using, but it took me another six trips through hell before this time around."

That horrifying sensation of having an invisible noose wrapped round my throat cinched a little tighter, remembering what had finally brought me to where I was today. "Three hundred and seventy-two days ago, I woke up naked in a bedroom I didn't recognize to the sound of gunshots. Not that waking up naked in an unfamiliar house was all that abnormal, but gunshots and a whole lot of yelling and screaming...yeah, that scared the living hell out of me. Worse, I was still fucked up enough I couldn't move very well and didn't have the sense God gave a goose. I ended up jumping out of the bedroom window half-dressed and earned myself a broken forearm and some pretty scars from broken glass."

I ran one finger across a particularly nasty one that cut across the back of my wrist, the blood that had covered my skin that day still vividly bright in my mind. "I spent a long time that day tryin' to call someone—anyone—to come help me." I shook my head at the empty center of the circle before I met the gaze of a late twenties or early thirties man right across from me. He didn't know me any more than I knew him, but he knew exactly what I was talking about. The recognition—the *understanding*—was right there in his eyes. "No one would take my calls. I had no money. Nowhere to go. No friends or family who'd have anything to do with me. The only thing I had to claim for myself was another fucked up situation…and that's when I hit my bottom. Not so much because of how banged up I was, but because I had nothing. No self-respect. No life. No love. No home. *Nothing.* And the really sad thing? I found out the next day that the house I'd been in? Whoever was shooting it up left no one alive. If the gunner had shown even a few hours earlier, a gunshot wouldn't have been loud enough to wake me up, and I'd be dead, too—with absolutely no one who'd mourn me."

Finally, some of the weight on my chest lifted and the air-conditioning finally registered against my clammy skin. I jerked my head toward Maggie. "I called my sponsor. Or at least she'd been my sponsor before the last time I jumped off the wagon. I wasn't too sure she'd be willing to talk to me after ignoring everything she'd shared with me before, but she told me she'd never walk away from me if I was willing to do the work. So, I started going to meetings again and really working the steps instead of paying lip service to them. Now, here I am a little over a year later—finishing my unpacking on Independence Day, which I think is ironic as hell—and ready to face my past by making some serious amends. And let me tell y'all… I'm terrified. I mean, it's one thing to own up to my character defects, but facing the people I hurt and seeing if they spit in my face?" I shook my head. "I'm not all that sure I'm ready for it. But I know I need to. I know working the steps and clearing out all the trash cluttering my life is the only way I'm gonna make it sober. And I want that. I really want it. I want healthy friends. I want a chance to have my sister in my life again and to show her there's more to me than just drugs and alcohol and problems."

I scanned the people in the circle and forced the muscles in my shoulders to relax. "So, yeah. That's why I'm here joining a new group and what I'm out to do. If you guys have a call list or some regular times you meet up for coffee, I'd sure appreciate healthy people to hang with while I'm looking for a job. And thanks for letting me share."

Maggie's hand covered mine and a host of people around the room offered a litany of *Keep coming back* and *Glad you're here.*

Yeah, ninety-nine percent of the people around me were strangers and their responses were about as standard at an AA meeting as a postage stamp on a letter, but I needed every one of them.

This was actually happening.

I was within short-range driving distance of all the bullshit I'd left behind and speeding toward very possible, if not probable, rejection.

But it was what I needed to stay sober, and this time I wasn't going to rob myself of the chance at a good life. Of having some self-respect and an existence I could be proud of—whether it meant staring rejection in the face or not.

Twenty minutes and a group recitation of the Lord's Prayer later, the meeting was over and the roomful of recovering alcoholics just like me were on their feet, sharing hugs and handshakes, and cleaning up.

Her red hobo bag already thrown over one shoulder, Maggie tucked her empty water bottle under one arm and folded up her chair. At sixty-two years old, she had the same or more energy than some twentysomethings and had a penchant for the gaudiest jewelry on the planet. She loved the sun almost as much as she loved to laugh and her skin showed it, the overexposure and constant smiles etching deep wrinkles on her face. "They seem like a quality group. Lots of sobriety in attendance. Got at least one meeting a day and it's close to your new place, too. That'll come in handy."

I snickered under my breath and followed her with my own chair to the rack designated for stowing them away until the next meeting. "Is that your crafty way of telling me I'd be wise to hit as many meetings as possible while I settle in?"

"No such thing as too many meetings, little girl. Not even for me, and I've been sober almost half as long as I've been alive." She paused and considered me, her brown gaze cutting right to the core of the matter in no time. "How ya holding up?"

Knowing my lifeline was all of ten or fifteen minutes from motoring back to Louisiana and leaving me without an anchor, the answer was a no-brainer. "Nervous as hell. Wondering why I had this stupid idea in the first place. Or if I'm even ready yet."

"You're ready. And you had the idea because your Higher Power gave it to you. Hard to make amends to people when you're in a completely different state. Especially the kind of amends you've gotta make." She slung an arm around my shoulder and steered me toward the long folding table near the room's entrance and the woman packing up all the welcome literature that had been laid out for newcomers. "Come on. Let's see if they've got a phone list handy before you walk me out to my car."

The midforties-looking blonde who'd also been the leader for tonight's meeting stacked all the meeting paraphernalia into the bottom of a two-drawer filing cabinet and punched the lock button at the top corner. She stood, surveyed the space around her as though double-checking for something, then threw up her hands and turned our direction. The second she laid eyes on Maggie and me, her eyes got big, and a chagrined smile warmed her face. "Darn it! I *knew* I was forgetting something!" She held up one finger, then dug a set of keys from the front pocket of her jeans. "I pulled a call sheet just for you, then stacked it on top of everything else while I was packing. Let me just grab it for you."

"No hurry on my account," I said with a chuckle. "The only thing waiting for me at home are boxes and maybe some fast food."

"At least you can eat fast food," Maggie grumbled. "The way salt hits my system, I eat so much as a French fry and I'm blown up like a puffer fish by morning."

I snorted at that. "Like that ever stopped you from a run through the McDonald's drive-thru. And, for the record, you're the only person on the planet who ever thinks you look puffy. You've got a metabolism most women would kill for."

She raised her hands in mock surrender and added, "What can I say? God knew givin' up booze was gonna be hard enough, so he gave me the means to scarf back my fair share of Big Macs."

"Okay!" the blonde said as she stood and locked the file cabinet once more. "Here we go." She handed over two sheets of paper. "One call list and a rundown of our meetings. We've got a lot of active members who've been in the program awhile and are fortunate to have a strong enough attendance to keep our own building running."

I took the sheet, glancing at the long list of meetings offered throughout the week before I folded the papers in half and tucked them in my purse. "You're Susan, right?"

"Yep. Secretary for our group. Been sober for coming up on seven years."

Seven years.

I'd barely wrapped my head around the fact that I'd actually made it past one trip around the sun without a fix. To make it as long as she had—or for that matter, as long as Maggie had—defied my somewhat vivid imagination. "That's really nice. Someday I'd like that for myself."

Her smile softened and warmed. "As honest as you were tonight, something tells me you're on the right track. Just one day at a time."

"Amen to that," Maggie added. She opened her mouth as though to say something else, but a man stepped close enough to catch her eye and interrupt.

"Excuse me." He looked to Maggie and Susan first before he centered on me. "My name's Jason. Sorry to interrupt, but I've gotta be someplace and wanted to give you something before I leave."

Whoa. He's hot.

Strawberry blond hair cut nice, a closely cropped beard to match, and a killer smile. I was so caught up in appreciating the overall package it took a sluggish few seconds before I figured out he was the same guy

I'd locked stares with across the room while sharing. "Something for me?"

Maggie dipped her head toward the business card he held extended out to me and raised an eyebrow.

"Oh. Right. Duh." I took the simple white card. Aside from the heavily slanted font for the business name, it was just his name and a number beneath it. "What's Street Dreamz?"

"It's where I work. We make custom cars and motorcycles for people. You mentioned you were looking for a job. As far as I know, my boss hasn't started looking for anyone yet, but there hasn't been a day in the last two months he hasn't said he needs an office manager. It's only a mile from here, so I thought you might wanna hit him up and see if he'll give you a shot."

"An office manager?" I glanced at Maggie before routing my attention back to Jason. "What do they do?"

He shrugged and chuckled. "Beats the shit out of me. I just work on the rides. But if I had to guess, it's mostly answering phones, ordering parts and inventory, and making sure the rest of us don't make the boss's life a living hell."

Hmmm. Office manager, huh? It sounded nice. Too nice, actually. I fingered the edge of the business card and peeked at Maggie. "Wouldn't I have to have some experience for a gig like this or something? I mean, if he's looking for a manager doesn't that mean he'd want someone who's done it before?"

It was Susan who answered. "Oh, honey. Don't get wrapped up in the title. First off, everyone's gotta start somewhere. Even managers. Second, it doesn't sound like you'd be managing people. Just organizing things and making sure the business runs smoothly."

"And trust me," Jason said. "My boss is about as chill as they come. Or he was until business took off and he opened up two more shops. All he wants is someone to take the paperwork off his back so he can get back to workin' on cars."

He lifted his chin toward the card. "Seriously. Stop by tomorrow if you get a chance and hit him up. Even if he's not ready to pull the trigger on some help, he's got a ton of connections with other people who might be looking for help."

An odd and completely foreign lightness stirred inside me, and for some stupid reason my lungs had a hard time doing their job. Like they were afraid to move for fear of screwing up the opportunity or something. Nodding, I awkwardly held out my hand. "Feels a bit like a Hail Mary, but what the heck, right? Thanks for the lead, man."

His smile really was a killer. A perfect mix of bad boy and momma's angel that would have had me doing everything in my power to latch onto him a little over a year ago. He shook my hand and dipped his head to Maggie and Susan. "No problem. Sorry to share and run, but good luck."

He'd barely turned away before Susan made her own hasty exit. "I hate to leave you hanging, too, but I've got two teenagers chomping at the bit to make the city's big fireworks display." With zero hesitation, she opened her arms for a hug and pulled me in tight. "My name's on the list. You need anything—anything at all—you just call." She backed away, gave Maggie a quick hug as well and then hustled off with a backward wave. "Y'all have a good night."

"Ahhh…" Maggie said on a happy sigh. "I'm so

damned glad my child-rearing days are over. I swear to God, every gray hair on my head came to pass because of adolescence and hormones."

The comment did the trick and pulled me out of my semi-stupor. "You're a brunette!"

"Only thanks to my hairdresser, little girl. Now, come on." She steered me with a hand at my arm toward the building's exit and the parking lot beyond. "Get me to my car so I can get on the road. I don't mind the long ride home, but those seven hours aren't going to drive themselves."

Outside, it was typical summer in Texas—hot and muggy. The sun made its last descent behind the AA clubhouse, casting the asphalt parking lot and all the people meandering to their cars in much welcome shade. To the east, the skies had darkened just enough to promise a few stars. "Gonna be a good night for fireworks," I said for no particular reason.

Well, that wasn't entirely true. It was more that I was scrambling for something—anything—to keep the woman who'd been my lifeline for the last year close to me a minute longer. Even if it was just small talk.

From the understanding on Maggie's face, she knew exactly what was going on. "You know, you could go back in the clubhouse and go watch the show with those people who said they were going. You might make some new friends and have some fun while you're at it."

I crammed my hands in the front pockets of my jeans and studied the pavement while Maggie unlocked the door to her old sky blue Cadillac and tossed her purse to the passenger's seat. "I thought about it. Truth is, I feel like some time alone tonight unpacking might be better for me. Give me some time to process every-thing I'm feeling."

As was her way, Maggie nodded. "Well, then, go with your gut. Just don't let those feelings lead you to the liquor store. Make a call instead."

"Yes, ma'am," I said with a mock salute.

She snorted and pulled me in for a hug. "Smart-ass."

For the longest time, she just held me, ever so slightly shifting from side to side.

Funny. Every time she hugged me like this, I found myself searching for one single time my mom had held me this way.

I always came up empty-handed.

My dad had been a hugger, but he was long dead and gone—a fact that still haunted way too much of my life. My sister, Vivienne, had been a hugger, too, when I'd dared to let her. But she'd stopped taking my calls after one too many drunk dials and me begging for money or a bailout.

My arms tightened of their own accord and that tight-ening in my throat came back with a vengeance. "Do you think she'll ever forgive me?" I whispered.

Maggie stepped back, holding me steady at my shoulders. "We talked about this, kiddo. Your job isn't to worry about whether or not she forgives you. That's your sister's choice to make. What matters is making your amends. Not just with words, but with how you live your life. How you change and grow. That's the part that matters. Everything else will work itself out like it needs to."

She was right. I knew it in my gut. Had felt the cleansing effect actually *working* the steps had had on my life the last year.

But that didn't make the fear and worry over what lay ahead for me lessen by any measurable degree. "Right," I said cramming my hands back in my pockets. It was either that or grab Maggie and refuse to let her go. "What did you think about the job Jason told me about?"

For a second, she looked at me funny, then let loose a full-bodied laugh that echoed across the parking lot. "Girl, for a second there, I thought you were asking me what I thought about Jason, not the job. Guess that shows where my brain was when he was talking to us."

"Well, he was pretty hot."

"He sure as hell was. And if you ask me, he seemed to take a healthy notice of you, too." She grinned huge. "Maybe you could see where *that* goes over the next few weeks, huh?"

Oh, no. No way was I muddying up my sobriety with anything related to males. "You and I both know I used men almost as bad as I used drugs and alcohol. The last thing I need right now is any kind of a slippery slope."

Maggie cocked her head to one side for a moment. When she spoke again, her voice was pure sincerity. "You know, a year ago, I'd have absolutely agreed with you. I'm a firm believer that people starting a program shouldn't make big changes or start relationships when they're just starting out. But the whole point of you coming here is to take the things you've learned and start applying them in your life. It's true you don't want to put yourself in slippery places, but relationships are part of life. A *necessary* part of life. It's not about putting half the population on the shelf the same way you do booze and drugs. It's about checking your motives before you take action and learning who's good for you and who's not."

Hmmm. At a logical level what she said made sense. But then again, most everything that came out of Maggie's mouth made sense. It was the rewiring process in my brain that usually took too damned long. "Not sure I trust my judgment on that playing field yet, but I hear what you're saying."

"Good. And as for the job—I'd jump on that opportunity in a hot minute. You mention in a meeting that you're looking for work and after the meeting someone gives you a lead—that's a prime example of your Higher Power working in your life if I've ever seen it. Regardless of if you get the job or not. Every single thing happens for a reason. If you can trust that and keep taking the best next-steps you can, you're gonna live a very happy, healthy life."

She tapped the roof of her car the same way a judge would tap his gavel. "Now, time for me to get on the road, little girl. You need me, you call me, but I expect you to start building up a support system here, too. Got it?"

Words weren't an option. Not if I wanted to keep my tears bottled up. So I nodded instead and swallowed past the lump in my throat.

Maggie slid behind the wheel, shut the door and fired up the engine. As she waved and started backing out of her parking spot, a part of me wanted to follow her. To find some excuse to make her stop and linger in the safety she represented a little longer.

Another part of me wanted to look away and stuff my fear as far down as it could go. To pretend everything was okay even though I was processing all the same emotions I'd wrestled the day my mom had walked out the door leaving me and Vivienne behind with Dad.

Neither approach was healthy, though. Maggie had taught me that. Had taught me that using was just a way to bury my feelings and ignore them, where healthy people faced them head-on until they passed.

This pain would pass. My fears would pass.

And I wasn't alone. Tonight's meeting had proven that. Not to mention given me a first step toward building my new life.

At the parking lot's exit, Maggie's brake lights eased and the engine to her Cadillac roared as she steered it onto the street and back to Louisiana.

A gentle breeze drifted across my face, leaving a subtle chill where it hit the tracks of my tears. It was the end of one chapter, but it was the beginning of another, too. An important one. Maybe the most important one of my life. And this time—*this time* I was determined to live it right.

Chapter Two

Danny

Six gallons of Purple Haze.

Six gallons of Kandy Apple Red.

Six gallons of Euro Green Metallic.

It had to be a fucking joke. *Had* to be. Either that or I'd lost my damned mind placing last week's paint order.

I thrust the clipboard with the invoice pinched to the top of it back to the delivery dude. "Man, you sure this isn't a computer glitch? Ain't no way we need that much for this week. That's a nine-car order and no way we'd do that many in the same fucking colors."

The delivery guy shrugged, obvi not giving two shits about who screwed up what and why. "Not my job to know what ends up on the truck. I just get it where it needs to go, and this says it goes to you." He shoved the clipboard in my direction. "You sign and then you can call the company and figure out what happened."

Digging deep for what little calm I had, I snatched the board out of his hand, pulled my pen from behind my ear and scratched out my signature at the bottom. The guy was right. It *wasn't* his job to know what was what. It was mine. And yet again, I'd come up too damned short of hitting the mark and costing myself at least a G on paint that wouldn't get used until I could find someone else interested in one of the colors.

I underlined my name so hard the ballpoint nearly cut through the paper, yanked my customer copy from underneath his original and tossed the board back to the driver. Not waiting for a response, I spun to the garage at large and bellowed my frustration to the guys working behind me. "Who's got orders with Purple Haze, Euro Green or Kandy Apple Red?"

Not exactly the classiest way to go about getting the paint in the right hands. I sure as shit couldn't envision any of my brothers barking at their employees, but my well was way past empty. I needed time alone with a car, my tools and room to let my brain unwind, and I needed it stat.

Even with the Strokes' newest release blasting from the speakers I'd mounted at either end of the garage, all the clanging and banging came to a standstill, and every head turned to me—most of them sporting a wary or confused expression.

Hard to blame them. With six bays and five solid workers, my shop in the Dallas suburb of Garland had churned out sweet custom rides nonstop for two solid years. Once upon a time, that had made me pretty damned happy and fun to work with, but considering the sixth bay was supposed to be for me and I rarely got to spend time in it anymore, I'd turned moodier than an angry old man with a bad case of crabs.

I held up my pink copy of the invoice and tried to make myself not sound like a royal dick. "Got the paint delivery for rides scheduled next week. Kandy Apple, Euro Green, and Purple Haze. Who needs 'em?"

Comprehension and a whole lot of relief settled on the collective faces, and Jason, Rick and Jamey stowed their tools and headed my way.

Letting out a huge, huffing exhale, I turned back to the stack of paint and planted my hands on my hips.

Jason reached me first and stated the obvious. "That's too big of an order."

"I thought you said only three colors came in," Rick added when he saw the pallet. "That's enough for nine cars."

Jamey just looked at all of us like we were nuts.

"Three colors," I said still staring at the delivery and trying to figure out what to do. "Three gallons each."

"Yeah, but I only ordered one of each," Jamey said.

I looked to Jamey at exactly the same time Rick and Jason snapped their gaze his direction. "You did what?"

"I took the stack of orders last Friday and ordered a gallon of each just like you told me to."

"Like *I* told you to?" I said.

"Shit," Jason muttered beside me. "I thought Danny told me it was my week to place the order. I did the same damned thing."

Rick cleared his throat, the look on his face saying the last thing he wanted to do was share what was on his mind. "I coulda sworn you told me to, boss. I made an order, too."

Well, hell.

Guess that explained how I'd ended up with three times the amount of paint we needed for the week.

Out of habit, my hands went to my head for either the beanie I usually wore through the winter or a fistful of hair. I came up empty on both—the skullcap getting ditched once temps had hit ninety-five last week and my long hair long-gone since my sister, Gabe, had talked me into cutting it over Christmas. I folded my fingers together at the back of my neck instead and stared up at the ceiling. "Right then. My bad."

Jason—cool head that he usually was—offered up a suggestion colored with a thread of humor. "Might be a good idea to write who's placing the order on the calendar by the desk, yo?"

"Yeah." I didn't dare take my eyes off the ceiling. How these guys tolerated my feeble attempts at management was beyond me. Maybe I just wasn't cut out for it. I'd thought for sure I could make it work, but maybe my brothers just made it look easy.

Overhead, the doorbell that indicated someone had entered the order room and the main office chimed. Malcom set his tools aside and took off at a jog to handle the meet and greet.

Thank God, I'd gotten scheduling right on that particular duty.

I forced a smile and scanned the guys. "I'll update the calendar and give everyone a week for ordering. In the meantime, if anyone has a job come in and you think you can peddle these extra colors, I'd appreciate it. Better that than letting good paint go to waste."

"They won't let you send it back?" Jamey asked.

I shook my head. "Not on hot rod colors like those, no."

Rick shrugged. "Kandy Apple won't be hard to sell. Euro Green might take a month or two, but it'll go. It's the Purple Haze that'll take a special touch."

He wasn't wrong. Anything purple took a special customer. One that wasn't afraid to be a little out-there with their rides. Which was exactly why I'd done my '69 Chevelle in something similar.

The door from the main office to the garage swung open just as the main phone line started ringing.

"Yo, boss," Malcom shouted from the door he kept propped open with one hand. "Some lady here to see you. Something about a job."

A job?

The phone kept ringing, an annoyance I wasn't up for right now, even if it was the order of a lifetime.

Rick must've read the frustration on my face because he did the one thing he always tried to avoid and volunteered for duty. "I'll get it. No worries."

Jamey and Jason started gathering up their share of paint.

I shook my head, trying to piece some logic into the situation. "A woman?" I shouted back to Malcom.

He nodded.

My brain still coughed up an absolute zero.

"Um, boss?" This from Jason, who stood next to me with three gallons dangling from his fingers. "I probably should have given you a heads-up, but I'm thinking the woman's someone I sent your way last weekend."

"A designer?"

"Not exactly." He hesitated and seemed to consider if now was a good idea to share what he'd done. "You keep talking about hiring someone to help in the office. You know—someone to keep shit straight. Well, this chick's just moved back to our neck of the woods. She's tryin' to get her feet under her and needed work, so I gave her my card and told her to hit you up." One side of his mouth curved in a wry grin, and he shrugged. "Might not be a bad thing to consider, you know?"

The suggestion might have been delivered in a teasing manner, but my insides took it like an undercut to the ribs. Every one of my brothers save Zeke and Ivan managed their own businesses and had a helluva lot more shit to juggle as a result than I did. Me? I had three shops with no more than twenty-five workers total and I couldn't even get a simple ordering system set up right.

I planted my hands on my hips and forced myself to look Jason square in the eyes. "I've been thinking about it, yeah. Just wasn't convinced bringing in someone who didn't know cars would make a difference."

"Well, she wouldn't need to know cars. She'd need to keep shit in line in the office and maybe free us up off phone and walk-in duties. Better still, she could take over all that accounting stuff that had you bitchin' at the computer last month." He shrugged and motioned toward the bay I'd actually hoped to spend some quality time in today. "All I know is you spend an awful lot of time lookin' at your empty bay and no time actually in it. If nothing changes, nothing changes, right?"

Fuck.

Jason was right. All of my brothers had office managers, too, and it wasn't like the shops weren't making enough money to cover a reasonable salary. The only problem—I didn't have a clue what made a person right for the job.

I dipped my head and thumped Jason on the shoulder. "All right, man. I'll talk to her. See what kind of vibe I get and go from there. No promises, though."

"Hell, no. If she's not a good fit, then better you look another direction. No pressure from me—I just met her on Sunday and it sounded like a win-win."

From the doorway, Malcom shouted, "You comin', or you want me to tell her to come back?"

Talking with an unknown wasn't really anything I was up for after the morning I'd had—interviewing someone even less so. But if fate was dumping a solution in my lap, I'd be stupid to pass it up. I grinned at Malcom then started toward the office. "Nah, I'm coming."

Malcom nodded, twisted and said something to the woman waiting in the office, then hustled back over to his bay. Like all the rest of my designers, Malcom was a laid-back guy with a ton of talent. A twenty-three-year-old kid who'd looked too scrawny at first glance to lift a fender on his own and sporting no past experience to speak of, I'd almost turned him away when he'd shown up in the office. But there was something in his eyes that had swayed me as we'd talked. Sincerity and a whole lot of hope.

Turned out, Malcom had proven his skills and his drive before his first day was over. So, yeah. I sure as shit didn't know everything. Maybe I'd be smart to give this chick at least a listen and see what my gut had to say.

The air-conditioning from the office hit me just a few clicks shy of a bucket of ice water, which was probably good for the eyeful I got as soon as my eyes adjusted to the room's decreased sunlight. The only thing better than sweet curves on a custom ride were righteous curves on a woman. One glance at the woman with her back to me and studying photos of my prize-winning work, and I was ready to run my hands across every beautiful line she had to offer. Especially, her outstand-

ing ass, which was perfectly encased by a faded pair of
jeans that made my heart weep.

Hold up.

I knew that ass. And if my brother Jace had any in-
kling I'd just thought the things I had about his wife,
Vivienne, he'd run me through with the first sharp ob-
ject he could find.

No, wait. It couldn't be Vivienne. I'd just seen her last
night and her hair was a whole lot longer. This woman
had dark curly hair just like Viv's, but only down to the
base of her neck.

I cleared my throat loud enough to carry over the
Stereophonics tune playing through the speakers. "You
here about a job?"

The woman turned and an entirely different stream
of thoughts and emotions did the equivalent of a highway pileup in my head and gut.

Callie Moore.

Vivienne's sister.

In the last six years, I'd caught up-close-and-personal
glimpses of her slow and painful descent into addiction.
The first time, I'd just carried her up a flight of stairs
as a favor for Jace and Vivienne after she'd passed out
from her New Year's Eve drunken escapades. I'd also
been booked in jail once because of her tryin' to pull
a fast one on a local drug lord—not that the cops had
been able to make the charges stick since I was more of
a bystander. Shortly after that, I'd driven her to Louisiana, where she'd volunteered for a treatment program.

I'd thought that would be the last time I'd see her, but
nope. I'd been a fool and given her my number. She'd
sure as shit used it, too. Twice. Once to get her out of
hot water money-wise with a loan shark, and then again

to bail her out of jail. Neither instance of which I'd ever shared with my brothers or Vivienne.

What shocked me the most about seeing her now was that she looked a whole lot different than the wastrel of a human I'd told to lose my number the last time I'd ridden to the rescue.

Callie's eyes widened. "Danny?"

Hmm. Guess the hair whacking Gabe had talked me into made more of a difference than I'd thought. "In the flesh."

The disbelief on Callie's face shifted to something closer to outright fear, and she zigzagged her gaze between the door and me as if measuring for how fast she could make it to the parking lot.

Most of me wanted her to run. She'd been nothing but bad news to me in the time I'd known her and watching anyone throw their life away pissed me off to no end. Still, for some stupid reason that defied logic, I engaged. "Your hair looks different."

Callie clutched the top of her purse and shifted from one boot-shod foot to the other. Honest to God, you'd think she was staring down the Grim Reaper instead of the guy who'd driven seven hours one way on two occasions to help her out.

"You gonna talk, or you gonna run?" I said a little sharper than I'd intended.

It did the trick, though, because she seemed to snap out of her stupor enough to replay my question in her head. She ran one hand down the side of her head as though trying to figure out what prompted the question in the first place, then apparently figured out the answer. "Oh. I uh… I let it go natural. Part of tryin' to figure out who I am." She wrinkled her nose and winced a little. "Probably sounds stupid to you."

No. Not stupid. Surprising as hell, but not stupid. And now that I really looked, there was more to the change in her appearance than her hair. As in the fact, despite her initial jumpiness, she didn't look like she'd been strung out for countless days and actually had some meat on her bones.

The most shocking change, though, were her eyes— a soft green color much different than her sister's gray, but the same doe-shape all the same. "You look good."

I couldn't believe I'd said it, even if it was true, but the pleasure that hummed through me when her cheeks turned pink was an even bigger shock. This was Callie Moore—a drugger and a drinker that would give my own mother a run for her money. And, considering my mom's using had cost her both her kids and her marriage and she still hadn't given a shit, that was saying something.

Callie pulled the purse hanging off her shoulder around to the front of her and grasped it with both hands. "You…uh…you cut your hair."

Much like I had out in the garage, one hand went reflexively for the hair I'd kept down to my shoulders for most of my life and came up empty-handed. "My sister, Gabe. She said I was due for a new look."

Fuck. What the hell was wrong with me? A new look? I sounded like a sixteen-year-old girl. Pissed off at myself and the direction the morning in general had taken, I hardened my voice. "I hear you're here about a job."

Callie ducked her head and nodded to the ground. "Yeah. Sorry about that." A thought seemed to nudge her into motion, and she dug a card out of the front pocket of her purse. She inched only the most necessary distance toward me and held out the card by the very tip. "I met Jason Sunday night. I'd shared I was looking for a job and he gave me this. Said you needed someone for the office."

I took the card, but looking at it was pointless. I knew what was on it because I'd made them. What was more interesting to me was the fact that she'd met him Sunday night. I tossed the card to the desk, and it slid to the center. "You sober?"

Her eyes went wide, and she glanced at the card. "Um… I am, but I'm not sure what that's got to do with meeting Jason."

Well, that was a small point in her favor. She could've played up where she'd met Jason in hopes of getting some compassion. Instead, she'd kept his anonymity. That was promising. "Got nothing to do with Jason. I just happen to know he normally hits his AA meetings on Sunday nights, and I put the pieces together." I paused all of a heartbeat. "How long?"

She lifted one shoulder in an awkward shrug. "Just a little over a year. I moved here last weekend."

"Why?"

"Why what?"

"Why move here?"

She pulled in a long slow breath, then let it out between parted lips. "Look, I know me showing up here today probably looks suspicious to you. If I were you, I wouldn't have even talked to me this long. Not after the predicaments I've put you in. But I promise you… I didn't know this was your shop." She twisted enough to wave a hand at the pictures she'd been looking at when

I'd walked in. "Hell, I didn't even know what you did for a living. I was just…" She raised her hands to either side of her in an exhausted motion of surrender. "Just trying to put one foot in front of the other. That's all."

"That's not what I asked. I asked why you moved here."

For the life of me, I didn't know why I was as abrupt with her as I was. I only knew the question came straight from my gut and that the answer was important.

Apparently, it was important to her, too, because she pinched her lips together tight and swallowed hard. Pain showed behind her eyes. Not the bullshit *please help me* pitiful routine I'd seen her use on people before—me included—but real, soul-cutting pain. When she spoke, her voice had lost its smooth edge, replaced with brokenness and a whole lot of heart. "I guess I finally figured out the only way to sober up was to face all the garbage I'd filled my life with and to try and make it up to the people I'd hurt."

I wanted to believe her. Not so much for myself, but because of how many times I'd seen Vivienne gutted after getting a drunk dial from Callie. More than that, I'd heard her voice out loud the terrifying possibility she might have to bury her sister way too young.

But my own background with my mom and how she still used and tossed people aside left and right in her never-ending quest for the next high made me jaded. Yeah, I'd seen guys like Jason make the most of AA and other twelve-step programs and end up with a decent life, but Callie? If I weren't seeing real physical differences in her right before my eyes, I'd have probably called bullshit already.

"You tell Vivienne you've moved home?"

Callie's face paled a little and she shook her head. "Not yet. I wanted to get my bearings first and get some good program contacts around me first." She hesitated a few seconds then added, "She's been jerked around enough already. I want to make sure when I call her, I'm solid."

Another interesting change. A smart one, too. "And you think you've got the skills to take on managing an office?"

For the first time since I'd laid eyes on her, Callie loosened up and let loose one of those ironic chuckles reserved for people who didn't have a clue what they were doing. "The truth? I've got no idea what goes into whatever it is you need. I know I can answer a phone. I'm decent with basic computer stuff. Not the techy stuff like networks, but using software." She scanned the room and pursed her mouth. When her focus hit the desk beside me, she hit me with a wry grin. "I'm pretty good about organizing stuff, so I figure I can help there for sure."

"What kind of jobs have you had before?"

"Entry-level stuff, mostly. A few convenience stores and fast-food places. Convenience stores were a pretty good match for me, but I'm not cut out for the food industry. Not if I can avoid it. I worked in a vet's office for about a year and that was cool. Got to schedule appointments and help the docs out with the animals. The last year, I worked on stocking and filling online orders at the Walmart near where I went to treatment."

"Any school?"

She hung her head for a beat or two before she faced me again. "I tried right outta high school. Went to junior college thinkin' I'd get a physician's assistant cer-

tification then work my way through nursing school."
She wrinkled her nose again and tacked on, "Late night
parties aren't great for getting to class or making good
grades. They kicked me out halfway through the second semester."

Silence settled between us. Which was good because
I needed at least a few seconds to figure out which
way was up. Christ, but I needed some downtime. Real
downtime where I could be quiet and let my mind unravel all the knots reality had me tied up in.

To her credit, Callie kept silent and held my stare.
No small feat considering most men I met couldn't do
the same. Not that the handy bit of information did anything to help me make a decision. So, I bought the time
I needed and stalled, digging through the stacks of paperwork on top of my desk. "I gotta be honest. I'm not
sure what to do. So, if you need an answer now, it's a
no. If you're willing to let me sit on it a few days, it's a
maybe." I plunked a notepad I'd fished out of the pile
and a pen on the edge of the desk. "If you're good with
a maybe, then write down your contact info, and I'll let
you know when I decide."

Letting out an exhale that said she'd been holding a
decent amount of breath, she nodded and crept closer.
"*Maybe*'s more than fair." She picked up the pen, sat
her purse on the desk and bent over to write.

Unfortunately, that particular maneuver did a lot to
accent what made up the top half of her hourglass. I
forced myself to focus on what she was writing instead
of the plentiful cleavage she'd unwittingly offered me,
but damned if that didn't make my nose wake up and
zero in on her perfume. Or maybe it was lotion. Whatever it was, it wasn't as overpowering as the stuff other

women wore. More like flowers you smelled walking through a garden when there was a decent breeze to carry the scent.

Christ, I had to be fucking nuts. The last person on the planet I needed to be noticing in any way other than polite distance was Calista Moore. Hell, even if she didn't have a history with booze, I was in over my eyeballs with work. A woman in my life was only going to complicate matters, not help.

I gave up looking at anything her direction and focused on the black-and-white checkerboard tile beneath my feet.

All of twenty seconds later, Callie peeled the paper she'd written on off the pad, straightened, and handed it to me. "Here's my number and my email. I put my address on it, but I need to double-check and make sure the zip code's right."

Yeah, definitely not perfume. Probably one of those girly lotions like my sister Gabe was always buying. Rather than take the paper she offered right away, I took the opportunity of having her closer to really look at the difference in her compared to the last time we'd met. It beat the shit out of me how it'd happened, but she really did look at least five years younger. In fact, the last time I'd helped her out, she'd had a cracked lip where some guy had backhanded her. Today her lips were free of any makeup and too damned kissable for comfort.

I shook my head to clear the stupid thought, snatched the paper from her fingers and took a healthy step back. "Not thinking a wrong zip code's gonna be a problem seein' as how I can't remember the last time I used a stamp." I dipped my head hoping that, combined with the rest of my words, would bring an end to the morning. "Appreciate you coming in. I'll call you in a few days and let you know what I decide."

For a second, she looked like she wanted to say something more, then appeared to think better of it and took a step backward. "Like I said—more than I could ask." With a small, rueful smile, she turned away. "Thank you, Danny."

Behind me, the chime that warned the guys out in the garage someone had entered or left the office sounded through the glass. For a long damned time, I just stood there, staring at the main door to the office.

I had no clue what to do.

I needed the help. Any idiot could see that, even if I was loathe to admit I couldn't do it all myself.

But did I really want to take a chance at bringing a recovering addict into my already chaotic business? Hell, with as many cash jobs as we did, just letting her around the customers was a helluva financial risk. And even if I wanted to take a chance and hire Callie, it'd mean me coming clean with my brothers about how I'd helped her twice before and not shared.

Yeah, this one was going to take some alone time with just me in my bay come hell or high water. I spun for the door to the garage and stalked for my coveralls in the far corner.

"Yo, Jason!" I shouted as I passed him by. "Do me a favor and make sure the phones get answered and the place doesn't go up in flames. You need me for an emergency, come get me. But try like hell not to have an emergency." I snatched my coveralls off the hook and unzipped 'em. "I've got some thinking to do."

Chapter Three

Callie

Downtown Dallas had some seriously screwed up streets with too damned many cars and impatient people driving on them. Which was kind of an ironic thought for me considering I'd used to love tooling around in this part of town. The frenetic energy had been a perfect partner for the artificial buzz I was usually riding. An extra fix on top of whatever binge I was on at the moment.

Now? Now I missed the small town of Ethel, Louisiana, with its limited number of stoplights and uncomplicated street layout.

By some miracle, I navigated the nightmare split off Gaston Avenue onto Malcom X Boulevard without getting me or anyone else killed and coasted toward Deep Ellum—a part of downtown I'd once spent a considerable amount of time in thanks to its lively bars and nightlife. Whether my heart was thrumming from the task ahead of me, or the fact that I was about to see my old stomping grounds through sober eyes, I wasn't sure.

One way or another, I was about to find out.

My first thought was that the place didn't look nearly

as sexy on a Saturday at ten in the morning as it did at ten o'clock at night. Yeah, some of the more popular places had fresh coats of paint, but a lot of the store fronts looked like they hadn't been updated in twenty years. Probably because the owners figured neon and streetlights did enough to camouflage a beaten-down exterior and didn't see the value in spending money they could otherwise keep in their pockets.

My second realization—it had been a long freaking time since I'd had to parallel park.

Oh, well. At least this time I'd be doing it sober, which upped the odds of me keeping my five-year-old Chevy Spark free of any dings. My girl might not have been the sexiest car in the lot when I'd finally had enough money to buy my own wheels a few months ago, but she'd been in my price range, had low miles and got freaking fantastic gas mileage. Plus, what she lacked in sexiness she more than made up for with her electric blue color and general road-zippiness.

Thanks to a huge crowd of kids and parents lined up on the sidewalk, I found the building I was supposed to be at pretty easily and parked. From the looks of everyone outside, the Deadpool tee I'd paired with my jeans and white slip-on Chucks this morning hadn't been a completely terrible idea, so that was a plus. I threw my fringy faux leather black hobo bag over one shoulder, locked up my car and jogged across the street in search of Susan.

"Back here, Callie!"

I spun toward my new AA friend's somewhat harried voice and chuckled at the sight. At fifty-two with two teenage girls of her own and seven years of sobriety behind her, Susan normally struck me as the type that could juggle a lot of things and make it look easy. This morning, though, her ponytail was anchored slightly off center and looked like she'd actually slept in it. Combined with her lack of makeup, my guess was she'd overslept.

"Hey," she huffed as she made it to me. "Sorry I'm late."

"Hit the snooze too many times?"

"More like I forgot to set my alarm." She blew her longish blonde bangs out of her eyes then fanned herself with one hand. "So? You ready for this?"

No.

I was absolutely *not* ready for this.

But previous attempts at sobriety had taught me that idle time wasn't my friend. Particularly when I spent it sitting around worrying about the future and things I couldn't control. So, here I was—volunteering for the most bizarre service work I could think of. "If you'd told me I'd be babysitting kids doing art projects for three or four hours on a Saturday morning *before* you'd asked for my help, I'd have given my answer deeper thought."

"Oh, come on. It'll be fun. And for God's sake, don't call it *babysitting* in front of the girls. Most of these kids have been self-sufficient out of necessity since they were tiny and could probably navigate this whole event solo, but Catherine's Kids require chaperones for every two to three attendees, so…here we are!"

Right.

Here we were. Heading into the Wild Wild West of childcare. "You do realize I've never *ever* in my life been responsible for the care and well-being of a minor, right?"

Susan laughed outright, steered me around so I faced

the door and wrapped an arm around me. "Relax, girl-friend. I used to bring my kiddos here when I was first getting sober. And if it helps you frame things up in that crazy head of yours—the kids you'll be helping have single moms who've struggled with sobriety just like you. Unfortunately, they've been out of the program more than in it, so these kids need a little bit of happy."

Hmmm. Shared from that perspective, it kind of made me want to make the day a special one rather than view it as a morning of uncertain torture.

Susan must've intuited my thoughts, because she chuckled. "Just be yourself and roll with it."

Ten minutes later, Susan and I had checked in with the organizers manning a wide folding table outside the front door and stood waiting on the sidewalk for our charges to arrive.

Susan inched a little closer and lowered her voice. "Hey, you ever hear back on the job with that old friend of yours?"

Well, crap. So much for keeping my mind busy and not thinking about things outside my control. "He texted yesterday. Said he wouldn't be able to give me an answer until tomorrow." All too keenly, the shiver I'd felt the second I'd locked eyes with Danny last Wednesday wriggled through me. I still didn't know if it was just the mega hot factor blazing off of him, or the fact that he scared the absolute shit out of me. The dude was seriously intense. "For the record, he's not my friend."

"He's not?"

"Nope. More like a friend of my sister's. He helped me out of a few jams in the last six or so years, but the last time he basically told me to lose his number." I fidgeted and crammed my hands in my back pockets.

"I put him in a really shitty place by asking him not to tell my sister I'd fucked up again the last time he helped out. He kept the promise. Or at least I think he did. But yeah...he still seemed pissed about it. So, I'm thinking this job is a long shot."

"So, what other ideas have you got?"

I shrugged. "I'm gonna start working through my runner-up list Monday."

"What's a runner-up list?"

"Gonna call my old boss at Walmart in Louisiana and see if he can put a good word in for me at the local Garland store. It's not a bad gig, really. I was just hoping for something new."

"And if that doesn't work?"

"Then it'll be time to hit the restaurants."

"Ugh. Waiting tables is tough."

"Tell me about it."

Across the street, a beat-up Honda Accord that should have been sent to the junkyard a few years ago came to a squeaky stop and two preteen girls filed out of the back seat.

Susan straightened and a genuine smile broke out on her face. "That's them."

The older woman behind the wheel didn't get out to see them across the street. Hell, she barely even glanced our way before she gave us a half-hearted wave.

It didn't seem to matter though, because the girls adeptly checked the traffic and made their way across the busy street like they did it every day.

"Hey, ladies!" Susan opened her arms and squatted down enough to give the new arrivals each a big bear hug. "You guys ready to have some fun?"

Neither of them answered, but opted for a much more

restrained head bob that spoke of uncertainty and awkwardness.

If Susan noticed, she didn't show it. "You guys are *so* in for a treat today. My friend Callie is gonna be your chaperone." Straightening to her full height, she placed a hand on the girl closest to her. "Callie, meet Sydney and Amy. They've been coming to the summer art fair for a few years."

The girl farthest from Susan eyed me a whole lot more suspiciously than a girl with braided pigtails should be capable of. "You've never done this?"

"Nope," I said. "Total rookie. But I've had people tell me I'm a quick study. Are you Amy or Sydney?"

"I'm Amy." She whipped her attention to Susan. "She's not gonna make us stop at every single booth the way the last girl did, is she?"

I looked to Susan almost as fast. "Booths?"

"This is an art fair," Sydney answered before Susan could. In truth, the name fit her serious and oddly worldly demeanor. She had dark brown curly hair and doe-shaped eyes just like my sister's. "They've got three floors full of artists for us to tour. After you tour them all, you pick the one you want to commit to and spend the rest of the morning experimenting with that kind of art."

Well, that didn't sound too bad. Assuming I didn't lose either one of them in the thick crowd. "Okay," I said to Susan. "So, we look, we dive in, and then what?"

"You get the girls back down here no later than two o'clock, wait for Amy's mom to pull up, and load 'em up. Simple." Susan looked down to the girls and nudged them my direction. "Other than that, you guys have fun."

Much like they had before I'd stepped foot in my first AA meeting, my feet refused to work, and my brain coughed up an absolute zero on next steps. Drunks I knew how to talk to, but kids?

Not so much.

Just as solemn as an angel, Sydney wrapped her tiny hand around one of mine and peered up at me. "Don't worry. I'll take care of you."

The world around me stilled and a heavy weight settled over my sternum, the crowd and the sounds of the street utterly forgotten. My voice cracked a little when I spoke. "You know, my big sister used to say the same thing to me all the time."

"She did?"

"Yeah. You look a lot like she did at your age, too. Except your eyes are a deep green and hers are pale gray."

For some crazy reason, that made Sydney smile huge.

Amy, on the other hand, wasn't amused. Grabbing my other hand, she groaned and pulled us toward the line slowly moving through the front door. "Would you two come on? I wanna get to the painting class."

Unlike some of the other early 1900s buildings up and down Elm Street, this one had been heavily renovated into a major creative Mecca. I'd expected to find a setup like the expo vendors at a state fair, but the "booths" Susan and Sydney had referred to were more like two-car-garage-size art rooms separated by slick partitions that could be opened and closed to fit different needs. The back half of each room sported all kinds of artwork with tags beneath them identifying the artist and if the piece was for sale. The front half was all glass so those meandering the halls wouldn't miss the activity going on inside. Across every stretch of the first floor were concrete floors boasting a high shine that was probably intended for easy cleanup. Of course, those floors were crowded with tiny feet and the little humans connected to them at the moment.

"So," I said to Amy while we waited for a large group to move out of our way, "if the whole purpose is to check out all the art options, why do you not want to stop at each class?"

"This floor is for the little kids." Amy kept her laser focused gaze on the stairwell at the center of the building. "The better stuff is on the second and third floor."

"And you're looking for the painting class?"

"The painting class has three different groups," Sydney said, just as matter-of-fact as could be. "Each one has a specific painting, and they walk you through how to do it."

"Yeah," Amy said. "And the last time we missed out getting a seat because we took too long getting there."

"Right," I said with a nod. "No screwing around with the first floor then." I frowned down at the two of them. "Um…am I not supposed to say things like *screwing*?"

Both girls laughed at my question, but honest to God, the sweet smile that lingered on Sydney's face made me feel like I'd just laid the foundation for world peace.

"Seriously?" Amy said. "My teenage brother drops the f-bomb in every sentence. I ain't got no problem with *screwing*."

Bonus.

I'd made it a whole five minutes into my first foray into childcare without sticking my proverbial foot in my mouth. Granted, I still had three and a half hours to go, but hey…a girl had to take her wins where she could.

The upstairs was a whole lot easier to navigate—partly because I'd finally gotten my initial jitters under control, but also because the lack of younger kids had significantly thinned out the crowd. An even bigger coup was the drop in chatter.

But the art was fantastic.

Origami...pottery...tie-dye projects. Every class we stopped in front of left me feeling a whole lot more optimistic about the time ahead of me. There was even a macrame section where the instructor was teaching the kids how to do wall art featuring a wicked crescent moon.

Much to my dismay, Sydney and Amy had their heart set on the painting room we'd yet to find and tugged me down the hall before I could think of a decent argument to change their minds.

Ahead of us, a group of teenage boys stood grouped in front of one glass wall, their eyes wide enough you'd think a live pinup model was sporting a bikini somewhere inside.

Amy took one look at them, rolled her eyes and tugged my hand as she had almost every time she'd learned we'd yet to find the right room.

Sydney, on the other hand, dug in her heels and crept close enough to see what the boys were looking at.

I chuckled at the sight.

Not a pinup model, but the next best thing for some testosterone-laden teens—good old-fashioned model cars and metal art. The metalwork was relegated to a standing workbench on the far side of the room and had a hot older guy with gray hair pulled back in a ponytail teaching about six kids. Whatever they were working with must've had some kick to it because they were all gloved, wearing heavy smocks to rival an X-ray routine and sporting goggles, but the finished products hanging on the back wall were kind of interesting. Kind of like they'd used products to strip away the metal's surface and caused colorful reactions in a spectrum of patterns.

Most of the focus, though, was on the group building model cars in the other half of the room.

Actually, now that I took a better look, they weren't just normal model cars like the ones you bought off the shelf. They were custom jobs built off a Camaro, Corvette or Ford truck base and the kids got to pick their modifications from a wide array of metal options offered in a rolling toolkit behind them.

Really. Freaking. Cool.

God, if my dad had ever had a chance to do something like that, he'd have blown off work for a whole day just to pull up a chair and play.

I maneuvered the girls and I to the front of the group for a better look at a purple Camaro a kid was putting together—and froze.

Sitting next to the focused teenager was none other than Danny Parker. And while his student might be fully engaged with the project in front of him, Danny's attention was locked squarely on me.

My heart kicked hard enough I flinched, and the once cool hallway suddenly felt like a stifling metal building in August.

Seriously? In a major city with almost a million and a half people I had to run into this one freaking guy at a kids' art event? He was definitely going to think I was stalking him. Or worse, pressuring him on the job.

Not good. Not even a little bit.

Though, I had to admit…looking at Danny Parker

would never *ever* be a hardship. I'd thought he was hot when he'd had long hair, but the shorter version he was rocking these days made everything about his facial features more intense.

As if he needed any more intensity.

Swear to God, I didn't know whether to run like hell in that moment, or throw caution to the wind and rub up against him.

Sydney was standing right by my side, but her voice sounded like it was coming from the far end of a tunnel. "Do you know him?"

Pulling my gaze away from his took everything in me, but I forced my attention to her. "Yeah. Sorta. It's a long story."

"Well, he's hot," Amy added in a tone that you'd expect to hear from a sixteen-year-old instead of a tween.

"How old are you?"

"Twelve."

"Is that old enough to call a guy *hot*?"

"Well, duh. Now can we go find the painting room before it's full?"

Right.

We were here for painting. Not ogling or irritating a guy that might be my last defense from working overnights stocking shelves or schlepping food. I tried for what I hoped was a casual smile and dipped my head in Danny's direction before steering Amy and Sydney out of the crowd. "Yeah, let's go find your stuff."

Chapter Four

Danny

I was less than thirty minutes away from putting my ass out on the line with the eight men I respected most on the planet and all I had to base my approach on was a situation with more questions than answers.

Not in a million fucking years would I have ever expected to see Callie Moore volunteering with a couple of young girls. At least not the Callie Moore I'd grown accustomed to. But damned if I hadn't watched her do just that at the tail end of the art fair. Granted, I'd had to have Rex cover both of our stations and find the class Callie and the girls had ended up in before I'd caught that observation, but it'd been worth the juggling to confirm my brief sighting of her hadn't been a fluke.

Even more interesting than her hanging out with kids? She and the girls had really seemed to enjoy themselves. Hell, just watching the antics when the three of them had posed with their finished pictures at the end had left me chuckling, too.

The problem was, I couldn't trust a thirty-minute glimpse of wholesome or a twenty-minute heartfelt interview as a basis for judgment. Not when I had six years of intermittent shitty history on the other side of the scales and a mighty big risk of Viv getting hurt if my judgment was off.

I turned off the country road onto the long and winding driveway to Jace and Axel's ranch in Allen, a place affectionately dubbed Haven. Considering that's exactly what it was to all of us, the name couldn't have been more appropriate. A safe place away from the bullshit that was the real world where we all could be ourselves—whatever that looked like. The sprawling home with its tumbled stone and brown trim always made me feel like I'd somehow been transported to a mountain chateau in France. Of course, it being July in Texas, it only took a second after I parked my Chevelle to one side of the wide circle drive and opened the car door before the idea of mountains and winter air got shot straight to hell.

I wasn't even to the wide double wood doors framed by a porch swing and two Adirondack chairs that the sound of laughter hit me. One thing about the family that had embraced me, my sister and a whole host of other awesome people—they knew how to live and how to laugh. More than that, they knew how to love and did it with a ferocity that still left me dumbstruck.

It was that last bit about love I was hoping would keep Jace from kicking my ass before the night was over. *If* I even decided to open my mouth and share that Callie was not only back in town but looking to stay awhile.

Ninette's voice rose above a fresh wave of laughter and floated to me as I wound my way through the living room toward the kitchen. "Rex Niland, don't you think for a second I don't know it was you who snagged the last slice of pepperoni."

"Now, Ninnie—"

"Don't you Ninnie me," Jace's mom fired back just as I ambled in the room. Despite the scolding words, there was laughter in her voice that matched the sparkle in her pretty blue eyes. "I claimed that last slice fair and square."

The newest brother to join the family, Rex was at the far side of the round kitchen table that barely fit the lot of us anymore. He smiled that ornery smile only he could get away with where Ninette was concerned and lifted the paper towel covering his paper plate. Lo and behold, there was the slice of pepperoni. "Now, I'm just downright hurt you'd think I'd do somethin' that low when all I was tryin' to do was make sure no one got to it before you."

Trevor chuckled, rocked back on the rear legs of his chair and lifted his longneck. "More like he was tryin' to get a rise out of you."

"Well, it worked, didn't it?" Axel said. He shifted his gaze to me and shook his head, only the barest hint of the Scottish brogue he'd picked up from his mother showing in his voice. "Wish I could tell ya better news, lad, but you're the last gettin' here. We're down to three slices with pineapple and Canadian bacon and a single of some shite with anchovies on it."

Fuck.

I was starving, too. And hell would freeze over before I ate anything with anchovies on it. "I still don't get why anyone would get a pizza with minnows on it."

With a brief nod to the rest of my brothers and their wives around the huge table, I snagged a plate and the three decent pieces of pizza still left and started a side convo with Axel while Jace and Trevor volleyed a debate about a new pub location. "Where's Lizzy and your mom?"

"Took little Colin, Levi, and Mary out for ice cream as soon as they blew through the pizza. Surprised you didn't see 'em in the Escalade on the drive in."

Well, that explained where all the kids were. It'd been a year since Axel and Lizzy had welcomed little Colin into the world, and I still couldn't wrap my head around Axel being a dad. Who knew the most dedicated bachelor of the group would be the first to procreate. "I was distracted drivin' in."

"You've been distracted all morning." Rex stood and gathered his empty plate and napkin. "Not like you to bail on the kids."

"I wasn't bailing. I had to check something out." Something I was still struggling to understand. So much so, I'd tailed Callie and the woman with her for a while after the fair just to try and get a better feel for how up-and-up Callie was operating these days.

"Everything okay?" Jace asked, suddenly dropping the convo with Trevor. I shouldn't have been surprised. Jace ferreted out trouble the way most mothers sniffed out a lying kid.

I nodded and kept my attention on consuming my next bite of pizza rather than risk his or Vivienne's scrutiny. "Nothing we can't talk about later."

Either Jace bought my nonchalance, or he copped to my dodging a real answer and rolled with it. "Right." He rapped his knuckles twice on the kitchen table and stood. "Let's get on with rally, then. Axel and I've got a big headliner tonight at Crossroads. I wanna be in the office before the crowd gets crazy."

And just like that, dinner was over.

The men filed down the back stairway to the basement, while the women cozied up to talk about God only knew what around the kitchen table. All the men knew was that, by the time we were done covering family business, every single one of them would have a feisty spark in their eyes and smug expressions on their faces. Unlike the original six brothers, me, Ivan and Rex didn't have women of our own, but knowing my sister, Gabe, finally had a posse of females she could not only count on but laugh her ass off with, made whatever they were up to more than fine with me.

Taking the time to give my sis a quick kiss on the cheek and polish off the last slice of pie made me the last one downstairs. Not that there was a shortage of space around the massive conference table on one side of the room. It wasn't a polished fixture by any stretch. More like a castoff from the mid-'90s that had seen its share of nicks and scratches. According to Zeke, Jace had saved it from his and Axel's early business ventures and moved it into the basement as soon as Haven was built.

I fucking loved it because it was the closest I'd ever come to anything resembling a boardroom. Or had been until I'd sat behind the table Jace and Axel had now at Crossroads. The chairs around it were as varied and historied as the men sitting around the table. Which made sense considering each of us had chosen our own chair when we'd been brought into the brotherhood. My humble opinion was that mine was the sweetest one of them all—a killer modification of a mechanic's creeper from my shop that I'd soldered up to table height.

Mega wicked.

Still feeling that stupid pride I'd felt the day I'd brought her down to the basement, I rolled her away from the side of the table, settled onto the padded leather seat and reclined back.

"So," Jace said from one end of the table. "Who's got the rundown of existing business?"

Sitting opposite me, Knox typed in something rapid fire on his Mac keyboard and started in.

A discussion started up about an expansion location for Trevor's pub. Next up was an outline from Knox on some new security software he wanted to install at the bigger clubs, followed by the details on a run-in that'd happened at Trident in Lower Greenville only a few nights before.

Under normal circumstances, I'd have perked up the second we'd switch to security topics. Day-to-day business and restaurant or club fodder wasn't really my deal, but the time I'd spent working with Knox and Beckett in their security business had been second only to my love of cars. With Beckett's expertise as a bodyguard and security systems and Knox's hacking background, I'd gotten comfortable with everything from software installs, wires and drills to covering my own fair share of VIPs.

Still, everything we covered was pretty average stuff for us. Matter of fact, since Axel had gotten hitched almost three years ago, things had turned kind of run-of-the-mill boring in the basement. Which might have explained why my brain took off on a side trip noodling what to do about Callie. My gut wanted to believe she'd finally found the right path, but my own personal history with my mom made me dubious. Yeah, I'd seen some friends turn their life around with AA, but they'd really wanted a better life. How the hell was I supposed to know if Callie was of the same mind versus just setting people up the way my mom always had?

"You know, ya could just stop fucking around and go for it with Ninette," Axel said. "Jace might pretend to give you the hairy eyeball, but deep down, he'd be tickled as shit to know his mom had a steady man she could count on."

What.

The fuck.

Had I missed?

I straightened in my chair. "Hold up, what?"

"Rex and Ninette," Zeke clarified beside me. "Rex mentioned helping Ninette build that big greenhouse she's been wanting out back instead of hiring it done. Axel jumped in and called bullshit foul the way the rest of us have wanted to for months." He grinned at me and added on, "Of course, you'd have known that if you hadn't been in a pizza coma."

"You kidding me?" I grunted and shook my head. "You keep forgetting, Gabe was cooking mine and Dad's dinners for a long time before she met you. Gonna take a whole lot more than three slices of pie to put me to sleep."

"Gabe knows how to cook, that's for sure," Jace said. "Doesn't explain what's got you distant today. Anything to do with why you were runnin' late this afternoon?"

Well, shit.

Just like that, decision time was squatting right in front of me. My whole damned body itched to get up and pace, and the food I'd scarfed down too damned fast sat anchor heavy in my gut.

Seated near the corner and closest to Axel, Rex gave me a cockeyed grin that said he was mighty glad the attention had shifted to me instead of him.

Hold up.

Zeke was right.

Rex and Ninette *had* been dancing around each other for over three years now. None of us had ever said a damned word because we all knew it was out of respect for Jace. That and we all assumed Jace would freak the fuck out at the idea of Rex making a move.

But Axel had just laid it out in front of everyone, and Jace hadn't even batted an eye. If anything, he'd side-stepped it and given Rex his space.

All my brothers were like that.

Never once in the seven years I'd known them had they ever cut me down.

They listened to each other. Built each other up and supported everyone's decisions. So, what were the odds they'd judge me for helping Callie and not sharing before? Especially if they knew I'd only kept my silence to keep Vivienne pain free.

Gaze back on the center of the table, I exhaled a good chunk of the unease I'd been carting around since I'd seen Callie on Wednesday. "I need to get something out in the open."

The room fell silent. Not that uncomfortable, stifling silent you'd expect right before a firing squad took aim. More like that time my dad sat me down when he'd learned I'd started dabbling in drugs and stealing in high school and needed a minute to gather his thoughts.

"Most of you know, Viv's sister, Callie, has been down in Louisiana for the last six years and hasn't been doing so hot with the sobriety thing." I turned my attention to Jace and laid the rest out as clean as I could. "What I haven't shared is that she called me a few times asking for help. Once when she found herself kicked out of her apartment for nonpayment and another when she got arrested bein' in the wrong place at the wrong time and needed bail."

Not surprisingly, Jace's expression stayed cool and calm. "Any particular reason you felt like you couldn't say something when it happened?"

I shrugged, feeling much the same as when my dad had had that talk with me all those years ago. "You asking now makes the reasons sound stupid, but mostly it was because I felt like I was weak for caving and riding to the rescue when we'd all agreed taking her to treatment was the last time we'd interfere."

Jace nodded. "I can see that point. But the line I drew was for me and Vivienne. Your choices are yours, and you're the one who's gotta live with them. Just sad you didn't feel safe enough to lay those decisions out here."

"I think I get it, though," Zeke said. "Knowing your and Gabe's history with your mom, walking away when a woman who's living an almost identical life asked for help would be damned hard to do."

"Hell," Trevor said. "I'm not sure I could walk away from any woman who needed help. No matter what condition they were in."

"Oh, you could have walked away from my mom," I said. "Knowing she willingly took my baby sister along for a fuck and drug deal that could have gotten Gabe killed was bad enough. But the end for me was the day she came back to visit Gabe after losing custody under the guise of rebuilding their relationship and had the balls to ask her for money."

That old simmering burn that never seemed to die out fired hot and painful beneath my skin and my knuckles ached from how tight my hands fisted in my lap. "That day broke Gabe. Made her question every fucking relationship that came after it until she met Zeke."

The same welcoming silence settled around the table for at least a handful of seconds before Jace gently added, "You said there were reasons. Any more we should be aware of?"

It was a fair question. Especially for a man looking to protect his wife from more pain than she'd already endured with Callie. "Mostly because I didn't want to hurt Vivienne by confirming that her sister was off the wagon again, but also because Callie asked me not to. Likely for the same reason." The memory of Callie's tear-streaked face the last time I'd told her not to call me again hit like an elephant kick to the gut. "She might've been on the wrong road, but deep down, she loves her sister. I believe that."

"Might've been?" Knox shut his laptop, crossed his arms on the table and cocked his head. "That makes it sound like you've got reason to think she's got her past behind her."

"And why you're wantin' to come clean now," Axel added.

I sighed and rubbed the back of my head with one hand, wishing I still had all my hair to grab on to. "That's the thing. She's back and stumbled into my garage asking for a job."

"Stumbled in?" Beckett said.

I nodded. "Yeah. She got the lead from one of my guys who's shared with me he goes to AA. He knew I was strugglin' to juggle the office shit while gettin' the other sites stabilized, so he gave her his card and sent her my direction for an office manager gig."

"You didn't mention you were strugglin'." Ivan leaned forward and mirrored Knox's position. "If you needed help all you had to do was say somethin'. I'd have pitched in in a heartbeat."

"Me too," Rex said.

"We all would've." Somehow, hearing it out of Jace's mouth—so solid and sure—I found myself asking why I hadn't bothered to mention it before.

But I knew.

Deep down I knew.

The real question was if I was gonna be man enough to admit it.

I looked to Zeke first, then to Beckett—who'd taught me a whole new set of skills in the field of security while I'd wrestled with whether or not I wanted to have a business of my own. "I guess it's just keeping all the balls in the air, ya know? Opening a shop is one thing. Havin' employees and multiple locations is somethin' else. Lately, I've been pulled so many different directions—especially with the Louisiana shop—I haven't had shit for time to work on my own jobs."

"Well, that sounds familiar." Knox chuckled, reclined back in his chair, and playfully backhanded Beckett's shoulder. "You remember how fucked up things were when we first opened until we hired Katy?"

Beckett grunted and lifted the longneck he'd brought down from dinner in salute toward me. "He's not joking. Before Katy it was a damned miracle we didn't install a system in the wrong house, or turn over background information to the wrong person. It was a fucking zoo."

"Same for Jace and me," Axel said. "Back when he

opened Trident, we tried for a solid year to keep things going on our own and then stumbled on to Shelly by dumb luck. She's been coverin' our asses ever since."

I looked to Jace, part shell-shocked and part intrigued. "No shit?"

Jace barked out a laugh. "You say that like you find it hard to believe."

"Well…yeah. You guys always have your shit together."

"No," Trevor said. "They have people who keep their shit together for them. Big difference. The only reason I didn't fall into the same trap was I'd watched my momma coverin' all the logistics for my dad on the ranch growin' up, so I knew better going in."

Zeke nudged me with his elbow. "Benefits of sharin' rather than clamming up, you know?"

Well, I'd be damned.

All this time I'd been too stubborn to say a word for fear of looking like a fool. Come to find out my brothers had already trudged the same ground in one way or another.

Granted, the revelation didn't address the two-hundred-pound doubt still squatting in the back of my head that I wasn't cut out to be a business owner in general, but it did go a long way to cutting through my most pressing issue.

At least one of them anyway.

"So," I said to the table at large. "Y'all think an office manager is a good thing. But what do you think about givin' it to Callie?"

Axel's gaze shifted to Jace as though assessing the wisdom of his words before he retrained his sights on me. "What's your take on her?"

Jace's expression might not have changed, but the dark of his eyes seemed twice as harsh as a minute before, which made me rethink whether it was my gut giving me input on Callie or my dick.

I opted for facts. "What I know is she *looks* a helluva lot different than the times since I first met her. Got rid of that bottled bleach color she was sporting and has dark hair to match Viv's now. Hell, her whole damned face is different. Like someone rolled the clock back by about five years."

"And you don't think it's fishy as fuck that she showed up in your shop of all places asking for a job?" Jace said.

I shook my head. "Nah. Weird as it looks on the surface, I trust the hell out of Jason. He told me straight up he'd run into her and given her the card on his own. Plus, no actress could have faked her surprise when she first laid eyes on me in the office. Now, what is weird, is the fact that I ran into her again today at the art fair."

Rex chuckled low in his throat. "Guess that explains where you had to run off to toward the end of class."

"That's exactly where I was. I saw her with two preteen girls walking by our class and wanted to figure out what was going on. I found 'em right before they finished at one of the painting groups."

"Callie?" Jace uttered the single word and stared me down like I'd lost my mind. "The same woman who left Viv to face an armed and pissed off drug dealer on her own was hanging with two little girls at an art fair?"

"Yeah. I had a hard time wrappin' my head around it, too. But she was into it. Laughing and doing her own painting between the two of 'em." A painting I'd honestly been hella impressed with if the truth be told.

I scanned my brothers' expressions one at a time. "I even went so far as to follow her and another girl after the fair was over tryin' to get a clue what her ties to them were. All I got was a dead end at the AA club-house Jason goes to—which at least solidifies where he met her."

"And the fact that she's genuinely getting sober," Zeke said.

Jace snorted. "It's gonna take a lot more from Callie than a few meetings to get me to buy her being on the wagon. The last time she called Viv, she was so fucked up she could hardly form a coherent sentence. Took Viv a solid three days to stop worryin' about her and let it go. And that was with her a full state away. Not thinkin' I'm eager to see how bad she fucks Viv up being back in the same state."

"Man…" I said, pausing for the right words to find their way up my throat. "If I were in your shoes, I'd feel the same way. Honestly, my gut reaction when I first saw her was almost the same."

Well, that wasn't entirely the truth. My first reaction had been wanting to slide my hands along the swells of her hips to her waist and pull her against me.

Definitely *not* something I was going to admit to this crew.

"Sure sounds like you're leading to a big *but* behind that statement," Ivan said.

I exhaled hard and glanced at Zeke. "Zeke's not wrong. My mom and her bullshit messed with my head for a long time. But after I talked to Callie… after she said she's finally on a good track and look-ing to straighten out her life and make amends… I got to thinking. What if my mom had actually pulled her head out of her ass? Could I actually live with myself if I didn't give her the benefit of the doubt?"

"There's givin' someone a chance, and bein' a doormat," Axel said. "But I get what you're saying. Gotta make decisions you can live with, and with you havin' demons of your own, they're gonna sway the direction you go."

"She say anything else?" Jace asked.

I paused long enough to think through the encounter, staring at my hands in my lap. "I asked her if Viv knew she'd moved home. She said she hadn't told her yet. That she wanted to get her legs under her and stabilized before she did." I looked to Jace. "Said Viv deserved that after everything she'd put her through."

Jace grunted. "If anyone thinks I'm gonna keep this from my wife, they're out of their fucking mind. Secrets don't work. Especially in a marriage."

"I feel you," I said. "If I had a good woman like you do, I wouldn't keep anything from her. So, if I do give Callie the chance, it'll be contingent on her coming clean with Viv. The question is—if I give her the chance are you all going to be on board with it?"

"You think she can do the job?" Knox asked.

I huffed out a harsh laugh. "I asked her the same damned thing. She said she honestly didn't know what an office manager did, but that she could answer a phone, work a computer and organize shit. Which, if I'm bein' honest, is more than I can do half the time."

Beckett grinned at that and took another sip of his beer. "I hear you there, brother."

"You know," Rex said, "I'm all for givin' someone a chance at buildin' skills, but in your line of work, the wrong person on the phone could drive away a lot of business. Also, you've got cash comin' and goin' out of that shop. You're gonna have to keep an eye on that flow and make sure she's as solid as you're hopin' she is."

"He's right," Ivan said. "I'm all about opportunity, but not about being stupid."

"Easy enough to deal with," Knox said. "You've got cameras and surveillance already. We could loan Katy out to teach her the basics on day-to-day management stuff. While she's at it, I'll have her put in some checks and balances with a secured drawer. If money goes missing, you'll know exactly where to look."

"Upside to all this?" Beckett said to Jace. "We'll know where Callie is and what she's up to."

Jace focused on the tabletop directly in front of him and pulled in a long, slow breath. Only after a decent amount of time had turned into thoughtful silence did he redirect his gaze to me. "Truth? I hope like hell you're right about Callie. Vivienne loves her sister, and I'd be tickled shitless if they could have a decent relationship. And, if the wildcard is gonna be this close to us, I'd rather know where she is and what she's up to than have her all over town doing God knows what.

"That said, it's your business and your decision. So long as she comes clean to Viv, I'll support whatever choice you make."

"Yep," Zeke said.

"Same here," Axel added.

The rest of the guys nodded, adding their unified agreement.

For the first time in days…maybe weeks…the tension that'd been riding my neck and shoulders finally unwound, and the nonstop jumbled thoughts in my head took a load off and got quiet. I was square with my brothers, they had my back, and I just might be able to turn an awkward as fuck situation into a win-win for everyone.

Maybe.

If I was willing to take the risk.

I nodded to the table at large and reclined in my chair. "Let me sit on it tonight. I'll make a decision by tomorrow."

Chapter Five

Callie

Noticing the world and all its details was a whole lot easier sober. Or maybe it was less about *noticing* and more about *appreciating*. Like how good an evening breeze felt through your open car window on a summer evening. Or how pretty the sunset looked when the orange and purple rays pushed through clouds scattered on the horizon.

I pulled my Chevy into a slot in my apartment's parking lot, shoved the gearshift into park and took a minute to savor. The last time I really remembered paying attention to a sunset was the year Dad had taken us to some big fireworks show. I was maybe eight or nine, and the only reason the sun got any of my attention was because I wanted it to *go away already* so the fireworks could start.

Folding my arms atop the steering wheel, I gave myself time and just sat there. Watching. Appreciating. Letting myself enjoy the moment. Funny how the big gold ball seemed to crawl across the sky during the day, but moved really fast sinking behind the horizon.

Kind of has a similarity to your hopes of scoring a decent job, doesn't it?

The unexpected negative thought zapped straight through my happy moment and left me chilled. I sighed and straightened away from the wheel. I would *not* let my stinking thinking screw me up again. Negativity, low self-esteem and my overinflated sense of entitlement were my three biggest fast-tracks back to drinking, and I refused to let them cause me or the people I loved any more damage.

I closed my eyes and took a long slow breath.

Then another.

God, grant me the serenity to accept the things I cannot change, courage to change the things I can, and the wisdom to know the difference.

Three more breaths.

Then a few more until a little of my peace returned.

I couldn't change the fact that I hadn't heard from Danny.

I *could* make a call to my previous boss first thing in the morning and ask for a reference. I *could* be grateful that I had someone to call for a reference, and I *could* have faith that my Higher Power would get me where I needed to be. And if I still felt shaky in an hour or so, I could call Maggie and stay on the phone with her until I got grounded again.

Nodding at my healthier resolve and opening my eyes, I powered up the windows, killed the engine and strode toward my upstairs apartment. At eight thirty at night, the skies overhead and behind me were just dark enough to show a smattering of early stars, and a hint of someone grilling steaks or burgers hung on the air.

I jogged up the stairs and dug into my purse for my

keys. I should really consider grilling for myself one of these days. I'd been to a million cookouts—usually with an end result of being blotto. It might be nice to change the script and do a special meal just for myself. Maybe save up and get one of those tiny grills for my balcony. Make it a date with myself, so to speak.

Smiling at the somewhat goofy idea, I let myself into my apartment, happy not just at the prospect of some wholesome self-care, but proud that I'd dodged my old behaviors and replaced them with the tools my program gave me.

I dropped my purse and keys on top of an empty box I'd turned upside down and placed by the front door as a makeshift entry table. The rest of the apartment wasn't much to speak of—a chambray flannel couch that was comfy enough to nap on, a cheapo flat-screen TV that was small enough to pick up with one hand and a white entertainment stand that was super plain, but functionally perfect. Every stitch of it plus my bedroom furniture was secondhand, most of it donated by my AA friends in Louisiana when I'd announced my interest in moving back to Texas. The rest of it, along with the mix and match dishes in the cabinets, I'd purchased in thrift stores or garage sales. The only décor I had to speak of was the Lady in Paris picture I'd done at the art fair yesterday with my tween buddies which was presently propped up against the far wall.

But every bit of it was mine.

Honest treasures gifted to me by awesome people or earned through hard work instead of scamming.

I opened the refrigerator door, snatched a can of Cubana La Croix off the top shelf then poured it into the stemless plastic wine tumbler Maggie had gotten me for my birthday.

Serenity now, dammit!

I still chuckled every time I read the bright turquoise script jauntily written at an angle on the side. The disheveled cartoon blonde next to the inscription no doubt looked a lot like me when I first returned to AA.

The fizz was still whispering to me over the rim when three firm raps sounded on my door.

Hmmm.

That was weird.

No one except Maggie and Susan knew where I lived. Maggie was seven hours away and hadn't mentioned road-tripping to Texas when we'd texted this morning, and Susan had been headed home to spend the evening with her kids.

I set my drink and the La Croix can on the impromptu coffee table I'd made out of two crates and a weathered piece of plywood and headed to the door. Maybe it was one of my new neighbors stopping by to introduce themselves.

Opening the door, I plastered on what I hoped was a welcoming smile—only to feel my jaw slacken at who I found waiting outside. "Danny?"

He huffed out a chuckle and scanned the parking lot behind him before turning his dark as night eyes on me. "You expecting someone else?"

"Um…no. Not really. I thought maybe it was one of my neighbors."

Danny looked down the walk that fronted the other three units on the top floor then back to me. "Doesn't really seem to be a very active place." He scanned the doorjamb, the doorknob, then scowled at the latch before returning his attention to me. "Not very secure either."

"Well, I'm not exactly in an income bracket that has a ton of high security options, ya know?"

He pursed his mouth to one side in what could have been a wry smile or a grimace. "Yeah, I get it." He cocked his head enough to look behind me. "You care if I come in? Or are you more comfortable talking with me here?"

Shit.

"Sorry. I didn't mean to be rude." I stepped out of the way and waved him in. "You caught me off guard."

He strolled inside, openly checking out everything from my meager furnishings to the windows and the cheap white blinds that matched the walls. His gaze landed on the wineglass for a solid two seconds, then shifted to me.

"Relax," I said, snatching the La Croix can off the table and holding it up so he'd get a better look. "It's not booze. It's flavored fizzy water."

The comment earned me a cockeyed smile that made my knees get a little shaky and unleashed a host of butterflies in my belly. "I know what it is. Just didn't take you for a La Croix kind of girl."

Okay, that was fair. And maybe I shouldn't have just assumed he'd think the worst of me either. I shrugged and topped off my wineglass a little more since the bubbles had settled down. "My sponsor loves the stuff. I picked it up from her and developed a taste for it myself. You want one?"

He shook his head and anchored his fingertips in the front pockets of his jeans. "Nah. Just stopped by for a minute to give you an answer."

This time the sensation in my stomach wasn't nearly as pleasant. More of a plummeting free fall than anything of the tingly variety. I nodded and focused on the toes of his black boots. "I get it."

"Get what?"

Fuck but this sucked. I'd tried really hard since Wednesday to keep my expectations level, but if my quickly sinking hopes were any indication, I'd banked a lot more emotion on landing the job with Danny than I'd thought. "I'm not exactly a safe bet in the employee scheme of things. At least not for someone who knows me."

Silence stretched for long enough that curiosity finally made me lift my attention back to Danny's face.

His eyes narrowed. "That's twice in under a few minutes you've assumed I'd think the worst."

"Well, don't you?"

He sighed and studied the floor for a minute before answering me head-on. "The truth? Yeah, I've spent the last few days figuring out if I could trust you in my shop. I've also been trying to figure out if giving you my time will be well spent or put to foul use. But if I'd decided neither were doable for me, do you think I'd have shown in person to tell you that was the case?"

No.

Fucking.

Way.

"Are you…" I snapped my mouth shut, then opened and closed it again when my brain wouldn't cooperate enough to give me any words. I blinked a few times while I waited for my thoughts to come online. "You're telling me you're willing to give me a chance?"

He tilted his head slightly and studied me in a curious way that made me want to fidget. Like he wasn't really sure if he was looking at the right person. Only after a good ten seconds of healthy consideration did he answer, and when he did, his voice was so warm I could've melted. "I'll give you a chance, if you'll give yourself one."

I swallowed hard, though it was really freaking hard with the lump jammed up in the base of my throat. "Not sure what you mean by that."

"I mean if I agree to believe in you, I expect you to believe in you, too, and stop cuttin' yourself short."

Had I been doing that?

My thoughts shuttled back to the negativity that'd kicked in while I was in the parking lot. Those negative thoughts were a constant in my life. Always had been. But I was learning to turn those things over to my Higher Power and was asking Him every day to take them away from me.

Now, here was a guy I seriously respected telling me not just that he was willing to take a chance on me, but that he wanted me to take a chance on myself.

Wow.

Talk about miracles.

Maggie was gonna laugh herself silly when I told her how all of this went down and probably throw in a few *I told ya so*'s for good measure.

I nodded as much as I could beneath the humbling emotions powering through me. My voice was almost as shaky as the rest of me when I answered. "Yeah. I can do that."

"Good." He dipped his chin in a that-was-that motion. "Glad we're in agreement. Though, there is one condition."

My already unsteady insides flip-flopped to match some wicked airplane turbulence, and for the first time in at least a month I wished like hell my La Croix was Grey Goose. "Yeah?"

My caution must've been written all over my face because his voice gentled just a fraction. "Before I made my decision, I talked things over with my brothers."

I nodded, not really knowing what to say or where he was headed.

"One of my brothers is Viv's husband, Jace."

Yikes. That couldn't be good. And it also made absolutely no sense. "Viv never told me that Jace was your brother. Neither did you."

For a second, Danny frowned at me then shook his head. "I keep forgetting you only met a few of the guys once and weren't exactly in a great place when you did. No, we're not blood brothers. My sister, Gabe, is the only blood relation I've got left. I'm talkin' about brothers by choice. Family by choice, really. Men like me who've made their way out of a tough beginning and who back each other up. You put us all together with their wives and Jace's and Axel's moms—we make one helluva brood."

A family.

A really freaking nice one, too, if the pride in Danny's voice and the fond smile on his face were any indication.

I'd found something of my own family in AA, but I couldn't say I wasn't still envious of the clan Danny described.

And Viv was part of it.

A weird combination of happy warmth and frigid loneliness hit me all at once. Probably because, while

I was happy as hell for my sister, I was a little jealous of the life she'd appeared to have found.

Of course, I could have been part of that if I hadn't screwed up so many times the last six years. But life was full of choices, and I'd made a long string of shitty ones all the way back to high school.

"Sounds nice." The words were there, but the tone didn't have as much conviction as it should have. "Doesn't really tell me what the condition is, though."

He paused only a moment. "Families don't keep secrets. Even more to the point, husbands don't keep secrets from their wives."

Shit.

Shit, shit, shit.

I put my La Croix down on the plywood and paced toward the kitchen, wiping my trembling, sweaty hands on my hips. "He wants me to tell her I'm here."

"He does. And honestly? If you're out to live a straight life, I do, too. I mean, to my way of thinking there's absolutely no downside. Whereas, if you waited, you'd run the risk of runnin' into her somewhere and making her wonder why you never told her you were moving back."

He was right. I knew it. Maggie had known it, too, and told me as much when I'd insisted on getting my bearings before reaching out to my sister.

But I hadn't listened.

I still didn't want to.

"You feel like sharin' why the idea of calling your sister just made you look like you haven't seen the sun in a month?"

I stared at the line where the kitchen's linoleum met the living room's somewhat tired taupe carpet and tried to find my voice. Tried to find any combination of words that could adequately describe the swell of terror I knew I was eventually going to have to face.

I wasn't sure how long I stood there, but eventually, the simplest of truths tumbled past my lips. "My sister doesn't even know a tenth of how far I've fallen. Of the bad things I'm accountable for. But for me to have any kind of a meaningful relationship with her—to really own up to who I am—I'm gonna have to come clean with her. And I'm not sure I'm stable enough yet for that."

Danny stared at me, the expression on his face one I wasn't sure how to interpret. If I had to go with anything, I'd guess I'd somehow shocked him. "That's a big step."

"Uh, yeah," I said with an ironic chuckle. "And I really don't want to face-plant when I take it."

That lopsided smile of his popped out of nowhere again, confusing me completely. "I wasn't talking about you coming clean with Viv. I was talking about you realizing it needed to happen."

Oh.

Right.

I looked back to my toes, my cheeks suddenly hotter than they'd been when I'd been running errands this afternoon in ninety-eight degree heat. Just to have something to cover my awkwardness, I hustled back to my drink and lifted it. "Yeah, well." I took a sip, both grateful for how it eased my suddenly parched tongue and irritated the familiar burn I used to rely on didn't blaze its way down my throat. "Realizing something and actually acting on it are two very different things."

"Maybe. But I'd say figuring out what needs fixing is

way bigger than doing the actual work. You can make a plan when you know what it is you need to tackle, but if you're in the dark, everything's a guessing game at best. And remember, no one says you have to do the work the second you talk to her. Hell, if anything, I'd say that'd be the worst move. She'll need time to ease in with you just as much as you'll need time to ease in with her."

Well, that made sense. Though, it didn't cover all my concerns. "But what if she doesn't want to talk to me?"

Danny shrugged. "What if she doesn't? Is your sobriety so shaky you think you won't know how to handle it? You think you'll go straight to a bar? Or are you in a place where you'd call one of your people and talk it through?"

"No. My sponsor and I already talked about that. We agreed I'd call her after the fact and talk it through."

"Then you've got a plan for handlin' that, too. And if Viv doesn't want to talk, then that decision's on her. But at least you'll have taken the time to be honest from the get-go instead of slinkin' around on the quiet."

My heart thrummed like I'd sprinted up two flights of stairs, but I was also keenly focused. As if everything Danny had said had reached inside of me and stirred long-buried hopes and dreams.

Much as I'd tried not to think about his job over the last five days, my mind had repeatedly wandered back to the idea. Imagined what it would be like to actually have some meaningful responsibility and all the things I could learn and leverage for opportunities in the future. I'd even gone so far as to Google what an office manager typically did for a company and had almost swallowed my tongue when I saw how much I could make if I got some real experience. Talk about a stroll past minimum wage…

I took another sip of my drink just to buy some time, then let out a slow breath while I sat it back down on the table. While I wasn't really sure I wanted the answer, I asked the question burning up my throat anyway. "Do you really think I can do this job? Or are you just doing this for Viv?"

Some men might have been offended by the question, but it bounced off Danny like I'd asked him if he had a preference between tan and taupe. "I love Vivienne the same as I love everyone else in my family, but I'm not gonna put my business or my reputation at stake just for a favor. And yeah, I think if you've got the right support and enough drive behind you, you can make it work. You just need to know going in that if you don't make the most of it, my support won't be there long."

"You mean you'd find someone else."

"Damn straight. It's the standard I set for my designers in the shop, and it'll be applied to you just the same. What you do with the chance is up to you." He paused a second and considered me. "Now are you in, or out?"

It was such an amazing chance. Especially with Danny's business being custom rides. That was a hell of a lot more my speed than the other industries I'd looked at when I'd combed the job boards. And the truth of the matter was—if I didn't tell Viv I was in town, Danny or Jace would anyway. Then I really would look like the chicken-shit he'd implied I'd be.

I nodded my head. Or at least I tried to. No small feat considering I had enough adrenaline flowing through me to light up a small village. "Yeah. I'm in."

"Good." He folded his arms across his chest and smiled. "Then let's get it done."

Huh?

I stared at him for a few seconds, waiting for some kind of clarification. When all he did was stare back, I went for something more tangible. "Get what done?"

"You calling Vivienne."

What that… "Now?"

"You got a better time? I'm here. You're here. You want the job and agreed to the terms, so…let's get it done."

Fuck.

A cold sweat broke out along the back of my neck and my ears rang with way too much silence. I didn't have a clue what to say to my sister. Let alone with a man as intimidating as Danny watching. "Can you just…" I waved him off and paced around my makeshift table to the sofa, dropping like a stone to the middle cushion. I planted my elbows on my knees and buried my face in my hands. "I'm gonna need a minute."

"Fine with me." His booted footsteps sounded on the carpet, followed by the scrape of my La Croix can being lifted from the table. I looked up to find Danny checking out the front of it. "On second thought, you care if I take you up on nabbing one of these?"

As if my brain needed one more hurdle to overcome in a minuscule chunk of time, I tried to wrap my head around Danny Parker sipping a La Croix in any flavor. "Uh, sure. In the fridge. Help yourself."

With an easygoing nod, he did just that, strolling into my kitchen and opening cabinets like he was a well-known guest instead of an acquaintance.

God, could this night get any more bizarre?

I shook my head to clear my thoughts, stood and strode to my purse by the front door. My trip back to the couch was a whole lot slower, the weight of my phone in my palm feeling twice what it normally did.

What the heck was I going to say to her?

Hey, Vivie! It's Callie. Guess what? I moved back to Dallas and wanted to see if you wanted to get together and catch up.

I cringed at the mock dialogue in my head, both because it sounded totally fake and because it masqueraded as something normal sisters would say. Thanks to my addictions, Viv and I were about as far away from a normal relationship as two people could get.

There was also the very real probability that she wouldn't even deign to answer the phone—not that I could blame her for sending me to voice mail.

I thumbed up my contacts and let out a harsh exhale.

In my periphery, Danny finished pouring himself a drink and leaned one shoulder on the wall that separated my galley kitchen from my living room. "That tough, huh?"

Vivienne Moore.

Her name stared at me from the screen. Such a pretty name. Both sophisticated and spunky. A name worthy of my sister. "I don't know what to say to her."

"Maybe just the simple truth."

The truth.

The *simple* truth.

I closed my eyes and clutched the phone tight. *God, I am terrified right now. Terrified that my sister will answer the phone. Even more afraid that she won't.* I paused a second and reached for the stillness that always came when I took the time and waited. *I don't know what to do or what to say, but I know You're giving me this chance for a reason. Please help me.*

Not giving myself time to think, I opened my eyes and punched Viv's number.

One ring.

Then another. And another.

With every single repeat, the muscles in my body tightened to the point where I wasn't sure they'd ever unlock.

"Hello, you've reached the voice mail for Vivienne Moore with Amaryllis Events. Please leave your message at the tone and I'll return your message as soon as possible."

My sister.

She'd always had a pretty voice. A perky one to match her indomitable spirit. But listening to it now, I noticed something I'd missed when I'd called before.

Happiness.

Yeah, it was a standard, businesslike greeting, but it was thick with peace. Like she'd finally let go of chasing whatever it was she'd been so damned determined to find growing up and had simply decided to enjoy the present moment.

The tone to leave a message jolted me out of my stupor. I still didn't have a clue what to say, but the one thing I'd learned in the last year was faith. So, I opened my mouth and leaned into it.

"Hey, Vivienne. It's Callie." I paused a moment and just let the silence be what it needed to be. "Listen, I know when we last talked you were really clear about me not reaching out again unless I was sober. I've honored that because I know me calling when I'm wasted hurts you really bad. I'm sorry for that. I really am. I also know that me saying sorry doesn't mean a damned thing and that actions are what really counts, so I'm working on that. I'm going to meetings regularly and have just over a year clean and sober."

The memory of standing next to Vivienne the day we'd buried my father surged up out of nowhere. I'd never felt such profound pain as I had that day. We'd stood together and watched the men lower his casket down into the ground and, more than anything, I'd wanted to throw myself in the hole with it and let them bury me, too. I didn't deserve to live. Not after what I'd set in motion.

The only reason I hadn't completely lost it that day was Viv's hand wrapping around mine. She'd anchored me.

She always anchored me.

But it was time for me to stand on my own.

I cleared my throat. "I also need to tell you that I moved back to Texas last week. Not Dallas proper where I was before, but over in Garland. The places to rent are a lot cheaper here and my sponsor had some friends who recommended a particular AA clubhouse that's got a lot of really healthy sobriety, so…"

I rubbed my free hand against my thigh. "Anyway, I don't expect you to do anything with any of this. I'm just trying to be transparent and let you know what's going on with me." The bridge of my nose burned with the threat of tears. "And that I'm trying to be a better person. To be me minus all the bullshit."

I swallowed around the knot in my throat, but the rest of my words came out scratchy. "Your message sounded really happy and I'm glad for that." My lips trembled. As though they were afraid to utter the rest of what I wanted to say. "I love you."

The tears I'd tried to hold back slipped free as I punched the end button. I cradled the phone in my hands and just stared at it.

Wrong or right, I'd tried.

I'd put myself out there. The rest was out of my hands.

Hushed movement sounded beside me, startling me so badly I visibly flinched.

Danny.

God, I'd been so focused on the call to Viv I'd completely forgotten he was there. I stood and pressed my palm over my heart like that had any prayer of getting it to settle down. "Sorry, I was kind of out of it."

Shaking the heavy residue of the call took a second or two, but by the time I'd stowed my phone in my back pocket and had the presence of mind to actually look at the man standing in front of me, I was a bit taken aback. Granted, I didn't know Danny well enough to claim any significant familiarity with his moods or what made him tick, but I'd sure never seen that particular expression on his face.

"You okay?" I asked.

His gaze held strong. Penetrating, but also gentle. As if he wasn't really sure what was going on himself. "Are you?"

My laughter mingled with what was also a lingering need to just sob like an overtired two-year-old. "Probably need to call my sponsor and have a good cry, but I'll be better for it in the end."

"Yeah," he said. Though, from the tone of it, I wasn't sure if the word was for me, or if he was answering an entirely different question running through his head. "I think you will be."

He blinked, shook his head as though clearing his own cobwebs, then downed what was left of his drink. Setting the glass on the plywood next to mine, he said, "Think I'd better let you get to that call." He straightened and cocked his head. "You good to show tomorrow around ten?"

Tomorrow.

At ten.

I was going to have a job.

A really good job that I might be able to make something positive from. "Yeah. Yeah, I can be there at ten. Earlier if you want."

He smiled at that and chuckled. "Yeah, we're not really early birds at the shop." With that he headed to the door, opened it, then paused at the threshold. "You're gonna make that call, right?"

I followed him to the door, pulled the phone free from my pocket and waggled it where he could see it. "Just as soon as I lock up, yeah."

Less than an arm span separated us. I'd always known he was a good foot or more taller than me, but standing this close I felt tiny. And, for some stupid reason, it was tempting as hell to just lean into him. To feel his arms around me.

For a split second, he looked as if he was thinking the same thing, but it was gone as quick as I'd had the thought. Or, more likely, it'd just been my wishful thinking. His voice, though, was as gentle as it had been right after I'd made the call. "See you in the morning, Callie."

Chapter Six

Danny

Walking into my own bona fide business and watching the rides each of my designers tackled take shape day after day never failed to stoke a deep sense of pride in me. But there was something about being one-on-one with a car—the feel of metal between my fingers or a tool in my palm...the steady rhythm of my breath... the time to let my brain just cruise wherever it wanted to—that centered me.

At least it usually did.

Today, even an early morning trip to spend some time with my newest commission hadn't given me any peace.

Keeping my eyes on the overlapping metal I'd anchored under the Vette's frame, I fumbled for my ratchet beside me. Sun slanting through the open bays behind me heated the back of my hand as it closed around my phone instead of my tool. My mind perked up, as it had countless times since last night, and started recounting yet again the message Callie had left for Vivienne.

I released my grip on the phone and patted the concrete, getting the ratchet the second time around, then quickly bolted the metal into place.

What the fuck was it about last night that had jolted me so bad? I mean, it couldn't be that I was shocked by what Callie had said. I'd obviously bought into the fact that she was on a better track for straightening out her life when I'd gone so far as to talk to the guys about giving her a job. All she'd done leaving that message was own up to where she was in life and shown some gut-level honesty.

That's a hell of a lot more than Mom ever did.

I laid the ratchet down like it was a live wire instead of an inanimate tool and just lay there a second, my brain scrambling to analyze what it'd just tripped on. Zeke had hinted of the similarities between Callie and my mom Saturday night at rally. Had even gone so far as to suggest that might be why I'd been unable to ignore Callie's calls for help.

Was that why Callie's message had hit me so hard? Because of my own relationship with my mom? Which was really more the *lack of* a relationship, if I called it what it really was.

My phone sat framed in the thick sunlight. Almost like an item spotlighted on display.

I went with my gut, swiped it up and rolled myself out from under the Vette's mostly bare frame. I was on my feet with a call to Gabe ringing in my ear before I got three steps into a steady pacing pattern.

"Whoa," Gabe said with the goofy tone she rarely showed those beyond family. "My big brother is calling before noon? Is the end of the world near? Is there a tornado headed my direction?"

"Hey, I only did that tornado gag once. Give a guy a break."

"You called me when I was in a deep sleep on a Saturday morning and yelled that a tornado was bearing down on the house."

"It was April Fool's Day! How was I supposed to know you weren't gonna look outside and figure out there wasn't a cloud in the sky before you took shelter in the tub?"

"It was still a shitty thing to do." The words were terse, but there was a loving smile in her voice that said she'd long let the prank go.

"Shitty, but funny as hell. Probably the only damned time in my life I've sent flowers to anyone, too."

"Seriously? You've never sent a woman flowers?"

I paused mid-trek to the opposite end of the garage and gave my memory time to stretch before picking up the pace again. "Nope. Just you."

"Hmmm." A swoosh that said she'd just dropped into someplace cushy sounded through the line. "Kind of sad if you ask me."

Was it? Or had I just not found a woman worth sending flowers to?

"Whatever," I said shrugging it off. "Wasn't calling to have you give me grief about my nonexistent relationship skills. Was callin' to ask you other deep shit."

"Oh…deep shit. I love it." More shifting sounded through the line, which gave me the image of her settling in for a deep conversation. "What's up?"

Across the street, the neighborhood 7-Eleven was doing gangbuster Monday-morning business. Giving up my back-and-forth routine, I leaned a shoulder against the bay's frame and watched everyone's comings and goings. "You said your trips to the shrink helped you see how Mom's bullshit impacted you growing up."

It took a beat or two before Gabe spoke. When she did, her playful tone had been replaced with one of concerned focus. "You having problems?"

Hell if I knew. But if I was, the one thing I was absolutely sure of was that I wasn't gonna push 'em off on my baby sister. She'd wrestled enough of her own shit. She didn't need mine, too. "Nah. More curious really. Been watchin' someone else going through some stuff, and it made me wonder. You know how my mind gets when I'm workin' on a car."

More silence. But if I knew Sugar Bear, she was thinking hard and trying to read between the lines. Gabe was a force of nature where family was concerned.

"Well, first of all," she finally said in a droll tone, "I don't think they like it when you call 'em shrinks."

I rolled my eyes even though she wasn't there to appreciate her brother's insensitivity. "Right. Therapists. Counselors. Whatever." I waved my hands in the air like the visual urging might help her stay on target. "So, what kind of impact was it?"

Gabe let out a slow sigh. "I guess if I had to pare it down to a simple description, I'd say I assumed anyone who got close to me would end up leaving me—so I used all kinds of techniques to keep most people away."

"So, abandonment issues."

She scoffed at that, but ended it with an adorable giggle that made me smile. "*Abandonment issues.* Aren't you just the closet therapist? Or did you pick that up on a rerun of *Dr. Phil* at three in the morning?"

"Man, why you gotta bust my balls?"

Gabe took it for the playful banter it was and fired right back. "Someone's gotta bust your balls. Everyone else except the brothers are too afraid to."

Under normal circumstances, the back-and-forth routine of trading jabs and innocent insults would've gone on for a good five minutes. But today? Today I was too busy trying to see how that particular puzzle piece fit on what I was feeling.

Unfortunately, I wasn't seeing it. I had lots of people I was close to. "So that's it. Just keepin' people at a distance so they won't leave you like she did?"

"Well, that and thinking I'd never measure up enough to be loved by anyone but you or Dad."

Hmmm.

Still no dice. I *knew* my family loved me.

But do you? Really?

The discomfort that'd been prodding me all damned night and morning grew a few new burrs and dug a little deeper.

If I was smart, I'd let it lie and let things be.

But Gabe knew me. And if I could trust one person without question in this world, it was her. "What about me?"

"What about you?"

Just forming the question in my head was a struggle. Which all by itself said maybe I was onto something. "Do you think Mom fucked me up?"

This time the silence between us was supercharged. So much so I was halfway tempted to tell her never mind and come up with some lame-ass excuse to get off the phone. Of course, Gabe would call bullshit foul on that action in a heartbeat. Hell, even if I tried, she'd be in the shop's office within thirty minutes picking up where we left off.

Gabe cleared her throat. It was the only warning I got before she laid it out in the gentlest way she could. "Danny, you just used the phrase *nonexistent relationship skills* with me not three minutes ago. Those were your words, not mine."

"So?"

"So, you don't think it's odd that you're thirty-four years old and you haven't had a girlfriend for longer than like a month at a time?"

I straightened away from the wall, a bristling sensation not unlike when some dumbass decided to get crosswise with me whispering along the back of my neck. "What the hell difference does that make? Other than I've got high expectations? I mean, look at all the women in our family. You really think I'm gonna settle for less than awesome when I can see how important finding *the right* woman is?"

"You've got high standards? Or you come up with a million reasons why they're not good enough so you don't have to get hurt?"

Sharp words that sliced deeper than I cared to admit, but delivered with the most sincere care. I stood there, so damned stupefied I didn't think I could've drummed up a response if I'd had to. Maybe I did have abandonment issues. Different in the way I'd gone about showing them, but a definite possibility all the same.

"Danny?"

"Yeah, Sugar Bear, I'm here. All good."

"You sure?"

Not really. If anything, I was more off-kilter than I had been when we'd started our conversation. But I'd figure it out. I still had thirty minutes before my staff started rolling in. Plenty of time to give my thoughts room to roam and settle down. "Absolutely. Good stuff to think about."

A blue Chevy Spark whipped into the parking lot, one I identified instantly after tailing Callie Saturday afternoon.

So much for room to process...

"Hey," I said to Gabe. "Someone just pulled up. I gotta run."

"Danny—"

"Not givin' you the brush-off, so don't even go there. It's a chick I hired to handle some office stuff for me. She just showed about thirty minutes early for her first day, and I gotta get my ass in gear."

She huffed but reined it in. Mostly. "You swear?"

"Promise. I'll follow up with you about it later, cool?"

"Tonight."

Right. Tonight. Like I'd be able to remember my own last name by the end of a Monday. But I went with it. "You got it. Call ya later."

With that, I hung up and jogged toward the office. I'd barely made it through the door that separated the shop from the office when Callie yanked the front door's handle and made the thrown dead bolt rattle. Why she thought she'd be able to see through the frosted film covering the glass entrance I had no clue, but she cupped either side of her eyes to block the sun and tried anyway.

I chuckled, flipped the bolt and carefully pushed the door open so I didn't whack her in the process. "You're early."

"First day, right?" She shrugged, then gripped the

strap of her purse. "I had no clue what traffic around this area would be like, and I figured better early than late." She eyed the space just past the threshold and raised her eyebrows. "Okay to come in? Or you want me to wait until ten?"

Christ, but the woman could *seriously* wear a pair of jeans. The way the ones she had on today hugged her hips, I was a little afraid to catch a view of how good things looked from the backside. Her T-shirt wasn't helping matters either. The turquoise color made her green eyes pop even more than they normally did, and the V-neck and tight fit made it hard as hell not to appreciate her amazing as fuck rack.

"Um...sorry if I pissed you off." Callie glanced at her car then jerked her thumb toward it. "I don't mind waiting. I know you've probably got other stuff to do."

The weird statement punched me out of my stupor. "What makes you think I'm pissed off?"

She looked at me in that sideways fashion reserved for lunatics. "Because you went from smiling to frowning in about two seconds?"

I had?

Shit.

I shook my head and opened the door a little wider, waving her through with my other hand. "No. Not pissed. Just up in my head this morning."

It took her another glance at the space inside and my face before she finally nodded and eased across the threshold.

Yep.

A *damned* nice view from behind.

And not at all what I needed to be thinking about with a new employee.

Or my brother's sister-in-law.

I cleared my throat and hustled around Callie toward the cluttered desk. "So, I've got someone comin' to help you figure shit out around ten thirty this morning. Until then, you're stuck with me."

"Someone to help me?"

"Yeah." I stacked up the invoices I'd left scattered haphazardly in the center of the desk along with a few legal pads I'd scribbled on and put it all to one side—not surprisingly on top of another stack I'd built over the last week or so. "Office stuff's not really my thing which is why you're here. I figured me teachin' you anything would be pretty fuckin' stupid, so one of my brothers is sendin' over their office manager to give you a leg up."

I turned to find Callie grinning up at me like a loon. "What?"

Her smile got bigger. "You just said *shit* and *fuck* with a new employee in less than two minutes."

Huh. I guess I had. "That gonna be a problem?"

She laughed this time and shook her head. "Nope. Not as long as you don't give me shit for doin' the same thing."

Funny. All of a sudden, I felt a whole lot lighter than I had all morning. Kind of like when me and my sister or my brothers were hanging out and having a good time. "Actually, I think if you don't use a few four-letter words in general conversation, the guys in the shop'll think you're an alien."

I waved my hand toward the bottom drawer on one side of the desk. "Pretty sure that one's close to empty if you want a place to stash your bag, then go ahead and have a seat. Might as well get you set up on the computer, then we can introduce you to the guys once they start showin' up."

Callie slid between the desk and the chair I'd pulled out for her and slowly lowered herself into the seat, cautiously taking note of all the papers still waiting for attention. "I'm gonna wager that making some kind of sense out of all this is one of my first jobs?"

"That'd be a good wager, yeah." I grabbed the old folding chair some of my guys used when they'd come in to take a break from the summer heat in the shop and planted it next to Callie where I could access the keyboard. "Like I said, office shit ain't my thing—especially paperwork."

I logged into the computer and pulled up the accounting software Knox had given me when I'd first opened the shop.

As soon as the main screen opened and displayed line after line of accounting entries, Callie leaned in for a closer look. "Whoa. That looks like some serious stuff."

It was on the tip of my tongue to throw out something crude like, *No shit, tell me about it* when that flowery scent she'd sidelined me with last week hit me again, and I lost my train of thought. The rows of charges and deposits stared at me from the screen while the hamster in my head ran wild on a spinning wheel to nowhere.

Fuck, I really needed to get my shit together with this woman.

Pronto.

I clicked a few menu headers until I finally remembered it was the admin function I was after and got busy making Callie an account. Getting into the mundane of showing her around the computer, what all was stored in and on the desk, plus where stuff was supposed to go in the file cabinets finally managed to get my personal chaos under control. Thirty minutes later, fate threw me another slow pitch when the speakers out in the shop fired up to a wailing guitar solo from a live version of a Tedeschi Trucks song, alerting me that at least one of the guys had shown for the new week.

I lifted my chin toward the shop and steered Callie by a hand at her shoulder toward the office's rear door. "Come on. You already know Jason, but I'll introduce you to the rest of the guys."

Outside, the sun had risen high enough the shop was in full shade, but the summer heat was definitely present. I led the way down the metal stairs. "We don't punch a clock here—everyone comes and goes as they need to, but I do ask the guys to share with each other if they're gonna be out more than an hour during normal business hours. I figure since you'll be in the office and taking calls, I'll have 'em change that up and let you know what their plans are in case you get any commission calls for 'em."

"Commission calls?"

"People who've made a down payment for a specific job. They call, tell us what they're after, and we work up a design. If they like it and want to move forward, they give us half down and we get to work. They pay the rest on delivery."

Callie nodded, but I wasn't sure how much of what I'd said had sunk in. Not with the way her wide eyes were taking in every detail. Honest to God, you'd have thought I'd walked her into a gold palace instead of an auto garage. Not at all what I'd expect of any woman.

Well, except my sister, Gabe. Gabe would've already

flattened herself out on one of the creepers and had herself under an engine—a side effect of growing up with only a dad and a brother in the house and both of them mechanics by trade.

Hmm. Kind of made me wonder if the similarity between Callie and Gabe meant the two of them would hit it off.

"This the new girl?" Malcom said as I hit the bottom landing.

I shook off the unexpected and kind of uncomfortable thought and waved a hand between them. "Callie, this is Malcom. He's been with me about three years now. Hadn't done custom jobs before I took him on, but he's gettin' a really good clientele on lowriders and flatrods."

"Oh, yeah?" Callie said to Malcom. "I saw a killer flatrod made out of a standard military jeep body at the Louisiana State Fair in Shreveport about five years back. Killer concept, but the guy who built it said the ride was rough as hell."

Malcom's jaw dropped to mirror his raised eyebrows.

I might have visually masked my surprise a little better than Malcom, but the shock was still evident in my voice. "You know custom rides?"

"Oh, yeah," she said smiling huge. "My dad loved 'em. Loved custom bikes even more. Always said he wanted to try it one day."

Just as quickly as the smile had broken out on her face, it flatlined. She jammed one hand in her back pocket and held out the other to Malcom. "Anyway... nice to meet you."

Odd.

I knew from Viv that their dad had died a long time

ago, but wasn't familiar with the situation behind it. Somehow I'd have to figure that out because whatever it was couldn't have been good if her sudden mood kill was anything to go by.

Malcom shook her hand. If he'd noted the shift in her enthusiasm, he didn't show it. Quite the opposite actually—he eyed her head to toe in a way that said he was considering how much trouble it would cause him if he cozied up with the new office manager.

I quenched that with a meaningful punch to his shoulder when Callie glanced away.

Malcom's eyes widened with genuine surprise for a second, but he clearly got the message because he lifted both hands in surrender and offered Callie a much more platonic smile when she turned back around. "Good to meet you, Callie. If you need anything when Danny's not here, let me know."

When Danny's not here.

Fucking punk.

Maybe I should have punched him harder.

Not giving Callie any time to respond, I grabbed her just above her elbow and steered her past Jason's bay where he was shimmying into his coveralls. "Jason you already know."

Callie waved at Jason and gave him a familiar smile.

Jason nodded in turn, then grinned at me. Whether it was because he was pleased I'd gone through with hiring her or because he'd seen the interaction between me and Malcom, I couldn't tell. Given the smirk in his eyes, I was gonna go with the latter.

Maybe it was time for a staff meeting. One without Callie in attendance and a single agenda item on

how it was definitely *not* okay to hit on the new office manager.

I paused between the empty third bay and the fourth one. "Bay three is Rick's, but he's more of a night owl and doesn't usually roll in until noon." I dipped my head to Jamey ambling toward us. "Bay four is for Jamey. Jamey, meet our new office manager, Callie."

Jamey wasted zero time openly giving Callie a languid once-over and finished it with a cockeyed grin he no doubt wielded on every pretty girl he met. "Hey, gorgeous. How the hell did we luck out getting you on our crew?"

Yep. We were gonna have to have a come to Jesus and sooner rather than later.

To her credit, Callie didn't backhand the buffoon. She did, however, cross her arms over her ample chest and cock her hip in a massive show of attitude. "Does that approach usually work for you, or have you just not thrown back enough coffee yet this morning to find a better groove?"

Jamey smiled, ducked his head a bit and brushed his chin with the back of his hand. "Yikes. That bad, huh?"

"Yeah, little bit. Not to mention I'm not in the market at the moment."

"Already got a man, huh?"

I might not have straightened to full attention externally, but my hearing got scary acute in like a nanosecond.

"Nah," Callie said. "Just got enough on my plate on my own. Not smart to add more to it right now."

The muscles in my shoulders and neck uncoiled at her pronouncement, but the reveal also plucked a nerve I hadn't expected. The upside—with or without a sit-

down with my team—I wouldn't have any office relationship bullshit to contend with. The downside? That
meant I was out of contention, too.

The realization piled on top of all the other unsettled
emotions I'd wrestled all morning and made my voice
come out a little harsh. "Not smart at work, period."

Shit.

Had I just said that out loud? Me of all people?

Callie and Jamey both looked at me like they'd
thought similar thoughts, but it was Jamey that jumped
in for damage control. "Hey, boss. That's all on me. I
should've known better."

The bell that indicated someone had walked into the
shop's office chimed overhead. Right at ten thirty, my
guess was my life preserver had just shown, and thank
God for that.

I waved a dismissive hand at Jamey and tried for
what I hoped was a casual smile. "Don't mind me. Got
too fuckin' much on my mind today and tryin' to teach
Callie things I don't even know how to do myself only
makes me worse."

Jerking my head toward the office, I guided Callie
toward the stairs. "Let's head up. Pretty sure Katy's
here to give you some advice you can actually use."

"Katy?" she said, hustling up the steps beside me.

"The office manager I told you about. Works for
my brothers, Knox and Beckett. They've got a security business, and she's pretty much the glue that holds
it all together."

Sure enough, Katy had not only shown, but had unloaded a few boxes of stuff and was glaring at the messy
desk with both hands on her hips. She turned as soon

as we made it through the back door and gifted Callie with a huge smile. "Hey there! You must be Callie."

Callie nodded and lifted one hand. "Guilty as charged."

Katy laughed at that and shook her head. "I think the guilty party is the one standing next to you." She looked to me, but the expression I got was something closer to exasperation. "I thought at least *some* of my office juju would rub off on you when you were working with Knox and Beck. This place looks like it's the Wild Wild West."

"Bustin' heads and installing security systems rubbed off on me." That plus a few other nefarious educational items, but I wasn't going down that road with either of these women. "Paperwork, not so much."

Katy pursed her mouth to one side, but there was still a smile in her eyes when she harrumphed and shooed me away with one hand. "Fine. Be gone with you. Let me take this poor girl under my wing and see if we can't right the ship in less than a year."

Thank.

Fucking.

God.

I twisted for the shop door, desperate for my tools, a car and a whole lot of quiet so I could unravel the shit tangling up my head. Something stopped me mid-stride, though, and had me turning back to Callie.

Sure enough, her narrowed gaze was centered square on me, her expression one of confusion and maybe a little bit of hurt. Either that or my erratic behavior had her evaluating whether or not I was nuts.

The truth was, I was beginning to wonder the same thing. And while I'd been out of sorts for a while where work was concerned, being around Callie had stirred up a whole host of new thoughts—the physical ones in particular something I definitely needed to get a hold on.

So yeah...distance was a good thing. Even if I did feel like a dick for the quick intro and subsequent bailing routine. But I could still give her the boost she deserved.

Smiling, I dipped my head and told her what I knew to be true in my gut. "It's not a job you've done before, but you've got a good head on your shoulders and a great teacher. You make the most of those two things, then you've definitely got this."

The parting shot worked and earned me a smile from Callie that made me feel like a giant and a superhero all rolled up into one.

Hmmm.

And why was that?

Nope. I wasn't going there. It wasn't right or smart. What was smart was me putting some healthy distance between me and Callie, pronto. So, I gave Katy a wink and made good on my escape.

Chapter Seven

Callie

"Well, I'll be damned." Just to make sure my brain wasn't making things up, I rechecked the ledger total on one side of the screen and compared it to the bank total on the website page next to it. "They match. They actually freaking match."

Katy snickered, grabbed a stack of the leftover notepads she'd brought from her boss's office supply stash on Monday and reboxed them. If anyone embodied the terms *spunky* and *stylish*, it was her. Kind of like Tinkerbell but with a wickedly cool pixie cut and flirty clothes that made me rethink my closet full of jeans and T-shirts.

"Of course they match," she said. "If you download transactions regularly and don't rush yourself, odds are they always will. It's when you get too far behind and try to hurry through the process that you screw things up."

"Right but…this is accounting stuff. Me and numbers—we haven't exactly been best friends, ya know? This is kind of a big deal."

"Then you should celebrate," she said, repeating the

boxing process with the pens and highlighters we'd decided Danny already had plenty of. "Treat yourself to something nice."

Oh, I was definitely going to treat myself. Maybe I'd stop at the Sonic near my apartment on the way home and order a large Reese's Peanut Butter Cup Blast.

I did a little happy wiggle in my desk chair—then froze.

Holy freaking cow.

My first reaction hadn't been about booze.

Or a party.

Or anything remotely sketchy that might lead to me drinking or drugging.

It'd been about ice cream and chocolate.

It'd been *healthy*...assuming you didn't count the calories.

An unbelievably powerful warmth blossomed beneath my sternum and a lightness I couldn't remember having since I was a little kid swept through me. Kind of like when my dad would throw me up in the air and then catch me, making me giggle until my stomach muscles ached.

Joy.

That's what it was.

Real, honest to God joy.

"Callie?"

Katy's voice ripped me out of la-la land in time to find her moving in close to me, a look of confusion and concern on her face. "You okay?"

I smiled big enough I felt it in my cheeks. "I'm grrrreat."

Better than great, actually. I was on cloud-freaking-nine and couldn't wait to get on the phone with Maggie.

And Susan. And anyone else in the program willing to listen to me.

But explaining what had caused my elation would undoubtedly be more than Katy was up for. She'd already unloaded a ton of patience in the last three days helping me come up with a system for managing Danny's office. So I waved my hands and chuckled. "Ignore me. I just had an *ah-ha* moment, that's all."

"Ahhh," she said going back to her task. Though I couldn't quite tell by her expression if she was buying it, or if she'd opted to bypass further questions in exchange for the fast track out of Dodge.

And that's when it hit me.

Tomorrow, my support system wouldn't be here, and I'd be flying solo.

Suddenly, my soaring childlike glee flatlined. "So, I can call you if I have questions, right? Like, that's not gonna bog you down or anything?"

"Girl, you can call me anytime you want. I've leaned on my fair share of people figuring out how to get stuff done, so I'm happy to pay it back. Plus, having a network to pull from makes you smart, not a burden. If I've learned nothing else from Knox and Beckett in the time I've worked for them, it's that. Their whole brotherhood is built on family and building each other up."

"Brotherhood?"

"Yeah, you know... Knox, Beckett, Danny, Jace and Axel...plus a handful of other ones I don't know as well." She paused long enough to grin at me. "You'll meet 'em and their wives eventually. If not through them coming to the business to see Danny, then at one of their parties. They might work hard, but they play hard, too, and make sure employees get a chance to let their hair down."

Ah, now I remembered. The family by choice Danny had mentioned. The one my sister was enfolded in the middle of and was fiercely loved by, the way she deserved.

A bittersweet pang wiggled through me. One I wasn't really sure I understood.

The shop door opened with a *whoosh* of hot July air and a swell of The Black Keys' "Gold on the Ceiling."

"What's up, my ladies?" Jamey strolled in sporting his usual laid-back, but overdone suave playboy routine, the bulk of his attention centered on Katy. "Everything good here in our little air-conditioned piece of heaven?"

"We're celebrating." Katy tucked the box flaps so they'd stay shut and slid it off the desktop, cradling it by either side on the bottom. "Callie's successfully graduated from Katy's School of Office Management."

"Right on!" Jamey held out his fist for a bump. "This means we're one step closer to a happier boss man."

I knocked my knuckles to his but rolled my eyes, too. "Let's not bank on *happier* just yet. My dad always said, *One ah, shit wipes out an awful lot of atta girls.*"

Jamey barked out a full belly laugh and casually slid his hands in the loose pockets of his coveralls. "Man, you are *not* wrong on that score. Still, you gotta take the wins where you can." He straightened and glanced out the window that overlooked the garage below. "You know, you should come with us after work. We always do happy hour on Wednesdays over at Rita's."

The shop door opened, and Danny strode through, headed for the file cabinets with a single-minded concentration reserved for a man on a mission.

Jamey ignored him and kept going. "They've got Corona longnecks on special for a buck apiece. Come with us, and we'll help ya celebrate."

Danny jerked open a drawer, then stopped midway through reaching for a file and zeroed in on us. "Hold up. Celebrating what?"

"Callie," Jamey said, either unaware of the scowl on Danny's face or just immune to it. "She's all done with Office Manager 101. I told her she should join us for happy hour at Rita's."

Danny's concentration morphed to a scowl, every bit of it directed at Jamey. "And why would she do that?" He looked to me. "You don't drink. Remember?"

Jamey might have considered the office an air-conditioned haven, but in that second, my cheeks burned like I'd been sitting in hell for a week, and I would have given a lot to hide under the desk.

But I was also pissed.

Past fuckups or not, my issues were mine to share and absolutely no one else's. I cleared my throat and squared my shoulders. "No. I don't drink. Not that either of them knew that until you said something."

Danny at least had the good sense to flinch and wiped the nasty look off his face.

I shifted my attention to Jamey. "Does Jason go with you guys to happy hour?"

Jamey and Katy both volleyed their gazes between me and Danny, but while Katy only looked mildly confused, Jamey seemed like he was ready to hightail it back to the garage. "Uh...yeah. Most of the time. Why?"

"Does he drink?"

"I don't know." Frowning, Jamey glanced out the window toward Jason's bay before answering me. "I guess not, now that you mention it. It's never been a big deal."

I aimed a cocked eyebrow at Danny, but otherwise kept the rest of my thoughts to myself for fear I'd push my righteous indignation a step too far.

"Yeah...uh..." Jamey backed up two steps toward the shop door. "I think I'll head back down with the guys. Callie, the offer's open if you wanna join us." He looked sideways at Danny a second, then tacked on, "I think."

Before he could get his fingers hooked around the door's handle, Danny uttered, "Hold up."

It took a second or two for Jamey to evaluate if it was wise to listen or leave anyway, but eventually he dropped his hand and waited with the rest of us.

Letting out an awkward sigh, Danny shoved the file drawer closed and faced us fully. "Callie, I'm sorry. Me saying that was out of line. Outside of the shop, it's none of my business what you do or who you do it with. I just..." He lifted his hands out to either side of him and let them drop heavily back to his sides. "Well, I meant it in a protective way. That's all."

His gaze shot to Katy. "And I heard all that grumblin' goin' on in here Monday when I walked through a few times. You should probably go with her and charge a round for yourself on my card for fixing all my accounts."

"Oh, Knox said you're gonna get a bill for that," Katy said. Given her sly smile and the edge to her voice, it was hard to tell if she was serious or just really good at razzing him. She hefted her box for a better grip, then looked to Jamey and added, "I'm in for happy hour, though. How about you help me haul these boxes out?"

Jamey glanced between me and Danny, then grinned

and headed for one of the two boxes stacked on the floor beside her. "Good idea."

Danny watched them go, but waited until the front door was fully closed behind them before he took a few cautious steps my direction. "I really am sorry. I over-stepped. Big-time."

Much as it had been the night I'd called Vivienne and left her a message, his tone was tender. Sincere, but also pitched low and smooth, so I pretty much for-got everything else except that finite moment. That and the fact that his eyes were really, really dark. More like black than brown.

I cleared my throat and licked my lips, reminding myself for what was probably the thousandth time that my boss was absolutely off-limits for the direction my brain was headed. "Thanks. Not just for saying it now, but for owning it in front of them."

"You should go. Have fun."

I wanted to. Wanted to be normal—whatever the hell that meant—and feel like I was part of the team. But I wasn't stupid either. I'd worked my ass off to get not just a year behind me, but a good quality program as well. "I think I'll talk to Jason first. See if he's going."

He nodded at that and gave me an unguarded smile I suspected was awfully hard to earn from a man like Danny. "Sounds like a smart plan."

My whole damned life, I'd been quick on my feet with the gift of gab, a skill I'd leveraged repeatedly through my party years to manipulate a host of situa-tions. But now? Now, I couldn't have thought of a topic even if someone had pointed a shotgun at my head. All I knew was I was content to be right where I was and do absolutely nothing if it meant being closer to Danny.

"So, you know your stuff now?" He motioned to the laptop on the desk beside me. "The software's all lined out and you've got the ordering plans figured out?"

Work.

I could talk about work. "Oh, yeah. After Katy got all the accounts and categories straightened out, she got you caught up to the beginning of the year, then showed me how to keep things going from there. On the ordering, you guys won't have to enter your own anymore. You just give me what you need, and I'll consolidate everything at once and check the deliveries when they come in. We even got all of your past invoices, commission slips and photos filed away, but you won't really need paper stuff going forward. We digitized everything as we went."

As soon as I mentioned the filing, I remembered how he'd been going for something in the file cabinets when he'd stormed in. "Did you need something?"

Danny's memory didn't seem to be as quick to catch up as mine, because he furrowed his brow as though thoroughly confused.

"When you came in," I said motioning toward the file cabinets, "you were looking for something. Do you need help tracking something down?"

"Ah, yeah," he said, finally cluing in and spinning toward where I pointed. "I couldn't remember some of the smaller details on the ride I'm working on."

Curious, I moved closer to him, but looked out the window to the modified Corvette parked in his bay. It'd only been three days, but he'd made a ton of progress on it. "Not sure they can ever top a C3 Widebody."

Stopping midway to pulling open the same drawer he'd gone for before, Danny snapped his head up and looked at me like I'd just spoken fluent Korean. "Come again?"

I jerked my head toward the shop. "It's a Widebody C3 Corvette base, right?"

He shook his head and chuckled, going back to searching through the files. "I forgot you're a car girl."

"And motorcycles. Probably more motorcycles than cars, if you wanna know the truth." I inched a little closer to the drawer he was leaned over for a better look. "You want any help?"

He frowned down at the files. "I could have sworn I put that file in here." He looked to me. "Did you guys move stuff?"

"Nope." I lifted my chin toward the third and last cabinet. "All of the stuff that was on the desk is organized in there. You got a system for these files?"

Danny grumbled something I couldn't make out then restarted at the front of the drawer, this time slowing his roll as he worked toward the back. "I've got a system, yeah. Problem is, I forget what my system is and then make a new one. So, when I need something from the old system, I can't find it."

I probably should have at least tried to hold back my chuckle, but it slipped out before I could. Fortunately, me opening the top drawer of the cabinet next to him covered some of the sound. "So, what am I looking for?"

"Well, I thought I'd filed it under his last name— Rodney Farewell. But maybe I did it by date?" He paused a minute and stared at the wall as though searching his memories. "Hell, maybe I filed it by the invoice number in the computer."

I peeked at the invoices slotted in my folders.

Last names: Smith... Bowles... Hall. So, definitely not alphabetic. Except maybe...

First name: Al... Ben... Brody... Charlie...

I leaned over for a better look at one of Danny's invoices.

Frank... Hal... Hal again... Jim.

I straightened and tapped the end of his drawer. "Try the next drawer down, under Rodney, not Farewell."

That lost and confused expression zipped across Danny's face for all of a second before he pushed the drawer closed and shifted down one with renewed determination. He did the finger walking thing a few times. Paused, pulled up a file, cocked his head for a better look and... "Yes!"

Straightening, he flipped the file open and thumbed through several pages with drawings on it.

I angled for a better look. "I take it that's the right one?"

"Hell, yeah." He snapped the folder shut, tucked it under his arm and shoved the drawer closed. "Girl, you're a genius. I could totally kiss you."

A right hook couldn't have knocked me stupider. In fact, I was pretty sure my jaw was hanging open.

The wallop must've carried straight through to Danny as well, because he froze as soon as he got a good look at me and grew a seriously alarmed expression. "I mean, I wouldn't really do it. It's just an expression."

Under normal circumstances, I'd have found the predicament funny as hell and laughed the whole thing off in a heartbeat. As it was, my heart couldn't decide if it was going to explode from beating too hard at the idea of a kiss from Danny, or stop altogether because he *wouldn't really do it*.

Either way, the awkward was…well, *awkward* enough that I pulled my shit together and waved him off with a *pshhht* and a forced chuckle. "Yeah, yeah. I know that. It was the genius part that shocked me. Pretty sure that's the first time anyone's ever tied that word to me."

It took him a few seconds cautiously considering me before he seemed to believe he hadn't really struck a nerve, but eventually he grinned and gave me a single pat on my shoulder. Kind of like what I'd seen him do with the guys a time or two, only with a lot less punch. "Something tells me you don't give yourself enough credit. You got this place lined out fast enough, didn't you?"

I shrugged. "Well, Katy did most of it. But I watched and learned. I've got a good idea of some other things I can do to help."

Uncomfortable with the topic, I dipped my head toward the folder under his arm. "Is that what it's supposed to look like when it's done?"

"Oh. Yeah." He slid the file free. "Wanna see?"

I did. Mostly because it'd give me an idea of how things transitioned from paper to real life. But also because that meant more time with Danny—a treat that'd been mostly absent since he'd turned my education over to Katy. "Yeah, if you don't mind."

With a level of enthusiasm I hadn't ever seen from him, he hustled toward the desk, then pulled the sheets out of the folder and laid them across the widest side of the L-shaped desktop.

"So, I usually start here," he said pointing to a simple

black-and-white stock drawing. "This is just a basic C3 I used as a reference when Rodney and I were throwing ideas around." He moved an image done on tracing paper on top of the stock photo. Then repeated the process with another. "From there we went through cycles until we ended up with a final product." He slid the last picture in place to cover them all.

And wow was this car gonna be spectacular.

I traced my finger along the specialized chrome pipes along the bottom edge of the car. The car's color was incredibly unique—not quite coral, but definitely not orange either. The modified fenders hugged the modern sport tires with their edgy rims to perfection, and the engine had been lifted so it was raised out of the hood. "You know what this reminds me of?"

"A sunset," he answered with zero hesitation. "That's the whole concept Rodney started with. Said he didn't want just a standard muscle car, but one that had that kicked back vibe of a summer sunset. Took me fucking forever to find the right color."

"If that's what you were after, it's perfect. But it reminds me of more than that." I pulled another version Danny had done from a different angle closer and pointed to it. "Makes me think of those badass Hot Wheels Tommy Langham used to collect when I was a kid." The memory was such a fond one. A time well before my mom leaving us and my dad dying had all but stripped away my innocence and steered me down any path that would offer options that numbed my pain.

I was so lost in the memory…the sheer guilelessness of the moment…that I forgot all about offices, and bosses, and appropriate distances and grinned up at Danny. "I had a *huge* crush on Tommy Langham."

Danny stared down at me.

Only he wasn't smiling. Not like I was.

He was studying me and doing it so intently I could have sworn little sparks were nipping at my cheeks.

And he was close.

Way too close, according to workplace etiquette.

My lungs hitched, probably because they'd forgotten how to function the same as my brain had, and I could have sworn someone had flipped the heater on in place of the AC.

What the hell was I doing? I literally had no context to work from; my repertoire of intimacy of any kind for as long as I could remember was all tempered by the haze of drugs and alcohol.

The ding from the front door sounded and the mingled laughter of Jamey and Katy almost violently cut through the moment. I took a step backward and quickly stacked the papers, my fingers shaking as I slid them back in the folder and handed them off to Danny. "Thanks for sharing them with me. Glad we found them."

Danny took the file, but did so slowly, his gaze still thoughtful—even if some confusion had crept in.

"Hey, boss," Jamey said as though he hadn't noticed anything weird. "You comin' to Rita's?"

Finally, Danny seemed to shake himself free of whatever had his thoughts so focused. He glanced at Katy, then gave Jamey a shake of his head. "No. Not today. But thanks for the invite."

With one last glance at me, he tapped the folder on the desktop and headed out the shop door.

Jamey scooped up Katy's last box. "I'll load this one up, then we can all head out. Sound good?"

Katy nodded, but kept her gaze on me, the look behind her eyes indicative that she'd caught the tension between Danny and I before I'd had the good sense to step away. "Works for me. Callie and I'll shut things down and meet you there." She waited until Jamey disappeared out the main door, then grabbed her purse from the bottom drawer, closed it and leaned a hip against the far end of the desk. "You okay?"

Was I? I'd sampled some seriously messed up substances since my latter teen years and never once had I felt like I was feeling right then. My arms and fingers were trembling like they'd been brushed with electricity, and my body was so jumbled up I wasn't sure it could navigate walking a straight line, but my brain was buzzing like I'd had nothing but coffee for eight straight hours.

I crossed my arms over my chest and rubbed the goose bumps that had flared over my upper arms. "I have absolutely no idea. Listen, would you mind shutting things down? I need to get home and make a phone call."

"You're not going to Rita's?"

Oh, no. Rita's was the last place I needed to be tonight. Not while I was feeling like a barrel of gunpowder in search of a gunfight. I shook my head, grabbed my purse and started fishing for my keys. "No. Not a good place for me to be right now. Alcohol and I have too much of a sordid past."

"Yeah, I got that from Danny sticking his foot in his mouth, but I'm gonna guess the real reason you're not going has something to do with the fact that Danny looked like he was about to eat you alive when we walked in here."

"He did?"

"Mmm hmm. And you didn't exactly look like you were all that bothered by the idea."

Wow. So I hadn't made it up.

I wasn't sure if that relieved me or scared me even more.

I blew my bangs out of my face, shouldered my purse and stood there like a lost puppy without a clue which way to go.

Katy chuckled and waved me toward the door. "Girl, go. Get whoever it is you need on the phone and get yourself figured out. I've got it covered."

Thank. Fucking. God. Because as wired as I was, I'd probably fry the computer on proximity alone.

"Thanks," I said headed for the door. My fingers curled around the bar that crossed the glass door and I gave it a shove.

Katy's voice cut to me before I could get all the way across the threshold, bringing me to a stop. "You just gotta promise me I get the deets first if that lip-lock ever happens. Deal?"

Kissing Danny Parker.

Christ. Why did she have to actually put it in words? I actually had to steer a car through rush hour traffic and having such a tangible image in my head wasn't going to help.

Still, Katy was willing to cover me at a time I really needed cover, so I gave her what she wanted before I headed to my car. "Deal."

Chapter Eight

Danny

One week.

It was the fastest I'd ever turned around a car. It was also the most I'd actually been available to work on a car since I'd launched my custom rides business a few years ago—thanks in large part to Callie sliding into overseeing the office like a perfectly lubed piston.

But Rodney's Malibu Sunset Widebody was done.

And she was *perfect*.

All shiny chrome with a killer paint job that had just a touch of gold at the front then faded to the same dark persimmon that stretched across the skies in summer just before the dark took over. Not the most outlandish design I'd ever done, but my customer was gonna be the envy of everyone who laid eyes on her.

I ran a fresh chamois over the back fender then up and over the trunk, making sure every spot was ready for Rodney's first look.

Hot Wheels.

The fucking phrase had been almost a mantra for me while I'd worked on the Vette. Half the time, it kind of made me wanna stop what I was doing and ask

Knox to find out who the hell Tommy Langham was so I could choke him with my bare hands. The other half—it'd pushed me to do some of the best detailing I'd ever done merely in the hopes I could get Callie to smile at me the way she had last week one more time.

Christ, that'd been a close call. So close that, for a few seconds, I hadn't given two shits when Jamey and Katy had walked in and seen us all of inches from crossing a serious line.

I tossed the shammy to my workbench, grabbed my half-empty bottle of water and spun my stool around so I'd get a full view of my finished product. Beat from the strengthening afternoon heat, I dropped to the worn, padded cushion and it *whooshed* out a tired protest.

Behind the office glass that looked out over the shop, Callie grabbed her cell phone and appeared to fire off a somewhat lengthy text. Whatever she was saying seemed to inspire a mighty intense level of concentration. What bugged me was she'd been on her phone a helluva lot since about mid-morning and had seemed disconnected when I'd passed through for lunch. Edgy and hyper focused.

Whatever it was couldn't have been about work. Not if what was going down was taking place on her cell phone. Plus, she clearly had work under control. Not only had she mastered the basics Katy had shown her last week, but she'd branched out to helpin' the rest of the guys with incoming calls on commission interests and proactively feelin' out what each guy needed where supplies were concerned.

Needless to say, the crew loved her. Spent their breaks in the office with her. Had taken her to lunch a time or two. Hell, Rick had even brought her some homemade smoked ribs on Monday.

Me, on the other hand—I kept my distance. Said hello and was friendly in passing, but kept my grabby hands well out of reaching distance.

The slick ride in front of me was the outstanding result.

"She's a beaut." Jason wiped his hands on a mechanic's rag and shoved it in his back pocket. "Your guy's gonna be over the moon."

"He ought to be. I've got half a mind to give him his down payment back and keep her for myself." And something told me a shrink would have a field day with that revelation, too. I shook it off and stood, motioning toward the office. "You talk to Callie today?"

"About what?"

"I don't know. Anything. She seems kinda off."

Jason looked to the office, then back to me and shrugged. "Seemed okay to me. But she was also on the phone talkin' to someone when I came in, and I've been under that pony for most of the day."

The beat-up shell of a Mustang Jason's client had wheeled in a few days ago was gonna need a major overhaul before it found new life, but if anyone had the patience to tackle the job, it was Jason.

I glanced up at Callie, who was back to texting again, and debated if I should drop the topic.

"Why?" Jason said, following my gaze again. "You think something's wrong?"

Hell if I knew. I just knew her behavior was different today—and I'd become a certified expert in watching Callie from my bay over the last week. "She just seems distracted. Or disturbed. It kind of makes me wonder if she's gettin' an itch for a drink. Or worse."

Comprehension widened Jason's eyes, but instead of mirroring the same concern back at me, he smiled. "Well, if she is, it's up to her and her HP to deal with it."

"HP?"

"Higher Power. Some people call it God. Some call it the Universe. Whatever works for 'em getting sober. But it ain't you, and it ain't me. So, let it go."

I frowned at that. Letting go wasn't exactly my strong suit. Fixing shit was more my style, or even strong-arming if I had to.

To my surprise, Jason actually chuckled. "Man, maybe I need to pick up a list of Al-Anon meetings at the clubhouse."

"Al-a-what?"

"Al-Anon. It's like AA, but it's for the people who have alcoholics in their lives. They go to meetings just like we do, 'cause the addiction affects everybody—not just the drunk or the druggie. The program helps family and friends deal with things in a healthy way."

Huh. I'd overheard Viv telling Jace she was headed out to a meeting a time or two after dinner at Haven, but I'd just assumed she had some late evening planning gigs to deal with. Maybe she was doing the Al-Anon thing instead.

I shook my head. "Nah, man. I'm just her boss. And distant family, of a sort."

Jason raised his eyebrows. "You sure?" He glanced back at Jamey's empty bay and then lowered his voice. "I mean, you gotta know all of us dig the shit out of her, but Jamey said he thought he walked in on some pretty fucking strong attraction brewing the other day."

I fought back a growl, but barely. "Jamey's speculatin' where he shouldn't be. I'm just a decent human being and don't want someone that's workin' for me strugglin' if I can do something to help 'em."

Jason's lopsided grin looked like he didn't really believe me. He chucked me on the shoulder and said, "Sorry, boss. If she's struggling, it's on her to figure out how to deal with it. I'm gonna take a late lunch. You let me know if you change your mind and want a list of Al-Anon meetings."

I watched him lazily saunter out one of the open garage doors, torn between dragging him back and demanding more information, and just firing him because I could.

Through the window, Callie snatched her phone up off the desk and started texting again.

Let it go, huh? Just trust that someone who'd struggled nonstop for years to keep away from booze was just going to magically get it all right without help? It made no sense to me. Jason, though…much as I wanted to kick his ass for the smirk he'd given me, he'd done nothing but show stability in the years he'd worked for me. So, maybe he was right. Maybe I needed to focus on my job and mind my own fucking business, even if it did feel twenty kinds of wrong.

Resolved to let things ride for now, I snapped a host of pictures of the killer car beside me, took some final notes and itemized the pricing, then headed up to the office. Callie was back on her mobile again when I walked in, but this time had it up to her ear instead of texting and was scribbling something on a notepad. She also nearly jumped out of her chair and fumbled the phone when she glanced over one shoulder and locked eyes with me.

"I gotta go," she said to whoever it was. "I'll be there. Thanks for bringing me in on this one."

Bringing her in? On what?

It took everything in me to skip those questions and keep things simple. I plugged my phone into the cord we kept connected to the laptop and started download-ing the pics I'd taken. "You see the finished product?"

I might have avoided Callie for the last week, but she hadn't avoided watching the Vette as it'd transformed day by day. More than once, I'd found her staring down at my bay and taking note of the changes. So, her dis-tracted response as she typed something else in her phone seemed odd. "The finished what?"

"The Vette." I unplugged the cord, tossed the fin-ished folder on the desk in front of her and gave Callie my full attention. "She's done. I need you to call Rod-ney and schedule a pickup time."

Either my stance or my tone finally got her attention because her head snapped up toward me. Her eyes were red, and her lashes spiked from recent tears. "It is?" She looked through the glass at the car beyond and for the briefest of moments, a wistful expression flickered on her face. "She turned out really pretty."

I didn't get it. Why was she sad? I would've expected her to be as pumped as I was. Maybe go down and see it for herself.

Instead, she shook her head as though clearing her thoughts and looked to me, all business. "Hey, I'm re-ally sorry to ask this, but I need to handle something. I'd say I'd make it back before the shop closes, but I hon-estly don't think I will." She opened the desk's bottom drawer and pulled out her purse as if my agreement was a foregone conclusion. "Everything's done. I can call Rodney first thing in the morning and ask Malcom or Rick to cover the phones until six."

I looked to the notepad she'd been writing on when I walked in.

2121 S. Glenbook Dr. #215

It wasn't such an odd request. Everyone had shit to take care of from time to time, and she'd been rock solid since day one. Plus, it was already three thirty. If any of my guys had asked the same thing, I wouldn't have even blinked before agreeing. So, why was I so hesitant?

I shrugged and forced myself to shake the worry climbing up my back as I moved away from the desk and headed for the shop door. "Fine by me. I'll hit Malcom up for you on the way back downstairs."

With swift, efficient movement, Callie shut down the laptop, and was rounding the desk for the front door before I'd even put one foot on the stair's top landing.

Weird.

Again, I tried to shake it off and finished my trek down the stairs. "Yo, Malcom. Callie had to run an errand and can't make it back before closing. Can you cover the phones?"

Malcom looked up from a sheet of metal that appeared to be putting up a hell of a fight rather than staying in place and frowned. "Man, I hope whatever she's doing chills her out. She's been kind of weird all afternoon."

I stopped dead in my tracks, the prickly unease that'd been fucking with me all day where Callie was concerned ramping up to a whole new level. "You caught that, too?"

"Hard not to. Probably just chick stuff, though."

Hmm.

Maybe. Everyone had off days. But what if it was more than that?

If she's struggling, it's on her to figure out how to deal with it.

Jason was right. If it was any of the guys acting odd, I'd give 'em space for a while. If they didn't straighten out, I'd talk to 'em after a day or two. Callie deserved the same treatment.

Back at my bay, I ditched my coveralls and started stowing my tools.

2121 S. Glenbook Dr. #215

For some reason that address sounded familiar. I'd grown up in Garland and knew most of it like the back of my hand, but since I'd branched out with the brotherhood, I'd spent most of my non-work time in Dallas proper or out at Haven. Curious, I snatched my phone off my workbench and looked it up.

My gut clenched, and a chill that balked the near triple-digit heat whispered against my neck. I definitely knew the place. Had hung at an apartment complex in that same neighborhood multiple times when I was in my senior year of high school—right up until my dad had all but put his foot up my ass for being an idiot and experimenting with drugs.

She's been kind of weird all afternoon.

Red eyes. Probably from crying.

On the phone texting.

Jumpy when I'd walked in.

Fuck.

I jammed my phone in my back pocket and high-stepped it to the stairs before jogging up them. "Malcom, I'm out. Anyone needs me, call."

"Everything okay?"

"Yeah, yeah. Fine." Which was complete bullshit, because if my gut was right, Callie was on her way to throw a solid year of sobriety out the fucking window. Maybe it made me the worst kind of meddling asshole on the planet, but if I could help her avoid taking that fall, I was damned sure gonna try.

Forty minutes and too damned much late afternoon traffic later, I pulled up in front of an apartment complex that was right next to the place I'd spent time at in high school. Built in a style I'd place in the mid-to-late '70s, the single-row multi-family was in desperate need of a paint job and had exterior lamp posts that'd probably looked classy in their day, but were mostly beat to shit now. And, sure enough, Callie's blue Chevy Spark was parked two slots down from me.

I tapped my thumb on the steering wheel, torn between calling her and demanding she come out, going to the door and knocking, and just waiting until she came out. Calling seemed easiest, but left the door open to a bunch of potential lies I wasn't eager to hear rolling out of her mouth. Waiting risked her taking whatever she'd driven here for before I could have a chance at stopping her.

So, going in it was.

The heat was a killer. A smothering weight that only heightened the suffocating fear I'd forced myself to breathe through on the drive here. I tagged the cheap black numbers *215* at the farthest end of the second floor and took the black iron and concrete stairs two at a time.

Logic pushed me to slow down. To think and double-check my actions before I committed fully to anything.

But somewhere between leaving the shop and driving down the sad, run-down roads I'd long forgotten, my adrenaline had taken over. I was all of two steps away when the door I was headed for opened.

I stopped hard, my right hand going for the Glock I carried when I was working with Beckett in the field only to come up empty-handed.

Turned out, the reaction was wildly unnecessary, because the brunette woman who stumbled out of the door first was so thin and out of it, a strong summer wind could have knocked her over. The woman who came out right behind her toting a duffel bag was none other than the blonde who'd hung with Callie the day of the art fair.

I was just about to throw out some bullshit line about being in the wrong place to cover myself when Callie came out behind them and closed the door.

She locked gazes with me almost instantly. "Danny? What are you doing here?"

Not only was she stone-cold sober, but I knew with absolute certainty I'd read a whole lot of wrong into Callie's actions. The question was if I was gonna be man enough to admit it, or try to bullshit my way out of the situation.

Before I could answer, Callie seemed to do her own tea leaf reading because her expression hardened with a whole lot of pissed off. She looked to the blonde and murmured, "Susan, you guys go ahead. I'll meet you there."

I stepped out of the duo's way and offered them both what I was pretty sure was a lame excuse for a smile.

Susan volleyed a look between me and Callie as though she wasn't sure leaving us alone with each other was such a bright idea, but then seemed to realize she was the only real support keeping the brunette upright. "No, Mia and I will wait on you in my car, and you can follow us to intake."

Intake.

Fuck. I'd not only jumped to all the wrong conclusions, I'd gone the exact opposite in direction. Callie hadn't come here to get drugs. She'd come to help someone else get off of them.

Christ, I was an idiot.

A meddlesome, hotheaded idiot.

And yet, Callie threw me a bone and waited until Susan and her woozy companion were well down the stairs and out of earshot before she lit into me. "You followed me."

"More like I googled the address, but yeah. Same thing."

"Because you didn't trust me."

"No." Where the hard-and-fast response came from I wasn't entirely sure. "It wasn't about trusting you."

"Oh? You just knew I was doing a twelfth step call and decided you'd be able to help out?"

"A what?"

"A twelfth step call. Helping someone who wants to get sober."

Oh. Right.

I rubbed my hand over the top of my head, missing the hell out of my beanie, and let out a long exhale. "Listen, Callie… I know this looks seriously bad, but I swear it wasn't about me not trusting you."

"You're right. It looks really fucking bad. Not to

mention it's embarrassing as hell. How am I gonna explain to Susan why my boss showed at a person's house when the people who reach out are supposed to be able to keep their anonymity? I mean, fuck, Danny. This was my first real twelve-step call. How are they gonna believe I'll keep private details to myself when other people need help?"

Shit. I'd known I'd blown it, but I hadn't even considered the anonymous part. "I honestly hadn't even thought about that. Hell, I didn't even think at all. I just put what I thought was two and two together, and I drove like hell to get here."

"Because you thought I was going for a score."

"Yeah. And if I could help you not blow a good year of sobriety, I wanted to help you."

"By what? Banging on the door and dragging me out?"

Well, yeah. Something like that. Though, from the look on her face, I was guessing that approach wouldn't have worked. Too frustrated to check my delivery, I barked my answer back to her. "Well, I had to do something!"

"Why? What fucking difference does it make to you if Viv's loser sister falls off the wagon again?"

"Because you're not a loser, dammit! You matter!"

The ire in Callie's expression fizzled and her jaw dropped open, the lingering power of my voice hovering around the two of us like some ominous cloud.

"I've watched you," I said, utterly clueless where the words were coming from. "You've worked your ass off since you started. Have been honest with me from the day you walked into the office. Made friends with the guys and stood up to my stupid ass when I was an idiot."

Callie still didn't say anything. Just stared at me, openly stunned.

"You forget," I said. "I saw you at your worst. I saw the emptiness in your eyes and the un-fucking-believably stupid shit you were doing. The sunken way your skin fitted around your skull and how thin you were. I see you now, and I *know* you're on a better path. In a better place. And God damn it, I want that for you. I want you to be happy and free of all that shit that almost killed you."

In just the barest of movements, Callie shook her head. Her voice was barely above a whisper. "Why?"

One simple word. One that should be easy to answer.

But I couldn't. Not clearly anyway. There was too much emotion tangled up in the situation, the power of it all something I wasn't sure I was prepared to unravel.

So, I gave her the one simple truth I could admit. "Because I like you."

Her eyes welled with tears and, while she tried to hide it by pinching her mouth tight, her lower lip trembled.

I glanced at the parking lot, suddenly very aware that—while I hadn't watched them load up—Susan and Mia were somewhere out there as an audience. I lowered my voice and inched just a little closer, wishing I could give Callie some kind of contact. Any type of comfort to ease the pain I'd caused. "Look, I know I fucked up. Again. I just felt…" I raised my hands out to either side of me and grappled for the right word. "I don't know… I was afraid if I didn't do something, you'd lose everything you worked so hard for."

"You can't save me, Danny." The strain in her voice was evident, but so was her resolve. "Neither can Vivienne. Or Susan. Or my sponsor, or anyone else. They can help. They can listen. But it's always going to be my decision in the end."

Sighing, I hung my head, Jason's admonishment to stay out of it taking a fresh lap through my head. "Yeah, I've got no clue how to support someone who's trying to change their life the way you are. And I get it—I should've minded my own business."

I scanned the parking lot once more and this time zeroed in on a white Honda with two occupants inside. From the looks of things, Mia was out cold in the passenger seat. Susan, on the other hand, had her gaze locked tight on Callie and me.

"Listen," I said. "I know you've gotta go. If there's anything I can do or say to Susan to let her know this was all on me, I'll do it. I know it meant a lot to you."

Callie adjusted her purse on her shoulder. "No. I'll tell her what happened. She'll believe me."

I nodded and again found myself staring at my boots. The last time I truly remembered feeling this hollowed out and humbled had been the time Dad had given me his come to Jesus speech about drugs. I probably should have stepped out of Callie's way and let her get on with business. Instead, I forced my eyes to her and found myself asking, "Let me make it up to you. Somehow."

"Danny, you don't need to—"

"No, seriously. Just let me take you to dinner or someplace where we can talk this through. I've put you in a shitty position twice, and I don't want it to happen again."

This time it was Callie who peeked at the Honda in the parking lot. At first, I thought she was subconsciously seeking some kind of guidance from her friend, but then I realized her gaze had gone distant. More like she was remembering something. When she faced me again, she gave me a short nod. "Okay. We can talk."

For the first time in hours, the muscles in my gut unclenched and, if there hadn't been two people out in the parking lot waiting on her, I'd have been inclined to linger in the moment a little longer. "Good. Dinner then. Tomorrow night after work?"

"Ummm…" She wiped one hand on her hip and before she ducked her head, I could have sworn her cheeks turned pink. "Okay. Sure." She jerked her head toward Susan's car. "I should probably go before Mia changes her mind."

"Right." I stepped out of the way and waved Callie ahead of me. "Take care of business, and I'll see you in the shop tomorrow."

"Yeah." For the briefest of moments, she glanced at me and smiled, then started down the stairs. "Have a good night."

I took my time following in her tracks and watched as she backed out of her parking spot and followed Susan out of the lot.

What the heck was going on with me? Yeah, I could be impulsive. I'd always had a hot temper, but I was usually pretty quick to cool, too. Today, I'd taken off like a rocket and hadn't found any semblance of a brake until I'd smashed headfirst into a horribly wrong conclusion.

Because I like you.

The words I'd said echoed back in my head, and I came to a dead standstill next to my Chevelle. At the time, I'd thought they meant that I liked her as a person. But what if there was more to it than that? Had I reacted the way I did because of my fucked up history with my mom? Or had I reacted because of Callie? God knew, I'd felt more than enough attraction where she was concerned in the last few weeks, so if that's where my instincts were headed, it wouldn't be a shock.

And that last glance I'd gotten before she'd headed down the stairs—her cheeks had definitely been pink. The kind of pink a woman got when she was flustered in a good way.

Sliding behind the wheel, I fired up my ride and left the old neighborhood behind. Maybe I'd made a serious blunder and hurt Callie today, but I had a feeling I'd also stumbled on something I needed to deal with.

One way or another, I was gonna dig into whatever that something was, and I was starting tomorrow night.

Chapter Nine

Callie

I had things to do. Important things that culminated in Danny paying me at the end of the week for a job well done.

And yet, here I was staring at my computer, too kerfuffled by what was supposed to go down at six o'clock to give a single stupid fig about what was on the screen in front of me.

Well, nothing except the clock's display in the bottom right hand corner.

4:37 PM.

One hour and twenty-three minutes to go.

At least I thought it was one hour and twenty-three minutes. Maybe when Danny had said *tomorrow after work* he'd meant later. Like seven or even eight.

Maybe I should go down in the shop and ask him for clarification?

But if I did that, wouldn't that make me look too eager?

"Bah," I said to no one and snatched my phone off the desk. I'd tried like hell not to bug Maggie since my post-almost-nose-to-nose-with-Danny freak-out last

week, but if I was gonna keep from going bonkers between now and the end of this shift, I needed an inter-
vention.

It took three full rings, but Maggie finally picked
up. "Heya, kiddo! How's the high life in the Great State
of Texas?"

I exhaled hard and relaxed against my seat back,
all the crazy gymnastics going on in my head taking a
breather at just the sound of my sponsor's voice. "Well,
overall, I'm pretty good."

Maggie snickered in that *don't bullshit a bullshit-
ter* way she had about her. "Yeah, that's got the biggest
lead-up to a heaping pile of trouble if I've ever heard
one. So, how about we skip right to the meaty part."

Checking over my shoulder just to make sure no
one was headed my way, I lowered my voice. "I uh…"
Shit. What was I supposed to say? I had no clue what
to call whatever it was I was doing later. "I'm going to
eat dinner with Danny. Tonight."

A whole lot of quiet answered back for a beat or two.
"You mean like on a date?"

"Well, that's kind of the problem. I don't know. And
it's making me freak out a little. Like, he said we'd grab
dinner *tomorrow after work*. Now, it's tomorrow. But
does *after work* mean it's at six o'clock when we shut
down the office? Or does that mean it's later? And was
he just wanting to shoot the shit and apologize again
for his colossal fuckup? Or was he asking me out on
a date?"

"Oh, my God, girl," she said in between chuckles.
"Leave it to you to turn a simple human interaction into
a full-scale crisis."

"Well, it *is* a full-scale crisis! I don't know what I'm

doing. I mean, if I was drunk, I'd know, but I don't know how to do this sober."

While her chuckles had finally subsided, there was still a huge smile in her voice. "And isn't that a divine feeling? To experience the thrill and excitement without having a bunch of booze to screw it all up?"

"Maggie, be serious. I can't get excited about something if I'm terrified."

"Terrified of what? Break it down for me."

"I already told you last week. He made me *feel*. Like *a lot*. And I don't know what to do with all that. It's too big to process."

"And just like last week, I'll remind you that emotions are normal. You've worked your way through sadness and anger and learned how to deal with them without a drink or a pill to numb your senses. Now you're getting something new to work your way through—the glorious beauty of intimacy."

Intimacy.

Maggie had used the same freaking word last week and I still didn't know what it meant. Not even after looking it up in the dictionary. "What the hell does that even mean anyway?"

"Oh, my poor girl." Finally, the humor was gone, replaced with the same patient compassion she'd shown me since day one. Even that last time when I'd had absolutely no one to call and had shown up bedraggled and broken on her doorstep begging for another chance. "Intimacy is the real beauty of life. It's closeness. It's being vulnerable with someone. Being genuine with someone. You already know what that is because you and I share it. It's just this thing with you and Danny has the potential to take that feeling to a whole new level. Or at least that's the way it sounds given what you shared with me last week."

"But what if I'm reading it wrong? I mean, I listened to what you said last time. I took it a day at a time. I came into work. I did my job and focused on being myself, but I got nothing back from him. Nada. Bupkes. I barely even saw him except for a hello and a goodbye coming and going in the morning and at night. Not until yesterday when all hell broke loose."

"All hell, you say?" I could have sworn I heard the leather from her favorite oversized living room chair shift, and I easily pictured her settling in for a good story. "Say more about that."

So, I did. Top to bottom. From the mostly nonexistent interactions all week, to the part where I'd mega carefully made my way down Mia's complex stairway for fear of tripping and making an ass out of myself in front of him. "This morning when he showed for work, he was just as casual and matter of fact as could be. Friendly, but not *too* friendly. So, what do I make of that?"

"What do you make of what? The fact that he asked you to dinner? The fact that he wants to know your situation better so he doesn't hurt you again? Or the fact that he said clear as fucking day that he likes you?"

"Yes!" I said, then realized I'd raised my voice and lowered it again, checking to make sure no one had noticed. "All of the above."

As was her way, she got quiet for a minute. I'd learned to appreciate those silent seconds. To trust that she was handling my emotions with care. "The truth? I can't tell you what's going to happen tonight. No one can. Probably not even Danny, because the way you described it, he sounds a little off-kilter, too.

"But," she said, "what I can tell you is that he appears to be a man who genuinely does care about you. Yes, he mangled the situation horribly yesterday, but he's willing to spend the time to learn how to do better. That's a good thing. It says he thinks you're worth the effort."

"But is it just because he wants to be a good friend? Or is it because of…well…*more*?"

Maggie sighed, but it wasn't one of irritation. More one that said she hated having to drive home her point. "I don't know, sweetheart. But what I do know is that life is meant to be lived. If he's a person who cares about you, then it's a relationship worth exploring. Maybe he'll just be a friend. Maybe he'll be something more. You have no control or way to ascertain that answer right this second. But what you *do* have control over is being yourself and opening yourself up to whatever your Higher Power gives you."

Ugh.

I hated being powerless.

I hated not knowing.

But I also knew that she was right. It'd been proven time and again to me over the last year—when I let go and stayed in the moment, everything worked out the way it needed to.

I blew my bangs out of my eyes and rested my elbows on the desktop, cradling my phone to one ear. "I just don't want to look like an idiot, you know? Every time he even looks at me, I feel like I'm a stargazing teenager. I'm afraid I'll read something wrong and let that part of me out, only to find out he only cares because of my sister."

"Well, now there's a crock of shit if I've ever heard one."

The sharp, matter-of-fact snip in her words had me snapping my head up. "Why?"

"You yourself just told me he used the words *you matter*, yesterday. And, for the record, he's right. You *do* matter. And people like you because you're a good and likable person. It's just the likable and valuable part of you isn't hidden beneath a bottle of Jack anymore. Danny apparently sees that."

A hum I'd come to know as an indicator of a crucially important moment purred through my body. A kind of tuning fork sensation that always seemed to come at a turning point. I'd failed for years to heed that sensation. Had run from it and hid with any mind-altering substance I could find. But it was exactly this hum that had led me to Maggie's door a year ago. What it was telling me now, I wasn't entirely sure, but I knew better than to run this time. Walking through it was the way I needed to go, even if I had no clue where it would take me.

"You're right," I found myself sharing on a raspy breath. "I'm just...scared."

"Nothing wrong with being afraid, little girl. But facing those fears usually generates the greatest rewards. Pray. Keep your eyes and ears open. Talk to me and the people in your new group whenever you need to. Remember that unhealthy motives usually come with a boatload of fear or negative internal talk and that healthy motives make you feel good. Otherwise, get out there and dance, girlfriend. It's time, and you've earned some goodness in your life. Whether that's in the form of a friend or a lover."

A lover.

The shiver that rocked me had absolutely nothing to do with fear and everything to do with the memory of Danny standing so close to me in this very spot barely more than a week ago. I nodded despite the fact Maggie couldn't see me and licked my lips. "Right. Just stay in the moment and let the Universe take care of the rest."

"That's exactly right." I couldn't see her, but I knew how much conviction was in her face. She believed it because she'd lived through learning that truth the same as I was. "Now, I'm gonna hang up and you're gonna say that prayer then get back to business. Just don't forget to call or text when you get home tonight so I hear how things turned out. An old woman's got to get her kicks somewhere."

"Okay. Thanks, Maggie."

"No thanks needed, kiddo. You'll get more opportunities than what you did with Mia yesterday to pay it back. I promise."

More peaceful than I'd been in probably two days, we said our goodbyes, and I did as she'd told me—mostly keeping to the serenity prayer and a general request for help. Then, I got back to work, telling myself all I had to do was focus for five minutes. If that didn't get me in the groove, well, I could always turn things over with another prayer. And another one after that. Whatever it took to keep me grounded in the moment.

Turned out the five-minute trick worked like a champ, because the next thing I knew, the shop door opened, and Danny walked through at 5:55 PM. "Yo. You ready for some chow?"

Super casual.

Friendly casual.

Not at all potential hookup or romantic interest casual.

Oh, no you don't. No overanalyzing. We're going to be present and just let things happen like they need to. No expectations.

"Definitely." I closed down the software I'd been working in and powered down the computer. "You got someplace in mind already?"

"A few." He crossed his arms on top of the raised receptionist ledge along the front of my wide desk and leaned into them. "I'm leaning toward Chamberlain's."

"In Addison?"

"Yep. They do a mean steak, but you can get chops and seafood if that's not your thing."

Shit. I'd never been to that place, but I'd heard it was hella expensive. I glanced down at my usual jeans and the V-neck Pink Floyd tee I'd picked this morning. "I'm not sure I'm dressed for a place like that. Hell, I'm not even sure I own clothes for a place like that."

For some crazy reason, Danny smiled at my remark. "That T-shirt rocks, so I really don't care what they think. If they want my money, then they'll let us in. Plus, you forget—I'm wearin' jeans and a tee, too."

Money.

Crap.

I'd forgotten all about that. I could cover someplace a little more normal if I needed to pay for myself, but forking over massive dollars for a place as high-end as I suspected Chamberlain's was could knock the wind right out of my bank account.

Rather than look at Danny, I trained my attention on closing the laptop and tidying my desk. "Maybe we should go someplace a little more…casual."

One or two seconds of silence drifted between us, enough that I ran out of things to do to cover my discomfort and ended up staring at my hands splayed wide on the desk.

"Callie."

A delicious quaver wiggled through me at the sound of his low and entirely too sexy voice. Worse, I was pretty sure if I dared to look at him my face would make my reaction all too apparent.

"Callie, look at me."

Fuck.

Hiding was better. Easier.

But if I hid, I couldn't grow. And if I didn't grow and change…well, I'd be throwing away a chance at what I'd told Maggie I wanted after I hit bottom. A real life. A new life. One I could be proud of full of people I loved and who loved me in return.

Hands still braced in front of me, I slowly raised my head.

Damn, but he was intense. Dark hair. Dark skin. Dark eyes locked squarely on me. Full lips framed by that sexy as fuck scruffy beard that made me want to explore with my fingers.

"I hurt you yesterday," he said. "Badly. So, unless you tell me you abhor steak, seafood or chops, I'm taking you to Chamberlain's and you're going to let me treat you to whatever the fuck you want to eat no matter what it costs. Understand?"

I nodded. Or at least I thought I did. I kind of lost touch with reality when he looked at me the way he was now. A look that was somewhere between tender, amused and hungry as all get-out.

"Good." He straightened from the desk and jerked his head toward the parking lot. "How about if I follow you to your place so we can drop your car off, then you can ride with me."

The temptation to dive back into analytical mode hovered like a ghost in my thoughts, almost as subtle as those unexpected urges I sometimes got to ditch reality and find the nearest liquor store.

I ignored the urge and grabbed my purse out of the bottom drawer instead. "Okay. Sounds like a plan."

In my car, I cranked the AC and the stereo the whole drive home—the former to keep my makeup from melting off in the summer heat, and the latter to keep my brain occupied. I parked in one of the few remaining shaded spots, sent another quick request for help upward and stepped out into the great unknown.

Surprisingly, Danny was already within five feet of my Chevy by the time I shut the door and clicked the remote to lock my girl up. "You need anything from your apartment?"

Was that a trick question? Had my AC failed me and left my mascara running down my cheeks? Maybe my hair needed a quick visit with a brush?

God, Maggie was right. I really could turn even the most basic human interactions into a crisis. It was *just dinner*.

I shook my head and dropped my keys in my purse. "No, I'm good."

"Cool. Let's go then. I'm starved." Rather than head back to his car, he waited in the same spot until I got even with him. Then, just as natural and nonchalantly as could be, he put his hand at the small of my back and guided me the rest of the way to his Chevelle. The badass purple ride wasn't nearly as modified as some of the jobs I'd seen photos of in the shop, but it was still a beauty. A 1972 model with a fat white racing stripe down the middle and two flared chrome pipes curved up and out of the hood.

I'd never once allowed myself to get close enough to the fine machine to really appreciate it for fear Danny would read the interest the wrong way. Under normal circumstances, today would have been that day, but with Danny actually touching me and being as close as that contact brought him, I found I had a hard time breathing. Let alone exercise appreciating his custom ride.

Fortunately, he opened the door and broke the physical contact before I could pass out from lack of oxygen. "Make sure you buckle up."

Tempting as it was to laugh at the comment my brain was all too eager to misinterpret, I somehow managed to keep a straight face and slid into the butter-soft black leather bucket seat without whacking my head on the roof. Lucky for me, the time it took for Danny to close the door and round the front of the car gave my curiosity time to take over.

Like the seats, the dash was covered in the same soft black leather with fat white stitching running along the edges. The speedometer and tachometer were both refurbished originals from when the Chevelle was produced in 1972, but had a cool purple backlight to them. And while much of the interior trended to all things vintage muscle car, Danny had incorporated a nod to the modern world with a decent-size screen for navigation and a backup camera and a seriously impressive-looking stereo.

"Nice, huh?" Already buckled up, Danny twisted the key and sent the engine roaring to life.

"How long have you had it?"

"She was my first." He put the car in reverse and got busy with navigating us toward Addison. "I started her my senior year in high school—needed something to occupy my mind after I split ways with some friends who weren't good for me and had always wanted a Chevelle. It took me two solid years and a whole lot of help from my dad to get her restored the way I wanted, but we got her there."

"How old are you?"

"Thirty-four, why?"

I pointed to the center dash. "Because there's no way they had that kind of tech fourteen years ago."

Danny cast me a quick appreciative smile before he goosed the engine and sent us barreling onto the highway. "Oh, I've reworked the interior a few times in the last ten years. After some of the work I did for my brother Zeke on his Camaro, I was inspired to do some updating. Vintage is always a classic way to go. Hell, I wouldn't dream of messing with the exterior. But sometimes a touch of today's world is nice, too."

I ran my hand along the stitching that lined the center console between us, quietly allowing myself to just appreciate all the craftsmanship.

"You really dig cars, don't you?" he said. Almost as if such a thing were hard to fathom.

"And motorcycles," I said.

"Because of your dad."

Easy as a spring breeze, my thoughts drifted back to when I was little and things were simple. The iron and oil smell of my dad's garage. How I'd sit next to him and listen to him ramble on and on about his job or things he wanted to do or see someday. "Yeah. We were pretty close. He was a mechanic and always talked about doing something like you do every day. Even started a few times."

"Yeah? How'd it go?"

The bittersweet reality of my father's faults mingled with my fond memories. "Nowhere." I tried for a smile, but I was pretty sure it came up as empty as my voice. "Dad wasn't very good at finishing things. Always had big dreams, but he also loved to party and that had a way of derailing his path to the finish line."

"Was Viv close to him, too?"

A pang I hadn't expected struck behind my sternum. "Yes and no. She loved him, and he adored her. Sometimes so much it made me jealous as hell. But the truth was, Viv was too busy trying to prove herself to Mom—making good grades, looking good, trying to hang out with the right crowd—that she didn't have time to really just sit and hang out with Dad like I did. Me and Dad—" I shrugged my shoulders like that had some chance of explaining what words couldn't. "I don't know. I guess we just didn't buy into Mom's expectations and were fine letting her rant."

"She left when you were little?"

"Kind of depends on what you consider *little*. She left right after Viv graduated, so I was just out of my sophomore year. Personally, I was fine with her leaving. As much as she yelled and belittled everyone, the place was a whole lot more peaceful after she left."

"How'd Viv take it?"

A good question. One I'd never really bothered to find out. But I would. Eventually. Assuming I could ever mend the bridge I'd burned between us. "Hard to say for sure. She enrolled in junior college right after graduation and got a part-time job, so I didn't see much of her. She moved out as soon as she could."

"How'd you feel about that?"

I didn't much care for the answer that came to me, but I shared it anyway. "The truth? It was kind of nice. Dad and I had a rhythm to us. Not an entirely healthy rhythm looking back at it, but a rhythm all the same."

"Not healthy how?"

All those painful sessions in rehab crashed down on me at once, and I clenched my hands in my lap. "Like I said, Dad liked to party. I liked Dad to be happy, so I learned to party right alongside him."

"He let you drink with him and his buddies?"

The caution in his tone pulled my gaze to him. "Yeah. But nothing bad happened. Not like you're thinking anyway."

"But it set you up with drinking."

"Yep. And while Dad and I mostly ignored my mom and her constant put-downs, she still left a legacy in my head. I figured out that I couldn't hear all those echoed put-downs when I drank. I felt great about myself and didn't see the point in thinking about plans for growing up like Viv had, or even how to make a living." I sighed and looked out my window. "You know how the rest ended up."

"When did your dad die?"

My blood turned cold in an instant.

Your fault.

All your fault.

For years, people in the program and in treatment had been telling me otherwise, assuring me that my father was a grown man capable of making his own decisions, but that never seemed to make a difference to my conscience. "About a year after Viv left."

I was so lost in my memories, I didn't realize how far we'd traveled until Danny put the Chevelle in park and twisted in my direction. "Listen, if you don't want to talk about something, it's cool for you to call a pass and we can move on. I just wanna get to know you a little better. That's all."

"Why?" I asked before I could stop it.

Sucking in a long slow breath before he answered, Danny stared at me as though he wasn't sure of the answer himself. "Maybe just because I think you're worth getting to know. Fair enough?"

Not because of Viv.

Not because he didn't trust me.

Just because he wanted to.

Why that concept didn't exactly slide neatly into something my brain could readily accept, I wasn't sure, but I nodded anyway. "Yeah. Fair enough."

He smiled at that. A big one full of teeth that knocked me even farther off balance. "Good. Then hold tight and let me get your door."

Hold up.

What?

Why?

He exited the car and rounded the back end of it so quickly that I was still wrestling those questions by the time he opened my door. I was pretty sure my expression mirrored that of a modern-day human coming face-to-face with a dinosaur as I stared up at him. "Why'd you do that?"

"Do what?"

"Open my door."

He frowned down at me for all of a second before he seemed to come to some unknown conclusion then held out his hand to help me out. "Because it's what men do. Now, come on. The steaks are waiting."

The only thing my brain could come up with in answer was an unhelpful *hmmm*, so I put my hand in his and let him guide me out. Of course, then he had to go and scramble what was left of my common sense by putting his hand at the small of my back again and walking me in, opening up the door for me when we approached to boot.

Weird.

Nice and super flattering in a *Princess Diaries* kind of way, but mega weird.

Come to find out, Danny had a reservation for us, and the host didn't give what we had on a second look before hustling us to a cozy corner booth covered in plush leather the color of milk chocolate. The room was pretty open with mostly tables and chairs between us and the door, but they were all covered in high-end tablecloths and full sets of cutlery and wine goblets.

"Wow." I touched my fingertips to the base of the two forks on the left and eyeballed the extra fork parked parallel to the top of my plate. "You get a bonus fork here."

"Dessert fork." Danny snatched the intricately folded napkin off his plate, shook it out and dropped it across his lap. "And don't read too much into the fact that I know that either. I only picked it up doing bodyguard work with Beckett, covering people who have ridiculous amounts of money to burn."

I mimicked his actions with the napkin and opened my mouth to find out more about him being a bodyguard, but got sidelined by a waiter with a whole lot of pep in his step.

"Good evening." Mr. Peppy gave us each a small, but formal bow. He handed Danny two menus before handing me one then filled our water glasses. "My name is Ravi, and I'll be your server today. Can I interest either of you in a cocktail?"

Danny answered before I could, handing the smaller of the two menus back to the man. "No drinks for me. Just a Coke to go with the water."

"You sure?" I asked, ignoring our audience entirely. "Just because I don't doesn't mean you can't."

Cocking his head, Danny seemed to consider me for a moment before turning his attention back to the waiter. "Just a Coke's good. And whatever she wants."

I shrugged and looked to Mr. Peppy. "You got any La Croix or flavored fizzy water?"

A weird look moved across the server's face. Kind of like I'd just asked him if they had Kool-Aid on tap. "We have Pellegrino, madam. Would that suffice?"

Bleh. I'd tried that stuff before, and it was all fountain drink without the good stuff. "Nah, just bring me a Coke, too." I waited until he gave us another bow and took his high-stepping self off to somewhere else, then wrinkled my nose at Danny. "I guess my taste in beverages is too unrefined."

"He'll get over it. Hopefully, before it's time for me to sign the tab." He opened his menu and scanned both sides. "So, what are you in the mood for?"

Holy freaking cow. The cheapest steak was $34.50. I could eat fast food out for lunch almost every day for a week at that price.

I scanned the choices for something cheaper that

wouldn't actually look like I was trying to go the cheap route. Wagyu Beef Bolognese? At $26 it seemed to be the best bet, but I had no clue what the heck it was, and I didn't think I was brave enough to try fish in my current scenario. That only left one thing. "I think I'll do the chicken breast."

Danny's head snapped up. "Seriously?"

Pointing to the header above the section with the chicken breast, I stuck to my guns. "Says right here it's a chef specialty."

"You don't like steak?"

"Are you kidding? I fucking love steak."

"Then get something good. Like the rib eye. That's what I'm getting."

"That's a $48 steak!"

"And it tastes like it, too."

As if on cue, Mr. Peppy showed up with our Cokes. "Are we ready to order?"

Danny gave a short, sharp dip of his chin. "We're both havin' the forty-day aged rib eye."

We were?

"Very good, sir." The waiter looked to me. "How would you like that cooked, madam?"

I was still swimming through the fact that he'd ordered the $60 upgrade and how I was gonna fork back a twenty-two ounce steak, so it took a minute for me to shimmy up to a response. "Um, medium, please."

He rapid-fired me a few more times for side and salad options, then repeated the whole questionnaire process with Danny. Before I knew it, he was gone, and I was still speechless.

A crooked smile crept across his face. "Girl, when's the last time a man took you out?"

The question hit me out of nowhere, and I'm pretty sure my head snapped back like it'd had a physical impact. "I don't know. A while?"

"How the hell can that be?"

I shrugged and gave him the truth. "I guess because I was more about finding a party and hooking up that way than ever really having a bona fide date."

Sipping his Coke, Danny studied me over the rim. From the sharpness in his eyes, I was guessing he had about another thirty questions lined up behind that one, so I did a volley of my own to cut him off. "Tell me about your family."

"Not a whole lot different than yours really. The players are a bit switched up, but similar. Dad was a mechanic like yours, but he was our rock. Great work ethic. Great life ethic, really. Loved the hell out of all of us. Mom, on the other hand, loved her drugs. Went so far as to take my sister, Gabe, out on a drug deal her two boyfriends talked her into handling and got busted. Once Dad learned about the drugs and the men she was banging, he kicked her out and got full custody of us."

"Damn. How old was Gabe when it happened?"

"Little. I was twelve, so she'd have been eight. Really did a number on her, too."

I got that. I'd been a whole lot older when Dad had died, but that night had cut and marked me so deep, I wasn't sure the wound could ever heal. "I take it Gabe's a nickname?"

"Short for Gabrielle, but Gabe fits her better. She's a hell of a mechanic and likes hangin' out with the guys way better than hanging out with chicks. Or at least that was the case until Ninette, Sylvie and the rest of the girls got ahold of her."

"Who're Ninette and Sylvie?"

"Jace and Axel's moms. Jace you already know from Viv, but Axel's one of my brothers, too. Big guy. Long, wild red hair. Has a Highland Scottish warrior meets Dolce & Gabbana vibe going."

"I can't tell if that's hot or scary."

The waiter showed with a basket of bread and some fancy butter that looked like it'd been freshly made and was formed in the shape of a flower.

As soon as he was off again, Danny picked right back up where he left off. "You'd dig him. All the chicks do. Or did. Now he's happily married to Lizzy—AKA Lizzy Hemming."

"Holy shit. Not Lizzy Hemming as in the one I hear on Spotify all the time."

"Yep. That's the one."

Wow.

I grabbed a roll—twenty-two ounce steak be damned—and knifed up a little of the mega creamy butter. "And all of these people are part of your and Viv's family. That's fucking wild."

And so it went. A few more questions from me. Another handful from him. Back and forth and back and forth until I was two-thirds through my steak and bursting at the seams. I set my fork and knife down and dropped against the booth's back. "That's it. I'm gonna have to box the rest."

Danny had long beat me to the finish line, annihilating every single scrap from his plate, but now he pushed his plate back and crossed his arms on the table. "You liked it?"

"Liked it enough *I'd* pay $60 for the stupid thing. That was fabulous. I'm officially fat, dumb and happy."

Rather than laugh the way he had all through dinner, he cocked his head and said, "You are many things, Callie, but fat and dumb don't make the list. You do look happy, though."

Too flustered by the scrutiny on his face and the shift in the mood, I folded my napkin in my lap. "Well, you know what I mean."

"I don't just mean tonight. I mean I think you look freer these days. Lighter, or something."

Grateful he'd lit into a topic I was familiar with instead of giving me compliments I had no clue how to handle, I shifted gears. "I think that's because I finally got desperate enough to really work a program."

"A program?"

I nodded.

"I've got no idea what that means."

Forcing myself out of my beached whale routine, I mirrored his pose and leaned into my elbows. "The steps. There are twelve of them. I guess if I was gonna describe them easily, I'd say the first three are about admitting you can't control things and making a relationship with something bigger than you."

"A Higher Power?"

The way he said it I couldn't help but smile, because he sounded like a kid in algebra who was definitely hoping he hadn't just embarrassed himself in front of the whole class. "Yeah. Where'd you hear that?"

"Jason told me yesterday when I asked him if he thought something was wrong with you. He told me if there was it was between you and your Higher Power."

I couldn't help but chuckle. "And then you promptly chucked that piece of advice."

He lifted one nonchalant shoulder. "Hey. What can

I say? My mom didn't hang around for me to learn any different, so I'm cutting my teeth on you."

For some reason, knowing that his mother had such a similar history to mine was both comforting and frightening. Comforting from the viewpoint that we had something so tangible in common, but frightening because a part of me was afraid his attention was more about exorcising the past than anything to do with me.

Rather than give my thoughts time to run, I kept going with my explanation. "Steps four through nine are the meat of the program. The parts where you dig in and figure out the defects in your life that keep you in a bad place and who you've hurt along the way. Ten through twelve are the maintenance steps. How you keep your life on the right track."

"What made this program thing stick this time?" he said.

I shared the story I'd shared many times before in meetings—how I'd barely escaped a deadly shooting and found myself wondering the streets of Ethel with absolutely no one to call for help. "I guess that's what made me hit my bottom—realizing I was completely alone. That absolutely no one would miss me or mourn me if I'd been in that house."

Out of habit, I stretched one arm out in front of me and ran my fingertip along the jagged scar on the back of my wrist.

"What's that?" he asked motioning toward the old injury.

"One of the parting gifts I earned from swan-diving out of a window half-naked. The others were a concussion and a broken arm." I lifted my gaze to Danny. "I'm glad it's there, though. Makes for a good reminder if I start entertaining bad ideas."

Danny's gaze shifted to my arm, still resting slightly outstretched on the table while I leaned into my other arm crossed in front of me. He reached toward my arm—the movement surreal as if it were in slow motion—and ran his thumb along the four-inch scar.

Goose bumps flared up my arms and across my shoulders, the heat of his touch and the rasp of his work-hardened fingertip ridiculously erotic. I couldn't move. Couldn't breathe. Couldn't think or reason. Which probably explained the uncensored question that whispered past my lips. "What are you doing?"

Not the least bit stirred by my question, he retraced the wound once more before pulling in a slow and amazingly sexy inhale that rustled across every inch of my body. He lifted his gaze to mine, dragging his thumb toward my palm until his hand covered mine. "Going on instinct."

Not really an answer, but my physical self didn't seem to mind in the least. Not if the shiver it generated was anything to go by.

He drew a tiny, almost comforting circle with his thumb against my palm. "If you're uncomfortable, all you have to do is say the word. You'll get no judgment from me. No pressure. I'll be your boss and hopefully your friend, but the truth—the more time I spend with you, the more I think there's the potential for more than that between us."

His words washed over me, warm and sultry as a summer evening breeze. Consuming and offering a promise to sweep me away if I'd just let go and roll with it. Not entirely different from the release that came from my addictions, if I was honest. Only this was so much bigger. More powerful because my senses were completely aware and marking every single second to memory.

Life is meant to be lived.

Remember that unhealthy motives usually come with a boatload of fear or negative internal talk and that healthy motives make you feel good.

Maggie's words whispered through my head.

Did I feel good?

Definitely. One hundred percent lit up from the inside. In fact, the only negativity trying to break through was the incessant voice telling me what he'd said was too good to be true. It was up to me—*my* choice— whether I listened to the shitty committee trying to rob me of happiness, or I turned the volume down on their commentary and moved forward with something new. Something potentially good.

Trembling despite his warm skin against mine and his heated stare, I gathered up what courage I could. "You mean like sex? Friends with benefits? Or like… I don't know what to call it. Dating?"

Danny shook his head. "Not a hookup. And I have plenty of friends. And since I don't have much of a track record on girlfriends to speak of; I don't know what to call it either. What I do know is that I want more time with you. I want to see you smile at me the way you did when you told me about Tommy Langham and his Hot Wheels. I want to make you laugh like the guys in the garage do when you're cutting up in the office. I want to show you the things I love to do and find out the same about you.

"More than that, I want to kiss you the way I wanted

to last week before Jamey and Katy broke the mood and see if it rocks me the same way you just looking at me did. The same way you're looking at me right now."

Wow.

Just freaking wow.

I swallowed hard and shared the only truth still holding me back. "I have no idea how to navigate something like that. It's taken me a year to figure out how to be a healthy friend to anyone. Let alone how to process something more."

His mouth crooked on one side. "That's not a no."

No, it wasn't. Not even close. Even if I didn't have a clue where to go from here. But I could let the outcome go and let things be what they needed to be. All I needed to do was take a deep breath and jump.

"You're right. It's not a no. Like I said, I have no clue what I'm doing, and I'm afraid I'll bungle things in record time…but yeah. I'm totally on board with something…*more*."

Chapter Ten

Danny

I'd always been a guy to go with my gut. Not in an irrational, hold-my-beer kind of way. I'd had a few friends like that in my early twenties and their antics reeked more of stupidity and overinflated egos to my mind.

No, my way was more about honoring those quiet, subtle nudges that popped up now and again. Taking a left on a country road when I normally went right just to see where it took me. Bending a piece of steel in a way I hadn't planned on when working on a car. Not taking my eye off someone when my instincts told me they were about to throw a punch or pull a weapon.

But what I was feeling now…this insistent push that had me ignoring all the ripples that might come later… it was powerful. An engine built with a scary amount of horsepower just begging me to press down on the accelerator.

I downshifted the Chevelle and took the exit ramp off the highway, stealing a glance at Callie just before I checked oncoming traffic from the access road. Most women I'd taken out wouldn't have dreamed of driving with the windows down. Especially in summer or on the highway.

But not Callie.

She'd rolled her own down as soon as I'd pulled out of the restaurant's parking lot and had given me that schoolgirl delighted smile again when I'd done the same.

God, that look.

That absolutely glowing, ear-to-ear smile that made her eyes shine ten times brighter.

Three times now I'd earned it and every single one of them had made me feel like I was the only fucking man in the universe. Like I'd somehow hung the moon with one hand tied behind my back. I'd never felt anything like it in my life, but I knew—hands down—it was precious. A gift I wanted to be worthy of and hoard for myself all at the same time.

Finally unhindered by the wind and highway noise when a red light forced us to a stop, I hit her up with the question that'd been circling in my head. "You heard from Viv yet?"

With her elbow anchored on the window ledge and her face lit up by the sun, the pleasure in her expression dimmed just a fraction. A soft wistfulness replaced it. "No, not yet." She faced me, her cheeks a little pink from the warmth of the sun. "I can't really blame her, though. I've kind of blown any reason for her to trust me ten ways to Sunday. Getting that back will take time. And space. Or so Maggie's reminded me every single day for the last eleven days."

"Maggie?"

"My sponsor."

I'd done my share of time on Google since making an ass of myself the day before and had finally figured out a sponsor was a person of the same sex who was your go-to while you figured out how to live sober. That was, unless the person getting sober was gay, lesbian, or bisexual. Then the name of the game was picking someone you didn't stand a chance in hell of being attracted to. Whatever it took to make sure romance didn't wander into the equation. "She live here, or in Louisiana?"

"Louisiana. Has a cute little farmhouse a few miles away from the treatment center you guys took me to. She's colorful, to say the least. Has a sky blue 1980 Seville Cadillac, which—if you ask me—suits her personality to a T. That and all the bulky plastic jewelry she wears. Great big bold stuff in vivid colors—just like the woman."

"She sounds nice."

"She is. Unless I've got my head up my ass…which is about every other day, sometimes. Then she's the most direct woman on the planet."

I hesitated with my next question, hating that I might stray into territory that caused her restored mood to tank again. Then I remembered—if I was gonna weigh in with Callie the way I wanted to, neither one of us could afford poor communication. "You talk to Maggie about us?"

A pretty blush stole across her checks and, for a brief moment, she looked away while she seemed to gather her thoughts. "Sort of. I told her what happened last week. Then I called her today because I was nervous."

"Nervous about what?"

She shrugged and traced an absent pattern on her thigh. "I wasn't sure what to expect tonight."

I chuckled at that and turned onto the road that would take us to her apartment complex. "Well, that makes two of us." I glanced at her long enough to find her peeking my direction with a whole lot of curiosity then turned my attention back to the road. "I'm gonna guess whatever you and Maggie talk about belongs just between you and Maggie, but any chance she offered up some words of wisdom I could use, too?"

If I'd had any doubt as to the depth of the bond between them, they were shattered by the fondness in her voice when she spoke. "She said that facing our fears usually generates the biggest rewards and that I should always check my motives. That I knew the difference between what healthy and unhealthy felt like now. And then she told me I should get out there and dance."

Callie wasn't wrong. Maggie sounded like a helluva woman. "Are you afraid right now?"

I made it into a parking space and had the gearshift in park before she finally answered. "A little."

I shifted in my chair to better give her my attention, appreciating how the sun setting in the distance set her up with a halo of deep auburn. "Of me? Or the unknown?"

"Not of you." She paused a moment, and her gaze grew distant until she seemed to find the right words. "Do you remember your first date?"

Whoa. Talk about digging back in the archives. "Uh, yeah. Rachel Wiseman. Assuming a clueless sixteen-year-old boy taking a fifteen-year-old girl to an arcade counts as a date in your book."

Her grin deepened at that. "That sounds like a killer date. Did you kiss her?"

Oh, I'd kissed her all right. Then I'd had to come up with about fifteen minutes of small talk while sitting in the car with her before I could walk her to the front door without a boner. But I figured that wasn't the best bit of intel to share right now. "Probably not my best showing in the history of kisses, but yeah. I stole one before the night was over."

"Were you nervous?"

"Oh, hell yeah. Didn't have a clue how to make that play. Other than a bunch of ideas my buddies had thrown around the day before. All of which ended up being utterly useless. Why?"

She hesitated only a second with her words, but uncertainty was written all over her face when she spoke. "Because how you felt then—not knowing how to go about things or what to expect? That's me right now."

I guess the fact that I wasn't exactly tracking was written all over my face, because her voice dropped in volume and she added, "I can't remember even so much as getting a single kiss when I wasn't drunk. Every bit of physical contact I've ever known I've processed through the haze of at least alcohol."

The weight of what she was saying hit me with the subtlety of a two-by-four. When she'd told me she had no clue how to navigate a relationship, she'd really meant she *really* had no clue. "So, in a matter of speaking, when I walk you to your door and give you a kiss, I'll be your first."

The minute the words were out of my mouth, something seriously primal inside me woke up and growled its approval. And, given the hungry look that had taken over Callie's face, I was thinking something inside her had heard it and agreed.

"If that's your plan," she said, "then yeah. I guess you could say that. In a manner of speaking."

I liked that.

Actually, I fucking *loved* it.

Loved the idea that I could be the one to mark her with all kinds of first-time memories untainted by booze. Memories that had the potential to be etched in her brain for a lifetime.

But it also meant I needed to exercise a hell of a lot of caution and care if I didn't want to scare her off or send her into a bad place.

Patience though…patience I'd clearly run out of because I found myself more than ready to get the fuck out of my Chevelle and on to memory number one. "Callie?"

"Yeah?"

"Unbuckle your seat belt. It's time to go inside."

A heady buzz I hadn't felt in years hummed beneath my skin as we made our way inside, and for the first time in more years than I could remember, an uncertainty I wasn't at all comfortable with dogged my every step. What if venturing down this path sent Callie off on a spiral that knocked her out of sobriety? What if it fucked up the good arrangement I'd finally landed at work having someone solid and capable managing the office? Even if things went well on a personal level, there was still no guarantee Jace and Viv wouldn't flip their shit and I'd somehow compromise the awesome family I now had in my life.

Before I could drum up any answers, we were at her front door, her keys jingling as she turned the bolt. She pushed the door open then seemed to second-guess the action and turned to me, a silent question that seemed to ask for direction written on her face.

Facing our fears usually generates the biggest rewards.

Was I afraid?

Was that why in the space of three to four minutes I'd started second-guessing where I'd been driving us both toward all night? And what were my motives? Were they based in self-satisfaction, or were they genuinely grounded in that voice that had guided me through all of my life?

I moved in closer and splayed my hand on the door, pushing it wider even as I guided her across the threshold with my other hand at her back.

I *was* afraid. Where I was steering things unquestionably came with responsibility. And with consequences. For both of us. But my gut was one hundred percent clear that I was on the right path. This wasn't about a quick hookup or even a casual physical relationship. There was something more behind it. Something I didn't have the experience yet to understand. Only the faith to follow where it took us. And if that meant facing my fears to honor it, then so be it.

I closed the door behind us and held my hand out to Callie. "Give me your purse and the leftovers."

She handed me the Styrofoam box, then hesitated a beat before following through with her bag. Once she finally did, I set both on the overturned box by the door and faced her. A smarter man probably would have come up with something to ease her obvious apprehension. Some clever line or lighthearted quip to make her laugh or at least fill the silence.

Instead, I let the quiet be what it was—a canvas to hold whatever the two of us created—and slowly stalked toward her. If I'd had any doubt whatsoever that what she'd shared in the car about not remembering any intimacy without alcohol involved, her expression and the way she held herself would have annihilated it in a second. Lips slightly parted. Hands loosely fisted at her sides. Her breaths quick and shallow and her beautiful green eyes wide and flooded with wonder.

I stopped right in front of her and cupped her shoulders, giving myself the time to take it all in. To let it mark me in a way I never allowed anyone to before.

And mark me it did. Buried itself inside in that sacred space that defied description and took on concrete roots. Deep roots I suspected I might not ever really understand, but didn't seem to mind one bit.

This was it.

The beginning.

One I hadn't seen coming and had no desire to turn away from.

I pulled her closer, the press of her breasts against my chest and the barest whisper of her ragged exhalation against my skin narrowing my focus. Sharpening my determination and an overpowering need to touch her the way she touched me with just a single look.

Holding her gaze with mine, I slid one hand to the back of her neck and pressed the other low on her spine, pulling her hips flush against me.

Her breath hitched and the innocent unknowing behind her eyes shifted to something far more primal. A hunger I found myself eager to stoke and feed even if it killed me in the process. I traced my thumb along the vulnerable stretch at her neck, her pulse a frantic rhythm compared to the insistent war drum beating behind my sternum. "You with me?"

"Yes."

Only a whisper, but there wasn't a single inch on my body that didn't feel it. I skimmed my thumb along her jawline and leveraged the seconds it took to cup the back of her head to make sure my memory never lost sight of the way she was looking at me in that moment. "Good, because I think this is gonna be a first for both of us."

Perfect.

The fit of her lips against mine. The plushness of her mouth and how she opened so naturally when my tongue swept inside. The taste of her and the needy mew that coupled with her hands at my back and neck pulling me closer.

I'd been wrong to call her hungry. Callie was ravenous. Fire and passion just waiting for the right tinder and air to burn and billow wild and free.

And I fucking loved it.

Loved the energy sparking between us.

Loved how naturally every touch materialized and the easy flow that seemed to carry us both despite the powerful current.

But more than that, I was grounded. A part of me filled and content when I hadn't even realized I'd been missing something or empty. It made me greedy. Drove me to let my hands roam and do whatever it took to get us skin to skin with absolutely nothing separating us.

Except you promised her slow.

Maybe it was my subconscious talking. Or maybe it was my own Higher Power looking out for both of us. Either way, the words put a leash on my escalating need and helped me ease us both back from the flame.

By the time I pulled away, her lips were swollen from my kiss, her eyelids heavily weighted, and a perfect flush painted across her freckled cheeks. More than anything, I wanted to see that same vision with her sprawled out on my bed, naked and languid after I'd filled her with my cock over and over and made her come.

But that was for later.

Much later.

After we laid a foundation.

Although, I suspected the journey between now and then might kill me. "You feel that?"

"Oh, yeah." Part playful. Part dead serious. But one hundred percent as shaken as I was if the husky quaver in her voice was any indication.

"Got it etched in the Hall of Firsts?"

I caught her smile right before she ducked her head and chuckled. "Oh, it's locked in for life, for sure."

"Good." Missing her expressive stare already, I steered her gaze back to mine with my thumb at her chin. "Then that's where we're gonna leave it tonight. And tomorrow...well, tomorrow we build on a little more."

Her eyes narrowed just a fraction and the muscles in her torso tensed beneath my palms. "You're leaving now?"

So sweet.

So vulnerable.

Yet another reminder for me to handle every single step of the path we were on with the utmost care. "Better I go slow and leave us both wanting for more than rush things and risk regret. We can build on wanting more, but we can't undo regret."

She nodded, but only once and a little jerkily at that.

"I mean that, Callie. Whatever this is, I don't want to rush it. I want to do it right."

This time I got a crooked smile from her and one of

those yeah-yeah-I-know-you're-right eye rolls. "I get it. I don't like it, but that's probably a good indicator that it's the smart way to go."

I chuckled at that. "Is that Callie logic? If old instincts say to go north, maybe you should go south?"

She pulled her hands from around my neck and rested her palms on my chest, shrugging along the way. "Well, when what you've been doing your whole life was a whole lot of wrong, then it stands to reason an opposite direction might not be a bad idea."

I could see that. But like her, I hated the idea of pulling away, so I pulled her in for a hug and held her tight. "Either way, I'm glad you get me wanting to go slow." I paused a second, sliding my hand to her nape and inhaling deep the flowery scent that clung to her hair. "While we're setting expectations, I want a promise from you."

She pulled back enough to meet my stare. "What kind of promise?"

"The next time that mind of yours starts trying to divine where my head is at, or you're uncertain about something between us—you ask me. I don't want you wondering what I'm thinking or walking on eggshells because you're uncertain. I want us to talk. Whatever questions you've got, I'll answer the best I can. Can you do that?"

She pursed her mouth to one side—an adorable mix of mischief and uncertainty mingling with the look she gave me before she answered. "Sounds like a leapfrog into advanced relationship skills to me, but I can try."

"Fair enough." I palmed the back of her head and pulled her in for a kiss to her forehead. "Now, I'm gonna step away and force myself out that front door before I make a liar out of myself, and you're gonna put those leftovers in the fridge and kick back for the rest of the night with a belly full of good food."

With a playful sigh, she nudged me away and put her hands on her hips. "Fine. I'll make like a beached whale and nurse my food coma over Netflix then. What are you gonna do?"

"Well, for starters," I said, forcing my feet toward the door, "I'm gonna figure out some plans for us for the weekend."

She followed behind me. "You are?"

"Well, it's gonna be kind of hard to start walking down this path we're on if we're not together, so yeah." I opened the door and faced her. "So, if you've got meetings to go to, or other plans to handle, text 'em to me before you go to bed." I snagged her around the waist with one arm, pulled her in for one last quick kiss and added, "And don't forget to text me good night before you turn in."

God, that smile.

It was blinding. Pure sunshine in feminine form.

"You want me to text you good night?"

"Yeah, peach. I do. At least until we get to a place where you can tell me good morning face-to-face." With that, I slowly let her go, grabbed the doorknob to pull it shut behind me and winked. "See you in the morning."

Chapter Eleven

Callie

In the last thirteen months, I'd had an awful lot of experiences redefine what happiness looked and felt like—but not a single one of them held a candle to kissing Danny Parker. At nearly eleven in the morning with a night of fluffy dreams separating me from the event, I was still buzzing.

And grinning.

And driving Susan *and* Maggie insane by equal parts via text. Maggie had carried the bulk of my delighted squealing last night, so it was Susan up at bat today.

The green text message bubble lit up my phone's screen.

Susan: So, what happened after he kissed you?

Me: Nothing! He said he knew I was new to doing the whole relationship thing sober and didn't want to rush me, so he went home. But he said he was going to make plans for this weekend.

Susan: He said relationship? Wow, that's big.

Wait a minute. Had he said *relationship*? Maybe I'd thrown that word in on my own. Maybe I was jumping the gun on things or had spun one too many fantasies while I'd lain in bed last night replaying the whole ordeal.

Me: Well, now that you say it... I'm not sure he actually used that exact word...

Susan: Oh, God. Don't go freaking out! You said he'd told you in no uncertain terms that he wanted more than a hookup. Just be happy. You are happy, right?

Me: Sooo happy. Like my cheeks are kind of cramping from how much I've been smiling.

Susan: Right! Then enjoy it!

The clock in the bottom corner of my computer screen showed 10:55.

Me: You don't think it's weird he's not here yet this morning?

Susan: Is he normally in by this time?

Me: Usually, but not always. Sometimes he has to run errands.

Susan: And if he hadn't kissed you silly last night would you be freaking out about him not being there yet?

Hmmm. That was a good point.

Me: If he hadn't kissed me silly last night, I'd be about ten times farther along on ordering supplies instead of texting back and forth with you.

Susan: Ha! Then you better put the damned phone down and get to work before he shows. But keep me updated when you hear what he comes up with for the weekend. So excited for you!!!

Right. I needed to work. To focus and stay grounded in the present. Not floating on memories from last night or fashioning all manner of possible future interludes. On the bright side, it was a lot less tempting to let my mind wander with a computer screen in front of me than it had been last night lying in bed.

Exhaling hard, I grabbed the stack of notes from the guys detailing what they needed for this week's work and typed in the URL for the main paint supplier we used. I made it two-thirds through Malcom's list when the front door's chime pulled me out of my search for a paint called Orange Beast.

Shit. You. Not.

Watching Danny walk through that door with the late morning sun glowing behind him I really did feel like I was thirteen all over again, complete with angels singing in my head and my heart going pitter-patter. God, was I glad he'd had the good sense to go slow last night. If only a kiss had me goo-goo, actual sex probably would have had me writing wedding invitations.

"Hi," I said with all of the aforementioned goofiness oozing out of the single syllable. My cheeks protested a little more than they had while I was texting Susan, which meant my full-tilt smile was back in place. So much for playing it cool on my end...

Danny got one solid look at me, and a look of pure male satisfaction overtook his face. He rounded the end of my desk and slid a letter-size business envelope on top of it. "Well, good morning, peach. You slept good, I take it?"

Sleep? What was that? Or why would I want to? Riding on giddiness was much better. Best drug I'd ever come across, hands down.

The fact that my mental train had jumped the tracks must've registered with Danny loud and clear because he chuckled, gave up waiting for an answer and pulled me to my feet instead. He released his grip on my wrist and smoothed his hands over my hips to rest lightly at my waist. When he spoke again, he was close enough the lingering scent of his shower enveloped me, and his voice dropped to that low and gruffly sexy voice he'd used after he'd kissed me. "You did sleep, right?"

His lips were so close the warmth of his breath whispered across my face, and I couldn't have looked away from his near-black eyes if I'd wanted to. "Sort of."

His grin got bigger, the scruff surrounding those divine lips showcasing a whole lot of teeth. "Had a hard time nodding off?"

"Something like that."

A little of his smile slipped, but his eyelids got sexy heavy. "Spent time thinking about things left undone?"

Boy, was that the understatement of the century. More like running every possible sexual scenario that could have happened through my head. "A little," I said instead.

His fingertips tightened at my waist, and my breasts

grew heavy and tight. As if they craved his touch as much as my mouth tingled for his lips. "Me, too."

He sealed the husky admission with an easy, slightly lingering press of his lips against mine, then slowly let me go. Not entirely ready for the loss of contact with him, I swayed backward. Fortunately, my chair hadn't budged, so I went with the movement and plopped back into my seat. "Well…guess that answers how you feel about whether or not we should keep personal things quiet at work or not."

The playfully wicked grin I was rapidly developing a craving for whipped back into place as he leaned back against the desk and gripped the edge with his hands. "Never have been much on hiding things. But if you think it's gonna create a problem for you with the guys or you're not comfortable with it, maybe we should talk it through."

Well, that was kinda cool. I'd known my history with relationships was built on dependency and generally poor decisions in general, but having someone actually look me in the eye and offer to talk something through really put a spotlight on how foreign my new terrain really was. "That sounds like a very adult and healthy idea."

He cocked one eyebrow. "Not doin' PDA in front of the guys sounds adult and healthy?"

"No, silly. *Talking things through* sounds adult and healthy. But to answer your question, I'm fine with it. I just…" I shrugged in lieu of finishing the statement.

"Were you up in your head again?"

I wrinkled my nose, but owned it. "Maybe a little. But mostly I was worried you'd gone home, changed your mind and decided to avoid work. You're not usually this late getting in."

"Ah," he said snatching the envelope he'd laid on the desk. "Not avoiding anything. Just had to stop and pick up a decent fucking dead bolt for your apartment on the way in. Speaking of—what are you plans after work?"

A dead bolt? Why would I need a different dead bolt? Figuring I'd misunderstood the statement entirely, I opted for answering the question. "Usually, I hit a meeting at seven. But I can go to the noon meeting and eat my lunch there instead if you had something else in mind."

"Nope. Keep your seven o'clock if that's the one you like best. I've got something I need to take care of around dinner time, so I'll be tied up until about eight. What time will you get home?"

"Eight thirty."

"Perfect." He straightened off the desk. "I'll come by after my deal and we'll make it an easy night of television. You got any streaming services or cable?"

"Just Netflix. Cable's too pricey for my blood."

"Right, so I'll grab my Fire Stick before I head your way, too. Got any more of that fancy fizzy water?"

I didn't, but you could bet your sweet ass I'd be hitting a Walmart between now and eight thirty tonight. "Sure. Do you want anything else?"

He shook his head. "Totally up to you. Whatever it is you normally nosh on when you're watching TV is fine with me. I'm not picky."

Hmmm. Watching TV wasn't exactly an exercise I'd done a lot of in the last year of my sobriety. Too much idle time gave my brain waaay too much room to run and rationalize actions that weren't good for me. "Okay. Got it. Eight thirty with snacks and fizzy water it is."

"Good. Then I'm gonna run over to the Ft. Worth shop and see if I can't start gettin' my arms around what the hell's going on out there." He handed me the envelope. "You mind droppin' this off for me when you head out for lunch?"

I turned the gold six-by-nine package around.

Nelson Ford
Straight-Line Services
7700 Lemmon Ave
Dallas, TX 75209

"Sure. What is it?"

"Rough drafts on a new commission. I was supposed to mail it a week ago and forgot all about it working on the Malibu Vette. I'd do it myself on the way to Ft. Worth, but Nelson says he won't be there until noon, and I hate waitin' another two or three days for UPS to do the job."

I stood, flipped the package over and went for the metal tabs holding the lip of the envelope down, then hesitated. "Can I look?"

An odd expression drifted onto his face. Kind of like he was amused and amazed all at the same time. The latter of which made absolutely no sense to me at all. Didn't he get how cool his designs were? I mean, he had awards and pics with beaming customers mounted all over the office walls. How could a person *not* want to look at his stuff?

"Sure," he finally said with a bit of a self-conscious shrug. "Go ahead."

Gently, I opened the flap and eased the folder inside free, mindful of the tracing paper I remembered from the last images he'd shared with me. The top image was a standard off-the-line red Dodge Charger. "I suck with years. Is it a 1970?"

Danny shifted so he was mostly behind me and peering over my shoulder. "1968. The '70s have a little bit wider front end with a whole lot more chrome. The body also angles a little more forward than the '68. Gives it a meaner look, I think."

At the wistfulness in his voice, I glanced up and scanned his face before carefully laying the first layer of tracing paper over the base image. "Sounds like you'd have gone with the '70."

"Not my money. Not my car. But yeah. I like the edge on the '70."

Another page.

And then another.

Until finally I got to the last one sporting the finished product. More than anything I wanted to touch the drawing, but I fisted my hand against my stomach instead for fear of messing up the image. "Wow...that's just...wow."

"You like it?"

I shook my head, absorbing every detail. "I think it doesn't matter that your guy picked a '68. You *made* it mean. And totally badass. I mean, all the basics are still there so it's all muscle car, but the way you dropped it to a low rider, smoothed out the edges and added those whacked-out chrome rims—*totally* awesome."

I twisted, expecting to find him eyeing all the same details I'd been *oohing* and *ahhing* over. Instead, I found his gaze locked solidly on me. And this time that look was searching. For what I didn't know, but I sensed it was big. Something important. "You're insanely good at this. You know that, right?"

His focus shifted to the drawing. "That's the part I love. The making. From the original to the final outcome."

Instinct pushed me to turn the rest of the way around and slide my arms around his waist, but my confidence wasn't fully on board with that bold of an action. So, I went with asking what I wanted to know instead. "What part don't you like?"

He met my stare again and tried for one of those killer smiles that always left me stupefied, but his heart didn't seem to be in it this time. "All the other stuff."

Before I could ask what that meant, he stepped back and shut whatever thoughts had been riding him down. "You sure you don't mind takin' them to Nelson? Love Field ain't exactly a quick drive from here, but maybe I could call him and ask him to show you his choppers."

"His choppers? Like motorcycles?"

Danny chuckled and shook his head. "You wish. But no. He's got a helicopter business. Kinda like my brother, Trevor, with his jets, but focused on shuttling people faster across shorter distances. The way he tells it, he's got some of the best out there."

"Okay, not as cool as motorcycles, but definitely worth the drive." Mindful of packaging everything up the way it'd been to start with, I tucked the drawings back into the envelope. "If you were asking me to go there between four thirty and six, I'd call it a detriment to my sobriety and politely pass, but at lunch with a chance at seeing something cool I'm good." I placed the envelope on the desk and faced him. "So, you're good to go wrangle whatever needs wrangling in Ft. Worth. Give me a shout if there's anything there I can help with."

For a second or two, he just looked at me, thoughts I had no way of interpreting moving behind his dark eyes. "You know what's nice about you, peach?"

Peach. An interesting endearment, but one I found myself liking very much. It was different. Kind of like us. "My spunk and stellar T-shirt collection?"

He smiled at my quip, but didn't let it derail him in the slightest. Rather, he moved in close and cupped each side of my face in his big, strong hands and murmured, "You're fresh air. Sweet, honest, fresh air." He pressed another lingering, soft kiss to my lips before he eased back and slowly released me. "Looking forward to testing my restraint tonight. You need anything between now and then, call me."

I stood there, part stupefied, part mesmerized while I watched him go.

Fresh air.

Such simple words. Words I'd imagine some women would find odd, or maybe too simple for their taste. But to me? To me, they were a badge of honor. Because I got it. Felt exactly what he meant every single time I went out into the new life I was creating and found myself truly experiencing every moment. When I rolled the windows down and let the wind do whatever it wanted to my already unruly curly hair. When I'd sat outside the AA clubhouse in Ethel during the wintertime and felt the cooler temps nip my cheeks. When I tried new food and took the time to really appreciate the flavors or took note of all the colors present in a well cultivated flower bed.

And he'd called me not just sweet, but *honest*. Definitely not a word anyone would associate with my name in the last fifteen plus years.

My goofy smile pushed my sore cheeks back into the place they'd spent most of the morning, and I snatched my phone up. I pulled up my chat with Maggie and started up where I'd left last night.

Me: Girl, you are NOT going to believe what Danny just told me...

An hour later, I'd not only given Maggie an earful about what had gone down with Danny, but finished placing orders for the guys. A glance at the envelope waiting for me on the far edge of my desk and a rumble from my stomach reminded me in no uncertain terms it was time for lunch.

So, I hit a Sonic on the way to I-635, knocked back the Car Hop Classic, then drove the thirty-five minutes to Love Field. And *wowza*, was it ever worth the trip. Yeah, I'd ended up tacking on an extra hour to the trip, but getting to fly in that helicopter? I was never ever gonna forget that treat.

On the downside, I'd probably gushed a little too much about Danny's work when I'd walked Nelson through the drawings, but hey—I was me. And, according to Danny, *me* was synonymous with *fresh air*.

Bebopping my head from side to side at the thought, I put my economy-conscious Chevy in reverse and got busy with the drive back to work. Or at least getting back to work was the plan until some yahoo was too busy texting at the left-hand turn light and missed the green arrow that lasted all of five seconds.

My first instinct was to honk my horn or let out some of the serious inpatient road rage comments I'd been prone to in my party life. But a second behind that urge was another far more powerful thought.

It's been a damned good morning. Lots of productive work down. Two more kisses from Danny. The promise of more kisses and some chilling time with him tonight.

And Danny thinks you're fresh air.

Yep. Lots and lots to be grateful for. Not the least of which was a working air conditioner when the temperature gauge on my dash said it was nearly one hundred degrees outside. Not surprisingly, most of the people coming and going from the businesses on every side of the intersection reflected the oppressive heat in their miserable expressions.

My gaze drifted from the people and the wavy haze pulsing off the asphalt to the actual businesses.

Walmart.

The digital clock in the center of my console showed just after two. Malcom had said he'd be good to cover the phones until at least three. If I stopped in now for a La Croix restock, I'd have more time to get gussied up before my meeting at seven.

A total win-win!

Five minutes later I'd made the gruesome trek across the parking lot into the industrial AC of my former employer and was trolling the bakery aisles for some form of inspiration. Out of nowhere, a push to dig my phone out of my purse and call Viv for some advice on what to get hit me. Viv was a master planner in situations like these. Plus, I kind of wanted to share some of the excitement I'd been sharing with Maggie and Susan all night and morning.

I paused at the cookie display, pulled out my phone and thumbed up her contact information.

Twelve days since I'd called her and not so much as a text message back.

It hurt.

Bad.

Not so much because Viv hadn't called, but because I knew I was the reason. I was the one who'd pushed her away, bit by bit. Drama by drama.

And now, here I was standing in a Walmart wanting to have a real moment with my sister, and I couldn't.

Give her time, Maggie had said.

Deep down, I knew she was right. Knew that changes hadn't happened in me overnight and wouldn't happen for Viv any faster. And besides, it was good for me to figure out what worked for *me* in situations like this. Not what everyone else would do. Even when it came to food.

A little disheartened by the turn of my thoughts, I tucked my phone away and got back to the task at hand. It took me three laps between the bakery and the chip aisle, but eventually I settled on a dozen pink iced sugar cookies, a party-size bag of Original Lay's, and a box of Pop Secret's Homestyle. Not *Lifestyles of the Rich and Famous* by any stretch, but it was all my kind of food and none of it would go to waste regardless of what Danny did or didn't eat tonight.

I headed to the beverage aisle and spied the La Croix smack-dab in the middle stacked up on the non-refrigerated side. Since they were a dollar off a twelve-pack, I grabbed two, spun to put them in my cart—and almost dropped them on top of the chips and cookies.

Modelo.

Blue Moon Belgian White.

Dos Equis.

And on and on, taking up nearly all of the refrigerated items until a daunting selection of wine took over.

All it would take to cover the rest of the afternoon would be a phone call to Malcom. And if he couldn't answer the phone, one of the other guys could.

Nothing beat a hot afternoon like a mega cool beer.

And no one would know.

Not if I was smart about it. I mean…one drink wouldn't hurt.

The weight of the twelve-packs still in each hand drew my focus away from the beer and back to the cart.

You're fresh air. Sweet, honest, fresh air.

Someone saw me that way. No, that wasn't true. Maggie had pointed out after the fact that lots of people saw me that way. Saw sober Callie that way. Did I really want to throw away my new healthy happy life for a drink?

I dropped the twelve-packs into the cart, grabbed the cart's handle for all I was worth, and spun so fast I literally whacked some poor dude reaching for a case of Miller Lite in the ass.

"Shit!" I backed away enough to right my cart. "I'm so sorry. I wasn't paying attention."

The truth was, I still wasn't. Was too deep in the need to get the hell out of the aisle and Walmart altogether that I nearly jumped out of my skin when he grabbed me with an uncomfortable grip at my upper arm. His eyes narrowed. "Do I know you?"

Dark hair, slightly receding hairline, six feet tall, slender and fit. Not a single detail triggered my memory. "No."

I glanced down at his hand—a hand I realized was mighty freaking strong for someone that was missing at least two fingers. "Uh, you wanna let me go?"

Something in his expression hardened, and the flight response that'd already been triggered in my near miss with going for the beer ratcheted up to DEFCON 1. "I *do* know you."

Fuck that.

Whether he knew me or not, I needed out of there now. I jerked my arm free despite the bruises I knew it would earn me and power walked me and my cart to the self-checkout line. I was back out in my car with the engine fired up and the AC blasting inside ten minutes, but instead of driving I locked the car, fumbled for my phone and speed-dialed Maggie.

She answered in just over two rings, but didn't even get a full hello out of her mouth before I cut her off. "I almost fucked up."

Chapter Twelve

Danny

The only thing worse than a day wading through bullshit was an evening driving through rush hour traffic *after* said bullshit wading. One would think after living my whole life in the DFW area, I'd have known better than to hop on Highway 121 right at five o'clock, but after a day of tryin' to make sense of my Ft. Worth shop manager's business logic, I'd completely spaced on what time it was. Plus, there was the one dreaded task that had been hanging over my head since I'd woken up. One that involved me talking to people who very well might not like what I had to say.

A sign marking Allen's exit as one mile away whizzed past me on my right, and the heavy weight that had been squatting in my gut all day got a little bit heavier.

I hated this. Hated the fact that I was in a position where other people's feelings or prejudices might force me to choose between loyalty and my instincts. Worse, I hated that me moving forward with Callie might do something to tank the chances of her reconciling with her sister.

But hiding where she and I were headed wasn't an option either. It reeked of guilt, and there wasn't a bone in my body that felt guilty about a single thing I'd said or done with her. Not to mention the fact I'd found myself pretty fucking proud going out with her last night.

So, yeah. Hiding was off the table, no matter where the aftermath ended up.

Coming up the drive, the circular path that ran in front of the main house's front door was free of any vehicles save Rex's truck. Not exactly my ideal situation. Hitting Haven on a Friday before Jace had a chance to head to their club without anyone else around had seemed my best bet, but I'd take what I could get.

I parked, knocked on the front door since I hadn't given anyone a heads-up I was coming, then opened it up and headed into the lion's den. "Anyone home?"

I made it about four strikes toward the kitchen before Ninette showed in the archway, her eyes wide with surprise. "Danny! You should have told us you were coming. We're working our way through dinner."

"Oh, yeah?" I gave her a hug, hoping like fuck it wasn't going to be one of my last where she was concerned. "Who all's here?"

Maybe she sensed my hesitancy—or maybe she was just being herself—but she squeezed my torso a little stronger before she let go and stepped back. "Axel and Lizzy. Little Colin, of course. Jace and Viv. Me and Sylvie and Rex." She waved me into the kitchen. "We kept it simple and grilled hamburgers tonight. I think there might be one left."

I shook my head, then followed her in. "No worries. I mostly came to talk somethin' over with Jace and Viv. I can grab somethin' on the way home if I need to."

She cackled at that. "Like you've got a fuckin' prayer of getting out of here without Sylvie putting something in your belly."

That was definitely true.

Although, the night wasn't over yet. She might not get a chance to ply me with her pantry full of sweets before I headed home.

All heads turned to me when I walked in, including Colin, who somehow managed to smile and give me a good view of whatever it was that was in his mouth at the same time. He then proceeded to bang his high chair with a huge serving spoon.

"Hey, Danny." Lizzy grabbed the spoon and sat it on the table well out of reach. "Sorry, little man fancies himself a drummer lately."

"Little guy fancies himself a ladies' man is more like it." Axel looked to me and kept on with the conversation like he'd expected me to show nearly at the end of dinner. "I've never seen the likes of it before. Ran to the grocery store for Ma and took the little tyke with me. The bugger had three of 'em lined up and *gooing* and *gahing* inside five minutes."

Jace laughed. "And you're fucking surprised? You ever heard about the apple not falling far from the tree?"

Viv smacked Jace on the shoulder. "You know he's starting to talk right? I don't think we want him dropping an f-bomb for his first word." She looked to me and motioned to the one lone hamburger patty on the serving plate in the middle of the table. "We've got one burger left if you want it."

"Right," Sylvie said sliding back from the table and heading toward the main part of the kitchen. "I'll get ya somethin' ta drink. What'll it be, love?"

"Whatever's easiest. Beer. Tea. Water." For some reason my eyes locked on Rex who was—not surprisingly—seated right next to Ninette. Maybe my attention had shot to him because, while he was usually the most laid-back man I knew, tonight he looked a little aggravated. "Everything okay, brother?"

His head swiveled from the blank stare he had aimed at the table to me. "Come again?"

I rounded the table to a seat between Viv and where Sylvie had been. "Just asking if everything is okay. Not often I see you without a smile on your face."

For the most part, he covered his reaction well, but I still caught the hardening of his lips before he spoke. "All good. Just thinkin' is all."

Ninette straightened in her chair and reached for one of the sugar cookies piled high in a bowl closest to Lizzy. "Y'all tried Sylvie's new cookie recipe yet? She added a little almond to the equation and now I'm guaranteed to go up a dress size."

Vivienne *harrumphed* and bit into a French fry. "You're not the only one, sister."

Funny. On the surface the comment seemed like she was agreeing with Ninette, but the droll humor behind it made me think she was referencing something I'd missed.

Actually, now that I thought about it, the whole room had a super weird vibe going on. Whether that was going to play to my advantage, I wasn't sure yet. But things were definitely not the usual warm and fuzzy around the dinner table.

I piled up my burger and took the glass of lemonade Sylvie handed me while Ninette quizzed Vivienne on what she wanted for her upcoming birthday. I was so focused on dressing then powering down my burger, it took about a three-second delay before I realized Viv had not only asked me a question, but that everyone was looking to me for an answer. "Sorry. I was somewhere else. What was that?"

Viv shifted a little in her chair and tucked her hands under her thighs. "I asked about Callie. I just... I haven't called her back yet because I wasn't sure what to do or what to say. I was wondering how she's doing."

Beside her, Jace stretched his arm out and rested it on the back of Viv's chair, but aimed his gaze at the floor. An unspoken yet unmistakable dismissal of all things Callie if I'd ever seen one.

I sat the last bite of burger down on my plate. No way it was gonna go down now anyway. Not now that the barn door was open and the cows were moseying toward the field. "Honestly? She's doing great. A whole different person than the one I've seen in the past. Looks healthy. Laughs a lot. Goes to meetings and says what's on her mind when she needs to. Even called me on my shit a time or two. The guys love her."

Right. Like they're the only ones who've been tripping all over themselves where she's concerned lately.

I ignored the jab from my conscience and refocused on Viv, who at that exact moment was looking at me like she couldn't decide if I'd gone crazy or like she wanted to cry. "She's really...for real this time?"

Man, but the place Viv had been in had to suck. Being not just stone-cold sober while you watched someone you love going slowly down the pipes, but doing it while your own life just kept getting better and better. Talk about a guilt-rich environment.

"Look," I said. "I can't tell you she's one hundred

percent never going to drink again. No one can. But what I can tell you is she seems to be putting the work in to stay that way a day at a time. For me, I finally got to a point that I decided I had to leave the past behind and focus on who she is today if I want to give her a fair shake. If she goes back out—well, I'll deal with that situation then."

Viv gave me a wry smile before ducking her head and dashing what I suspected was an unwelcome tear from her cheek. "You sound like the people at my Al-Anon group."

"You've been going?"

She nodded before meeting my gaze again. "I started going a little over a year ago. Right after the last call from Callie. They said I needed to detach and let her find her bottom on her own." She paused a moment, scanning everyone else at the table, then seemed to dismiss the fact that she had an audience. "The thing is—now that I've put that space between us—I don't know how to step back into talking to her. I'm too afraid she'll just start using and drinking again, and then I'll have to feel all that awful fear and disappointment all over again."

Man, I totally understood. Had asked myself the same thing about fifty times between when I'd walked out her apartment door last night and this morning when I walked in, and she looked at me like I was Superman. "No one blames you for being afraid. Not even Callie."

The comment was apparently strong enough it got Jace's attention. Though, he didn't get a chance to comment before Vivienne did. "You really think that?"

"I don't think that, I *know* that. She's told me she's

accepted the consequences for the person she's been in the past. I think it's part of the program she's working."

"That so?" Jace said, finally weighing in. And, judging from the disdain in his voice, he wasn't weighing in from Callie's corner.

I shrugged. "She's a different person. Or maybe a better way to say it is, she's able to be the person she was supposed to be without the booze."

Jace cocked his head just a fraction, and his eyes narrowed. "Sounds like she's got herself a champion."

The statement got my back up and had me answering on instinct. "Everyone needs a champion now and then. Even the person who's lost every right to one."

Silence swelled and swallowed the table.

Viv volleyed her attention between her husband and me, her expression one of cautious uncertainty.

I couldn't say I blamed her. Like me, Jace had a powerful temper once he reached his tipping point and there was nothing faster at triggering a man's anger than protecting a woman he loved. An interesting observation considering I'd just jumped to Callie's defense without a beat of hesitation.

And...since I'd stuck my neck out this far... I figured I might as well see if the guillotine was gonna leave me walking out headless.

"Speaking of Callie..."

"I hate to break things up," Ninette said at the same time, "but I..."

We both paused and grinned at each other, but it was me who spoke. "Sorry, go ahead."

One of Ninette's eyebrows shot high, the suspicious nature of her look squarely aimed at me. Then her lips curved in a sly smile, and she waved me ahead. "No. No. You first."

Damn it. She'd clearly caught my mention of Callie. Though, why Jace hadn't done the same and called me out as well had me stymied.

I cleared my throat, wiped my hands on my napkin and wadded it up before throwing it onto my plate. "I came out here tonight to talk to Jace and Viv…just to lay something out there…but I figure you're all here, so I might as well rip the Band-Aid off with everyone."

Aside from Lizzy, who had her hands full trying to wipe Colin's mouth and hands, every gaze locked on to me. And even Lizzy managed to glance my way after enough silence settled around the table.

I took a breath and threw it out there, tact and delicacy be damned. "I took Callie out on a date last night. And after that date, I'm inclined to do more exploring where she and I are concerned."

Lizzy smiled.

Axel chuckled. "Must've been one helluva date."

"That does sound promising." Sylvie crossed her arms on the table and leaned in. "What happened?"

Ninette shared some kind of silent eye to eye communication with Rex that I didn't have a prayer of interpreting, but looked pretty interesting.

Not surprisingly, Viv had her wide eyes aimed at Jace who shook his head and blurted, "You're fucking kidding me. Callie? The bitch who left Viv with a drug dealer holding a gun in her face and cost me a shitload of money to keep her from getting whacked?"

Shit.

I'd known about the money since I'd been a part of the hand off to Moreno, but back then I hadn't been voted in as a brother yet, so Viv staring down a gun-man was a detail no one had seen fit to share.

Still, I wasn't ready to back down from where I was. Especially not with the name throwing. "She's not a bitch. She's an alcoholic. One who's finally got some time behind her and is trying to get her life back on track. We've all fucked up. Even you. And while I can't change the fact she left Viv in harm's way more than once, I *can* cover the money if that's gonna help you let go of the past."

Stunned and absolute quiet pressed on all sides of me.

Even my own brain flatlined for a good second or two until it figured out what I'd just offered on a finan-cial spectrum. Yeah, I was more than comfortable with the money the shops brought in, but a hundred G was nothing to sneeze at.

I forced myself to hold Jace's stare even though his anger was palpable enough to leave a few bruises with-out physical contact.

When Jace finally found a voice to speak, it came out low and with the most dangerous edge I'd ever heard. "It's not about the money. It's about disrespecting Vivi-enne and what she's been through. It's about disrespect-ing this family and—"

"Now, hold on just a damned minute." Ninette sat up tall in her chair and faced her son in a way only a mother could do. "Don't you *dare* jump in and start throwin' around *disrespect* specific to this family. Not until you ask how me and everyone else feels about it. And as for Vivienne, I'm pretty sure she's got a mind and a backbone of her own. She doesn't need you beatin' your damned chest and fighting all her battles."

Well, fuck me.

I'd seen Ninette put people in their place a few times, but this time she was fired up like I'd never seen her before.

But Jace wasn't backing down. "You're gonna tell me you think this is right?"

"I think family doesn't get to dictate who does what with whom. It's called a *personal* life for a reason. It means each person gets to do what they think is right and abide by the consequences, good or bad. Now, I get you and the boys wantin' to keep Haven only to those that are in it for the long haul, but you ask me—you're crossing a bullshit line when you start telling people who they can and can't date." She paused only a moment to drive her point home with a ferocious stare at Jace, then shifted her attention to Vivienne. "How do you feel about all this?"

Vivienne blinked about four or five times, scanned the table and swallowed hard. "The truth? I'm kind of in shock and haven't had a chance to process yet. I mean, I love Danny. And while I'm pissed at Callie for a whole lot of reasons, she's still my sister, and I want her to be happy." She hesitated a beat and glanced at Jace before continuing. She covered his fist where it rested on his lap with her hand and her voice got a whole lot softer. "I guess I'd say if either of them has a chance at finding what I've found with Jace, I'd want them to give it a go."

Jace's jaw dropped.

Sylvie, Rex, Lizzy and Axel all smiled.

Me? I was still braced for Jace to shoot across the table for a takedown.

"Right," Ninette said, clearly still on a roll. "Then if it's *her* sister and Danny's offerin' you an out on the cash, then I'd say your beef is a nonissue. It's out there, Danny's doin' his thing, and let the pieces fall where they may."

She sat back in her chair with a *hmmph* and crossed her arms. "And by the way... Rex and I have a thing goin' on, and if anybody gives me or him shit for it, I'm liable to cut someone's nuts off. It's our life. No one else's. We clear?"

She looked to Jace, then to Axel—both of whom appeared to have lost the ability to speak. Though, it did kind of look like Axel could bust a gut laughing at any moment. Which was probably why it was him who broke the silence with a solemn dip of his head and an ornery smile on his face. "Duly noted. No one's gonna give you or Rex the least amount of shite for doin' the dirty on the sly."

"Oh, bollocks on that." Sylvie stood and rounded Colin's high chair, deftly undoing the belt that kept him from doing an escape act mid-meal. "I've been givin' Ninnie shite since the day I met her. Not gonna stop that just because she's officially out on knockin' boots with Rex." When she'd freed the kid and had him on her hip, she ducked closer to Ninette as she rounded the table and murmured, "And for the record, I already knew. So, don't be thinkin' you were passin' one off on me, aye?"

For the first time since she'd waded in, a little mischief flickered behind her sky blue eyes as she looked up at her best friend of God only knew how many years. "Would've been worried your nosey skills were wearin' thin if you hadn't."

Sylvie laughed, snatched a sugar cookie off the table and headed toward the pantry still lugging Colin on her hip.

Rex straightened off the back of his chair and leaned both elbows onto the table, zigzagging his attention between Axel and Jace. "I'd apologize for not sharin' sooner about your mom and me, but the truth is… I kind of agree with her about the personal stuff. You start into something new with someone, the last thing you want is an audience readin' your every move."

Mouth pinched like he'd swallowed a mouthful of bitter beer, Jace shook his head and met Rex and Ninette's stares one after the other. "Never would've stepped between anything between the two of you. You're both due whatever happy you can get." His gaze lingered on his mother before his voice dropped. "You in particular."

All of two seconds passed before he frowned at me, leaned over to give his wife a kiss on her cheek and muttered something I couldn't hear, then stood. "Think I'm done with family shit for the night. Gonna take the long way to Crossroads and give myself time to unwind."

And then he was gone, all the tension of the last fifteen or so minutes was replaced with the same easygoing banter Haven's kitchen was known for. But I couldn't help feeling I'd dug up some nasty skeleton and fractured the family I'd grown to love.

I reclined against my chair back and gave myself time to recalibrate, floating on the chatter around me even though I had absolutely no fucking clue what a one of them were saying. Before I knew it, Rex's chair legs scraped against the kitchen tiles and ripped me out of wherever my head had drifted to find Ninette clearing the table with Vivienne.

Rex waited until I met his gaze and dipped his head. "You did the right thing, brother. The honest path is always the right one, and the last thing a man like you needs in his life is regrets. If your gut is tellin' you to go for it, then that's what you need to do."

"He's right." Axel pushed Colin's high chair back so it no longer separated him from Lizzy, dragged her chair closer and wrapped his arm around her shoulders. "Jace is pissed now, but he'll come around. Just give him time."

Time.

Shit.

What time was it?

7:57 PM.

Damn, I'd spaced longer than I thought I had. Thankfully, the drive to Garland from here was no more than twenty minutes or so this time of night.

"I hope you're right," I said, pushing back from the table. "Love the fuck out of this family. It'd suck if I found one thing new only to lose something else that's important to me."

"It won't come to that, brother," Axel said. "We're family. Sometimes that means we butt heads, but all in all, we come together when it's important. Jace'll see that."

I gathered up my plate and utensils, did my thing with loading the dishwasher and said my goodbyes, making damned sure I gave Ninette an extra-huge hug for the solid she'd thrown me before I headed for my car.

I'd barely made it halfway to the driveway when Vivienne's voice cut through the night. "Danny!"

I stopped and faced her as she hurried my direction.

"Hey," she said, a little out of breath. "You seem like you're in a hurry."

Great. Just what I needed. Another awkward moment. I cleared my throat, but manned up. "Yeah. I…ah…

told Callie I'd meet her after her meeting was over to-night. Gonna hang out and watch some television."

Viv surprised me with a blinding smile that reminded me a helluva lot of Callie's. "Netflix and chill, huh?"

Honest to God, I couldn't remember the last time my cheeks had burned with embarrassment, but having Callie's sister call it out like that brought the sensation back in a heartbeat. "Not thinkin' we're to the *chill* part yet, but yeah. We're gonna hang out a bit."

She nodded at that and stuffed her hands in her back pockets. "Well, I don't want to keep you, but… I wanted to ask you…do you think I should call her? I mean, will it screw things up for her?"

Man, talk about your double-edged sword. The self-ish part of me wanted to tell her to give it more time before she reached out to Callie so I'd have more time to get to know her before the rest of the family waded in. The other part of me knew Callie would be over the moon just to hear her sister's voice. To have a chance at making things right.

I opted for something I hoped was a lot more dip-lomatic. "I think you have to make the decision that's right for you. If you're ready for it, then call her. If you're not, then wait. But whether you do or don't won't have any bearing on whether or not Callie stays sober. That's all on her."

Viv cocked her head. "You sure you haven't been going to Al-Anon meetings? 'Cause that sounds a lot like what they'd say there."

I huffed out a chuckle at that. "Wish I could say I had. More like I've learned a few hard lessons in the short time since she started working for me. Even went so far as to follow her one afternoon 'cause I thought she was about to buy drugs. Turns out she was meeting one of her AA buddies to help out someone who wanted to get sober."

"How'd you find that out?"

"Because I was just about to knock on the door of the apartment she was in when she walked out with her friend and the lady needing help. Made for one hell of an awkward moment. For both of us."

Viv smiled and studied me a moment. "You really like her, huh?"

Such a simple question. I wished my answer was one that was equally simple, but the truth of it was, I was still trying to sort out what was different about Callie. "She's different. Or I guess I should say things feel different when I'm around her. There's a balance—an ease, or something—that I only feel when I'm around Gabe or you guys. I don't have to think about what to talk about. Hell, I don't even have to talk because she's comfortable with silence, too. It's just…fluid." I hesitated, uncertain if I should share the rest or keep it to myself. "When I'm around her I feel one hundred percent whole and accepted. Which is probably fucked up considering she only wandered into my shop about three weeks ago."

A deep understanding settled behind Vivienne's gray eyes. "I wouldn't call that fucked up. I'd call that a blessing." She opened her arms, stepped close on her tippy toes and pulled me into a tight hug with her arms around my neck. "You keep doing what you think is right. No matter what Jace might say right now, he'd do the same thing."

The unease that had tormented my insides all damned day settled in a heartbeat, and I tightened my arms around Viv on instinct. "Thanks for that. The last thing I want is to stir a bunch of shit with the family, but I don't think I could stand it if my actions caused you pain."

"No," she mostly whispered. "No pain. If anything, I'm hopeful for my sister for the first time in years." She let me go and stepped away, dashing a tear from her cheek with the back of her hand. She shooed me toward my car. "Now go. Enjoy some happy. I'd say you've earned it after the night you've had."

Walking away from any female with tears welling in their eyes wasn't normally my MO, but I also knew the value of having a minute alone to get my shit together. "Thanks, Viv. For everything."

And with that, I got in my car and headed to Callie.

Chapter Thirteen

Callie

What was it about a serious sob session that completely wiped a person out?

I trudged up the concrete and iron staircase to my apartment, the muscles in my legs sapped from the emotional wringer of the last six or so hours and the late July heat. The twelve-pack of La Croixs in one hand and the three plastic grocery bags filled to the brim dangling from the other sure didn't help matters. But more than that, my eyes burned with the need to let my eyelids close and my body drift until I found the sweet release of sleep. In the morning, I'd feel about seventy-five times better. Lighter. I'd learned that much from the other near misses with drinking and the crying jags that had followed over the last year.

But I couldn't go to sleep just yet.

Not until I got to enjoy just a little time with Danny watching TV. Not even a head-to-head with booze was going to rob me of that simple pleasure, even if the interaction re-fired all the crazy emotions I'd finally managed to even out over the afternoon at Susan's house.

Inside my apartment, the air was uncomfortably

stuffy—the byproduct of trying to save a few bucks in
the thick of a Texas summer in a run-down apartment
with air conditioners older than I was. I unloaded the
groceries on the kitchen counter, stashed my purse and
phone in their usual spots and adjusted the thermostat
before getting busy with unpacking my loot. By the
time I finished, the digital readout on the microwave
showed 8:25. Just barely enough time to run a brush
through my crazy as fuck hair and see if I couldn't do
something to make my eyes look like they hadn't just
watched *Steel Magnolias* three times in a row.

Halfway to the bathroom, three solid knocks sounded
on the front door.

Well, shit.

Looked like Danny was going to get his first dose of
seeing me and my best drowned rat routine.

I combed my fingers through my hair on the way
to the door and pulled in a few slow breaths before I
turned the knob and opened it.

Man.

Bedraggled and weary or not, seeing Danny and all
his handsome goodness outside of my apartment was a
serious jump start. And not in a bow-chicka-wow-wow
way either—though I imagined if those full lips of his
got involved that would change.

No, this was more of a cozy, easy feeling. Like
when you walk out into the first sunny spring day after
months of cold and cloudy. I smiled at the thought, but
my cheeks quivered in the process. "You, sir, are a sight
for sore eyes."

The rakish grin that had been on his face when I'd
opened the door had slowly disappeared, but shifted to
open concern at my greeting. "What happened?"

Damn. I must've passed drowned rat and transitioned to death warmed over sometime on the drive home.

I stepped out of Danny's way and waved him in. "Kind of a long story. You might wanna come in and grab a cookie. Crazy is a lot better shared with snacks."

For a second, he looked like he wanted to argue and demand an answer right then and there. But then he glanced over his shoulder and seemed to remember neither of us were really in a great position for any lengthy conversation. "How about you talk first," he said, taking over with closing the door and dropping a plastic bag he'd carried in next to my purse on the upended box. "We'll figure out if cookies are the right next step after I hear what's got you looking like you've been to a funeral."

Yep. Definitely death warmed over.

Great.

On the bright side, if he was seeing me at my worst now, I'd know sooner rather than later how high up on the list of importance physical appearance landed on his list. Which was kind of an important thing when you considered how scary my bedhead could be.

"Fine," I said, headed to the kitchen. "You skip the cookies. But I'm definitely in a place where eating my emotions is warranted. You want one of those La Croixs, at least? I just put 'em in the fridge ten minutes ago, but they're still pretty good over ice."

Danny eyed me fighting with the label that was keeping me from popping open the plastic container filled with sugary goodness and seemed to decide it was better to go with the flow than argue. "Yeah, but I'll get it. And one for you, too."

"Cool." I gave up trying to peel the blasted label out

of my way, snatched a knife out of a drawer and cut the stupid thing. "'Cause I've got Original Lay's and my favorite homestyle popcorn, too, and they're gonna get their time in the limelight just as soon as these babies take the edge off."

And with that, we got our first couple's kitchen tango—him doing his thing finding the glasses, filling them up with ice and pouring the bubblies while I plated up one more cookie than was good for me. I liked it. Liked the naturalness of it. How moving in such close proximity not only didn't feel awkward, but felt good. Like we'd been doing it for years rather than minutes.

Finally done, I sat on one side of my couch and dug in just as he set each of our glasses on my makeshift coffee table. Danny plopped right-smack dab in the middle of the couch, reclined back and stretched one arm on the back of the couch behind me. "Okay, we're loaded up. Now, talk."

I frowned and talked with too big of a mouthful for good manners. "You're kinda pushy."

"You haven't seen pushy yet, but if you keep dodging, you might."

Hmmm. "Are you pushy because you're irritated?"

"I'm pushy because the woman I've been looking forward to seeing all day looks like she spent the whole damned afternoon falling apart, and I'm worried about why that same woman doesn't feel comfortable sharing what caused it."

Oh.

Well, that was nice. Especially the part about looking forward to seeing me all day. I sighed and set half of an uneaten cookie back on the plate. "I'm comfortable sharing with you. I'm just not sure how well I'm gonna be able to share in a way that'll make sense, or so you won't freak out."

At the mention of him potentially freaking out, his eyes narrowed. "How 'bout you start at the beginning and let me handle how I respond?"

He had a point. I had no control over people, places or things—including Danny. So, I ran it down. How I'd stopped off at Walmart for snacks and drinks and floundered around a bit before giving up trying to figure out what he'd like and opting for my favorite TV watching food. "Before I knew it, I was just standing there eyeballing case after case of beer and rationalizing how I could easily pick one up for myself, take the afternoon off to enjoy a few and no one would be the wiser."

"But you didn't, right?"

I shook my head and picked up the cookie. "Nope. I hightailed it out of the store, called Maggie and stayed on the phone with her until I could get to Susan's house. Then I spent the next four or so hours crying like I'd just been given a fatal diagnosis of some kind."

Danny frowned. "You cried because you almost drank? I would've thought you'd have been happy you didn't."

"Yeah, it's not quite that simple." I dusted the crumbs off my fingertips then leaned back and twisted so my leg was partway bent on the sofa between us. "The truth is the last three weeks have been *a lot*. A lot of good—no doubt—but it's still been substantial stuff to process. Moving…calling Viv…starting a new job and meeting new people—there and at the clubhouse. And then the whole thing between you and me started. You mix those super high emotions—all the excitement and curiosity and newness—with the sadness and worry I've been stuffing when it comes to Vivienne and you end up with a powder keg just waiting for a match."

In my mind, the case of Modelo was still as clear and crisp as it had been when I was standing there. The refrigerated air still whispering against my skin and the hum of the machines that handled the cooling still droning in the background. "I could have lost everything today. By the grace of God, I didn't. But the impact—that minute when everything I thought I'd been handling so well came crashing through all at once— it shook me up. So, I spent the afternoon purging it all with Susan."

He studied me for a minute, thoughtful as though he was replaying everything I'd said and formulating an evaluation. "What are you worried about with Vivienne?"

I shrugged one shoulder and started fiddling with the hem of my jeans. "Wondering if I'll ever have a chance at mending my relationship with her. If I'll be able to measure up and be good enough if she does give me a chance. I mean, I know she's angry. She's got every right to be. A lot of people do." I glanced up at him. "You included. Sometimes just carrying that around... knowing how badly you've hurt people or been an imposition...it's a lot."

He inhaled long and deep, then let it go just as slowly. "Not sure if it's a good thing to share or not, but she asked about you tonight."

"Vivienne?"

"Yeah. She wanted to know how you were doing."

My heart kicked out an extra beat, and my breath caught in my throat. "She did?"

A soft smile curved his lips. "You say that like you didn't think such a thing was possible."

"Well..." I said with an ironic chuckle. "Let's be honest. I've pushed the patience envelope with just about everyone." I paused a second, weighing if it was too much to ask for details, or if I'd be smarter to take comfort in not knowing.

"You might have pushed it maybe, but I don't think you've burned it." He lifted his arm off the back of the couch and cupped the side of my neck. The stroke of his thumb along my jawline was pure velvet, as was his lowered voice. "And for what it's worth, I told her you're really doing well. That you look great and are happy. That you've jumped into the job with both feet, the guys love you, and that you really seem to have gotten your life on track."

The words were beautiful. A comfort after a rough afternoon facing emotions I'd thought I'd been dealing with well, but had apparently buried and ignored instead.

But his touch...

The warmth of his skin and the tenderness in the way he touched me...

All of my emotions and physical weariness settled in an instant. He calmed me in a way I couldn't easily describe. Even more surprising was that what he'd said registered as more important than any interest in hearing Vivienne's response. "That's the person you see? Someone happy who's got their life together?"

His smile deepened. "You think I'd be here diggin' deeper to get to know you if I didn't?"

My cheeks burned, but I held his gaze rather than ducking my head the way I wanted. "Sorry. Just hard

for me to wrap my head around the idea other people
might see me in a good way. I've been *Callie the party
girl and general fuckup* for a long time. You know?"

It took him a good three or four seconds before he
answered, but when he did, his fingers at the back of my
neck tightened. "You ask me, knowing what I've learned
of you so far, you weren't ever a fuckup. You were just
a scared girl who didn't have a whole lot of guidance
starting out, and alcohol helped you bury all the fears."

One second, and I was sixteen again, feeling that
first buzz and floating on a high that had me strutting
my stuff like I was a runway model instead of the gan-
gly girl with pimples I really was. I'd been confident.
Funny. The life of the party.

And I'd loved it. Loved being the apple of my daddy's
eye. The center of attention instead of a daughter that
had been cast aside by her mother. "Maybe at first, that
was the case. But alcohol is a greedy master. Once it
got its hooks in me, why I started drinking didn't matter anymore. Only getting that next high."

He nodded. "I think I get it." He hesitated a second
and shifted his arm back to the sofa. "The question I
gotta ask, though…you said all the emotions you've
been feeling where we're concerned contributed to a
near miss today. Is this thing we're pursuing gonna put
your sobriety on the line?"

It was a good question and one that had been the
topic of conversation this afternoon. "I thought about
that and talked to Maggie and Susan. Both of them
agreed—emotions are part of life. Ups and downs are
gonna happen no matter what, and it's not feasible for
me to hide in my apartment to avoid them. What I don't
want to do is look back and regret exploring the gifts

my Higher Power gives me. And before you ask—we talked about the downside, too. If you and I only last a few days or weeks…or if we last a few years or more… I'm okay with that. I can't control life or outcomes, but I can control how I react to things. How I face things. So, no. I'm not walking away from whatever it is we're doing because I'm afraid of alcohol."

God, I loved the sexy glimmer in his dark eyes when he smiled like he was right now. A glorious mix of naughty and delighted that left me feeling like I'd somehow done something special to create it.

"Sounds like you've given this ample consideration," he said almost playfully.

"Oh, it was ample, all right." I picked up a second cookie and bit into it, again talking with too much of a mouthful. "Enough so, poor Susan told me she was gonna treat herself to a bubble bath after I headed home." I swallowed and paused when his gaze narrowed on my mouth. I brushed my lips with my fingertips, expecting to see crumbs fall into my lap. "What? Is there icing on my face?"

His mouth twitched as though fighting back a smile. He took the cookie from between my fingers and slid it onto the plate. "Nope. No icing." He planted one hand at my waist and cupped the back of my head with the other. "But I gotta confess, I wanna know how that cookie tastes on your lips."

Oh. My. Lord.

Three times now I'd felt his mouth against mine and my senses still hadn't adjusted to the impact. Not even a little bit.

I leaned into the kiss and opened for him, glorying

at the deep growl the action earned me and the exhil-
aration that came when he pulled me astride his lap.

It was so easy to kiss him. So easy to let go and get
utterly lost in the moment. In the confident way he held
me close—one hand firmly at the back of my head and
the other low on my spine. With each passionate glide of
his tongue against mine and the skillful way he coaxed
my lips to engage with his. Before I knew it, his hands
were beneath my tee, his calloused palms coasting along
my sides and his fingertips and thumbs teasing my skin
until goose bumps flared in all directions.

My breasts tightened and a kittenish sound I hadn't
known I was capable of making eked free.

Danny pulled his mouth from mine with a grated
fuck and rested his forehead against mine. His breath
was ragged, and his hands gripped my hips like they
were the only thing holding him steady. "Callie…"

The frustration in his voice pulled me out of the
haze he'd created, and I lifted my head to see if my
eyes could make sense of what the rest of my senses
couldn't. "What?"

He dropped his head back on the top of the couch
and pulled in a long breath. Beneath my palms at his
chest, his muscles were fully flexed, and his eyelids
stayed shut.

An uncertainty I hadn't felt in a very long time crept
the length of my spine, and a chill my air conditioner
wasn't capable of generating whispered against the back
of my neck. "What's wrong?"

Something in my tone must have reached him, because his eyes snapped open. "Nothing." He added a
small smile to his response, but there seemed to be pain
behind it. "Not a damned thing." His fingers tightened

just a touch more before he released my hips and moved his hands so they rested on my thighs. "More like what's right. What's very, very right."

"Oh." I sat back on my heels and covered his hands with mine, not just relieved, but also pleased to hear the need coursing through my body echoed in his voice. "I thought that was supposed to be a good thing."

His long, drawn-out inhalation as he deftly shifted our hands and curled his fingers around each of my wrists sent a quiver straight to my sex. "It's fantastic." At my pulse point, he drew slow, mesmerizing circles and slowly lifted his gaze to mine.

God, I loved his eyes. So dark and deep it looked like they went on forever and ever. "Then why did we stop?"

He shook his head and slowly slid his hands up my arms. "Because we've got time. And we're gonna take that time and do things right. Even if it kills me." He punctuated that last bit with a gentle squeeze around my upper arms, but immediately let go when I flinched.

"What was that?" He lifted one arm of my tee and checked the skin underneath it.

"I don't know." I twisted for a look as well when he shifted to the arm that had actually protested. "It felt like a bruise."

Turned out, it was. A fairly faint one considering how much I'd jumped, but still about three inches long and the width of a finger.

"Oh," I said, mostly thinking out loud. "I bet it was when that dude grabbed me."

Danny's gaze shot to mine and the room turned eerily still and supercharged in a second. "What dude?"

Uh-oh.

I'd always sensed Danny could be intense on a frightening scale. Kind of like how you knew a tiger could take you down, rip out your throat and eat you for a snack even when they were behind a Plexiglas wall and acting like a kitten.

"It's not a big deal. I bumped into him with my cart mid-freak-out on the booze. It was totally my fault."

"And he grabbed you hard enough to bruise you?"

"Well, in his defense, I whacked him in the ass pretty hard. Plus, I think I startled the shit out of him, because he thought he knew me."

Yeah, in the realm of things to say to get your tiger to calm down, that apparently wasn't one of them. "He said that?"

"Yeah. A few times. But let's face it…he was in the beer and wine aisle. Odds are good he was already lit up, and I just reminded him of someone. Honestly, I jerked my arm free of his hold—which is probably how I got the bruise—and got the hell out of there. I never thought a thing about him again until just now."

"You're sure he didn't follow you out of the store?"

Uh, no. Watching for stalkers while I'd done the fastest self-checkout of my life and all but sprinted to my car hadn't exactly been the top thing on my mind at the time. But given the way Danny was looking at me in that moment, my very inadequately trained feminine instincts said admitting such a thing was the worst idea on the planet.

"Nope," I said instead. "Didn't see anyone following me." Which was the honest to God truth. I *hadn't* seen anyone following me and barely saw a single person on the road, I was so focused on getting to Susan's.

The technicality seemed to be a good choice, because the tension in him abated, and he relaxed a little deeper against the sofa.

Eager to get us back on a topic less riddled with land mines, I got back to what he'd said before the whole stranger danger thing had come into play. "So... when you say we're gonna do things right...what's that mean?"

A little of his playfulness crept back into his expression. "It means today was an emotionally shitty day for you. One where a whole lot of other firsts stacked up and left you on uneven footing that almost fucked things up for you. So, the last thing we're gonna do tonight is heap more firsts on top of the pile, because I promise you—the first time we get our clothes off and get serious, it's gonna be an off the chart experience you'll need time to level out from."

"It will?"

He cocked an arrogant eyebrow. "Was that you that was arching your back and practically purring for me to touch you a few minutes ago?"

Oh, wow. I knew I'd made some funny sounds, but... "I was arching my back?"

"Oh, yeah. Took everything in me not to say to hell with the consequences and give us both what we needed."

My heart sped up again at just the thought of his hands gliding over my breasts. And, from the way his eyelids got a little heavier, I suspected his brain had headed off in the same direction. "So? What are we gonna do instead?"

He reached around, grabbed the back of my head and pulled me in for one of those sexy, lingering kisses he'd given me in the office. When he was done, he kissed the tip of my nose and leaned back again. "Well, for starters, you're gonna hop up and we're gonna make the rest of those snacks you got at the store. Then we're both gonna lose our shoes, plug in my Fire Stick and find something we can turn our brains off watching. Sound good?"

Honestly? After the time I'd spent in Danny's company, I was starting to realize I could probably watch paint dry with him, and I'd have a damned good time. Though, that was probably too much to admit just yet.

Instead, I swung one leg off of him and stood, grabbing a cookie on the way up. "That sounds divine."

Chapter Fourteen

Danny

This was different.

Not the actual act of lazing in front of the TV and letting *2 Fast, 2 Furious* drift by while my thoughts veered off in all directions. That I'd done many times over. And the fact that a female was curled up next to me...that had happened once or twice, too.

But being here with Callie?

Totally different.

I slid my hand from between her shoulder blades down the length of her spine, sorely tempted to go a little farther and rest my hand on her gorgeous ass.

But we'd have time for that. Because the one thing I knew with absolute certainty after tonight was that I needed more of Calista Moore in my life.

More of *us*.

The bowls of Lay's chips and popcorn sat empty on the coffee table, and only two of the dozen sugar cookies remained in the plastic container. We'd killed the lights over two hours ago, and Callie had nodded off halfway into a movie. Now here she was, curled around me with her head on my chest, and I'd never been happier.

Or maybe it wasn't so much happy as it was content. Peaceful.

In the short evening, we'd laughed, debated and shared perspectives on everything from cartoons we'd grown up on to the state of the world and where we thought things were headed. And while the topics had covered the board, not once had things turned dicey or uncomfortable. In fact, you'd have thought we'd have both grown up in the same household with how similar we viewed things.

But the most humbling part was her attention.

Her complete focus and the smile in her eyes every single time she looked at me. I'd never felt more seen or heard in my life. More valued. And all she'd done was given me her time and herself.

It'd made for a precious night. The most stellar second date I'd ever had even if it'd been the simplest.

Even more staggering—the last thing I wanted to do was leave. That was undoubtedly a first for me where women were concerned, and it gave me pause like nothing else about Callie had before. Which was saying something considering she'd given me a lot to pause and think about since she'd shown back up in my life.

I kissed the top of her head and drew that flower garden scent of hers deep in my lungs. It would be so easy just to close my eyes and drift off to sleep with her, but that wouldn't make for a good night's rest for either of us. Getting her to the bedroom and stretching out next to her was an option, too, but the idea of me and Callie in a bed together before we were ready for that kind of intimacy seemed akin to putting out a cigarette in a gasoline tank. Especially when I reflected on how fast things had ramped up between us the two times we'd locked lips.

That meant there was only one option left, and I was mighty damned grumpy about it, even though I knew it was the right thing to do.

I lay there a few more minutes, plotting my approach. Across the room, the plastic bag with the new dead bolt inside it sat untouched and drew to mind the asshole who'd left a bruise on her arm this afternoon. Not that the dead bolt would have done anything to change that situation, but I could all too easily imagine some dickhead like that following her home and taking in private what he hadn't been able to land in public. For now, I'd have to leave it. Tomorrow I planned on inviting her out to my place. Maybe I could have her bring a bag and she could stay the night in Gabe's old room. That would give me until Sunday afternoon to get that task squared away.

Decision made, I carefully extracted myself from under her arm and tucked a big throw pillow back under it while I got busy stacking dirty dishes in the sink, pulling back her comforter and sheets, and finding paper for a note—the latter of which was pretty fucking easy considering how organized she was.

I chuckled a bit as I wrote. Of all the things we'd had in common, organization wasn't one of them. Unless you counted my tools. Then I could put the most uptight individual to shame in a heartbeat.

I flipped the ringer on her phone to silent and left the device on the stacked milk crates serving as a nightstand with my note beneath it. Turning off the movie left the room too dark for me to navigate with an armful of woman, so I flipped on the tiny light over the stove before carefully lifting Callie in my arms.

Turns out, she was one hell of a sound sleeper. Either that, or the day's events had just been too much for her and had KO'd her hard for the night, because the transition from the couch to her bed was a piece of cake. Or was mostly a piece of cake, anyway. The fact that she seemed to reach out to me in her sleep as I pulled away made for a hellacious final temptation. Plus, I kind of hated leaving anyone to sleep in their jeans. At least I didn't have to deal with shoes. She'd kicked those off as soon as we'd settled in with the snacks, giving me a peek at her pretty, pink-painted toenails.

I huffed out another chuckle at my wonky mind and pulled the covers up to her shoulders. Seriously. Who knew toes could be so sexy? I sure as heck couldn't remember noticing them on any other women, but with Callie I'd been pretty damned appreciative.

Crouching beside her, I gave myself one last indulgence and smoothed her wavy hair away from her cheek. The moonlight on her face suited her and seemed to accent the slight angle of her eyes at the outside corners. Her button nose was adorable as fuck, too. And while I couldn't see them in this light, I really loved the freckles that dotted the bridge of her nose and tops of her cheeks.

Christ, I was a goner.

What other excuse could I have for ogling a woman like this in her bedroom?

You've got high standards? Or you come up with a million reasons why they're not good enough so you don't have to get hurt?

Gabe's words had unsettled me for days. Had made

me truly wonder if my mom choosing drugs over us had been the barrier between me and any kind of a serious relationship.

But what if I really hadn't met the right person? Because, honest to God, *good enough* hadn't seemed to factor with Callie. She'd been...well... Callie.

Funny.

Focused.

Adorable and honest.

Quick to learn and curious.

She wasn't perfect, but...

She's perfect for you.

The quiet voice inside me struck thunderbolt deep and sent me full vertical beside her bed. Part of me wanted to all but sprint out of the place, but another part—the part that'd voiced the thought, I suspected—kept me right where I was long enough to breathe through the panic.

Eventually, I leaned down and placed a soft kiss to her lips before I stole out to the kitchen for a dinner knife and the living room for her keys. I worked the right key off the key chain, then headed out, locked the POS dead bolt behind me, and more easily than I should have been able to, used the knife to shove the key back under the door. I jogged down the stairs to my car, lighter on my feet than I'd been in a very long while. But more than that, I was hopeful.

I'd had a great night.

So had Callie.

And both of us were comfortable taking our time and doing things right. If that worked out, it'd be amazing.

If it didn't—well, I'd have finally taken a step toward learning how to be a better partner to someone else.

That was a win-win no matter how I cut it.

Chapter Fifteen

Callie

My underwear was seriously unsexy.

The white, tan and black cotton options were all neatly stacked in my top dresser drawer, practically yawning back at me while I tried to figure out what to pack for my second Saturday night trip in a row to La Maison de Danny.

Once upon a time, I'd had at least three or four matching lacy bras and panties, but *practical* and *inexpensive* had been more the name of the game getting sober over the last year, so I'd gone from knockoff silk in a variety of bold colors to…well…boring.

Oh, well.

I snatched both of the black sets I had, put one on the counter for after the bubble bath I had planned for later this afternoon, and stacked the other on the bed with the rest of my stuff to put in my backpack. It wasn't like Danny hadn't already been slowly introduced to my cotton Hanes specials. Between my first trip to his house last Saturday night and last night's Friday night TV binge, we'd been slowly working our way through the bases—culminating in him deftly maneuvering me right out of my tee and Snoozeville white bra—the latter of which he didn't seem to be even remotely turned off by.

So… I'd just keep being myself and let things go where they needed to. Although, I seriously hoped they'd go farther this weekend than second base because I was horny enough from all the kissing and petting that I could probably bottle my pheromones and market them for a profit.

I hustled to the closet, snatching my phone off the side of the bed on the way and checking the time.

10:17 AM.

Still plenty of time to finish packing, get a snack, get dressed and get to my noon meeting.

The rockin' selection of tees I'd built over the last year via consignment and thrift shops hung nice and neat on the plastic hangers Maggie had stocked me up with pre-move.

Did they still call things *bases* when it came to intimacy? Maybe there was a hipper term I should be using. I'd have to remember to ask Susan after the meeting. Surely her teenagers kept her in the loop with all the latest and greatest terminology.

A knock sounded at my door midway through my tee review.

Hmm.

It wasn't Danny. He'd never knock that quietly. And it wouldn't be Susan. Not this early in the day.

Quietly making my way to the living room so I wouldn't feel obligated to answer if I didn't want to, I peeked through the peephole.

Holy freaking shit.

I dropped to my heels, stunned more than a little

stupid at the sight of my sister waiting on the other side of the door.

God, I looked like hell, too. Complete with navy blue and red cotton plaid pajama bottoms and a plain white top that made it more than a little evident I didn't have a bra on.

Well, you were *in bed up until an hour ago, and it's Saturday morning. And it ain't like she hasn't seen you looking a lot worse.*

Hmm.

A little on the sad side, but also very true. And to be fair, I'd seen her with bedhead more than a few times, too.

I wiped my suddenly very sweaty palms on my hips, took one calming inhalation then eased the door open.

Yep.

It was definitely Vivienne, sporting a pair of jeans I was willing to bet cost a mint and a formfitting white top that probably came from a designer store I couldn't pronounce. Unlike the tennis shoes or sandals I stuck to with my everyday casual attire, her shoes were a moderate-height cork wedge with gleaming black leather straps. Her nervous smile was as wobbly as my insides, but she was carrying a box of donuts in one hand and a tray with two coffees in the other, so whatever she was here for couldn't be all bad.

"Hey." She lifted the box of donuts. "I probably should have called first, but I was hoping the donuts would make up for the bad manners."

"Are you kidding? I'll forgive anything for a donut on a Saturday morning." I stepped out of the way and waved her inside. "Come on in. Sorry I'm not dressed better. I wanted to get some packing done before I hopped in the shower."

Hesitantly, she eased through the doorway and scanned my meager abode, waiting just inside the living room while I shut and locked the door.

"It's nowhere near as awesome as your Uptown pad," I said, stating the obvious. "I always thought the way you finished it out was super slick. Even if I did like the flirty room you let me sleep in the best."

The comment earned me my first genuinely big smile. "Yeah, that was my favorite room, too." She motioned toward the sofa with the drink tray. "You wanna just dig into these over there?"

That was my classy Vivienne—acting like there was some kind of choice in the matter when the reality was there was nowhere else to sit save my still-unmade bed.

"Works for me." I led the way and dropped down on one side. "You don't live at the Uptown place anymore?"

Vivienne unloaded all the goodies on the table and eased onto the sofa a whole lot smoother than I had. "Hmm?"

"The place in Uptown. You said the room *was* your favorite. Past tense."

"Oh." She carefully pried out a coffee and handed it to me. "I still own it, but I moved out to Haven right before Jace and I got married."

As I took the coffee she offered, my gaze locked on to what I'd originally thought was a fancy black cuff around her wrist. "Damn, Viv. You got ink!" I sat the coffee down and grabbed her hand for a better look. The cuff portion was somewhere between lace and a jewelry filigree design, but the center showcased a tribal-styled tree and a badass H surrounded by the tree's roots. "That is legit the coolest-looking tattoo I've ever seen."

Her expression turned to one of tender fondness, and her voice softened. "Yeah. I got that the weekend Jace and I eloped to Vegas with the rest of the family. The H is for Haven."

I could've studied the artwork a whole lot longer, but figured I'd already pushed some boundaries grabbing her the way I had after not seeing her in person for so long. So, I gently released my grip. "What's Haven?"

"Jace and Axel's ranch. It's out in Allen. Probably one of the last patches of land that hasn't been gobbled up by developers. Their moms live out there with us."

"Oh, right. Axel's married to Lizzy Hemming. Danny didn't tell me they had a name for the place, but it sounds really cool."

Viv bit her lip, reached for the box of donuts and held them out to me, opening the lid as she did so. "I hear things with Danny are going well."

Oh man. She'd really gone all out at the donut shop and picked my favorites. I took my time picking between a classic chocolate glaze and a tasty-looking cake option with thick vanilla icing and multicolored sprinkles. "You mean at work?"

A sly smile tilted her lips—one I hadn't seen since I was probably thirteen. "Oh, I've already heard work is going well. I meant with you and Danny giving things a go."

Wow. He'd actually told the people he considered family. Maybe it was silly, but knowing he'd laid it out there made the time we'd spent together over the last week and a half feel even more special. "I didn't know if he'd told anyone or not."

She laughed and grabbed her coffee. "Yeah, he told us. Some of us anyway. About a week ago when he came over for dinner." She studied me over the rim of her cup as she sipped it, then added, "He sounds like he's really into you."

A warmth stirred behind my sternum and the tingle of impending tears danced across the bridge of my nose. Not so much at hearing Danny had sounded into me—though, I had to admit that was pretty damned nice, too. But more because I was sitting in my living room, eating donuts on a Saturday morning, and talking about life stuff with my sister. In the last year, I'd wanted this moment…imagined it and prayed for it countless times.

I swallowed around the huge lump in my throat and stuffed my emotions with another ridiculously large bite. "The truth? I'm stupid into him, too. I told my sponsor Maggie after our first date that my cheeks hurt from smiling so much. Come to think of it, I smile almost all the time around him." I nudged the box a little closer to her. "Aren't you gonna have one?"

She looked at the donuts and her smile wavered for a second. Still, she rallied pretty quick and went for a cake option with chocolate icing and nuts on the top. "So, how'd it happen? You and Danny, I mean."

I finished my last bite, licked the icing off my thumb and headed to the kitchen for a few paper towels. "It was kind of weird, honestly. He was super cautious around me at first. Kind of leery, like he was waiting for me to screw up. Which of course makes sense given my background. But then we started this weird dance of butting heads one minute and ending up in tight proximity the next. And by tight proximity, I mean you could have jump-started a car with the sparks coming off of us.

The yo-yoing kept going until one day he followed me when I was headed out on a twelve-step call thinking I was going to buy some dope. I sort of yelled at him for assuming the worst and making me look untrustworthy in front of my AA peeps. He said he wanted to make it up to me and, the next thing I knew, we were out on a date."

I handed her a paper towel of her own. "Sorry. I haven't quite worked my supplies up to real napkins, yet."

"Oh, please. I might have more in the bank now than I did once upon a time, but I still make paper towels do double duty." She took it, laid it on the table in front of her and set her donut on top of it. Only a quarter of it was gone.

I motioned to it and plopped back into my seat. "Is it not good?"

Vivienne followed the direction of my gesture and straightened a little taller. "Oh. No, it's fine." She waved her hand dismissively. "My stomach's just a little off this morning. I'm not sure hitting it with seven thousand grams of sugar first thing is the brightest idea."

"You? You'd live on pastries and chocolate if you could."

She chuckled at that and scootched back a little farther on the sofa, making herself more comfortable. "If you ever meet Sylvie, you'll realize I'm pretty much surrounded by dessert options 24/7. The woman never met a recipe for sweets she didn't try. It's a Haven life hazard."

"That sounds like a perk, not a hazard."

Laughing, she raised her coffee in salute. "Fair point." After taking a sip, she rested her cup on her thigh. "So, you guys are moving along pretty quick, huh?"

Was it quick? I'd spent so much time focused on navigating the emotions and learning to take things at face value that I hadn't really thought about it. "I guess so. I mean, one minute he was my boss, and the next minute he was a whole lot more. We've spent time together pretty much every day since then. Why? You think that's bad?"

Viv's eyebrows shot high on her forehead. "Me? Good grief, no. I'd be the world's biggest hypocrite if I did."

"You would?"

"Oh, yeah." She paused a minute, as though considering whether or not to share what was on her mind. "You probably don't remember this, but the first night I met Jace was also the same night you first met Danny."

"The night you saved my ass from the guy I stole the drugs from?"

For a second, she looked a little nonplused. She shook her head. "No, that wasn't the first night you met Danny. The first night was the one he carried you into my house when you were passed out. It was Jace who had him follow us home. You were at The Den celebrating New Year's Eve. Jace saw us take a fall when I was trying to get you out to my car, and he stepped in to help. Like I said, though. You were pretty out of it. But that was the night I met Jace. We were married just over a few months later, so I'm the last person to judge how fast people get together. To my mind, if people click easy, there's probably a reason for it."

All of a sudden, the donut in my stomach felt like it not only weighed ten pounds instead of ounces, but was acting like it wanted to surge right back up my throat. I grabbed my coffee and took a drink that burned my tongue in the process.

Vivienne pushed away from the back of the couch and leaned in a little. "Hey. You look upset. I would've thought me sharing about how fast Jace and I got together would have made you feel better. Not worse."

When the time is right, you'll get your chance.

Maggie had preached that phrase over and over again when it came to making amends. She'd said it when my chance to make those amends wasn't sitting right next to me, so I'd been fine with it at the time. Even comforting. But it was a whole lot different echoing in my head when *the right time* had actually shown up bearing donuts and coffee.

I took another, smaller drink, then set my cup on the table in front of me. "It does make me feel better. About me and Danny, anyway. It's just…"

All of a sudden, my living room was as hot as Danny's shop in late afternoon, and my tongue literally seemed like it'd lost all of its fluid, despite the drink I'd just taken.

God, please help me.

Please, just help me do this right.

"I hurt you," I finally managed, keeping my eyes on my coffee cup. "So many times. Half of them, I'm embarrassed to admit, I don't even remember. Like the night you just told me about. All I remember is waking up with only bits and pieces of the night before in my memory and thinking *I won't do that again.*

"But I always did. Always found that next party. That next high. And took for granted that you'd always be there to bail me out physically or financially when I was irresponsible or just plain stupid." I forced my gaze to hers. "I took advantage of your kindness. I took advantage of your love. And for that, I am *so* very sorry."

Vivienne stayed completely still, her eyes a little wider than normal and her lips slightly parted as though I'd not only completely caught her off guard, but had stolen her capacity for speech.

"I know that doesn't make up for what I've done," I said. "The only thing that has a prayer of really making amends is to change my life. And I'm trying. One day at a time, I'm trying to be a better person."

"Callie," she finally said on a broken rasp. "You were never a *bad* person. You're a person fighting a disease." She paused a second and shrugged one shoulder. "I didn't realize that before. I thought you were selfish. I thought you just lived for the next party like Dad did. But you're not the only person who's been going to meetings. That last time you called, I started going to Al-Anon and they taught me about how addiction is a family disease. How we all end up playing a part in the process and how it pulls us all down. I didn't *have* to bail you out. I *chose* to. Even when the reality was that my doing so probably contributed to you not getting sober sooner. So you're not the only one with amends to make."

Holy. Freaking. Cow.

This was really happening. Me and Viv were talking. Really talking.

The tingles on the bridge of my nose started up again and this time I didn't even try to stop them. "You don't hate me?" I whispered.

"Oh, Callie." Viv set her coffee next to mine, shifted closer and pulled me into a fierce hug. "I've never hated you. Never. I hurt for you. Feared for you. Wanted to fix you and got mad as hell more times than I can count. But hate was never a factor. Not once."

I hung on tight and let my tears fall, thanking God He'd given me this chance and given me the right words to say. "I was so afraid to reach out to you. My whole life you've been this smart, perfect ideal I knew I'd never measure up to. But when I drank, I felt pretty. Interesting and funny."

Viv chuckled against me, but the raggedness in it made me think she was as teared up as I was. Sure enough, when she pulled away, there were wet tracks marking her cheeks, and her nose was as red as mine probably was. "Callie, you *are* interesting and funny. And absolutely gorgeous. What on earth ever made you think otherwise?"

This time it was my turn to shrug. "I just heard how Mom was always praising you. Listened to Dad bragging to his buddies about how awesome Vivienne was. I never heard them say those things about me. At least not until I turned into Dad's drinking buddy, and then he told me I was awesome all the time." I sniffed and dashed a tear from my cheek. "I guess I should have considered the source."

"Oh, I think Dad loved you—booze or not. You were always his favorite."

A sharp stabbing pain jabbed deep beneath my heart, and the elephant-size weight that squatted on my shoulders when no one else was around grew a little heavier.

But I couldn't deal with that right now. I'd deal with that in a few weeks. Right now, I needed to keep my head in the present and make the most of what I'd been given. "I think he loved us both."

I patted her knee before I stood and darted for my bedroom. "Stay here. I've got something for you."

It took me three attempts before my shaking hands cooperated enough to get the thick pink card I'd purchased for her a few weeks ago into its matching envelope, but after I got the job done, I rejoined Viv in the living room.

"It's not much," I said handing it over, "but happy birthday."

Surprise lit Vivienne's face once more, but this time there was a smile to go with it. "My birthday's not for almost two more weeks."

"I know." I sat on the couch and watched her open it. "But I've also been too stinking drunk in the past to remember it, and this time I wanted to make sure I remembered."

"Callie…"

Thank you for being my sister and loving me, even when I wasn't much of a sister in return and couldn't love myself.

It had taken me forever to settle on that sentence. Forever and about thirty text messages to Maggie, but now I was glad I'd gone with it.

Vivienne closed the card and stared at the top, running her finger along the outside edge for a few seconds before she redirected her gaze to me. "I really wish I hadn't been such a chicken and had reached out to you after you'd called. Or even answered the phone, for that matter."

"Well, let's be honest. I gave you a lot of reasons not to pick up the phone."

She smiled at that, but kept going. "The thing is… I was afraid, too. I'd detached and focused on letting you do whatever it was you needed to do to hit your bottom for so long that, when you called, I wasn't sure how to react. I wanted to be happy, but I was also afraid that…"

"It was like all the other times I'd tried?"

She chuckled and hung her head. "Yeah, pretty much."

"I get it. But I'm really fucking happy you brought me donuts today and gave me the chance to tell you how sorry I am."

Gripping the card a little tighter, she rasped, "I'm glad I came, too." When she looked up, her mouth was pinched together tight—that same look of determination someone might make just before they took a huge leap of faith. "You know…the family is doing a big birthday thing for me the weekend before my birthday. Saturday, the fourteenth. We're doing it at the Main Event so the kids can play games, then we're gonna see how competitive the men can get with bowling."

"Bowling?"

She giggled and tucked the card in her purse. "I know, it sounds goofy. But you don't know how goofy until you meet all these guys."

"Are they all like Jace and Danny?"

"Yep. Pretty much. Add on their moms and their wives and it's guaranteed to be at least a few hours of serious entertainment." She hesitated a beat and lowered her voice. "I really would love it if you could come."

Meeting the family.

Viv's *and* Danny's.

No wonder she'd looked like she was ready to jump out of an airplane. This was huge. At least it was in my book. "I think I'd like that. Very much."

"Good." She stood and looped her purse over her

shoulder. "And if you have any questions or need to get ahold of me in the meantime, you've got my number. I promise this time I'll answer or call you back in less than a month."

A month?

Had it seriously been that long?

I stood as well and pulled her in for another hug before I could overthink it. "Thank you. For being so gracious. For taking a chance on me again." I tightened my hold and whispered, "Just for being you."

Her hold on me tightened as well. "It's good to have you back, Callie. I mean that."

We stayed like that, both of us content to just let the past slip away and stay in the moment. Grateful and quiet.

Until a thought jolted through me.

I gently eased away. "Hey, I'm gonna drive to Tulsa the day after your birthday party and visit Dad's grave. If you wanna go, I'd love to have you tag along."

"The fifteenth?"

I nodded. "Yeah. I owe him an amends, too. I thought that would be a good day to do it."

For a second, she seemed confused, but then appeared to put the puzzle pieces together. "He died August 15th."

I shrugged, wrestling internally to keep the oily sludge of guilt from swallowing me whole. "I thought it would be good timing. Maybe put things to rest. You know?"

It took her a few seconds before she answered, but when she did her voice was soft and understanding. "Yeah, I think I do." Her gaze went distant for a second, considering, then refocused on me with a little bit of a troubled smile. "Let me think about it, okay?"

I shouldn't have been surprised. Where Dad and I were thick as thieves, Viv had been a one-man show. Particularly after Mom took off. "Sure. No pressure at all. Just..." I held up one finger and hustled to my room. "Let me get my shoes on, and I'll walk you out."

"You don't have to do that," she answered while I stuffed my feet into my fuzzy lined moccasins.

"No seriously. You're leaving seven thousand donut calories behind." I hurried back out into the living room. "I'm gonna need all the exercise I can get, right?"

Whatever had caused her mood to go sideways unraveled and she laughed hard. "Well, all right. When you put it that way..."

Outside, the heat was in full gear, but the skies were gloriously clear blue. Not a single cloud to be found. The parking lot was empty of anyone else coming or going, the decent number of parking spaces indicating most people had already hustled off for the day.

Weird.

I paused two steps off the sidewalk and onto the lot's asphalt and studied the tail end of the black Porsche Cayenne parked in the otherwise empty back row.

Vivienne stopped beside me. "Something wrong?"

"I guess not. It's just no one ever parks on that farthest row. And people in my complex don't exactly drive Porsches."

"Maybe it's someone visiting and they didn't want to risk a door ding."

I spun to Vivienne. "Oh, my God. Is that your car?"

She laughed at that and pointed in the opposite direction in the second row. "No, that's me."

A spotless black Fastback Mustang with a gleaming chrome front bumper and equally sparkling rims and white rally stripes low on each side sat between two empty spots.

"Damn, Viv." I hurried that direction and paused at one corner to take in the sleek lines. "That's a '67, right?"

"God, no wonder Danny's nuts for you. You know cars as good as he does. And yes, it's a '67." She stood beside me, appreciating the sleek lines, and sighed. "It's gonna suck letting her go."

"Wait—what?"

Keeping her eyes on the car, her mouth crooked in a wry mew. "Yeah. I'm gonna have to sell her. Get something a little more practical." She looked to me. "I was thinking about one of those Audi SUVs. Like the Q7 or something. You like those?"

"Uh… I guess? I've never been in one, but they look really cool. Super safe, too, from what I hear."

"Oh my God…and they drive like a dream. Not kidding, when I test-drove one a few weeks ago, I thought I was in a hover craft or something."

Man, things had really changed for Viv. All of it in a very good way from what I could tell. "Well, you only go around once. Might as well get whatever lights your fire."

She fished around in her purse for a second and pulled out a set of keys. "You got that from Dad."

Yeah. I had. And in many ways, his viewpoint was right. I'd just abused the notion and used it as an excuse to throw away years of my life, drowning my low self-esteem and using people along the way. "He might not have been the most ambitious man, but he wasn't bad. He was just—simple."

"I was nowhere near as close to him as you were, but at least he hung around. That's more than either of us can say about Mom."

So much pain in that statement. And here I'd thought she and Mom had been close. "I still hear her in my head. A lot. Usually asking me why I can't do something better. You ever talk to her?"

Vivienne shook her head. "No need or desire to. I've got two awesome moms at home who are a lot more supportive. You?"

"Nope. I left a message for her about six months ago. I never heard back. But like you said…not a loss." I dipped my head toward her Mustang. "You better get in there and get the AC going. If your stomach's off, the heat isn't gonna help."

"Thanks. And don't forget about the party. I think you'll like meeting everyone. Plus, you'll have Danny there."

That would definitely be a plus. Being the new kid in a big group still wasn't easy for me without alcohol propping me up and, from the sounds of things, her family was an extremely big group. One that no doubt knew about my bumpy past.

Still, I'd walk across hot coals if it meant rebuilding what I'd broken with my sister. I waved as she slid behind the wheel and gave her the truth. "I wouldn't miss it for the world."

Chapter Sixteen

Danny

I was failing.

I hated to admit that particular truth, but as far as owning and running multiple shops was concerned, I didn't appear to be entrepreneurial material. Which was kind of an ironic realization to have at the exact time in my life I finally appeared to be getting my groove on where relationships were concerned.

Turning off Miller Road, I steered my Chevelle toward the home I'd lived in my whole life—a simple, single-story ranch that only clocked about fifteen hundred square feet total. The subdivision was a holdout from the '70s and was the only one I knew of around Lake Ray Hubbard that hadn't sold out to big developers eager to raze and rebuild with newer and bigger houses. The fact that mine was only five hundred feet off an isolated cove made it prime real estate—a situation that had almost cost my sister her life when a crooked developer thought it'd be a good idea to try and force us out.

That'd been when the brothers had fully invited me into their family. It was also when Gabe had found

Zeke, which had led to her moving in with him shortly before they got hitched.

I pulled into the two-car driveway and put my car in park, giving myself a little bit of time to appreciate the simplicity of the pale yellow paint and the shallow-pitched gray roof.

Callie had loved the place. Had acted like I'd invited her to the Taj Mahal instead of an old but well cared for home. And the Sunday morning we'd spent out on the covered back porch nursing coffee and talking about anything and everything…that'd been golden. The closest thing to perfect I ever remembered being a part of.

After the day I'd spent in the office, on the phone dealing with pissed off customers from my Louisiana office, I couldn't fucking wait for Callie to show and for us to have a stellar repeat of last weekend.

At least I hoped it would be a stellar repeat.

Maybe I needed to dial back my expectations a bit. The last thing either of us needed was pressure, and I was mega mindful of how too much too fast could have a negative impact on Callie's sobriety.

I killed the engine, gathered the groceries I'd bought on the way home and made my way inside. The clock on the wall behind the four-person glass and brass table showed just after five. Callie was supposed to be here at six. That meant I had thirty minutes, at most, to get everything put up and me showered before she showed.

I shook my head at the thought and started unpacking.

My girl. Always early.

I hesitated midway to stashing the Lay's I'd gotten for her in the pantry.

Was she my girl?

I didn't hear the answer so much as I felt it—a re-sounding *yes* that came from a place inside me that was fundamentally primitive.

When had that happened? And more importantly, how did I feel about it?

Stuffing the spent plastic bags in the holder Gabe had hung for me on the back of the pantry door, I tried to pinpoint when I'd crossed the line of exploring and entered into something more definitive. I still didn't have an answer on the timing by the time I was out of the shower and dressed in a clean pair of jeans and a soft T-shirt. But I was damned sure how I felt about it all.

I was happy.

Happier than I had been in a long fucking time, if I was honest. And the really interesting thing about it all was that being around her brought an extra layer to life. Like going from a black-and-white existence, to full-blown vibrant color. I'd never minded the black-and-white before. It was all I'd ever known, so it'd never bothered me.

But now I had *more*.

More color. More laughter. More ease and balance. And I liked it *a lot*.

The storm door squeaked, announcing Callie's arrival before she could knock on the door. She opened it and poked her head through the small gap as I exited the hallway. "Hello?"

Goofy girl.

I made it to the door, guided her through the rest of the way and shut it behind her. "I told you last time you didn't have to knock."

"Well, what if you'd been streaking through the living room or something?"

I chuckled at the image. "If you were worried about that, you wouldn't have poked your head in."

God, but the woman could blush in a nanosecond, but whatever embarrassment she felt didn't damper her sass. "Maybe deep down I was hoping you were streaking?"

Oh, yeah. Life was a whole lot lighter around Callie. Lighter and strangely liberating. So much so I had a mind to showing her how much I appreciated having her around with a kiss, but was presently blocked from doing so by a Dunkin' Donuts box between us. "This your idea of dinner?"

She smiled huge and handed the box to me, then proceeded with shrugging her backpack off and piling it and her purse to one side of the front door. "No way. That's for breakfast tomorrow. Figured they'd be perfect out on the patio with coffee. Even better…ask me how I got 'em."

I strolled to the kitchen with her trailing behind me and slid the box onto the counter. "I'm gonna go with a drive-thru."

"Nope. Way better." She waited until I faced her, then dropped her bomb. "Vivienne brought 'em to me."

"No shit?"

"No shit! She showed up at my apartment this morning with a whole dozen and coffees. And it was *awesome*. I gave her that birthday card I told you about and made my amends. Even better—she invited me to the family birthday shindig on the fourteenth."

Damn. That *was* a lot. No wonder she was beaming like a toddler hopped up on a sugar high. "Peach…" I wrapped my arms around her and pulled her in tight. "That's great news."

I held her there for long seconds, letting the happiness pouring off her steal straight to my heart. Only when her arms loosened around me did I kiss the top of her head and pull back enough to see her face. "If she invited you to the birthday thing, I'm gonna take it the amends went well?"

"Better than I ever thought it could've gone." She hesitated a beat and bit her lower lip. "You're not weirded out? About me going to the family thing?"

"Weirded out?"

"Well, it's your family thing, too. I thought you might find it awkward or something."

God, she was sweet. Honesty and vulnerability might not have been her thing for a long stretch of her life, but without the alcohol and drugs twisting her thoughts and actions, she was pure goodness.

I smoothed a wavy wayward strand of hair away from her cheek and cupped the side of her face, keeping her close with my other arm at her back. "Not awkward." Not for me anyway. Though, I had a feeling Jace and I might end up toe-to-toe before it was over if he was a dick to Callie. "If anything, I'm lookin' forward to bein' able to be with you around the people I love most. And I think they'll love you, too."

"You do? Even after…" She wrinkled her nose in that funny way I found adorable. "Well, everything?"

"You're not the same person you were then. I see that every day. Vivienne must have seen it, too, or she wouldn't have invited you. So, yeah. I think they'll give you a fair shake and get to know you the same way I have."

Her expression softened, so much of the emotion that had no doubt come from the morning she'd had shining back at me. When she spoke, her voice was soft and a little shaky. "It was a *really* good day."

There was probably a smarter response I could have given—something wise and heartfelt I could have said to support everything she was feeling. Instead, I sealed my lips to hers and let my actions do the talking.

"Whoa," she rasped when I finally lifted my head. "That was some kiss. I take it you had a really good day, too?"

I gifted myself with a few seconds of admiring her big green eyes staring up at me and the wonder they always seemed to have behind them.

"My good day started when you walked in the door," I said, finally releasing her. "If you'd been here about an hour ago, you'd have turned around and run home."

"Why? I thought you were gonna take advantage of a Saturday and get some alone time in the garage."

I snatched my phone off the kitchen table and thumbed through my apps as I headed for the sofa. I dropped down in the middle of it. "I got a few hours in from ten to noon, but then I ended up getting a call from a seriously pissed off customer in Louisiana. Turns out my shop manager has gone AWOL, and two out of four of the other guys have taken advantage of him being gone to turn the whole damned place into a zoo. I spent the rest of the afternoon talking to the two guys who don't have their heads up their asses and VPNing into the office computer to see what state the accounts are in. Turns out, the shop manager was AWOL for a reason."

"Oh, no." She eased down next to me.

"Oh, yes." I pulled her close to my side and slung one arm around her shoulders. "Looks to me like my main account there is at least three large lighter. Maybe more."

"Shit."

I shook my head. "Doesn't matter. I'll deal with it later. Right now, I'm starving, and you've got a day worth celebrating. You good with another DoorDash?"

"Sure. Which restaurant?"

That was another thing I appreciated about Callie. She not only admitted her cooking skills were limited, but she actually preferred eating out. While I appreciated a home-cooked meal and had been spoiled rotten by Gabe, Ninette, and Sylvie with their love of time in the kitchen, I never saw the point. Why buy the groceries and spend the time and effort when you could spend as much or less than you would at the store and get what you wanted made to order in a fraction of the time?

Chinese, comfort food, sushi, Mexican...

I stopped on a mom-and-pop Italian place that'd just opened about three miles away. "How about this place. I heard their pizzas are pretty good. New York style."

"I wouldn't know a New York style from anything else, so I think it's safe to say I'm universally okay with pizza. You sure you don't want me to go pick it up? A $5.99 delivery fee is stupid high."

No way in hell.

Just having her beside me had scrambled all the thoughts and pressures that had pelted me all day and left me with blessed calm and quiet. "It might be stupid high, but it's worth every penny. We can strategize our TV watching while someone else does the cooking and driving."

"Well, all right then." She toed off her cute sandals

and stretched her legs out so they were crossed at the ankles on top of the coffee table to match my own.

"Pizza preferences?"

"Anything but olives, anchovies or barbecue sauce."

Another thing I'd found to be a relief about spending time with Callie. She knew how to say what she wanted as much as what she didn't want. Sometimes she was super picky—as in when she ordered her hamburgers—and sometimes she had looser limits. It made it easy as hell to be around her because you always knew one hundred percent who and what you were dealing with.

"They've got a special on two larges. How about we mix it up? One large cheese and one large with chicken, jalapeños, onions and bell peppers."

"Two larges?"

"I'm hella hungry."

Her eyes narrowed, and for a second, I thought she was gonna tell me I was nuts. Instead, she threw me some of that mock seriousness that never failed to catch me off guard. "Me, too. Let's do it."

Sure enough, it worked. I barked out a laugh and got busy placing the order, the dregs of my shitty day slowly disappearing with every minute.

Three hours later we'd polished off three-quarters of the food—me doing most of the heavy lifting in the pizza department—dipped into the donuts for dessert, and had made it to the end of Marvel's *Avengers: Endgame.*

"Third time I've seen it and I still get choked up." Callie pushed herself up from where she'd nestled into the crook of my arm and twisted enough to face me. "How the hell can you kill off Iron Man? It's just wrong on so many levels."

I had to agree. Iron Man made the series what it was. Him and Scarlett Johansson. "Yeah, but they brought time travel into the equation, so you gotta ask…is he really dead?"

She raised a suspicious eyebrow. "You say that like you've got a theory."

I chuckled and stood, grabbing the can of La Croix I'd polished off as I did, then headed to the kitchen. "No, not really. But my brother Knox has several he's shared with anyone that would listen ever since the movie was released." I tossed the can in the trash can. "Honest to God, I can't follow a single one of them. The whole mul-tiverse thing kind of warps my simple brain."

"Simple brain? That's the last thing I'd ever call—"

Her words were cut short by my cell phone, which I'd inadvertently forgotten to silence when the movie started. I glanced at the screen long enough to note it was one of my guys from the Louisiana shop—spe-cifically one of the ones I'd been told had been hosting parties in the garage after hours for a few weeks now.

The anger I'd nursed all afternoon fired up fast and hard, and I was sorely tempted to punch the answer button and give the guy a serious piece of my mind.

"Everything okay?" Callie sat up on the sofa and muted the movie that was still running through the credits.

It had been.

And it still could be, if I chose to ignore the moron and save the headaches that came with him until later.

I punched the decline button, tossed the phone back on the coffee table and dropped down next to Callie. "Just more shit from the Louisiana shop."

Callie reclined back once more, but this time twisted

enough she could see me head-on and pulled her knees up so her cute feet were propped on the edge of the couch in front of her. "You wanna talk about it?"

"Not much to talk about. I mean, I know I can hire someone to manage those offices the same as I hired you and at least some of the chaos would stop, but the guys I hired in Ft. Worth and New Orleans aren't carryin' their weight the way I need 'em to."

"You don't have to hire someone else to manage the offices. I could take those on, too, I bet. We'd just have to change up some of the processes for when the guys have orders and get me access to the other office accounts."

I shifted to match her angle, grabbed her ankles and stretched her legs out so they draped over mine, a posture that got her nice and close to me. Not surprisingly, the angry edge the phone call had created flatlined the second I touched her.

"I thought about it." I tucked a lock of her hair behind her ear then dragged the back of my finger along her jawline. "It'd fix part of the problem, but not the root of it."

Her voice took on a sexy rasp and a shiver worked through her torso. "What's the root cause?"

Just say it.

Get it out there and be done with it.

I smoothed my other hand along the outside of one leg, my gaze on her jeans while I tried to form the words. "Pretty sure it's me."

Her hand covered mine and she squeezed. "What do you mean it's you?"

The truth was right there, poised on the tip of my tongue and ready to fly. But it still took me a good ten or so seconds before I found the courage to voice it. "I think I'm just not into it." I shifted my gaze to hers. "I love doin' the cars. I dig the shit out of the guys I work with here in Garland. Hell, I've known most of 'em for years and can trust their work. But the other two shops? I could give two shits less about what's going on at either one of them and don't know the first damned thing about the men. And it shows. In the product. In the unhappy customers. In the bottom line. So, yeah. I think the problem is me."

Her eyebrows pinched tight together in that way they did when she was on the trail of tracking something down for me in the office. "This might be a really stupid question, but if you're not really into the other locations, why have them? I see your books on the Garland shop every day and you're turning a sweet profit even with me on the payroll. Why add the extra headache if it's not making you happy?"

And there was the million dollar question. The answer to which I hated even thinking about. Let alone saying it out loud. "I guess because that's what I thought I was supposed to do. You get one good business running, then you launch another one and make it successful, too. That's how you build a big bank account. Right?"

"According to who?"

My brothers.

They hadn't said that with actual words, of course. But that's what they'd done. How they'd made their mark after being born into all manner of unprivileged circumstances.

Never once since the suspicion had settled in my

head had I ever said it out loud. Hell, I wasn't even sure it'd make sense to someone if I did.

But Callie was sitting there, looking at me with those big green eyes of hers like there was absolutely nothing I could say that would be wrong.

"Every single one of my brothers came from some seriously shitty circumstances," I said. "Heck, I think I might've had the most balanced upbringing of any of them. But they all found their niche and worked their asses off to make their mark."

"And you thought you had to make a statement of your own with your cars to measure up."

No judgment. No snark or pontificating about what I should or shouldn't do.

Just understanding.

A soft, simple place to lay it out there.

My voice came out a little grated, but the weight I'd been carrying around for months seemed to fall away when I spoke. "They're the most amazing men I know. And they accepted me. Taught me new industries. Showed me how to start my own business. Invested in me so I could take that step. All I wanted was… I don't know…maybe to show them I could make the most of all they'd given me."

"And you thought success meant having a lot of shops?"

"I wouldn't exactly call three a lot. Hell, Jace and Axel have five clubs in the Dallas/Ft. Worth area alone. They've got more in all the surrounding states and their fingers in all kinds of businesses outside of entertainment."

"But that's what feeds *them*. What you do—that's art. It's not the kind of thing that can be replicated and mass-produced. Not and still be able to have it mean something special."

Weird. I'd never thought of what I did as art before. When I'd first started, what I was out to create was just a dream. The passion of a sixteen-year-old boy who wanted a killer ride no one else could match.

"Look." Callie ran her hand up my arm and squeezed my shoulder. "I don't really know these guys, but I've listened while you've talked about them. From everything you've told me, they don't seem the type to lay expectations on anyone. If anything, they sound like they buck convention and follow their guts."

"That's exactly who they are. Who we are."

"Then maybe what you need to do is ask yourself what would make you happy. I mean, if you could do anything, what would that look like?"

I huffed out an ironic chuckle. "That's a no-brainer. I'd shut those other two shops down, go back to just focusing on the Garland one, and throw in with Beckett and Knox whenever they need me at Citadel."

"Their security place?"

I nodded, but my brain had drifted off to three or four years ago when I'd had the best of all worlds. "It was nice. My days were simple. I'd work on my commissions most of the time, but could freelance with Knox and Beckett whenever they needed muscle on a detail or had a big install. Kinda broke things up, you know?"

"And the guys in the Garland shop…would you keep them?"

"With you there? Hell, yeah. Their commission percentages added to my bottom line make my income pretty cozy, and you doin' the books, the ordering and covering all the other office shit makes my life a breeze.

Plus, five of us working in the shop adds more word of mouth and demand for work."

Callie cocked her head and raised her eyebrows in that sweetly smug way Gabe always did after she'd deftly trounced me in a debate. "Sounds to me like you've got your answer."

I did.

And more than that, the relief of saying everything out loud and wading through the bullshit I'd fed myself had me breathing a whole lot easier.

Not giving myself time to second-guess myself again, I cupped the side of her face, claimed her lips and got us both horizontal on the sofa.

Christ, but I loved the taste of her. Loved how easy her lips yielded and followed my lead and the slick glide of her tongue against mine. Craved the feel of her lush body pressed against mine and those sweet keening sounds she made when I pressed my palms against her bare flesh.

I skimmed my thumb along the lower swell of one breast and she gasped against my mouth, arching into the point of contact.

So responsive.

As quick to react to my touch as a flame was to gasoline.

My cock throbbed with the beat of my pulse, straining against my zipper and urging me with a single-minded focus to take her. To feel her heat. To hear what sounds she made when I pressed inside her.

To claim what was mine.

I broke the kiss at the thought and rested my forehead against hers, my breaths coming hard and heavy. Deep down, I knew I needed to stop, but couldn't resist the temptation of circling the distended nipple through the cotton beneath my palm.

"Danny…" Her hands at my shoulder blades slid down to my ass and her eyelids opened, meeting my gaze head-on. "Please don't stop this time. I know you want to go slow because you're worried about me, but I swear to you… I'm ready."

So tempting.

Her lips swollen from my kisses. Her face flushed and her eyelids heavy with need. I couldn't have stopped my hand from sliding beneath the cotton and feeling her skin to skin even if I'd wanted to. The one time I'd allowed us to get skin to skin from the chest up had damned near broken my restraint, but now…feeling her beneath me…the press of her hips against my aching cock and the quiver that moved through her torso when she did…

"I want this." Her hands stole beneath my tee, the heat of her palms branding me. "I need this."

So do you.

No hesitation.

No indecision.

Just pure instinct acting on an undeniable truth.

"Wrap your legs around my waist and hold on," I demanded, barely waiting for her to comply before I lifted us both from the couch. I barely made it clear of the coffee table before I claimed her mouth once more and walked us to my bedroom. By some miracle, I maneuvered the path without slamming us both into any walls or doors and hit the light switch before I tumbled us both to the bed.

From there it was a free-for-all. A frantic mix of touching, tasting, and discarding of clothes—right up until I peeled her panties and jeans over her hips and my eyes got their first full look of Callie in all her gloriously naked splendor.

I was dumbfounded.

Awed by the sheer beauty of her.

Her creamy skin framed by the blue comforter beneath her. The sultry curve of her hips. The fullness of her breasts and the dusky tips of her nipples.

"Callie..." I crawled toward her, eager to explore every curve with my hands and mouth.

I managed to tease my lips just below her simple silver and rhinestone studded navel ring before Cassie shivered and shoved my shoulders. "Oh, no you don't. Not before you lose your jeans, too."

Fuck.

I reversed my path and shucked the confining denim in record time, an act that brought her up on her knees almost as quickly and had her palming my cock in the next heartbeat.

It was my last conscious thought.

With my mouth against hers and our bodies connected skin to skin, there was nothing left but instinct. A primal drive so powerful and fluid it bordered on spiritual.

I gloried in it. Feasted on every inch of her. Suckled her nipples and savored her sweet pussy. Fisted her silky hair and all but roared at the feel of her warm mouth around my aching cock.

"Callie." I squeezed her shoulder, skating dangerously close to the edge. "Love your mouth, peach, but the first time I'm with you, I'm coming inside you."

She lifted her head, a shy but insanely sexy smile

tilting her lips and her wild, sex-mussed hair framing her flushed face. "Condom?"

"Nightstand. Top drawer."

"Right." She rolled, made quick work of finding one, then rolled back to me.

I snatched it from her, gloved up in record time...

And then I was inside her.

So fucking perfect.

Heaven.

Her heels digging into my ass as I pumped inside her, and her nails biting into my skin at my shoulders.

But it was her eyes that held me.

The deepest green I'd ever seen. Open and locked to mine. Showing me everything. All her fears. All her hopes and everything in-between.

This was what it meant to be connected. Bound to someone in the most fundamental way.

My balls drew tighter, release pushing closer even as I felt her pussy tighten around my shaft. Holding myself above her on one arm, I speared my other hand beneath her and pressed her hips upward, grinding my pelvis against her clit with each thrust. "Get there, Callie. Get there and take me with you."

Her lips parted on a gasp and her legs tightened around me. The walls of her sex fisted tight, and her eyelids fluttered closed, the reflexive pulse of her release dragging my own free with it.

The waves went on forever, every roll of her hips as she rode her pleasure, heightening mine as well. I gave up trying to keep my weight off her and blanketed her completely, burying my face in the crook of her neck while I tried to catch my breath. "Please tell me I'm not too heavy for you."

"God no," she whispered, dragging her fingertips along my spine and spawning goose bumps along my skin. "You're perfect. Besides, if you move, I might float away."

I barked out a laugh, wrapped her up tight and rolled us both so she was on top of me. "I'll make sure you don't."

I didn't know how long we lay there, and frankly, didn't care. I hadn't exactly been a player since losing my virginity eons ago, but I hadn't been a monk either. Callie and I had amazing chemistry. Mind-blowing chemistry, to be honest.

But as I lay there and just let myself absorb it all, I accepted it was something more. Something deeper. Something I knew would mark me as a fool if I ever lost it.

I tightened my arms around her and pressed a kiss to her temple. I'd been many things in my life, but a fool wasn't one of them. Whatever it was we'd found— I was keeping it.

Chapter Seventeen

Callie

Everything was going to be fine.

No matter what happened, I had everything I needed in my life to survive. My program. My meetings. My sponsor.

It would all work out exactly as it needed to.

At least I hoped it would…

I did a deep inhale then let it out between my lips just as slowly, focusing on the cars behind us in the side mirror and the aggressive way they zigged and zagged between lanes.

Several clips back, a small- to mid-size black SUV held steady in the same lane as us, the sun reflecting hard off its windshield. I chuckled to myself, the image drawing to mind the spotless Cayenne that'd been in my parking lot off and on ever since I'd first seen it two weeks ago. I guess I'd been wrong about no one in my complex being able to afford that kind of a ride. Either that or one of my fellow dwellers had hit the lottery, or something.

Danny glanced at me from the driver's seat, the busi-

nesses along the George Bush Turnpike whizzing behind his window. "You're fidgeting again."

I was?

Oh. My leg.

I pressed my foot more firmly against the floor mat
and forced myself to stop the nervous jangling. "Sorry.
It's a big day."

"Why? You've been trading texts with Viv the last
two weeks. You can't be worried about seeing her
again."

"A few texts, yeah. Nothing major, though. Just easy
stuff like what to wear today and which location we
were going to. And that last text was a *duh* moment
on my part. I mean, I should have known you'd know
which one we were going to. You're family, and I'm
not. I guess I was just trying to find something to talk
about. Which is all about me trying to control the situation, when obviously I can't."

Eyes on the road, he grinned and shook his head.
"And now you're rambling."

He was right.

Again.

He took his hand off the gearshift and rested it on my
thigh. "It's a family birthday party. We'll eat until our
eyes bug out, embarrass the shit out of ourselves with
bowling, then we'll head back to my place and unwind."

His place.

Shit.

"I forgot my backpack." My watch showed 1:34 PM.
There was no way we'd have enough time to go back
beforehand and not be late for the party.

This time his grin got bigger, and he squeezed my
thigh. "Relax. We'll grab it on the way to my place. It's

not a big deal." He gave me another sideways glance before he released me and steered us into another lane. "Have I mentioned you look hot in that getup?"

"You have. Three times now. The first two are the reason we were late getting on the road to begin with. Fixing lipstick is tricky business."

"Yeah, but you stopped worrying for at least five minutes after the fact."

"That's because of the kisses. The outfit—I don't know. I'm not sure it's me." The outfit in question being a sleeveless taupe-ish top I'd treated myself to at TJ Maxx a week ago. It buttoned down the middle and flared out at the waist. It had a bit of a sheen to it that made it look almost satiny and flowed the same way as well, which appealed to my inner flower child. The collared neckline gave it a nod to sophistication. I'd paired it with my nicest jeans that were fitted at the top but looser at the bottom and a pair of chunky cork sandals that reminded me of Vivienne's. I'd picked those sandals up at TJ Maxx, too, for a song.

"It's totally you," Danny said. "It's got attitude, but class."

"Good. That's good." I clenched my hands in my lap and stared out the windshield, not really seeing anything. "I'm still nervous."

"About?"

All too easily, the night Jace and Viv had drawn a line and told me I either had to go to treatment in exchange for them bailing me out of hot water or to face the mess I'd created with a drug dealer showed like a movie reel in my head. "These people—all the brothers, the wives, the moms—they're important to Vivienne. And to you. Most of them I've never laid eyes on, but have heard amazing things about for weeks. The rest of them have only seen me looking like death warmed over after that stupid thing I did trying to steal drugs. I'm sure they all know about my past in some form or fashion."

Danny kept his gaze locked dead ahead and it took him a second or two to answer. "Yes, they know."

Shit.

I mean, I knew that would be the case. Families talk, and I'd produced a lot of opportunity for fodder for years. Still, I think a part of me was hoping he'd say something different.

I opened my mouth to say I understood, but Danny kept going. "Just because you behaved a certain way before doesn't mean that's how you are now. Everyone in my family has been through hard times. If there's one thing I'm confident of, it's that they'll give you a fair shake."

"You really believe that?"

"Absolutely." He signaled for the exit and looked over his shoulder before changing lanes, glancing at me in the process. "Though, I'll be straight up—some of them might need more time than others."

"Is there someone particular you're thinking of?"

His face got hard. "Jace, mainly. But that's mostly because he's crazy protective of his wife."

That sounded nice. Not to mention reasonable. "Mostly?"

It took several seconds of him giving a ton of attention to exiting the highway and navigating to the turn lane, all of which I suspected was a cover for him to carefully form his words. "How much of the night Jace bailed you out of trouble do you remember?"

The nervous jitters in my stomach shifted to more of a sludgy churn looking for an upchuck opportunity. "I remember getting the bright idea to try and nab more Ecstasy from a dealer, then getting good and lit before I headed out to do the job. I remember hiding in a closet and calling Viv for help, then running for all I was worth when the dealer found me. The next thing that's really clear is bein' in the car with you and getting out at that fancy house where your doc friend looked me over."

"You remember what happened when you were running for it?"

I stared at my thighs and pushed my brain to work through the fog. "I think I remember seeing Viv and running her direction." I retrained my gaze on Danny. "Everything else is too hazy."

"Well, I wasn't there, but Jace told me the story." His face looked pretty similar to someone who'd drawn the short straw on being a mortally bad news messenger. "The short version—Viv was tryin' to help you out, but you were so messed up, you fell and dragged Viv down with you. The dealer caught her, and you took off running."

"I left her there?"

Danny nodded and steered us into the Main Event's parking lot. "Fortunately, Jace got there right when the dude had a gun pointed in her face."

My face went cadaver cold in a heartbeat. "I left my sister," I whispered. "She came for me, and she could've died."

"She could've, but she didn't." He pulled into a parking spot a few rows away from the door, yanked the parking brake and swiveled to me. "Look. You ask me, this is a shit time for you to be finding out all this shit, but I don't want you goin' in there without knowing."

I nodded. "God, yes. What if I'd said something flippant? I had no clue." The dashboard loomed in front of me, but it was the conversation I'd had with Viv in my apartment that was the main focus of my thoughts. "She was so gracious. Never once told me what I'd done to her."

"Because to her, it's over. But for Jace—he loves the hell out of that woman, and he came awful damned close to losing her that night."

Bits and pieces of me sitting in that gorgeous living room all those years ago started filtering back to me. How pissed off I was about the way everyone was treating me. How I had no clue what I was going to do for money now that my plan had gone south. But more importantly, how the hell I was gonna get the hell out of Dodge and take the edge off again.

"God, I was so self-centered," I said mostly to myself. The wiser part of me—the one that had done the hard work of getting sober over the last year—knew it was that entitled self-centeredness that had gotten me where I was. But actually remembering it at such a visceral level... I kind of wanted to cut my heart out. "I wasn't even thinking about Viv. I was thinking about how I was gonna get out of that house and get back to not feeling again."

Cupping the side of my face, Danny lowered his voice. "It's behind you. You know that. I know that. And from the sounds of how things went when you made your amends to Viv, she knows it, too. So, let it go."

Easier said than done. But I had the tools to work through it now. Positive ones that focused on taking all the ugly things that had weighed us down and shedding light on them instead of drinking until I couldn't remember them.

I exhaled hard and nodded. "Okay. One step at a time."

Danny grinned, leaned in, and pressed a tender kiss to my lips. "That's the spirit."

Inside, the Main Event was...well...a zoo. Voices echoed in all directions. Arcade games pinged, zinged and ponged across a long stretch of the building to my left. Above the gaming area, kids in full harnesses and headgear teetered on nothing more than a single rope. A wide stretch of bowling alleys covered the entire far end of the building, and up on my right was a sizable ice cream parlor.

"Come on." Danny put his hand low on my back and steered me forward. "Pretty sure they've got a table near the bowling alley."

Sure enough, we rounded the ice cream parlor and found four serving tables that had been pushed together to make one big rectangle.

And it was packed.

"Oh, great," I said. "We're late."

Danny huffed out a laugh and steered me forward. "Hardly. Beckett, Gia, Knox and Darya don't look like they're here yet. You're not late until they beat you somewhere."

I gripped the strap of my purse a little tighter and pasted on what I hoped didn't look like a painful smile.

Please, God. Just help me through this.

I heard Vivienne before I actually laid eyes on her. "Callie!" She scooted back from the far side of the table, stood and started my way. "I was wondering if you'd changed your mind."

"Yeah, I think that was my fault," Danny said. "Something about me causing her to pause for a lipstick fix."

Vivienne laughed as she approached and wrapped me up in a big hug. "I think Jace has made us late a time or two for the same reason." She pulled away a little, but kept her hands on my shoulders. "I'm so glad you made it."

"Me too." I scanned the sea of people with heads all craned my direction. "I think."

"You'll be fine," she murmured low enough only Danny and I could hear. Then she raised her voice and took over steering me to the table. "Let me introduce you to everyone."

Two women sat side by side at one end of the table, both of them older than the rest of the crowd, but enviously gorgeous. One looked like she'd once been a fashion model and had platinum gray hair halfway down her back. The other had that cool black cherry hair color and had an impish aura about her.

Viv started with them. "These ladies are the matriarchs of the family. Sylvie is Axel's mom, and Ninette claims Jace."

Ninette raised one eyebrow and glanced at Jace, who I'd noted sat right next to the chair Viv had vacated. "Well, most of the time I claim him. Every now and then I have a mind to put him on eBay."

Jace chuckled, but the look on his face didn't match the sound. I also noted his gaze never fully met mine.

"It's nice to meet ya, lass," Sylvie said. "Danny's

had quite a pep in his step the last several weeks. I'm lookin' forward to learnin' what's got him so fired up."

An older man with shoulder length gray hair and a mustache that belonged in a Western sat next to Ninette. "Pretty sure we all know what's got him fired up, but I'm lookin' forward to gettin' to know you, too." He gave me a mock salute and a wicked grin. "I'm Rex by the way."

Viv stepped in and pointed to the toddler in a high chair next to Sylvie. "That's Colin—Axel and Lizzy's little boy."

My gaze drifted to the couple on the other side of Colin. Like all of the men except Jace had done when I'd approached, the burly man with the wild, long red hair stood behind his wife. "You're Lizzy Hemming," I said to the black-haired singer I'd know anywhere, then shifted my gaze to her husband. "So, I'm going to guess you're Axel."

"She's got good deduction skills," Axel said to Danny as he held out his hand to me. "That'll be a plus for her when she finds out we're all about bustin' each other's balls and tryin' to pull a prank wherever we can."

Oh, thank God. He was funny and had just referenced busting balls at the dinner table. Maybe I wouldn't fall flat on my face before I made it to a chair of my own. "Nice to meet you both."

"You already know Jace," Viv said, almost skipping him completely, then pointed across the table to a blond man who looked like he'd just walked out of a Brad Pitt cowboy movie and a brunette woman who could land a Miss Clairol ad gig in a heartbeat. A boy that looked to be closing in on his preteens sat next to them. "This is Trevor and Natalie and their son, Levi."

Trevor dipped his head in lieu of a handshake since there was too much space between us and Levi followed suit, but it was Natalie who spoke. "My God, you can definitely tell you and Vivienne are sisters. Same hair. Same amazing eyes." She rolled her eyes. "Same amazing figure."

Trevor pulled his chair out, settled beside his wife and grinned. "Not thinkin' I've ever given you cause to think your figure is anything but stellar, darlin'."

"You're biased."

"Maybe. But I've also got damned good taste."

"Aww man." Levi sat and faced the girl I'd place at maybe three or four years younger next to him. "Wanna go play games while we wait on the food?"

"No," the man next to the girl said, then waved at me. "I'm Ivan and this is my daughter Mary," he looked to Levi and finished his sentence, "who'll be staying here for Aunt Vivienne's birthday dinner."

Mary giggled.

Levi groaned, but then seemed to realize I might take offense. "Sorry. It's not you. I just don't like it when they get all googly-googly."

"Mmm hmm," Ninette said, sipping her water. "Let's see how many more years it takes before you get all googly-googly with someone."

"Oh, my God," Natalie said. "Now *I* wanna go play arcade games."

A mix of chuckles and outright laughter circled the table and, for the first time since I woke up this morning, my insides relaxed enough for me to pull in a decent breath.

"Um, hello…" The feminine voice came from someone I couldn't see with Danny and Viv both on my right.

Or at least I couldn't until she leaned out enough to peer around them and waved a hand. "I'm Gabe. Danny's sister. And this," she jerked her head toward the dark-haired man standing beside her, "is my husband, Zeke."

"Wow," I found myself saying out loud. "Danny's said so much about you, but I…"

Well, shit. Now what was I gonna say?

"Not exactly spitting images are we?" Danny slid his arm around my waist. "Gabe looks like Mom, and I look like Dad."

Well, then his mom must've been a female Abercrombie model, because this lady had wide, pale blue eyes, pouty lips and sun-kissed blond hair to die for.

"Sorry, Callie," Zeke said, a healthy amount of mischief glinting in his eyes. "One of us had to get the better end of the family genes."

"Cut it out, Dugan," Danny said. "If it wasn't for me, you wouldn't have even met Gabe." Danny pulled a chair out for me next to his sister. "Sugar Bear, do me a favor and make sure Zeke doesn't fill her ear with a bunch of bullshit before we're done eating."

Danny sat on the other side of me, and the rest of the table slowly settled into smaller conversations.

I leaned closer to Gabe and lowered my voice. "Sugar Bear?"

She grinned huge. "I had a thing for Sugar Crisp cereal when I was little. Sugar Bear was the guy on the box. Don't ask me why, but it stuck. At least for Danny and Dad, it did."

"It's cool," I said. "We never had nicknames in my house. Not unless you count the ones Mom had for Dad, but those weren't the type you wanna remember."

Okay. Probably not the best conversation to bring up, so I shifted gears. "Danny says you're a mechanic."

"Not like I used to be. Zeke got me a garage where I can go and tinker with a car I'm restoring when I need time to think. Mostly now I'm focusing on graphic arts."

"That sounds fun. Is it hard to learn?"

She shook her head. "Not really. I mean, it's part creativity and part technology. I can show you some time if you want. Let you play around with some of the tools?"

"That'd be great!"

A wave of *hellos* and *heys* drifted up from around us and all the men stood once again—this time Jace included.

"Yo, yo, yo," a seriously built man with dark hair and a near-buzz cut bellowed. Beside him was a knockout brunette that was tiny in comparison size-wise, but had a presence about her that made her seem just as powerful. The man fist-bumped Axel, waved at Jace across the table then did that manly half hug, half back slap thing with Danny. "What have we missed?"

"Nothin' much," Danny said. "We just got here ten minutes ago." He turned to me. "Callie, this is my brother Beckett and his wife, Gia."

Danny stepped back to let another couple I hadn't initially seen move into view. The man had tousled dirty blond hair and a graphic Marvel tee I was tempted to try and barter for, and the woman was tall, lithe and sporting some seriously platinum blond hair. "This is Knox and his wife, Darya."

I stood, uncertain if I should do the shaking hands thing with everyone, so I looped my thumbs in the belt loops at my waist instead. "I've heard a lot about you guys from Danny. Well… I've heard about Beckett and Knox." Realizing how that sounded, I winced and looked to the two women. "Not that he doesn't talk about you guys, too."

I scanned the table like there might be a lifeline hanging around to bail me out of my awkward rambling, but the unhelpful hits from my brain kept coming. "He's always telling me how great the whole family is. Though, he kind of forgot to tell me that all the guys were hot and the women beautiful."

Shit.

I really needed to stop talking.

My cheeks burned despite the fact that my blundering comment had generated a mix of amused reactions. Including an indelicate snort from Gabe. "Oh, my God. Don't tell these ding-dongs they're hot. They've already got egos bigger than Texas."

"Girl, that's the truth." Gia pulled me in for a hug. "And relax. There are a ton of us, but we've all been the new kid at some point."

Knox barked out a laugh as he passed, guiding Darya to an open set of chairs farther down the table. "Bullshit. I have it under good authority that Axel *does*, in fact, bite."

This time it was Lizzy who guffawed loud enough to carry well beyond our immediate group. "Yes. Yes, he does. And I'm grateful for it."

"Well," Darya said, gracefully sliding into a chair next to Knox's. "If she's going to call me beautiful, I'm a fan of the new girl already. Plus, she's Vivienne's sister, so she must be awesome."

A scoff sounded from the opposite end of the table.

I swiveled my head to find the source and caught Vivienne giving Jace a nasty nudge with her elbow.

The whole table got quiet, only the crash of falling bowling pins and arcade games sounding around us.

Beside me, Danny tensed and locked eyes with Jace.

"Did I say something wrong?" Darya asked the table at large.

"Oh, no." Ninette crossed her arms on the table in front of her and threw out a droll "...this is just one of those times where I think I'd be better putting my son up for auction on eBay." She eyed Danny as only a seasoned mother could. "Have a seat, Danny. You want to say your piece with Jace, you can do it after we get some food in our bellies."

As if nothing at all were wrong, Jace dropped his arm along the back of Vivienne's chair and gave his mother a long-suffering look.

Sylvie scooted back from the table and stood. "I think I'll just go run down our waitress and let her know everyone's finally here."

With one last glare at Jace, Danny pulled my chair out and waited for me to take my seat before he did the same. "Sorry," he murmured low enough only I would hear. "I don't know what's up his ass lately."

"Well," I answered just as quietly, "considering what we talked about in the car, I'm thinking it's kind of a reasonable response, don't ya think?"

Knox cut into our side conversation. "So, Callie... how's the new gig going? Katy says you took to everything pretty easy."

"Well, she's a great teacher. Plus, she spent a good part of the first two days helping me get things organized. Overall, I think things are going great."

"The guys love her," Danny added. "That first day when she started talkin' shop with Malcom about a flatrod she'd seen at a state fair, I thought his eyes were gonna pop out of his head."

Beckett finished placing his drink order with the waitress, then jumped into the conversation with a question for me. "You know custom cars?"

"Not like Danny and the rest of the guys. But my dad always had a thing for them and motorcycles. I guess it rubbed off."

"Well, that's gotta be handy working in the office," Gia said.

"More than handy," Danny answered. "I think she's upped mine and the rest of the guys' commissions over the last month talking with our potential clients."

"Gives the customers an extra vote of confidence," Rex said. "Happens all the time with the stuff I put in a gallery. If I tell a buyer it's a good piece they'll consider it, but if a second person comes along and says it's awesome, too, they'll lay down money a hell of a lot faster."

"It's validation," Zeke said. "Everyone wants to feel like they're doing the right thing."

And just like that, we were in the zone. The conversation easily moving back and forth from one person to the other and from one topic to the next. Before I knew it, the pizza was gone, everyone was halfway through the huge birthday cake Sylvie had custom baked for Vivienne, and the party planner was finishing up getting team names for the big bowling head-to-head of men versus women.

"All right. I think that does it." The planner straightened from where she'd been writing names at the head of the table. "I'm gonna set you guys up on lanes nineteen and twenty. As soon as I get your names entered in the system, you'll be free to find a ball that suits you and can start on a few warm-up rounds."

"Hey, Uncle Knox," Levi said. "After we finish bowling, you wanna do the gravity ropes with me?"

"Only if you do laser tag with me after that."

"Oh, fuck that," Zeke said. "We're all doing gravity ropes and laser tag."

Gabe leaned into me and murmured, "Zeke's a bit of a thrill seeker. If your heart ends up in your throat or you wanna toss your cookies, he's generally into it."

"Which is kinda ironic considering he's a trauma doc," Danny said. "Half the people he sees in the ER are probably there because they were out doing the same nutty shit he was doing."

"Not so," Zeke said as if warming up for a debate. "Thrill sports generally have much better safety protocols than your average dad who thinks it's a great idea to fix an electrical outlet with a live current and no shoes on."

Viv cut into the conversation. "Hey, Callie. You still going to Tulsa tomorrow to visit Dad?"

For the first time since Danny and Jace had had their starefest, Jace actually deigned to look my direction, then promptly recentered his attention on Viv. "Your dad's dead."

"Yeah. Tomorrow's the anniversary of the day he died. She's going up for a visit." Viv smiled at me. "You still going?"

Whether he was doing it out of habit or as a silent show of comfort I wasn't sure, but Danny rested his arm on the back of my chair and affectionately cupped my shoulder.

"I'm still going. You wanna go?"

"No," Jace said. And it wasn't a polite no either. More like a judge throwing down a death sentence for a killer who'd not only confessed to what they'd done but was happy about it.

Viv's head snapped to Jace.

The rest of the table got scary quiet.

Danny's hand at my shoulder got tight. "What the fuck is wrong with you, man?"

Viv leaned into Jace and said something none of the rest of us could hear. All of a second later, Jace pushed back from the table, stood and stormed toward the front of the building.

Apparently eager to get an answer to his question, Danny pushed back in his own chair and stood as well.

I started to do the same. "Danny—"

Gabe caught my hand before I could stand and squeezed. "Let him go. Danny's right. Jace has been in a weird fucking mood for weeks. Whatever it is that's going on, they'll work it out."

"Possibly on each other's faces," Gia added, "but they'll work it out."

"See what I mean?" Zeke said to me. "It's the average idiot that keeps me in business. But not to worry, I've got a kit in the car. Won't be the first time I've patched either of them up."

Well, hell.

At least everyone else seemed calm about the situation. Both of the mothers included.

Except, it seemed, for me and Vivienne. "Whatever it was I said, I'm sorry."

"Don't be," she said. "They're right about Jace. He's had a lot on his mind lately."

Lately.

Or, to Gabe's definition—for weeks.

Which suspiciously synced with my return to Dallas. A coincidence?

Maybe.

But if I were in Jace's shoes and I'd had to sit around the table with a woman who'd left my soon-to-be wife facing a drug dealer with a gun I'd be pissed as hell.

Viv stood and pushed in her chair. "Okay. Time for men versus women. Everyone head to our lanes and I'll go wrangle Mr. Crabby Puss."

"I'll go with you." I stood and tossed my napkin on my empty plate.

"Callie," Viv said, "I don't think—"

"Let's be honest," I said. "He's got a lot of reasons to be pissed at me. If that's the case, then let's get on with it and let him say what he needs to say. Because the truth of the matter is—I screwed up. A lot. Particularly where you're concerned."

Viv shook her head. "I really don't think—"

"Viv, I want you in my life. And I'd really like to have you in my life without you or me having to worry about your husband growling every time I come around."

"Honestly, might not be a bad idea," Ninette said. "Jace might be a hothead, but he's also honest and direct. If he's got something up his ass and Callie's willing to hear it, then let 'em clear the air."

Thank God. Because this was definitely a situation I wasn't eager to repeat. Even if I was looking forward to staring down the bear even less.

Viv sucked in a huge breath, considered for a minute then swept her arm toward the front of the building. "Okay. Let's go."

Finding the two men took all of three steps around

the corner. Framed by the two sets of double doors that made up the entrance, Jace and Danny were just behind Danny's Chevelle, Danny ranting about something with a whole lot of hand gestures while Jace glared at the asphalt, hands on his hips.

Viv pushed through the glass doors first and I followed, hearing Danny's voice above the drone of cars on the highway a few blocks away.

"Give me one fucking good reason why she doesn't deserve a fresh chance just like everyone else!"

"You want a reason?" Jace said. "My wife! *That's* the reason. And if that's not enough, I've got about a hundred thousand more on top of that."

Viv came to a stop so fast in front of me, I nearly slammed into her back.

"Are you..." Danny said. "Is this about the money? I told you I'd pay that."

Their voices kept streaming, but something about the situation triggered my memory. The elegant living room with its fancy wood floors and high-end furniture. The pool beyond the window wall. And me—sitting on a plush couch with everyone looking at me while Jace gave me my options.

"I'm willing to bail your ass out of hot water. In exchange, you agree to detox at a place well out of sight of Hugo's reach and straighten your shit."

"I don't need your help."

"If you want to keep breathing, you do. The way I hear it, you're in for at least fifty grand for the X you stole. Now, unless you've got about three times that floating around, the odds of you coming out from any altercation with his men are slim to none."

"I just need to find the X."

"See, that's what you don't get. Hugo's going to want to send a message to you and any other idiot fool enough to steal from him. So you don't just need what you stole. You need more. You get me?"

"Callie?"

My sister's voice felt forever away, but I knew she was close. Could have sworn I heard Danny's right after and footsteps coming closer. The afternoon sun beat down on me and the heat from the pavement wavered upward. Almost as if hell had opened its mouth and was swallowing me completely.

I shook away the haze of years ago and the present came into focus, Danny right in front of me and Viv beside him. Jace stood beside Viv, his expression one of open concern.

"You bailed me out." I'd heard the word *bail* at the time, but hadn't bothered to really think about what that entailed.

The concern in his dark eyes shifted to regret. "Let that go. I'm all about you owning what's on you to own, but me putting up money was on me. It was my choice. My actions."

"The X was worth fifty grand, but you paid him more to keep them from making an example out of me."

"Callie…" Jace stepped a little closer.

Danny shifted so he stood slightly in front of me.

Jace stopped and held up both hands, eyes locked to Danny. "I'm not out to hurt her. I know I haven't acted right about her lately, but you know I'd never hurt a woman. Especially not Viv's little sister." He shifted his gaze to mine. "What I said, that was just me being pissed about being powerless. It had fuck all to do with you. I swear on everything that means anything to me, my only beef with you is Viv not hurting again."

"Me, too," I whispered. I swallowed hard and gripped Danny's forearm to hold him in place as I moved next to him, bringing me closer to Jace. "But what you did for me… I was so out of it. So focused on just getting out of that house. On doing whatever I had to to be free to scheme and get my next fix… I didn't think." Tears welled so quickly I had no hope of holding them back. They spilled down my cheeks, the hot summer breeze against them the only cool relief to be found. "Maybe I just didn't want to remember. But I do now, and I promise… I'll find a way to pay you back."

"No," Viv said. "You don't have to do that. We don't need it."

"She's right," Jace said. "Every dollar I gave Hugo was worth it. It gave Viv peace, and it got you in to treatment."

Danny shook his head and pulled me deep into the crook of his arm. "You're tellin' me *now* you're feelin' supportive of Callie getting sober? I'm not buyin' it, brother."

Jace muttered under his breath, glanced at Vivienne then spun and fisted his hair on top of his head, his focus on the clear blue sky above as though praying for guidance. When he spun back there was genuine vulnerability on his face. "I ran up on a man holding a gun to my wife's face—the woman I love—and you'd left her there. So, do I trust you yet? No. Am I happy to see my wife so glad to be talking with you and seeing good things from you? Hell, yes. Do I believe people deserve second chances? Yes. Abso-fucking-lutely yes.

But when you asked about her going with you to Tulsa alone, I flipped my shit."

"Because the last time we were alone together I left her."

"Yes."

"No way," Danny said. "I'm not buying it. It's not like Callie's using. She's sober and—"

"I'm pregnant."

Viv's quiet yet unmistakable announcement shot through Danny's tirade and left a tender silence hovering between us. She looked to each of us, an almost guilty expression on her face before she gripped Jace's arm and moved in tight to his side. "It's still early. Not through the first trimester yet. But I'm thirty-seven as of Wednesday, and the doc says that every year over thirty-five the risk for miscarriage in the first trimester goes up. I didn't want to risk everyone getting excited until we cleared that hurdle, so, I asked Jace not to tell anyone. Not even his mom."

Jace pulled his wife in tight and buried his face in her neck, such an obvious display of devotion mixed with fear my heart ached for him.

"That's why you've been on edge," I said.

It took many long, quiet seconds before he finally lifted his head, cupped each side of Vivienne's face and kissed her forehead. Finally, he pulled her into the circle of his arm beside him and answered. "Even leaving for work in the morning is hard. Not because I'm worried about the baby, but because I'm worried Vivienne will need me, and I won't be able to get there fast enough." His gaze landed on me, and his voice grew gruff. "You didn't deserve me treating you the way I did." He shifted to Danny. "You didn't deserve my shit either. For that—for how I treated you both—I am genuinely sorry. I just… I'm havin' a hell of a time keeping things in check. Being this powerless…it doesn't sit well with me."

"Ah, man." Danny released me and pulled Jace into a hug that left zero doubt of how close the two really were. "I wish I'd known, but I think I get it." He pulled away and slapped Jace's shoulder hard enough it would have knocked me over. "You're still a dick and overprotective as fuck, but considering the circumstances, it's forgivable."

"Totally forgivable," I said, moving in to hug my sister. "And so exciting." I held her tight a moment and whispered in her ear. "You're gonna be a mom."

"Maybe," she whispered back. Her grip around me loosened and she eased back enough to see my face. "But let's not go there for a while, okay? Not until we're on safer ground."

"Fair enough. And mum's the word until you tell us otherwise."

Danny tugged me backward so my back was against his chest and kissed my temple, but his words were for Jace. "You're gonna be a dad."

"Whatever, Parker. Let's get the hell out of this heat before Vivienne passes out and I have a solid reason to bust your ass."

Danny barked out a laugh and spun me for the entrance. "Man, I cannot wait to see you up to your elbows in shitty diapers. That's gonna be better than the day Colin upchucked on Axel's favorite cashmere sweater."

I had to confess, as dark and brooding as Jace was, I was kind of hoping I got to see that, too. But that was months away and we still had a lot of memories and future hurdles to overcome between now and then.

Right now was for being happy. For putting the past behind all of us where it belonged and enjoying today. After all, as Maggie was always telling me, tomorrow would take care of itself.

Chapter Eighteen

Callie

It'd been sixteen years since I'd visited the city where I'd been born. A considerable amount of time when I considered it as a unit of measure, but driving into Tulsa and seeing things in person, it seemed almost negligible. Like all I'd done was blink before finding myself back in comfortable terrain.

Yeah, some of the businesses had been replaced with new ones, and the ones still thriving were a little more weathered, but the bulk of the foundation was the same—a mix of small town and urban city.

I slowed for an upcoming red light at 71st and Memorial and ended up hitting the brakes too hard when Vivienne gasped and pointed at Woodland Hills Mall across the street from us. "Oh, my God. Look. It's still packed."

Doing my best to bring the black Escalade I'd driven us here in to a somewhat smooth stop while my heart recalibrated from the jolt she'd created, I rolled my eyes. "It's August in Oklahoma. It's only two degrees cooler than Texas at best. What else are people gonna do but swim or shop?"

Vivienne grinned at me and reclined back into her cushy seat. "You're too uptight."

"I'm driving a car that costs close to eighty grand and is about ten times bigger than my little Spark. So, yeah. I'm uptight. Jace'll kill me if I put a ding in it."

"No, he won't. And it's not Jace's anyway. It's part of Knox and Beckett's security fleet."

The light turned green and the uber-sensitive accelerator shot us forward. "They've got a fleet of these things?"

"Well, they call it a fleet. I think there are five or six of them. So, technically, anything that happens is a business write-off."

"Yeah, not sure I'm finding much comfort in that. Beckett looks like he can be worse than Jace when he's pissed—and that's sayin' something."

"Nah. He's a teddy bear."

"To you, maybe. I'm still the outsider who out-bowled him yesterday."

"Oh, my God, those three strikes you nailed in the last round were awesome. Sylvie and Ninette were still bragging about it last night when Jace and I finally headed to bed." She pulled in a long breath and let it out with a refreshed *ahhh*. "I'm so glad I came."

"Me, too. Though, I'm a little surprised he let you out without an armed guard."

"I think he considered it. The Escalade was a trade-off—it being bulletproof and tracked by GPS and all…"

My head snapped Viv's direction, my brain boycotting all attention on the road in front of me long enough to gauge her face for any signs she might be teasing. "You're joking, right?"

"Nope. Like I said…it's part of Beckett and Knox's fleet, and they do personal protection, so…there you go."

"Wow." I shook my head and stared at the back of the minivan all but crawling the last mile to the cemetery in front of us. "Danny said he did security stuff with Beckett, but I thought he meant like those guys at concerts who guard the backstage area or club security."

"They do some of that, too, but Beckett and Gia typically shoot for the higher-end clients. More cash for less work. He conveniently leaves off the fact that it's more risk, too."

My knuckles protested my much tighter grip on the steering wheel and the Slim Jim and barbecue chips I'd polished off an hour ago did a whirligig routine in my stomach. "That kinda scares the shit out of me."

"Because of Danny?"

"*Yeah*. I mean…"

What did I mean?

I scrambled for an answer, but neither my brain nor my mouth had much to offer.

But Vivienne did. "Maybe because the thought of something happening to him scares you?"

It absolutely did. But it was the why behind the answer to her question that had me both shaken and awed. "Wow…"

"Wow, what?"

"I just realized… Okay, this is gonna sound nuts, but growing up, I always felt different from everyone else. Like I was so drab that I blended into the background, and no one could ever really see me. When I drank, it was like the alcohol gave me color. Vibrancy that made me visible and interesting."

"So, without the booze you felt invisible?"

"Exactly. When I finally got serious about working the program this time around and identifying all the negative beliefs I'd been operating under my whole life, I figured out that invisibility was one of the big triggers that contributes to me drinking again. So, I've been working on it—not just accepting myself, but reframing how I talk about myself."

"And?"

"And I just realized—ever since Danny and I started spending time together—I don't feel drab anymore. I feel alive and colorful and happy. And it's not because he's a fix like booze was, but because we're so much alike. It's easy to be with him because he gets me, and being accepted at such a fundamental level, I think he's teaching me how to really love myself."

Silence filled the car's interior for so long, I glanced at Vivienne to make sure I hadn't put her to sleep.

She wasn't, but her eyes were wide and her mouth slightly parted.

"That probably sounds nuts, doesn't it?" I said, wishing I'd thought through things a little more before I'd blathered on. "Especially with us knowing each other for such a short time?"

Vivienne shook her head, and her voice was a whole lot softer when she spoke. "Actually, I think it's beautiful."

It was beautiful and, honestly, nothing short of miraculous from where I was sitting.

"And stop worrying about how long you've been together," Viv said. "I already told you—Jace and I might not have set the world record for number of days to the altar, but we didn't lollygag either. I think when it's right, it's just *right*."

The entrance to the cemetery came into view about a block away, the aged gray stone and wrought-iron railings that ran the perimeter a stark contrast to the modern buildings and business around it.

I signaled for our turn and all the fluffy warm feelings my big ah-ha moment had generated dissipated, replaced with the cold, hard reality of what I needed to say out loud before the afternoon was over.

There was no way I was backing out now, though. Vivienne was here and, in a matter of speaking, Dad was, too, so it was time to put my wrongs to bed. I just hoped what I had to share wouldn't make for a painfully quiet ride home and a shattered bridge between me and Viv.

It took a whole lot of guessing from each of us and multiple wrong turns through the maze-like roads before we finally found the plot we were looking for. A black marble bench with *Moore* emblazoned in white script sat just beyond the flat grave marker I'd painstakingly selected all those years ago.

All your fault.

It'd been a nonstop loop in my head from the day he'd died, one that I'd only begun in recent months to address.

But today I was going to let it go.

Or at least try to and ask for forgiveness in the process.

I put the gearshift in park and stared out the driver's window at the summer-stained grass covering Dad's grave. Tension gripped my shoulders, arms and stomach in a paralyzing vise, and my throat felt so constricted it was a wonder my lungs were able to function.

"You okay?" Vivienne asked.

The dashboard vents funneled a steady stream of chilled air at my neck and face, dancing across the fine sweat that rose across my skin and sending goose bumps out in all directions. My voice croaked when I finally found the determination to speak. "I will be."

Forcing myself to move, I killed the engine and jerked the door handle open.

Heat enveloped me before I could even get the door closed behind me, a thick, humid cloud of awfulness paired with the blazing sun overhead. At the far end of the cemetery, a mausoleum stretched like a wall between us and the real world. Behind me lay the graves of people who could afford to be buried with their own private crypts or gargantuan headstones. Between it all was nothing but flat, nondescript land broken only by flat markers that dotted the landscape in a neat and tidy hyphenated trail.

Vivienne's quiet voice pulled me out of my stupor. "I don't remember us paying for a bench."

The black marble stood out amongst the rest of the plots. Almost like someone had thrown down a dying dare for the rich folks on the other side of us by breaking the norm. "We didn't. Randy did."

"Randy?"

One word, but the incredulousness behind it may as well have said, *Randy? As in the guy who actually killed our father?*

The fact that she was so easily triggered by his name made me question how well I'd fare with my sister in the minutes in front of us. "Yeah. He called me about a month after we buried Dad. Only a few days before I finished the sale on the house and moved to Dallas, actually."

"That's bold."

Bold wasn't exactly the word I'd have picked. More like *gracious*. Or even *forgiving*. "He felt awful. Said he wanted to do something for Dad and thought a bench so you and I could visit him would be nice." I huffed out a sad scoff. "Maybe I should have told him to save his money seeing as this is the first time I've been back in sixteen years."

Viv threaded her arm around mine so we were linked at the elbow. "You say that like you blame yourself."

I did. And had almost every single day I'd been gone. "That's because I do blame myself."

"Um, hello? I didn't visit him either. I was too caught up in being Mom's mini-me and trying to be someone I wasn't."

The truth prodded me between my shoulder blades. A rapier too dull to actually break the skin and pierce my heart, but still sharp enough to make me wish it would all just be over. "I wasn't talking about visiting him." My throat constricted, fighting back the words even as they burned the back of my throat. I swallowed hard and forced myself to get it over with. "I was talking about being the reason he's dead."

A hot gust of wind tossed my hair across my face, and from somewhere nearby two car doors slammed shut.

Beside me, Vivienne scanned the cemetery in all directions. As if she were waiting for someone to hop out of nowhere and pronounce she was being punked. "Callie, it's not your fault. Dad's dead because he was a hothead who couldn't think straight when he was drunk. That's why we agreed to drop the charges on Randy.

They were both just idiots who were too messed up to think like adults."

"You're right. Dad had a temper." I pulled in a slow breath and turned enough to meet Vivienne's stare. "But I used that temper. Knowingly. Randy might have pulled the gun, but I may as well have pulled the trigger."

Viv frowned and her voice dropped so low I barely heard her over the workmen that had fired up their Weedwackers only a stone's throw away. "I don't know what you mean."

Sixteen years later and I could still feel the righteous indignation I'd nursed for less than twenty-four hours before hatching my stupid plan. It'd been an itchy fire in my blood. A fixation that had worked like razor blades against my wounded pride.

God, I'd been so stupid. Shortsighted and embarrassingly self-centered.

I stared at the water-starved grass in front of me. Better that than to witness Vivienne's expression. "Did you know Randy and his wife were having problems around the time he and Dad got into it?"

"No. I didn't talk to Dad too much after I left. Every time I tried to call him, he seemed like he'd rather be doing anything else than spending time on the phone with me."

She'd read that one right. For weeks after Viv had left, Dad had ranted about how Viv was just like Mom— too focused on money and what everyone else thought. "Well, they were. Everyone was shocked and talking about it when we got together at night. I think a few of the guys even had betting pools going to see when they'd get back together or if they would."

"Okay, so what's that got to do with Dad dying?"

Man, this sucked. Not just because of what I'd done, but because the whole thing was so ludicrous, I was embarrassed to admit what I'd done out loud. "A few nights before Dad died, he'd had a few as usual. We were all hanging out at the club just down the street from the house. Dad was playing a round of pool with his buddy Ned from work. I was talking to some girl whose name I don't even remember when Randy and the whole betting thing came up in conversation." I shook my head, replaying the scene in my mind for what I hoped was the last time. "Dad told Ned there was a new scenario everyone should start betting on. Specifically, that Randy and Bess would officially split, Randy and I would get hooked up, and we'd all live happily ever after. *Fuck Bess and her old bratty ass*, he'd said."

"Wait—you and Randy? He was almost as old as Dad. That's like—gross."

I shrugged. "Yeah, he was older, but he wasn't exactly ugly either."

Viv's expression sobered, an understanding creeping into her gaze that gave me goose bumps despite the heat. "Don't tell me you seriously considered anything with him."

"Oh, I considered it all right. If there was one thing I'd learned early on it was that making Dad happy earned me a whole lot of praise. Praise I never seemed to get from anyone else. So, I learned to drink like a pro long before I was legal. Learned to play pool. Learned motorcycles and cars. Anything that would end up with me getting an *atta girl*, I did it." I sighed and tacked on, "Even hit on Randy."

"Oh, no." She faced me fully. "What happened?"

I chuckled, but the sound was full of self-disgust.

"Turns out Randy loved Bess a lot. So much, in fact, that he was appalled by my over-the-top seduction and all but threw me out of his house." I shook my head and focused on the ground, my mind tumbling through the memories over and over again. "I'd never been so mortified in my life. So ashamed. But do you know what fixes that feeling?"

"Booze."

"Yep. And I had a lot of it that night." A knot swelled at the base of my throat, and my heart rate increased with every word, but I kept going. "The more I drank the more my embarrassment shifted to bitterness and anger. By the time morning rolled around, I'd formed a plan to get even."

"Oh, no."

"Oh, yes. I waited until Dad got off work, met him at the club and told him all about it. Except the story I told Dad wasn't about me all but throwing myself at Randy." I hesitated only a second, but my voice quavered with the rest of it. "It was about how Randy lured me back to his house then tried to force me to have sex with him."

"Oh, my God." Viv covered her mouth with her hand for a moment, as though trying to hold back any other condemnation that might slip out. "Dad would have killed any man that tried to hurt either one of us."

I closed my eyes and let my head drop forward, the shame and guilt I'd carried around for years finally exposed to the two people who mattered most. The image of my dad when I'd first walked into the bar that night blasted in my mind's eye. "He'd been so happy that night. It was a Friday, and he was ready for the weekend. Laughing loud with his buddies and trading bullshit stories like he always did."

All the pain and terror of that night blazed a path up through my chest and to my throat, tears pushing past my closed eyelids to spill fast and heavy along my cheeks. I kept the image of him in my head. His huge smile. His burly laugh. "I'm so sorry. It was so selfish of me. So foolish. And worse, I knew what I was doing was wrong, but I did it anyway. All because I was embarrassed and afraid of what Randy would say to everyone."

The breeze whipped my hair across my face, the fine strands clinging in the tracks of my tears. Heat blasted my shoulders, and the drone of the Weedwackers drew slowly closer, drowning out my quiet sobs. Just like I had the day we'd buried my dad, I wanted to be beneath the grass with him. Wanted the weight of the soil to cover me completely until I couldn't breathe or feel anymore.

I startled and opened my eyes at Vivienne's touch, her hand tenderly sliding against mine and grounding me exactly as she had that same day. Tears streaked her face, too, but it wasn't horror or disgust in her expression as I'd expected. It was sympathy. And even more surprising, understanding. "You were barely eighteen, Callie. Eighteen with very little in the way of positive role models. And while what you did was absolutely manipulative and wrong—it doesn't absolve Randy or Dad of where things went from there."

Swiping one cheek with my free hand, I glanced at the workers, who'd now grown close enough they were annoying, then refocused on Vivienne. "You don't hate me?"

She shook her head and cupped our joined hands with her other one. "No. I don't hate you. But I do hurt for you. Hurt that you've carried so much pain and guilt around with you all this time and that you didn't have someone there to talk you through things."

I looked to the flat marker just in front of the bench Randy had bought, then to the stretch of grass between. "Do you think *he* hates me?"

Vivienne sighed and aimed her direction toward Dad's grave as well. "I wasn't as close to him as you were, but my guess would be no. He adored you. Would have probably forgiven you anything. Even this."

I wanted to believe it. Needed to.

Squeezing my hand, Vivienne added, "But I think the person who needs to do the most forgiving is you. You were young and doing the best you could with not the best circumstances. Maybe you could consider that and forgive yourself."

Maggie had said the same thing. More times than I could count. But until this moment, I hadn't been able to. Or maybe hadn't been ready to. But here, standing next to my sister and finally being back in the place where everything had started with everything out in the open, my heart felt a little lighter. The tether that had kept me anchored to the past strangely absent.

"It's weird," I said. "For months, I've thought about this moment. About facing what I'd done. Actually saying it out loud. Now that I'm through it… I don't know what to do."

Vivienne smiled, so much love and understanding in her eyes my knees nearly buckled. "I think you take that as a sign it's behind you and start over with a clean slate. One you take a day at a time."

I half sobbed, half snickered. "You really have been going to Al-Anon."

"I know, right?" she answered with the same emotional laugh. "Look at us, exercising emotional health and all that!" She released my hand, opened her arms and pulled me in for a tight hug. "I'm so proud of you, Callie. Proud of all the work you've done and so hopeful for what your life holds in store. Hopeful for you and Danny."

"Me, too." I squeezed her a little tighter and whispered close to her ear. "Thank you for coming. For not judging me and accepting me. Fuckups and all."

Inside my arms, Vivienne's body tensed and the whole loving, peaceful vibe she'd been projecting shifted to something far less pleasant. Her voice barely carried, but was thick with urgency. "Where are the keys?"

I tried to release my hold on her so I could get a better look at her face, but she held me fast. "Huh?"

"Don't move. Don't even act like anything's wrong. Just tell me where the keys are."

My heart took off at an uncomfortable jog. "Um. They're in my pocket."

"Okay, just follow my lead and when I ask for them, give them to me." Before I had a chance to respond, she released her hold, smoothing her hands down my arms until she held both of my hands. She smiled huge, but there was no mistaking it was one hundred percent fake. "A van just pulled up behind the Escalade. White. No markings."

Her gaze briefly cut to a worker I heard even closer behind me. "Those men. They shouldn't be this close, and their work truck is parked on the other side of the SUV. Where are the other two men?"

I quickly scanned the terrain behind her and the mild

surge of adrenaline her anxiety had created spiked to dangerous levels in a single heartbeat. "One's just two graves over, but the other one is in the work truck."

Viv dipped her head. "Hand the keys to me as casually as you can, then get your ass to the passenger's seat. Okay?"

Right. Calm, cool and collected. I could do that. What I wasn't sure of was how well my feet were going to cooperate.

I dug my hand in my pocket, slowly handed over the keys...

Then all hell broke loose.

Chapter Nineteen

Danny

"I'm gonna sell."

It was the first lull we'd had in conversation since rally started half an hour ago, but the words had been on my tongue and poised for launch since I'd set down. Given the eight men staring back at me with confused expressions, I was thinking I should have added a little more to the message. "The businesses in Ft. Worth and New Orleans. I'm gonna sell 'em."

My brothers looked to each other as though still struggling to find context.

"Unless," I said, "someone else has a better way to handle getting out of them other than selling. I thought about just liquidating, but my guess is, I won't get as much out of the assets as I put into them. So, if anyone's got ideas, I wanna hear 'em."

Already reclined in the gaudy bloodred velvet barrel chair he'd chosen for his own however many years ago, Axel anchored an elbow on the armrest and fiddled with his beard. "Might be more prepared to offer advice if you back up and start at the beginning."

"Yeah," Zeke said. "I thought you were all about

expansion and being the biggest player in the custom car market."

I dropped back against my chair on a huff and scratched the top of my head, trying to figure out how to share what I needed to. "Yeah, see that's the thing... I'm not sure that's what I want."

"Not what you want anymore," Knox asked, "or was never what you wanted?"

I looked to Zeke, then to Beckett—both of whom had been my staunchest supporters from day one, but the person that came most to mind was Callie. How much honesty and bravery she'd shown in the time since she'd been back. How she'd laid herself bare repeatedly and always seemed to come out stronger on the other side because of it. "The truth? I think I got caught up tryin' to be what you guys thought would be successful."

"What *we* thought?" Trevor said.

The rest of the men didn't echo the surprise out loud like Trevor had, but their expressions said as much just the same.

"Yeah," I said. "I mean, it's not like anyone actually said or implied I needed to. It's just..." I motioned to the table in general. "Look at all of you. Axel and Jace own more businesses than I think either of them can name off the top of their heads. Zeke's got a stellar rep as a doc. Trevor's got two different kinds of businesses he's juggling. Knox is a go-to guy for the government when it comes to hacking, and Beckett's on speed dial for people who've got enough money they need protection going to the grocery store."

Rex chuckled and hung his head. "I think I get it."

"Second that," Ivan said, raising one hand. "You guys

might be chill and hella supportive, but you also set the bar mighty damned high."

Yes.

Exactly that.

After yesterday's head-to-head with Jace and the subsequent clearing of the air, I'd felt a shit ton of relief. But right now? Right now, I felt like I was gonna float out of my chair from all the relief of just unburdening myself of the false beliefs I'd carted around. No wonder Callie had learned to be fiercely honest. The shit was liberating as hell.

I pulled in a deep, lung-filling breath and let the rest of it out. "I guess what I've figured out is—I'm not a businessman. I'm an artist. I like takin' one gig at a time, comin' up with a vision, and then makin' it happen. I like metal in my hands. I like taking things apart and then figuring out how to put them back together.

"What I don't like is managing people. Or paperwork. Or bank accounts and P&Ls. It pisses me off. What's worse is, it keeps me from doing what I love which is workin' on cars."

"But Callie's doing all the shit you don't like, right?" Knox said. "She's pulled the load off there?"

"On the one office, yeah. And she's offered to take on the other two, but that doesn't make the managing piece go away. I'd still have to listen to clients who are pissed off about a job I had nothing to do with because it's my name that's behind it all. I just…"

I looked at each man around me. Really let myself take in their open and focused attention. "It ain't me."

The silence lasted only a second before Jace broke it, his voice steady and even. "If it ain't you, then it ain't you. Life's too short to spend it on anything that doesn't fill you up."

Axel dipped his head. "He's right, brother. And it sucks that you spent the last three years chasin' a dream that wasn't yours." He shifted his gaze to Ivan and Rex. "And for the record, I could give two fucks how much any man around this table makes, how many businesses they own, or how well their name is known. I only care about who they are and what they stand for."

"Amen," Knox said. "And FYI, the government only comes to me when they're out of options. They think I'm arrogant and difficult to work with."

Beckett swiveled enough to face him. "You *are* arrogant and difficult to work with."

"Well, I'm already brilliant and good looking. God had to even the deck somehow."

Jace rolled his eyes, but he was chuckling just like everyone else when he rotated his chair at the head of the table toward me. "So, what do you wanna do with the shops? Sell all three, or keep the Garland one?"

"Oh, I'm keeping the Garland one. Callie's solid on the bookwork and handling clients, and I like workin' with the guys I've got right now."

"What if they leave?" Trevor asked.

I shrugged. "Doesn't matter. I own the shop, so the only overhead I've got is Callie's pay and my expenses. If I actually have time to work on a car, I'll be able to cover it all easy."

"So, you want out on the other two," Axel said.

I nodded. "Like I said—I thought about just liquidating rather than deal with the hassle of brokering a sale, but that seems like I'd be throwing good money away."

"You don't have to broker it," Jace said. "I know a

few people who can handle it for a fair commission. Lots of people looking for opportunities like this one. We'll get it sold easy enough."

And just like that, the gnarly beast I'd wrestled and tried to best for the last few years was gone. Handled with just a few honest sentences and subsequent conversation.

All because Callie had dared to call me on it.

It was one of the things I loved about her—her call-it-what-it-was attitude about everything. That and her laugh.

And her goofy sense of humor.

And her love of junk and fast food.

Hell, if I was honest, I just loved being around her, period. Life was easier with her there. Not because of any one thing she did or one characteristic she brought to the table. It was just because she was there. Breathing and being her one hundred percent authentic, no bullshit self.

I loved that.

You love that? Or you love her?

The thought registered for all of a few seconds before I subsequently realized everyone around the table had gone silent and had perked up from their relaxed posture.

Knox cradled his phone between his ear and shoulder, opened his ever-present laptop, and started working his fingers on his keyboard. "When did it come in?" he said to whoever was on the phone.

"What's up?" I said to Zeke beside me.

Zeke shook his head. "Don't know. Something came in from the monitoring station."

That was weird. The monitoring station never called Knox directly unless—

Knox's gaze shot to Jace. "Viv hit the panic button on the Escalade's key chain."

Jace was on his feet in a second, followed by the rest of us. "Where? When?"

Gaze back on the screen in front of him, Knox ignored Jace and fired questions at whoever was on the other end of the line. "Did you call her cell?

"Right. No more calls. If someone's got it, I don't want them knowing she tripped an alarm, but monitor that signal. If you see it move, I want to know." He hung up and volleyed his attention between me and Jace. "The Escalade's in a cemetery on the east side of Tulsa. There's no answer on her cell. GPS is still pinging so it's not powered off and can be traced. Tulsa PD's been engaged, and a car is on its way to research."

"Could be an accidental push," Beckett offered. "It wouldn't be the first time we've had one of those."

"Not with Viv. She's too careful." Jace looked to me, a mix of pure fear and fury on his face.

The same protective instinct that had fired hot and fast yesterday leapt to the surface before I could check it. "If you're thinking Callie did something, you can drop that shit right now. She wouldn't hurt Vivienne. She was too fucking happy when Vivienne called last night to make plans. I mean, my God, they talked like two teenagers for half an hour about it."

Jace stood absolutely still, his hands fisted at his sides and his posture oddly reminding me of a pissed off bull contemplating a waving red flag right in front of him.

"Brother," Axel said low and cautiously. "You need

to think. You saw them together yesterday. They were happy. The lad's right. Callie wouldn't hurt her."

It took another handful of stressful seconds, but Jace finally spoke. "Let's say you're right. Let's say this has fuck all to do with Callie. I can't think of a single person who'd want to hurt Vivienne. Can you say the same thing about Callie?"

"Man, you gotta drop this. She's not the same person she was. Her past is where it should be—in the past."

"For her, maybe," Trevor said. "But they're back in Tulsa. Could she have run into someone she crossed there? Someone she pissed off?"

"How the hell would I know? She doesn't talk about any of the people there, and everyone she meets here loves her."

"What about someone from her past here?" Zeke said.

My pulse throbbed at my neck and temples, a fiery rage building with every second until I thought I'd explode. "Why the fuck is everyone focused on Callie? Yeah, she's got a past, but so does everyone in this room. Hell, Jace, you've probably pissed off twice as many people as Callie ever did."

"Brother, calm down." A hand clamped onto my arm, and I jerked it away, spinning to find Axel next to me.

Arm.

Bruise.

I bet it was when that dude grabbed me...he thought he knew me.

"Knox, does Walmart have security cameras you can access?" I said.

"Why?" Jace said.

Knox answered at the same time. "Yeah, sure."

I ignored Jace and rounded the table headed toward Knox, mentally trying to calculate what the date had been when she'd had her near miss at the grocery store. "Pull up a calendar."

He did, and I leaned in for a better look. "Friday, July 23rd. Somewhere between noon and three o'clock. The Walmart over by Love Field."

"Right, but what is he looking for?" Beckett said.

I straightened and focused on Jace. "It could be nothing, but Callie had a near miss with drinking that afternoon. It was the same day I came here and told you we'd gone out. She'd been out buying stuff for us to eat later that night and found herself in the beer and wine aisle. She almost buckled, but instead she decided to get the hell out of there and accidentally hit a guy when she was leaving with her cart. He grabbed her—hard enough to leave a bruise. When I pushed her for details on the guy, she said *he thought he knew me*."

I scanned the faces of the rest of the men, most of them aiming dubious expressions back at me.

Jace, on the other hand, started barking orders. "Pull it up. See if you can get an image and any records of the guy."

"What about her house?" Beckett added. "You think we might find anything there?"

My anger fired up all over again. "Fucking A. You, too? I told you—this doesn't have anything to do with Callie doing anything bad to Viv."

"Not saying it does, but what if the guy followed her home and she didn't know it? How secure is her apartment?"

"No way anyone got in. It's a second story. Window access would take a ladder on the outside of the complex, and I put a Medeco dead bolt on it—" Hold up. Actually, I hadn't.

"What?" Beckett said.

"I didn't get the new dead bolt on it until Sunday. I stayed late with her the night it happened, then she spent the night out at my house Saturday."

Beckett dipped his head and focused on Knox. "You got her address?"

"Already sending it to you."

His text alert chimed all of five seconds later. Beckett checked it and headed for the door. "I'm on it. Let me know if you get a hit on the footage."

"GPS is on the move," Knox said, eyes locked on his screen, "but the Escalade is in place. Whatever they're doing, it's not in the SUV."

"When the police get there, I want details, and I want to know exactly where that cell phone ends up," Jace said, headed in the same direction. He paused long enough to lock stares with me. "I'm going to Tulsa. You in or out?"

My feet were in motion before my mouth was. "Oh, I'm most definitely in."

Chapter Twenty

Callie

"God damn it, let me go!" I thrashed against the man above me, the unforgiving ridged flooring of the van I'd been thrown into digging into my back as I tried to wedge my knees up for leverage to push him away. My sight was useless, hindered by the bag that'd been jerked over my head before I'd even managed to get halfway to the Escalade's passenger seat. From the grunts and shrieks of Vivienne outside, she wasn't in much better shape, but at least she wasn't in the van yet.

I got one knee up, pushed with all I had and—"Ooph." My forehead knocked hard against the van's floor, and I found myself on my belly, my arms stretched out in front of me and held together by someone else while the man I'd wrestled pinned me down.

"Hold her still," a man barked.

The *screeetch* of duct tape unwinding sounded a second before my hands were bound together. Before I knew it, the weight was off my back, and I was dragged backward and tossed aside like I was nothing more than a duffel bag.

Another thud similar to mine landed somewhere near

me, paired with a pained "*Fuck*" that unmistakably belonged to Vivienne.

"Vivienne!" Dried crumbles of dirt bit into my palms
as I braced against the floor and tried to scramble toward her labored breaths.

The roll and thud of the van's door slamming shut
blocked out most of the light that had filtered through
what I guessed was burlap sack.

Braced on my knees the best I could, I patted the air
in front of me. "Vivienne, where are you?"

"Here," she huffed all of a second before my hands
connected with her body.

Two doors opened up front then shut again quickly.
The van lurched forward, knocking me off balance and
throwing me backward. The back of my head slammed
against something as unforgiving as concrete.

"Shit! Callie!"

Dimly, my brain noted Viv's huffing and shuffling,
but between the sharp pain my tumble had created in
my head and the frantic way whoever was driving navigated the twists and turns in the old cemetery, my body
wasn't up for doing the same.

"Callie." Viv's voice was closer this time. "Callie,
wake up."

I'd been asleep?

No, that couldn't have been right. Or maybe I had
blanked out for a second, because the van wasn't making a million turns anymore. "I'm awake."

"When you fell, it sounded bad. Are you okay?"

Fuck no, I wasn't okay. My head felt like a bug who'd
gone one on one with a windshield. "I'll live," I groaned.
"Maybe."

More scooting sounded and then Viv whispered from

close enough she had to be right beside me. "Did you get a look at any of them?"

"Ummm." God, my mind just didn't want to work.

"Callie, you have to focus. Think. Did you recognize anyone?"

The scent of damp earth or mulch filled my still-struggling lungs, probably from whatever had been in the bag before it'd become my hood. I licked a tickle along my lower lip and tasted blood. "Dark hair. Shitty beard or bad stubble. Strong as fuck. Other than that, no."

"He didn't look familiar at all?"

I shook my head and instantly regretted it. "No. You?"

"No."

"Are your hands taped?" Vivienne asked.

"Yeah. You?"

"That and a hood."

Great. We were twins. Though, I was hoping she hadn't earned a knot on her head like I had.

"Listen to me," she whispered even quieter. "I punched the panic button a few times before they got me."

Jesus. I really must have whacked my head hard when I'd fallen because Viv was talking some seriously weird shit. "You what?"

"Shhh," she whisper reprimanded me. "The key chain. It had a panic button on it. All the women in the family have one."

Wow. As unexpected surprises went, that was enough to get my brain at least a little bit online. "No shit? The little white thingy?"

"Yes."

Totally cool. "I thought it was one of those Apple AirTag things."

"Kinda. But they took the keys from me when I was trying to get away."

I shifted and tried to sit up.

Viv's hands pressed against me. "No. Stay down. Better for them to think you're hurt or you've given up. But you've gotta be ready, okay? The guys are gonna figure this out eventually, and we'll get out of this."

I rolled to my back and winced as gravity did its thing. "You sound way too practiced at this shit."

"Not really. Just have listened to one too many of Beckett's lectures."

Right. The badass security dude. "Well, he would know..." I tried to swallow and got a serious protest from my dry throat, making me cough hard. My head ended up not being too crazy about that development and let me know it with an ice pick-worthy stab low at the back of my head.

I lay there until the pain was somewhat bearable, the drone of the van's tires against the pavement ebbing and flowing between stoplights. God, this sucked. Not just because my body hurt everywhere, and I had no clue how things were going to turn out, but because my first one-on-one time with my sister had turned into an absolute nightmare.

A tear slipped from the corner of my eye. "I'm sorry."

"For what?"

"For bringing you. If I hadn't brought you, you wouldn't— Oh, shit."

"What?"

"The baby." I rolled back to my side. "Do you think

it's okay? Did they hurt you anywhere? Did you fall bad?"

The hitch in her breath told me plenty. "Let's not think about that right now, okay? Just stay sharp. Remember our surroundings and look for opportunities."

"We're hooded and in a dirty van."

"God, don't be a wiseass. Stay positive."

I snickered, the sharp movement earning me a fresh wave of pain.

"What's so funny?" Viv said.

"You," I said, wanting to sob as much as I wanted to chuckle. "Me. Us." The tears hit me hard all at once, and I curled deeper into a fetal position. "Christ, I didn't even get to have more than a day with you before I fucked everything up."

"Shit." It was said more to herself than to me, but I felt her move closer to me right after she said it. "Callie, listen to me. Listen to my voice. Everything is okay. You're just overwhelmed with everything and maybe having a panic attack. So, breathe. Long deep breaths, in and out. Okay?"

I hurt so bad.

Physically.

Emotionally.

Viv's hands found mine and she gently squeezed. "Callie, I'm right here. It's been a shit day, but we'll get through it. Both of us. Together."

Her hand in mine.

Her voice in my ears.

Steady.

"Just breathe," she said. "In through your nose and out through your mouth."

I did it.

Then did it again.

And again.

I don't know how long we lay there, but eventually my mind cleared, leaving only the painful throb in my head. "Sorry," I said again. "I don't know what happened."

"Well, let's see. You spilled your guts about Dad, then got abducted and got body-slammed onto the floor of a van. Coupled with everything from yesterday, I'd say a little emotional breakdown was called for."

The van slowed and came to a stop. Two front doors opened and closed.

"Be ready," Viv whispered. "Whatever happens, stay sharp."

Right. No more freaking out and losing my shit even if it had been the toughest day of my life so far.

The sliding door whooshed open, and the van shifted as heavy footfalls sounded against the metal floor. The next thing I knew I was up and over some dumbass's shoulder, blood pooling into my head and sending my pain level to full shrieking mode.

I tried to focus on the sounds around me. A grunt or two from Vivienne and footsteps behind the buffoon carrying me. No cars. Concrete or some other solid surface beneath their feet.

The buffoon stopped, and metal against metal sounded. A second later we were on the move again, but the temperature shifted. The heat was gone, replaced with a wealth of air-conditioning.

"Over there," a man said. "In the middle. Leave their hands taped."

Weird. That voice sounded familiar.

The world went right-sided, and my feet hit the floor,

but then I was promptly shoved down until my ass hit smooth concrete. A weight pressed against my right side.

No, not a weight.

Vivienne. Shoulder to shoulder against me.

"Leave 'em," the same man said. "Wait outside, and I'll pay you what we agreed to."

Goose bumps that had nothing to do with the air-conditioning lifted up and down my arms and along the back of my neck. My head throbbed, but something else prodded me, too. Something not unlike being nudged from a deep, dreamless sleep.

The door opened and shut, leaving nothing but an echo and subsequent silence in the room.

Movement and the rustle of cloth sounded to my right.

"Oh, my God," Vivienne said beside me, her voice filled with shock.

Bright light blinded me a second later. I squinted my eyes and shielded them with my bound hands in front of me until my surroundings came into focus. A concrete floor. A metal building. Windows up at the front that filled the otherwise empty room with sunshine.

"Oh, my God," I echoed when I got a look at our captor. Only my words weren't shocked like Vivienne's. They were incredulous. Which was probably stupid considering he had a gun in one hand. "Are you fucking kidding me? I said I was sorry!"

Viv's head snapped my direction. "What?"

"I hit him with my grocery cart, but I told him I was sorry."

The man crouched between us, a self-satisfied grin

on his face—the type you wanted to slap on instinct. "I *knew* I recognized you."

"You most certainly did not," I fired back, "because I don't know *you*."

"Yes, you do," Vivienne whispered.

I looked to Viv too fast and winced from the pain my movement created. "What are you talking about? I don't know this guy."

Viv smiled, but it wasn't the good kind. More like a sad one that came paired with a *bless your little screwed up heart*. "Yes, you do," she said, softly. "He's the one you stole the X from."

My brain shot back to Danny's recap of that night.

So long ago.

Eons ago.

Viv was tryin' to help you out, but you were so messed up, you fell and dragged Viv down with you. The dealer caught her, and you took off running.

I'd hidden in a closet and called Viv.

I'd sat there for what felt like forever listening to a man rant and rave at the dude who rented the apartment. The apartment where I'd stolen the drugs. Then Viv had texted me and—dumbass that I was—I hadn't muted my phone.

The closet door had swung wide only seconds later.

The same face I'd seen that night stared back at me now.

"Startin' to come back to you, blondie?" His gaze shifted to my hair. "Though, you're not blonde anymore, are ya? That's why it took me so damned long to figure who you were. But I got there. Followed you out of that fucking Walmart and found out where you lived."

He held up the hand without a gun and spread his

fingers wide—or more like the fingers he had left. "You cost me two fingers, you little bitch. Two fingers, the loss of my wife and kids, and twenty years indebted to Hugo's bullshit."

Holy shit, this was bad.

Hugely bad.

Because the years I'd been gone had done absolutely nothing to dampen this guy's anger. If anything, time had only fueled it.

He turned his head to Viv. "And that asshole husband of yours…if he'd butted out and turned your sister over, I wouldn't be where I am today." He jerked his head my direction. "This bitch would be dead, I'd have my fingers *and* my family, and I'd be long gone livin' a life back on the East Coast."

"Jace made everything even," Viv said. "Hugo got twice the value of the drugs Callie stole."

The man stood and glared down at both of us. "Yeah. He made shit even with *Hugo* and bought blondie here a free pass. But he didn't buy one from me. Hugo still had a message to send. Needed somethin' to make sure none of the other dealers dared to lose product again. So, he made me choose. I could send my family away and work it off for twenty years, or they could take a bullet. I sent 'em off, but he took the fingers as a reminder that he could find 'em any damned time he wants."

Shit.

Shit, shit, shit.

I wanted to do something. Anything to get this guy's focus off Viv and onto me. Better yet, I wanted her out of here and somewhere safe. "This is all on me. Don't hurt her because of something I did. I own it. It was a

fuckup on my part, and you paid a high price, I get it.
But please don't hurt my sister."

"Oh, you're gonna pay." He nodded Viv's direction.
"And thanks to you two and your little road trip, her
husband's finally gonna pay, too. Been tryin' to catch
that asshole away from his usual haunts and out someplace where Hugo doesn't have eyes or ears for years."

"Wait." I volleyed a look between him and Viv. "How
did you know we were coming here?"

"Fuck, girl. Don't you listen? I said I followed you
home. Waited until you were gone, got one of my guys
to pick the lock and drop a bug—and boom. There ya
go."

A bug.

And I'd blabbed and blathered on and on about our
plans on the phone last night. All the information he'd
needed, I'd provided. And now look at us.

"What makes you think Jace will come here?" Viv
said.

The man pulled a phone from his back pocket. Viv's
phone. "He'll come because I'm gonna call him and tell
him I've got his wife. Make him think I want a ransom."
He eyeballed me, pure hatred filling his eyes. "It'll be
nice and clean. The people I want isolated in one space
and well away from Hugo. It won't get me back what
I've lost, but it'll feel fucking great."

"It won't work out the way you think it will," Viv
said.

Either the guy was a complete idiot, or we were both
missing some critical element in the overall picture, because the guy laughed like he was an untouchable in-
ternational kingpin. "What? You think your husband
is such an ace he can save the day twice?"

"I think you abducted two women in broad daylight on a last minute scheme. Even if we do all end up dead, someone somewhere is going to piece together all the information, and it's going to come back to you. You'll either end up in a cell or Hugo will deal with you."

If I hadn't been so terrified, bound and fighting back the agonizing pain building in my head, I'd have likely thrown in with some anticlimactic *Yeah* and high-fived my big sister for her lecture.

Some of her bravado must have made it through to the idiot, too, because—while he still had a little bit of a smile on his face—a bunch of it had slipped. He sneered, took two steps backward and waggled the phone in front of us again before he turned and headed for the metal door at the far end of the building. "I guess we'll just have to wait a few hours and see what happens then, won't we?"

Chapter Twenty-One

Danny

"Somethin's not right." My abrupt interruption into whatever it was Jace had been saying to Zeke garnered an instant silence inside the SUV we'd commandeered from Ninette on the way out the front door.

Jace, who'd not so unsurprisingly insisted on driving, first looked to Ivan in the seat directly behind him, then glanced at Zeke behind my front passenger seat before giving me his full attention. "Pretty sure this whole scenario is fucked up. You wanna be a little more specific?"

"It's the GPS on the phone."

"Yeah, what about it?"

I twisted in my seat enough to be able to see Ivan and Zeke as well. "What kind of idiot snatches women in broad daylight and doesn't either power their devices down or ditch their phones altogether?"

Ivan huffed out a chuckle. "The stupid kind."

"One could only hope that's the kind behind this," Zeke said. "Ought to make this easier for us to figure out."

Jace shook his head. "No. Stupid people do stupid

things. I'd rather have someone with brains who thinks shit through."

He had a point. But I still couldn't shake the idea that we were missing something. "You don't think it's odd whoever got 'em wouldn't cover that detail? That's a big oversight."

"Unless he wants you to track 'em," Ivan said. "That what you're gettin' at?"

"Like a trap?" Zeke said.

I raised both of my hands. "Who the fuck knows. Maybe. I'm just sayin', we'd be fools not to consider everything at play here."

The Tahoe's Bluetooth system kicked in and sent an incoming call ringing through the cabin. The display showed Knox.

Jace hit the answer button on the steering wheel. "Yeah."

"The cops found the Escalade," Knox said. "Keys were on the ground. One purse was found on the pavement near the front passenger door. ID inside it shows it to be Callie's. No other personal effects, so I'm gonna guess they've got Viv's purse along with her phone. No other signs of the girls."

"The GPS still moving?" I asked.

"Nope. Stopped about five minutes ago. Got the coordinates, but now I gotta know—you want the Tulsa PD in on this, or not?"

"Why wouldn't we?" Zeke said. "They're there and we're what—three hours away?"

Jace raised his hand as if to stall Zeke's train of thought. "Hold up. Any news from Beck?"

"He just got there about ten minutes ago," Knox said. "Shouldn't be too much longer."

"What about the footage?" I asked.

"Brother, that was a bigger order than you think. Walmart's just like all the other big players—they've upped their security in the last few years. Took forever to find a way in, but yeah, I got there. I used a Facebook image of Callie and have a facial recognition program running at the office. Katy's monitoring results while I drive to the office in case I need more horsepower than a single laptop and monitor."

Shuffling sounded in the background, then Knox added, "Hold that thought. Beckett's on the other line."

Silence filtered through the SUV's interior, so I took advantage and looked to all three men with me. "What if they kept the phone powered on to pull us away from Viv and Callie?"

Jace dipped his head in acknowledgment of the idea, but from the look on his face he didn't like it much. "Or maybe Viv hid hers and they don't know she's got it."

A blast of road noise shot through the SUV's speakers followed by Knox's voice. "Beckett, you're patched in. Tell 'em what you found."

"She was definitely bugged. Worst job I've ever seen, though. Only one device, placed in the living room under the sofa. It's a cheap piece of shit, too. Looks like something you'd buy at one of those so-called spy shops. It couldn't have transmitted much farther than the parking lot."

Ivan scoffed. "Startin' to think callin' whoever this is an idiot isn't much of a long shot."

"Hang on," Knox said. Movement sounded in the background. When he spoke again a hell of a lot of excitement filled his voice. "We got a hit on the facial recognition. Katy sent a screenshot of the guy who grabbed Callie. Who's free to get a pic?"

"Me," I said. "Jace is driving."

I pulled my phone out of my pocket, and Ivan and Zeke both moved in for a look over my shoulder. All of five seconds later, the pic came through. Zooming in, I shook my head. "Never seen the guy." I held the screen out for Jace. "You?"

In all the time I'd known Jace, I'd only seen him upset twice and both of them had revolved around Viv either being in danger or actually getting hurt. Seeing him now, I added a third instance to the list.

"Knox," Jace barked, "run a sheet on this guy. It's the fucker Callie stole from. One of Hugo's guys."

"No way," Zeke said, angling for a better look. "Hugo's a dick, but he'd never go back on an agreement. Too bad for business. Not to mention, he wouldn't be able to call me when he needs a bullet fished out of one of his guys."

"Who says Hugo knows about it," I said.

Beckett piped up. "He's got a point. Hugo made out pretty good on that deal, but I doubt he went easy on whoever it was that lost the product in the first place."

"Gotta make an example," Ivan added.

A flood of adrenaline had kept me pumped from the moment Knox had shared about Viv's panic button going off, but looking at the picture in front of me and the narrowed focus on the man's expression, my entire body went cold. "Hugo's nasty. If he did make shit run downhill, it would not have been pretty. Even if he did end up turning a profit." I looked from Zeke, to Ivan, then to Jace. "If we're right, Callie's fucked."

Jace shook his head. "Don't go there. Not even for a second."

"Mathew Allen McKipsy," Knox cut in. "Last arrest was two years ago. Possession with intent to distribute. Looks like he got off on a technicality, though. Represented by Deitz & Deitz."

"That's the firm Hugo uses," Beckett said.

"Right," I said. "So, we've got a name and a possible motive. What's our next move? Bring in TPD, or bring in Hugo?"

The line went silent, Zeke, Ivan and I trading looks, while Jace glared at the road.

A ring sounded in the cabin, jolting all of us at once.

The display in the center console flashed Viv's name as an incoming call.

"Knox," Jace said. "We've got an incoming from Viv."

"It's him." I knew it down to my toes. "Probably wants a demand and *that's* why he kept the phone."

"Take the call," Knox said, "but take it off speaker. As it stands right now, he shouldn't know we're on to him. No point in making him consider why you're in a car."

"Right. We'll call you back." Jace punched the button that transferred his phone off mobile then answered after a brief pause. "Hey, babe. Tried to call you a while back. You guys on the way home yet?"

How he'd managed such a nonchalant voice was beyond me. At best, I'd have probably sounded like a demanding tyrant with a stick up my ass.

"Who the fuck is this?" Jace said with a level of anger that matched the glare he had aimed out the window. Whatever the person said in response had Jace turning to me long enough to nod his head.

I texted Knox and Beckett.

It's him.

"Yeah, I remember who you are," Jace said. "Now put my fucking wife on the phone."

All too easily, the guilt and shame that had crept into Callie's expression when I'd told her how she'd left Viv to face the dealer on her own came to mind. She'd been so excited when Viv had decided to make the trip with her. Had seen it as a divine opportunity to finally put her past out there and get it solidly behind her. Now I imagined she was second-guessing everything and piling more guilt on top of what she already had packaged up.

Shit.

What if Callie wasn't even there? What if this asshole had already taken his revenge on her?

"Is Callie there?" I said low enough it wouldn't carry through the phone.

Jace frowned at me. "Let me get this straight," he said into the phone. "You want me to get my hands on a million in cash after three o'clock in the afternoon? You got any idea how impossible that is?"

All of ten seconds later, he rolled his eyes. "Right. I got the demand, now let me talk to Viv. And Callie." He paused, listening. "Bullshit. I'm not wiring a goddamn thing until I'm there and can make the trade. Plus, I want visual proof you're legit."

Whatever the guy said got Jace's attention quick. He swerved off the highway onto the shoulder just as the black screen disappeared. "He's gonna show 'em on FaceTime."

A ringtone sounded through the speakers.

Jace held the camera up close enough none of his surroundings would show in the background then hit the answer button. From where I sat, I couldn't see the image, but I damned sure heard Vivienne's shaky voice. "Hey, Jace."

Jace swallowed hard, but somehow managed to put on a good game face. "Hey, sugar. How you holding up?"

"I'm okay. The day didn't quite turn out like we'd planned."

"So, I'm gatherin'. How's Callie?"

The camera shifted and in the background the asshole barked, "Say somethin'."

"I'm fine," Callie said, though from the slight slur in her voice she sounded a little like she was drunk. "Got a headache from whackin' my head, but I'll live."

"That's enough," the man said. The way Jace flinched then scowled at the screen, I assumed he was face-to-face with the asshole. "You've got what you wanted. I'll text you the address, but I don't want any cops. If I so much as smell anyone but you anywhere near this warehouse, I'll cut my losses and off 'em both like I should have years ago."

With that, the screen went black.

"Motherfucker!" Jace threw the device toward the center console. It bounced off and tumbled to the floor near my feet. "I'm gonna kill him."

I scrambled for the phone. "Easy, man. You forgot Knox and Beckett. We gotta tell 'em what to do about the cops." I waited until he seemed to have his shit back together then handed him back the phone.

Ivan leaned in. "So, it's a ransom?"

"Yep." Jace thumbed through his contacts, punched a button on the screen and slid the phone back to where he normally left it cradled before navigating back onto the highway.

"What happened?" Knox said in the way of a greeting.

I answered before Jace could. "The guy wants a million wired. Jace said he wouldn't do it until he was there in person and could make a trade. Got a visual of both of the girls."

A chime sounded through the speakers.

Jace picked the phone up long enough to scan the screen. "Just got the address of the place and the wire info. He said on the call he knows we've got hacker connections that could handle any kind of transfer after hours."

Knox huffed out an ironic chuckle. "Not exactly one of those times I'm grateful for my reputation, but he's right." He paused a beat. "So, what do you wanna do? TPD is waiting on direction."

"He said no cops," I said to Jace. "We can't risk it. I say we wait until we get there and handle it ourselves."

"We can't wait." This from Zeke, whose voice was scarily low and measured.

I twisted in my seat to better gauge his face. "What do you mean we can't wait?"

His mouth was a tight line, his eyes full of compassion. "Brother...did you hear Callie?"

"Yeah. She said she had a headache, but she'll live. She's tough. She'll make it."

Zeke's gaze cut to Jace as though gauging how much he should say with a crazy man driving well over the speed limit before shifting back to me. "That's what she said, yeah, but did you hear how she said it?"

I thought back to her voice. She had sounded weird. "Sounded like she'd been drinking. Surely you're not thinking—"

"No, not that, but you couldn't see her as good as I could from back here. There was a lot of light wherever they are, but not enough to make her squint the way she was. Like she was having a hard time seeing. Vivienne didn't look anything like that. Callie's skin looked paler than Viv's, too. You add all that to her saying she whacked her head and that she's got a headache? I don't like it. Not when we're this far away."

"Why? What do you think's wrong?"

He pulled in a slow breath. "Head trauma of some kind. Could just be a bad concussion, but it could be a subarachnoid hemorrhage or hematoma, too. If it's either of the latter, we don't wanna mess around getting to her."

"Fuck!" I spun back in my seat, nearly tearing the damned headrest off the back of my chair in the process. "We can't just send strangers in there. What if they fuck it up?"

"Knox," Jace said. "I'm gonna forward you the address and account info. We gotta know everything about the building they're in. Who owns it…who might be a reasonable person to show unexpectedly…anything and everything. Then get Beckett on the phone. We gotta pull some strings with TPD and first responders and do it fast." He glanced my direction. "We've got a miracle to negotiate and a short time to do it in."

Too far away.

Too fucking far away to do anything. Hell, we couldn't even have Trevor circumvent the distance without a runway for his jets—

"Knox, hang on!" I said. "I got another idea. Trevor's trained for helicopters, too, right?"

"Are you kidding?" Zeke answered. "Trevor can probably fly anything, but he doesn't have copters in his fleet."

My heart kicked on a fresh flood of adrenaline and hope, the relief that mixed with it so thick I got a little light-headed. "He doesn't, but I know a guy who does."

Chapter Twenty-Two

Callie

My head hurt.

Bad.

Worse than any hangover I'd ever had, or the brutal headaches that had come with the multiple times I'd detoxed. On top of that, I was pretty sure if I moved too fast, I was gonna upchuck on anyone within three feet of me.

Unfortunately, Viv was the only person who met that criteria, and she'd already been through enough. What I really wanted to do was puke all over that smirking bastard who'd brought us here, then kick him squarely in the nuts for good measure.

I squinted, trying to bring said bastard into focus. With him bein' up at the front of the warehouse staring out one of the windows, that was no easy task, because the bright light made the throbbing pressure in my head even worse.

"How long has it been since?" I whispered to Viv, trying to hide the conversation by averting my face.

"Since he called Jace?"

I nodded and immediately regretted it, my stomach lurching at the same time as a fresh stab of pain hit me.

"I'm not sure," she said. "An hour? Maybe a little longer, but not long enough for them to get here."

"You sure you punched that panic thingy?"

"I did, but you heard what the guy said about cops. There's no way Jace would send them in if he thought it would risk us."

Slowly, I twisted toward the back of the building. As if I might see something this time that either one of us might have missed all the times we'd looked before.

But it was the same damned thing. Nothing but metal walls, metal framing, and a single metal door held closed by a thick padlock just above the handle. "I gotta do something."

"No," Viv said. "You're hurt."

I was, and the longer I sat here, the more the feeling of doom I'd been wrestling felt like it would consume me.

But I was done sitting on the cold floor like a worthless lump. My whole fucking life, I'd waited for people to rescue me or bail me out of the shitty situations I'd created. Maggie always said, *If nothing changes, nothing changes.* So, this time, I was gonna do something different.

"Listen," I said. "Whoever he had with him when we got here, I don't think they're here anymore. That means it's just us against him."

"Yeah, except he's got a gun. One I'd like to point out he hasn't put down since we got here."

I'd noted that, too. But I'd also noticed he was a twitchy fucker, which made me think, deep down, he wasn't as confident as he pretended to be. "He might have a gun, but he's in this thing on his own. If we throw a wrench in his plans, he might bail rather than risk getting caught."

"What kind of wrench? There's nothing for us to use."

"See the fire alarm to the right of the front door?"

Viv's gaze darted to our captor before shifting to the alarm. It was one of those lever mechanisms with a plastic see-through cover that prevented people from accidentally engaging it. "Yeah, what about it?"

"So, what if I get up and pull it?"

"Are you nuts?"

"No, think about it. Fire alarms are hooked up to a monitoring center, right? He doesn't want cops because he knows he'd be outnumbered. If I pull that lever, it won't take him long to figure out someone will be here eventually. He might just bail and leave us here."

"Or he might shoot us before he does."

She had a point.

I sighed and closed my eyes, that awful, prickling foreboding I couldn't shake sinking a little deeper into my bones. The bastard across the room might be holding a gun, but I would swear the grim reaper had the nose of a shotgun barrel pressed at the base of my neck. "Okay then, I'll distract him. You get out the front door and run for it."

"And leave you here?"

I didn't quite know how to tell her I didn't think it was going to make a difference. Hell, I wasn't even sure my body would cooperate enough for me to be a distraction. Let alone do any wrestling. "You've got to think about the baby. About Jace. If you get out of here, it'll be worth it."

"I'm *not* leaving you."

God, I was so tired. All I wanted to do was lie down for a minute and take a nap. Maybe see if I'd wake up from all of this and find myself waking up next to Danny at his awesome little lakeside house on a Sunday morning.

"Viv." Even whispering, my voice snagged in the back of my throat. "I know I've asked you for a lot. Put you in dangerous situations and never ever thought about the consequences. But the mess we're in today is because of me, and you know that asshole isn't as much out for money as he is blood. So, I'm asking you—begging you—please, let me try to put you and your family first."

My sister had aimed a host of expressions my way over the years. Incredulousness. Fear. Anger. Love. Pity. But I couldn't put my finger on what emotion stared back at me now. Of course, it didn't help that my vision was getting blurry up close. "You can't ask me to do this."

"I can. I am. And if it sways you even a little bit, I'll add that I think I did some serious damage when I hit my head."

"What do you mean *serious damage*?"

"I mean, if we were at home, I'd have gone to the ER or at least a minor emergency clinic about an hour and a half ago because I'm nauseous, I'm tired, and I'm not seeing things so good. So, if it makes you feel better making it about me, you gotta make a run for it and get me help."

Okay, *there* was the anger. Finally. "Why didn't you tell me?"

I would have laughed if I'd had the energy, but as

it was, just keeping my head upright was a challenge. "We're gonna talk about that now?"

Frowning, Viv looked to the asshole, then to the fire alarm, then back to him. "Okay. You make a distraction. Something so I can pull the fire alarm and then bolt. That'll trigger someone to get here, hopefully quick. But you gotta swear to me that you're gonna hang on. You gotta think about the life you've got in front of you, too. Especially Danny."

Danny.

I'd give a lot to see him one more time. Just to hang out with him a little longer. Talking about anything from cars and motorcycles to our ever evolving bizarre humanity. Watching movies and binging series. Maybe a chill Sunday morning out on his back porch drinking coffee and eating donuts while we looked out over the lake.

But I'd give everything for my sister.

No, more than that. For my sister and her little baby.

They mattered more than anything.

"I'll hang on," I promised. "So long as you run like hell."

She nodded. "What are you gonna do for a distraction?"

I had absolutely no idea. But what was becoming more and more apparent was that I needed to get a move on before my arms and legs wouldn't cooperate anymore.

Slowly, I straightened from my hunched over posture, uncrossed my legs from in front of me and braced my bound hands to one side while I slowly shifted to a kneeling position.

"Hey!" the asshole barked. "What are you doing?"

Considering how much the movement had cost me, I gave him the truth. "I don't feel so good." I got one foot braced on the ground in front of me, my whole torso wobbling from side to side for a few moments while I tried to balance. "I think I'm gonna puke."

"Sit down!"

My ability to gauge distance was for shit, but I could still make out shapes and movement enough to know he'd pointed that fucking gun my direction.

I was past caring. Past fear and second-guessing myself. Past everything except this single moment. I shoved with everything I had and got both feet planted. "Dude, I'm not joking." I staggered a step forward. Then another. "I think something's wrong."

Farther away from Viv. Just get farther away from Viv.

Dumbass kept yelling, but he didn't move away from the window. Maybe because he was afraid he'd miss Jace showing up.

I tuned him out and repeated the mantra in my head. I had one job. One fucking job, and I was gonna do it the very best I could.

For Viv.

For her little kiddo.

The sun cut mercilessly through the cheap windows, nearly blinding me.

"You little cunt. Get back over there with your sister."

Ugh, I hated the C word. Maybe I *would* puke on him. Puke made everyone freak out.

Okay, I'd clearly lost my ability to think if I was thinking about vomit with an idiot pointing a gun at me. I stopped with the nose of the gun no more than a few feet away from my chest. "I'm not joking. I'm—"

Man, my vision was seriously messed up, because I could have sworn I saw something black cut between the row of metal buildings opposite this one. I squinted, trying to make sense of what I was seeing. Maybe we were in an industrial park or something?

Dumbass turned, dropping his gun arm just a fraction.

Go!

Where the impetus came from, I didn't care. I just went with it, lifting my spaghetti weak arms up and over dickhead's head, so my duct-taped hands ended up around his neck and jumped on his back, wrapping my legs around his waist.

And then I did what I promised I'd do.

I hung on.

Put the whole weight of my flagging body into it.

An alarm blared.

A loud bang ricocheted against the metal walls and sent my ears ringing.

Water sprayed from overhead.

Dumbass thrashed harder, and another shot fired.

Don't let go.

Think about Sunday mornings.

Think about coffee and donuts.

Think about waking up next to Danny.

My arms trembled and the pressure in my head became unbearable. So much so, I couldn't help but sob.

The world shifted sideways, and my body jolted, the unforgiving ground pressing along one side of me and the unmistakable snap of a bone welcoming me back to the earth.

Something loud crashed behind me, and I could have sworn there was a whole lot of yelling.

"Callie!"

I knew that voice. A safe voice.

Danny.

But I was done. Hurting everywhere and so very tired.

I gave in and surrendered to the dark.

Chapter Twenty-Three

Danny

I hated hospitals.

Hated the smell.

Hated the beeping machines.

Hated the rules restricting the number of visitors and the uncomfortable furniture.

Aside from the day little Colin had been born, I couldn't think of a single good reason I'd ever been to one. Though, I had to give the people at this one credit—they were fucking amazing at their job.

Perched on the edge of a chair next to Callie's bed, I squeezed her hand and kissed her scraped knuckles like that might somehow stir her to life.

It wasn't right, seeing her like this. Callie was bright. Alive in every sense of the word. Even when she was asleep, she had a certain animation about her. As if even her dreams were a vibrant place where adventures were a certainty.

But the woman lying in bed was too still for me to draw a decent breath. Not at all like Callie.

The sliding glass door of her ICU room *whooshed* a little wider, and Zeke came in. The neurologist that had done the emergency surgery to relieve the pressure from the blood built up in her brain had let him scrub in and observe, but Zeke had long tossed his scrubs in favor of the jeans and tee he'd worn up here. He circled the foot of the bed and stood next to me. "How ya holdin' up?"

"Better if she'd wake up."

"Yeah, that's gonna take a while. She just had a hole drilled in the back of her head." He paused, looked at Callie and shook his head sporting a lopsided grin. "She's earned some time off if you ask me. Not too many people who'd be willing to wrestle a man while they've got a subdural hematoma."

All too easily, my brain called up the image of her riding that moron drug dealer's back like a wild woman, her dark hair plastered to her forehead and his face beet red and bulging at the eyes. A TPD car had met us at an open field maybe a mile away and we'd pulled into the industrial park to find five more units and an ambulance waiting. Five minutes later, we'd been mid-preparations when the shrill peel of a fire alarm had cut through the air and Viv had come sprinting out of the building. We'd been dicey on how we were gonna infiltrate the place without tipping anyone off to the fact we were there, but Callie had ended up saving us the trouble of figuring it out.

Not daring to let go of her hand, I wiped my face with my free one like it had some prayer of erasing the stress of the last twelve hours. "How's Viv?"

"Totally good. OB hospitalist is gonna keep her overnight for observation just to be sure, but the baby's heartbeat is solid. Right where it should be."

"And Jace?"

"Somewhere on par with an overprotective grizzly bear."

I huffed out a chuckle. "So…he's back to normal."

"Mmm hmm. Though, I wouldn't throw too many stones if I were you. You yelled at one of the paramedics when they were loadin' Callie in the ambulance and scared a few of the nurses in the ER just lookin' at 'em."

"You blame me?"

Zeke shook his head. "Nah. I don't think any of us do. But remember, her prognosis is good. Could very well be she'll just need a little therapy to get up and around after she's had time to heal."

Yeah, that *could* be what happened. But the neurosurgeon had been clear we wouldn't know if there'd been any brain damage from the bleeding until she woke up.

If she woke up.

Worse, she might have seizures to contend with even if her brain was otherwise fine and dandy, and she had a gunshot wound to her calf and a broken rib on top of it all. "You always this positive with your patients, or are you workin' on your bedside manner?"

Zeke clapped a hand on my shoulder. "Just stayin' focused on the positive and tryin' to keep you there, too. How about you stretch your legs a bit? Head down to the cafeteria and get something to eat. Ivan and Trevor are down in the ICU waiting room. I can hang here and call you if she wakes up."

"No." I braced my elbows on the mattress and cradled her tiny hand between mine. "Not gonna leave her. Don't want her wakin' up without someone she knows close by."

Zeke squeezed my shoulder a little harder and, for

a second, I thought he'd argue. Instead, he patted me again and stepped away. "Fair enough, but you do need food if you're gonna do a marathon bedside run. Let me know what you want, and I'll bring it up."

God, I was ready for the sun to come up. The fluorescent lights behind her bed made her skin tone look too damned pale. I couldn't hardly even see her freckles, and for some reason that seriously pissed me off. "Whatever's easy. Plus, coffee. A lot of coffee."

"Done. But I'll warn ya. The whole crew is headed up from Dallas. You might be able to push me off when it comes to takin' care of yourself, but I'm not thinkin' you'll be able to fight Ninette and Sylvie as easy."

Chapter Twenty-Four

Callie

Bernie's Bar & Grill.

I hadn't stepped foot in the place since I'd left Tulsa, but not one bit of it had changed. Same Budweiser and Coors neon signs behind the bar. Same dark wood barstools with the thick, green-topped padded tops. Same two pool tables with the worn felt. It even smelled the same—a weird mix of beer and cigarette smoke. Though, it seemed there was a faint hint of disinfectant behind it all. Which was weird, because I was pretty sure Bernie didn't have disinfectant behind the bar.

But what the heck was I doing here? I didn't drink anymore, and Maggie had warned me a jillion times to stay the heck away from slippery places. As old haunts went, this place was a ginormous slip and slide.

Oddly, though, the place was empty save one lone person at the far end of the bar, their back to me where I stood at the entrance.

No bartender.

No music.

Totally weird.

And what was that beeping sound? Not constant.

*Just every now and then. But the sound was strangely
out of place.*

I ambled toward the dark-haired man at the far end
of the bar. "Hey, where is everyone?"

The man spun on his stool, a Budweiser in his hand
and a smile on his face. "Heya, peach. 'Bout time you
showed up."

Holy shit.

My dad.

I had to be dreaming. And why was he calling me
peach? Dad never called me peach. Only Danny did.

"Um, hey?"

"Helluva day you've had."

I had?

Dad answered even though I hadn't spoken my question out loud. "Yeah. Don't ya remember? Took ya long
enough to pay me a visit and make your peace, but it
all worked out."

The cemetery.

I'd gone to visit Dad. To make my amends and share
the truth with Vivienne.

And then everything had gone to shit.

"Boy, that's puttin' it mildly," Dad said. "Though,
I gotta give you props, girl. You rode the back of that
motherfucker like a champ! Kind of a downer Danny
didn't get to maim the asshole like he wanted. Kind of
hard to do that with Tulsa's finest watchin' on, but I
got a feelin' the douche bag's boss will handle that for
everyone once the dust all settles."

He took a long pull from his beer, let loose an appreciative ahhh, then smiled at me. "How's your head?"

Something told me I didn't really want to dig up the

answer to that question, so I answered with one of my own. "What are you doing here?"

He shrugged and tipped his longneck toward a bar-stool near his. "What? A father can't visit his kid when he gets a chance? Have a seat."

Okay, this was seriously the most peculiar dream in the history of dreaming. But, me being me, I sat.

Dad cocked his head to one side, considering. "You know, I'm glad I got a chance to see you. I wanted to let you know...this place...it's nice."

"Bernie's?"

He frowned then looked around him like he wasn't sure what I was talking about then chuckled. "Nah, this ain't Bernie's. I'm dead. Dead people don't go to Bernie's. I think you're just seeing what you need to see. Funny how shit around here works."

I sat, oddly uncertain what to say. "So, you know you're dead?"

"Oh, yeah. And about that spiel you gave at the cemetery...you gotta let that shit go. I mean, yeah, makin' a pass at Randy wasn't your smartest idea ever, but you'd have probably never done it if I hadn't planted the idea in your head. So, if you're gonna place blame, put it with me.

"Plus, I'm a grown-ass man. Or I was." He laughed at himself, then kept going. "It was me and Randy in that fight, not you. So, there's nothin' for you to be carryin' around. Ya hear, peach?"

He'd heard me.

I kind of liked that.

No, actually I loved that.

Except—"Why do you keep calling me peach?"

"Well, that's what your man calls ya, yeah?" He

waggled his eyebrows and got a seriously ornery grin on his face. "I dig it. Suits you. And girl, that man has got a gift for a custom ride."

He picked his beer up and pointed it at me like he always did when he got fired up. "Say, you remember that custom Stingray we saw at the Tulsa Fair that one time? Bloodred? Had those wicked spoke rims and the shiny chrome piping all the way around the bottom?"

Oh, yeah. I remembered that one. "It was a '63, right? Had the cut out windows in the back and looked like something from a James Bond movie."

"Yeah, yeah! That one." *Dad raised his beer as if he'd just finalized a fine idea.* "Danny'd be able to nail that one, no doubt. You should tell him about it. You'd look sweeet behind the wheel of that baby."

I shook my head, a bittersweet sensation swirling behind my chest. "No. Cars are an art for Danny. He needs to be able to do whatever he dreams up. Not copy something someone else did. And besides, you're assuming after everything that happened with Viv, I'm ever gonna see Danny again. I mean, come on... I almost got her killed. Again."

Dad snickered at that, but there was a certainty in his expression I don't think I'd ever seen before. Like anything that had clouded his thoughts before he died had been stripped away and replaced with a wisdom I couldn't grasp. "You weren't alone. I was there with both my girls. And you're not givin' yourself enough credit, peach. You were meant for Danny. And him for you. It just took you a while to shake yourself free of all the bullshit your momma and me heaped on you and be ready to meet him. Now ya have."

Meant for Danny.

Now that he'd said it that way, it fit. Maybe not so much when I'd been using, but I'd been so full of myself I couldn't have recognized a good connection if someone had smacked me in the face with it. But after? Once I'd pulled my head out of my ass and gotten my life together? There'd never been a time I didn't feel easy in his presence.

At home.

At peace.

"Yep, exactly that," Dad said as though he'd heard my thoughts. "The kind of relationship you're buildin'—that's the kind that's true. The kind you can trust and grow a life around."

My lip quivered and my heart ached with the need to touch him. Just to hold his hand. I stood and took a step toward him, my hand outstretched. "Dad..."

He held both hands up and leaned back as though he was afraid to touch me. "No, no, Callie. You stay back. With me isn't where you're supposed to be."

I stopped and just drank him in. His bright eyes so much like mine, but free of the weight he'd always carried in life. His huge smile.

"It's good to see ya, peach. Good to see you happy and know you've got a bright and beautiful future in front of ya. So, how about you wake up, and give your poor man a break, huh?"

Happy.

I wanted to be happy.

My dad smiled at me and winked. "Love you, kiddo. Never forget that."

That annoying beep in the background piped up again for a second or two.

The space around me got a whole lot colder, and my dream world faded, replaced with a whole lot of black.

And pain.

A lot of it.

Everywhere.

Especially in my head.

Christ, had I been hit by a truck?

I tried to move, but my body was too freaking heavy. Even my eyelids seemed weighted. And what was that smell?

Oh, right. Disinfectant.

The beep sounded again. Three annoying blasts from somewhere on my right. Then everything was quiet again.

No, not entirely quiet. There were voices coming from somewhere, but they were muted. Where the heck was I?

I forced my eyelids open.

A small bed. A TV up on the ceiling with the sound muted. An IV in my arm. Danny on my other side, his forehead resting on the back of his hand, which was holding mine. Behind him, Viv was curled up on what looked like a pullout sofa bed, her head resting on her hand beneath her temple. The window behind the sofa showed a solid swath of black dotted by a few building lights.

I gotta give you props, girl. You rode the back of that motherfucker like a champ!

Oh, my God.

The drug dude.

We'd freaking lived through it! Though, from the hundred-pound anvil knocking around in my head, it hadn't been without its consequences.

Part of me wanted to go back to sleep. Just to close my eyes and settle back into that weird freaking dream I'd had. Just let go and hide from the pain.

With me isn't where you're supposed to be...you've got a bright and beautiful future in front of ya. So, how about you wake up, and give your poor man a break?

"Dad..." At least, I tried to say it. My lips didn't move all that great and barely any sound came out.

Danny. I needed to focus on Danny.

I tried to wiggle my fingers and gasped at the unpleasant jolt that shrieked its way through my muscles.

Danny's head snapped up, his eyelids as heavy as mine probably were, but the whites around his dark eyes shot with red. "Callie..."

He stood so fast the recliner he'd been sitting in slid back.

Viv startled upright. "What? What's wrong?" Her gaze settled on Danny, then me. A second later she was in motion, tossing aside the hospital blanket that had covered her and finding her feet. "Callie, you're up!"

"Hey, peach," Danny said low and quiet, leaning in. "How ya feeling?"

"Hurts," was the best I could manage.

"I'll get the nurse," Vivienne said and shot out into the hall.

I tried to swallow, hoping it would get my mouth cooperating a little better, but my tongue felt like it'd grown to the size of a football. "She's okay?"

"Oh, yeah," Danny said. "Doc says the baby is fine. Still had a great heartbeat. Only another week and they're out of the first trimester."

Thank God.

We'd really made it.

All of us.

At least I thought that was the case. Getting a closer look at Danny and seeing how fast Viv had stood up, I was starting to wonder if I'd made it out whole. "How bad?"

His smile was a tired one. "You fucked up your head pretty bad when you hit it. Zeke said it was a subdural hematoma."

My confusion must have shown on my face because he added, "Basically, means you were bleeding between your brain and your skull. The blood puts pressure on your brain the more it builds up, and your body starts shutting down. They drilled a hole in your head to drain the blood out and relieved the pressure."

Ah, well that explained the anvil.

"You got a bullet wound in your left calf, too. Went straight through, but it bled like crazy. Got a cracked rib when you took him down right after we charged in."

I wanted to laugh something awful, but the best I could manage was a slight lift of my lips and something that sounded like a gurgle.

The nurse hustled in with Viv tight on her heels. "Hey there, Miss Callie. 'Bout time you decided to wake up and say hello. My name's Beth, and I'm the RN taking care of you tonight. Can you tell me what your pain level is on a scale of one to ten?"

Was she kidding? I pulled in as deep of a breath as I dared. "Twenty." Thanks to my football for a tongue, it came out like *twunty*, but Beth seemed to speak my current language pretty well because she patted my hand and scanned the monitor beside me. "Well, all right then. Let me get the doc on the phone and we'll see about taking that down a notch or two."

She moved away from the side of my bed and pulled a tray out from under a computer I hadn't noted yet and started typing like crazy.

Viv moved into the space the nurse had vacated and gently grasped my hand.

"How long?" I croaked.

"Since you turned crazy rodeo queen?" Viv said. "That was yesterday afternoon. It's almost four in the morning on Friday."

Okay. That was more math than my brain could do.

"You've been out about a day and a half," Danny thankfully added. "I got into your phone and found Susan's and Maggie's numbers. Susan got here last night, and Maggie should be here by noon tomorrow."

"Plus, the whole family came down," Viv added. "I think they're drivin' the cafeteria staff crazy trying to feed everyone."

"Family?" I murmured.

"Yeah, Ninette and Sylvie," Danny said. "All the guys. Lizzie stayed home with Colin, Mary and Levi, but all the other wives came."

Oh, *his* family.

And Viv's.

"Worried about you…" I said. "That's nice."

Viv chuckled and leaned in enough to smooth her fingertips across my cheek. "They're not worried about me, goof. They're here for you. Not sure you realize it yet, but your family has grown a lot in the last week."

You've got a bright and beautiful future in front of ya.

My vision blurred with tears.

"Hey," Danny whispered so close I could feel his breath on my cheek. "It's okay. Everything's gonna be okay. You'll see. We just gotta give you time to heal. You'll be back on your feet in no time."

I hoped he was right.

I hoped Dad was right, too.

Because I wanted that. Wanted to finish what I'd started with getting sober. Wanted to live the life I'd always wanted.

"Okay, Miss Callie," the nurse said, returning with a syringe in her hand. She pulled the top off and went for my IV line. "We're gonna get you fixed up with some morphine. Pretty soon you'll feel a whole lot better."

Danny kissed my cheek, his voice low and gruff near my ear. "Just hang on, Callie. Hang on and we'll get through this. You and me. Together."

The powerful throb in the back of my head started to ease and with it the soft sweet comfort of darkness. Before I let it take me, I squeezed his hand as much as I could. "Not letting go. Not by a long shot."

Epilogue

Callie

"I love it!" Ninette declared from one side of me.

Positioned so her reflection was right beside mine in the mirror, Sylvie nodded her head. "It's perfect."

On my left, Vivienne had her back to the mirror and her eyes right on me. While her voice wasn't as emphatic as the other two women's, it was definitely genuine. "I think it's fabulous. Very smart and sexy."

The woman in the center of the mirror stared back at me. I mean, I knew it was me, but it was like seeing an alternate me. A me that was way more grown up and a whole lot more stylish.

I reached for the back of my head and tenderly felt for the squarish spot where my skull had been cut and put back in like a puzzle piece. Sure enough, the hairs around where everything had gone down were the same length around it as the ones on top of my square. "You can't see it?"

"Only if you're the guy cutting your hair," my new stylist chimed in. He'd given up trying to keep his position near the chair the second he'd pronounced himself done and was cleaning up the station that held all of his tools. "Maybe your man'll know. But no one else. Promise."

"Oh, my God!" Maggie's voice cut from the back of the salon where the bathrooms were located. "Did I miss it?" A few seconds later she wedged herself between Ninette and Sylvie—who, it turned out, got along famously with Maggie—and beamed down at me. "Now, that's a smart fucking haircut right there."

"Of course, it's fabulous," Nathan said with a roll of his eyes. "I did it."

I still had a hard time looking away from the new me in the mirror, but like everything else over the last four weeks, I rolled with it. "Okay then. It's got the posse stamp of approval, so I'll consider myself well and truly ready to face the real world."

"Ready to face, maybe," Ninette said, strolling to the sofa where her purse was stashed. "But that doesn't mean you're facing it yet. You've got two more weeks before you've got the green light to do more than bed rest."

My gaze cut to Vivienne who promptly mashed her lips together in a knowing grin. "I wish I could tell you these were extenuating circumstances, but the truth is, they're in everyone's business all the time." She hesitated for a second and lowered her voice. "It's great, isn't it?"

It was great.

It'd taken a week before they'd let me out of ICU and transferred me from the Tulsa hospital to one in Allen. Then another week in a normal room and two more in rehab.

But the whole Haven clan had been with me every step of the way. Bossing me. Pampering me. In gen-

eral, talking my ear off and doing their best to *ra-ra* me
through all the times I ran out of optimism. And while
I hadn't been able to prove it yet, I was pretty doggone
sure the zero balance medical invoices that kept showing up at the house had been paid by Jace.

Total. Teddy bear.

Most of the time, anyway.

"You ready for a rest, kiddo?" Maggie said. "This is
the most you've been up in a while."

I was getting tired, but there was no way I was gonna
show it. Not if it put me getting to go to dinner tonight at
Haven at risk. So, I wrinkled my nose and held out my
hand to Viv. "Nah. I'm good. Just help me up and get
me to the car. I gotta change my clothes before Danny
and I can head out."

The discreet chime that heralded another client coming through the front door sounded.

I'd barely gained my balance when Sylvie's voice
rang out. "Danny! Perfect timing! She's all ready!"

I tightened my grip on Viv and whispered, "What's
he doing here? I wanted to get my makeup on before
he saw me."

She turned to me and cocked an eyebrow. "You seriously think makeup is gonna make a difference?"

"Honey," Maggie said, moving in to stand between
me and my guy. "He's spent more time in the hospital
than half the people who work there. You could have a
unicorn horn comin' out of your head, and it wouldn't
make a bit of difference."

She was right.

I knew she was.

But I was also tired of him having to look at me all

bedraggled and bedheaded and had hoped to make it a nice surprise.

Danny moved in close enough Maggie couldn't hide my new hairdo anymore. He smiled big enough to show a whole lot of teeth and an appreciation that said he was thinking about how to get his hands in my new do. "Damn, peach. I didn't think you could get any sexier."

"You were supposed to meet me at home." Home now being with Danny—a pronouncement he'd made about a half hour after they'd gotten me situated in my new room at the Allen hospital. "I was gonna get all gussied up first."

He scanned me toes to nose, slow and steady. "Sweetheart, you're already gussied up in my book. Now, we're gonna get you home so you can rest. I don't want Zeke ridin' my ass about you doin' too much your first full day home."

Oye. Zeke was a handful. Smart as hell as a medical professional went, but good freakin' grief, he was a taskmaster.

It'd paid off, though. The rehab therapist I'd worked with the last two weeks said, considering how much I'd been through and my drinking history on top of it, my level of recovery had been nothing short of a miracle. Of course, it hadn't hurt that Zeke had had a good hunch about what was up with my head and had had paramedics on standby when they'd charged the place. The neurosurgeon had said another thirty minutes or so and I probably wouldn't have been so lucky.

"Come on, peach." Danny pretty much took over on Maggie's side of the balance equation and scooped me up in his arms.

"What are you doing?" I said, squeezing my arms around his neck. "I need to practice walking."

"You walked all the way in here," he said, totally ignoring everyone else and heading toward the door. "That's enough for today."

Behind us, Ninette was paying Nathan a huge chunk of cash while the rest of the salon looked on, a mix of *oohs*, *ahhs*, and dropped jaws on everyone's faces. In front of us, Sylvie pulled the door wide. "Take it slow to the Escalade, and I'll get the door for you there, too."

"Nope." Danny turned left outside the door and headed to his Chevelle. "Takin' her home in my ride. You guys are gonna go home and give us a little time to unwind."

"Mmm hmm." Ninette's drawl followed behind us. "Not thinkin' what you have in mind is allowed under doctor's orders."

"Oh, leave 'em alone, Ninnie," Sylvie said. "They've barely had a hot minute since she got home yesterday. Maggie, Viv—pile in the truck. We got a whole lot of prep before dinner. We can fawn over Callie with everyone else later."

I was cradled against the soft black leather of Danny's passenger seat less than a minute later and the two of us rumbling toward home in no more than two.

"I take it Sylvie is the one who called you?" I said.

Danny glanced at me and grinned. "You kiddin' me? I had her in my camp before you even went to sleep last night. I know those women too damned well to think they wouldn't start scheming and taking over the first free minute they got. So, I called her after I tucked you in and asked for a solid."

That was sweet.

But then again, he'd been a lot of sweet over the last four weeks.

So had the guys at the shop.

And all the brothers and their wives.

"Yeah, but someone had to have tipped you off."

He smiled at the road. "You think I'm gonna share my inside connection?"

It was Jace. I knew it, and Danny knew I knew it. Outside of Danny and Viv, Jace had been the most protective of all of them. A fact that still made me choke up when I dared to think about it.

"So, you really like it?"

He faced me long enough to give me one of those wickedly smoldering looks I loved. "Oh, hell yeah. Smart and sexy as fuck. Kind of lookin' forward to gettin' my hands in it, if you wanna know the truth."

I *knew* it.

Of course, that meant I was gonna have to try my hand at styling my new pixie before dinner. If it went south, I could always snag a ball cap and call it good.

Danny pulled me from my thoughts. "You know what? Now that I think on it, it's really gonna look hot with the new thing I got you to wear."

I snapped my head his direction, an ill-thought-out action that made the world spin a little more than I preferred. "You bought me something to wear?"

He nodded and draped his wrist over the steering wheel. "In a manner of speaking."

Okay.

Something was definitely up.

I mean, first the girls showed with their grand idea for a haircut.

Then Danny showed when he was supposed to leave the navigating to them.

"What are you up to?"

"Me?" He glanced at me, all schoolboy innocence. "I'm not up to anything. Just got you something I thought would look nice on you, that's all."

"Dude, you're not a shopper. Hell, *I'm* not a shopper."

"Who said I went shopping?" One look at the scowl on my face and he started laughing. "Oh, relax, would ya? Go along for the ride and just enjoy the surprise."

He was right.

I was too uptight. Too wound up and trying to control things. But in my defense, I'd had enough of not being in control of things in the last month to last me a lifetime.

"Okay, fine. I'll roll with it. Just wait to mess my hair up until after dinner. I'm not one hundred percent sure I can get it back to looking like this before everyone sees it."

"Deal. No hands-on until after dinner."

With that, he turned the radio up and drove us the rest of the way home, the latest from Greta Van Fleet filling the Chevelle's interior.

I closed my eyes and just let go. Enjoying the moment. Enjoying the cool air drifting from the AC vents against my cheeks and the rumble of the motor in my ears.

Twice now, I'd come close to death. The first the day I'd nose-dived out of that window, and the second the day I'd whacked my head getting kidnapped with Vivienne. The first had brought me to my bottom. The second had earned me peace with my past and a solid appreciation for today and my future.

The kind of relationship you're buildin'—that's the

kind that's true. The kind you can trust and grow a life around.

My "dream" of Dad hadn't faded one bit. Truth be told, I thought about it a lot. Had even written it down so I wouldn't be able to forget it as time passed. I'd thought about sharing with Vivienne. Maybe I still would. But for now, I was keeping it close. Appreciating it for what I suspected it was.

A gift.

A divine one.

I still wasn't sure I deserved it, but I thanked God every day when I woke up that He'd given it to me. That He'd given me the time with Dad, Danny, my sister, my sponsor and yes—my new, boisterous, meddlesome family.

I loved it. Every second of it.

"Hey," Danny said, turning down the radio. "You asleep? We're almost home."

I opened my eyes and looked out the passenger window. "Nah. Just thinking."

It hit me then that he'd come in the circular subdivision a different direction than he normally did, the change in route putting my side of the car in better view of the house. About a nanosecond after that realization, my eyes locked on to a killer red Vette parked right in the middle of the drive. "I think we've got company?"

"We do?" He straightened and frowned out my window. "What makes you say that?"

"Because we don't know anybody with a Vette like that."

"Oh, that..." He pulled in behind it and put the Chevelle in park. "Nah, that's not company." He twisted

enough to look at me. "I told ya I bought you something to wear."

No. Freaking. Way.

"Danny! You can't wear a car."

He laughed at that. "Peach, I promise—you get in
that car you will most definitely be wearing it." He
opened the door and put a leg out. "Hold up, and I'll
come get ya."

Honest to God, I couldn't move. Couldn't peel my
eyes off the beautiful machine right in front of me.

And then it hit me.

*Say, you remember that custom Stingray we saw at
the Tulsa Fair one time? Bloodred? Had those wicked
spoke rims and the shiny chrome piping all the way
around the bottom? You'd look sweeet behind the wheel
of that baby.*

"Dad..." I said to no one.

A second later, my door opened, and Danny gently
lifted me out. By the time he put me on my feet off to
one side of the car for a better view, tears were streaming down my face.

"Callie..." He stepped between me and the car and
wiped the tears away with his thumbs. "What's wrong?
I thought you'd love it."

"I do." The tears kept coming, even though I was
smiling. "I just...where'd you come up with an idea
like that?"

Danny's smile was so big and so bright I felt it warm
and huge in my chest. "You're gonna laugh and say I'm
crazy, but shit you not, I dreamed about it. Every freaking detail. As soon as I woke up, I sketched it out." He
moved to the side and wrapped his arm around my
waist. "I was with you at the hospital most of the time,

so the guys did the majority of the work. But it was Jace that found the stock model. Jumped all over tracking it down as soon as I showed him the designs."

I inched forward, carefully placing each step one at a time so I wouldn't lose my balance. Zeke and all my other docs had assured me that, over time, I'd get better. Stronger and more stable. But for now, I wasn't pushing it.

As soon as I got close enough to brace a hand on the side, Danny opened the driver's door. "Here, let me help ya get inside. The leather is wicked soft."

It *was* soft.

Soft and—aside from some modern technology they hadn't had all those years ago at the fair—it was a dead replica of the one I'd seen with Dad.

Amazing.

Miraculous, really.

Kind of like my life over the last fifteen months.

Through my tears, something sparkly caught my attention—a ring dangling from the rearview mirror on a silver chain. I sniffled and dashed my tears away with the back of my hand. "What's this?"

Danny crouched next to me. "What's what?"

I cradled the ring in my palm. It was gorgeous. A single, but pretty damned big round solitaire surrounded by lots of little ones on what I'd guess was white gold. The band was interwoven like a braid. "This…" I looked to him. "What is it?"

The smile on his face softened, and his hand covered my free one resting on my thigh. "I told ya I got ya something to wear. I mean—you totally own the Vette, but I liked the idea of you wearin' something I gave you all the time. Somethin' that would let people know you were with me all the time."

Holy.

Freaking.

Shit.

"Danny…" It was a whisper. Barely more than I'd managed when I'd woken up in ICU.

"Marry me, peach. Wear my ring, and be my wife. It'll be me and you. A solid team. Always."

You've got a bright and beautiful future in front of ya.

Dad had been right.

I did have a beautiful future in front of me. A life free of all the old shit and awful beliefs I'd grown up with. A life with a man I could trust. A man who fit me. Him for me, and me for him.

I released the ring and covered our joined hands with my free one and squeezed. I'd hung on this long. No way in hell I was letting go now. "Hell, yeah, I'll marry you. We'll make a hell of a team. Me and you. Always."

* * * * *

Author Note

Obviously, alcoholism and drug addiction play a key role in Callie and Danny's story. While the actual events and people are purely fiction, I have personally been impacted by alcoholism and addiction from the day I was born. The struggles and perspective I've represented in the story are founded on my own experience.

What's important to remember is that, despite the fact that alcoholism and addiction are family diseases, no two stories are the same. If you've been impacted by family or friends who struggle with addiction, your story may look and feel completely different. And that's okay! The key takeaway I hope everyone will find in this story is that there *is* help. And hope. Miracles (and serenity) are possible, and I guarantee you that there are people out there whose stories *will* resonate with yours. All it takes is the first step.

I promise you, you're not alone.

Acknowledgments

Getting this book across the finish line was tough! It seemed like every time I managed to get my fingers on the keyboard the universe sent me yet another reason to set my laptop aside and deal with something else.

But the usual suspects (Kerri Buckley, Cori Deyoe, and Juliette Cross) somehow always stepped in and finessed my brain back to the right place so I could get back to work and *finally* get Danny and Callie's story done.

The biggest heroes, though, are my family—my beloved husband, Joe, and my amazing daughters, Addison and Abegayle. No matter how low I got, or how certain I was that I should scrap every single word and start over, they always picked me up and reminded me why I started this writing thing in the first place. I love you all so very much. Thank you for always having my back and believing in me even when I didn't believe in myself.

About the Author

Rhenna Morgan is a happily-ever-after addict—hot men, smart women and scorching chemistry required. A triple-A personality with a thing for lists, Rhenna's a mom to two beautiful daughters who constantly keep her dancing, laughing and simply happy to be alive.

When she's not neck-deep in writing, she's probably driving with the windows down and the music up loud, plotting her next hero and heroine's adventure. (Though trolling online for man-candy inspiration on Pinterest comes in a close second.)

She'd love to share her antics and bizarre sense of humor with you and get to know you a little better in the process. You can sign up for her newsletter and gain access to exclusive snippets, upcoming releases, fun giveaways, and social media outlets at www.rhennamorgan.com.

His world. His rules. Her love.

Though his methods may be rough, when it comes to protecting what's his, Russian vor Sergei Petrovyh's heart is always in the right place. That's never been more true than when the gorgeous Evette Labadie asks him for a job. He knows enough to keep his hands off someone as beloved by the locals as Evie, but there's something about her that calls to him—no matter how badly he burns to make her his.

Keep reading for an excerpt from His to Defend, *book one of NOLA Knights, the heart-stoppingly sexy spinoff series by Men of Haven author Rhenna Morgan*

Chapter One

$480.

Evette pinched the business-size check from her former employer a little tighter and glared at the cleaning company's logo in the top corner. On any other Friday, the money would have meant inching closer to some semblance of security for her and her son, Emerson. A step toward unraveling the mess she'd created for her life. Today, the unexpected termination that had come with her weekly pay felt more like a sucker punch to the gut. Yet another obstacle to overcome after too many damned years running the gauntlet and never even glimpsing the finish line.

Maybe she could get a job cleaning at one of the hotels. God knew the French Quarter was packed with them, and she was pretty sure she could count on regular shift work, like the office cleaning crew she'd been on. Though, how she was going to land one by Monday when it was already close to 4:30 on a Friday afternoon was beyond her. And landing something quick was the only way this latest setback wouldn't force her into dipping into Emerson's school fund. Plus, there was the hurdle of what would happen if they called her old company for references and found out she'd been fired for a security breach.

Not. Good.

The commuter bus swung onto Tulane headed toward Mid-City, and Evie's spirits sunk a little lower. If someone had told her when she was growing up that she'd be a single mom living in one of New Orleans's rougher parts of town at twenty-eight years old, she'd have laughed in their face. She was going to be a fashion retail buyer—or at least have some kind of career in fashion. She was going to travel the world. See things. Know people. Adventure her way through life and suck it dry.

Then her mom had died, and she'd gone off the rails.

She sighed and slunk a little farther down onto the hard plastic bench, the run-down stores, bars and restaurants along the roadside passing in a blur while the vibrations from the bus's engine rattled clear to her bones.

Get knocked down seven times, stand up eight.

If she had a dollar for all the times her momma had said it and all the times Evie had echoed it in the last eight years, she'd be driving a Porsche toward the Garden District right now instead of heading to a barely livable apartment.

But her momma had made it.

Mostly.

Raised Evette through her tumultuous preteen years after her daddy's death and made it look easy. It hadn't been until a year after Emerson had been born and Evie had found the courage to read some of her mother's journals that she'd realized just how much of a challenge her mother had really faced. How much she'd given up and how alone she'd felt through every second.

Evie understood it now. Knew to her very marrow the sacrifices that had been made on her behalf.

And she'd thrown it all away nursing her grief.

Resolve and a whole lot of stubbornness revved her energy and forced her taller in her seat. Pity was what had gotten her into this mess to begin with, and she'd be damned if she went that route again. Labadie women didn't quit. Didn't give up. They faced whatever they needed to face, and they smiled doing it. Eventually, she was going to find a way to give her and Emerson the world. She just might have to scrimp a little longer and get more creative to make it happen.

The bus's brakes whined, and the older lady seated next to Evie leaned into her.

Evie braced herself enough to keep them both upright and smiled down at her fellow passenger. "You gettin' off here, Miss Arnold? You know Dorothy's Friday specials are always the best ones of the week."

Miss Arnold beamed a smile at Evie and hugged her grocery bag a little tighter to her chest. Her blue eyes might have turned murky in the last few years and the wrinkles lining her pale skin etched a little deeper, but her kind heart was still as strong as ever. "No, no, Evette. Trips to the grocery aren't as easy as they used to be. Better I get my tired bones on to the home before the sun goes down."

A smart move. Especially in this part of town, because a woman like Miss Arnold after dark was a mugging waiting to happen.

Once certain the older woman had her balance again, Evie stood, shouldered her purse and took another stab at the same argument she'd been having with the neighborhood woman for the past year. "Seems to me, you could use that fancy shuttle van all the other residents use for your errands and not have half the hassle."

Miss Arnold lifted her chin a little higher, the epitome of a Southern woman with an iron core. "Seein' to myself is a privilege. Gonna take advantage of it as long as the good Lord'll let me." She dipped her head toward the door at the front of the bus. "Best get yourself to Dorothy's and that handsome boy of yours."

Damn. Shut down again. "All right, but don't think we're not gonna talk about this next time."

"Lookin' forward to it, beautiful girl."

Evie shook her head and headed to the door.

"Evette." Miss Arnold's sharp voice halted her just before she took the first step down. She waited until Evie met her steady stare before she spoke again. "Gonna be all right. Whatever it is…it's not gonna beat you. You just keep on remembering that."

A tightness noosed around Evette's throat, and tears tingled along the bridge of her nose. Maybe she *wouldn't* have another chance to talk Miss Arnold out of taking the bus to the grocery store. Not unless her next job took her to the same part of town she'd been working in. She clenched the handrail beside the steep steps and forced a smile she didn't feel. "Don't you worry, Miss Arnold. Gonna take more than a kick or two to keep me down."

The older woman nodded as if she'd expected such an answer, then went back to staring out the window opposite her seat. "Good girl. Now get on to that boy of yours and tell Dorothy I said hello."

Outside, the temperature still hovered near eighty-five degrees. Not exactly an unbearable number at the tail end of September, but the humidity from the gulf and the subtle stench that last night's rains had stirred from the Quarter didn't exactly make for an ideal stroll on the streets either. She hurried past a cheesy souvenir shop, a convenience store and a pub—the latter leaving the faint scent of cigarette smoke on the sidewalk despite the front door doing its best to trap the conditioned air inside. At the end of the block, Dorothy's Diner sat like a neighborhood beacon. The entrance was right at the corner, two long walls of windows stretching for a good twelve feet on either side so those moseying past could get an easy view of the crowd inside.

And there was always a crowd at Dorothy's. As diners went, it was an institution. A safe haven in the middle of hell and a slice of soul food heaven all rolled into one. Per usual, Emerson was at the soda-shop-style counter perched on the barstool closest to the front door, his shoulders slightly hunched forward and his forearms around his plate like a linebacker braced to protect his food. His dirty blond hair was a nod to her daddy's side of the family and was a tad too long and tousled like any other seven-year-old boy's probably was at the end of the school day, but his expression was far too empty. His hazel eyes too void of emotion for someone so young.

She forced another bogus smile and shoved the glass door open. The bell overhead gave a cheerful jingle, and two or three of the waitresses on the floor called out a greeting.

Evie gave them all a polite wave, but went straight to her kid and added a little extra mess to his hair with a playful ruffle. "Hey, champ. How was school?"

For the briefest of seconds, her little boy stared back at her. Not much more than a hint of a smile, but enough to let her know the kid who had curled so innocently in her lap a few years ago was still in there somewhere. The openness was gone again in a blink, the sullen scowl she'd grown to hate aimed back at a plateful of turkey and dressing. He shrugged and stabbed a bite of turkey. "Just a day."

"Yeah, but it's a *Friday* and everyone knows Fridays are always better by default." She slid onto the barstool next to Emerson and let her purse drop to the raised step beneath her feet. "Anything big go down at recess?"

Emerson shook his head.

"Any surprise tests?"

Another shake.

"Meet any cute girls?"

To that, he simply lifted his head and looked at her like he was torn between walking home without her and suggesting she have her head examined.

"Well, at least that got your attention," she said. "You know, when I was your age, my momma couldn't get me to shut up."

Emerson pushed a green bean that had strayed too close to his dressing back to the exiled portion of his plate. "No point in talking if there's nothing going on."

"Hmm." She crossed her arms and pretended to check out the rest of the diner's patrons while her brain scrambled for any clue on how to engage with her son. He might be only seven, but he talked with more sophistication than most adults. Barely any slang. No Creole mannerisms and definitely no profanity. More like a gentleman stuck in a child's body. So, why she thought some shocking revelation on how to talk to him at his level was gonna plow its way to the forefront of her thoughts right this second after over a year of searching was beyond her. "Well, if you're not gonna talk to me, maybe Miss Dorothy will. You seen her?"

Emerson politely wiped his mouth with his napkin and dipped his head toward the kitchen. "She disappeared in there right before you came in. Table seven didn't like their special."

Evie glanced at the turkey and dressing on Emerson's plate. "Someone's complaining about the cooking? Are they high?"

Miracle of miracles, Emerson's mouth twitched with a smile that didn't quite break free. "Not everyone has good taste, Mom."

"True dat," she fired back, wishing with everything in her she could get her kid to let go and be a kid again. She swiveled toward the kitchen and waved her hand at her bag. "Watch that for me. Don't want our payday finding legs and running off without us."

"Yes, ma'am."

Yes, ma'am.

Evie meandered toward the kitchen, her son's perfect reply echoing in her head. If she'd been that proper growing up, her momma would have celebrated with street parties and however many charitable contributions for the offering plate their bank account would allow. Instead, she'd been sassy. Never disrespectful, of course. That would have earned her a butt whoopin' or boxed ears. But an *okie dokie pokey* or a *you betcha* was way more common than a proper *Yes, ma'am*.

The scrape of metal chair legs against the black-and-white industrial tile shot through the diner.

Evie paused at the end of the counter and turned toward the sound.

Backing away from the popular round booth in the

back corner was a slightly balding fortyish-looking man with a short-sleeve checked button-down barely covering his paunch. His black pants were a tad too short in the length, but they were clean and well-pressed. He clenched some papers in his hand and executed a semi-bow that could have been interpreted as fear or extreme respect. Maybe a little of both.

One glance at who was sitting in the booth and the tense gesture made sense.

Sergei Petrovyh.

She'd missed seeing him on the way in. Which said a lot about how distracted the new twist in her life had left her because just thinking his name made her flush. Actually looking at him made her and three-quarters of the female population too tongue-tied to talk. The other quarter mostly threw themselves at him and prayed to any god who would listen for a chance to hear that deep Russian accent of his up close and personal. Preferably in a situation where no clothes were involved.

Rather than butt into Dorothy's rant with the chef in the kitchen, Evie waited near the register and straightened a stack of menus.

The balding man said something to Sergei, took two more steps backward, then turned and quick-stepped it toward the front door.

Her gaze drifted back to Sergei, though she covered her leisurely perusal by thumbing through an order pad near the register. Dark wavy hair to his shoulders, sharp facial features, one of those sexy-as-hell tightly cropped beards and a deliciously tall and fit body to go with it.

But it wasn't just his looks that left women wanting. It was his power. A charisma burning behind his dark blue eyes and a graceful yet predatory edge behind every movement. In short, Sergei Petrovyh was the kind of man who could make any female forget her problems for at least a few precious moments with a single look.

Actually, if she was honest, Sergei could eradicate her problems completely. It was what he'd done for a long list of people in her neighborhood since he'd moved to New Orleans a little over a year ago—traded fixing untenable situations in exchange for obligations owed.

More to the point…he was a mobster.

A damned good-looking one, for sure, but a seriously dangerous man all the same.

Footsteps and muffled grumbling registered a few seconds before Dorothy's droll voice cut through Evie's ogling. "Girl, I've seen star-struck groupies act less obvious than you right now."

Evie crushed the urge to flinch like a guilty schoolgirl and gave Sergei another thorough once-over just to prove to both of them she could. Seriously, the man was like a Greek god. Maybe it was all that olive skin. Or the fact that he moved like a panther. The custom-tailored suits he wore definitely made the fashion lover in her want to stretch out and purr.

So, yeah. She was old enough to ogle all she wanted and wasn't about to apologize to anyone for doing it. Especially not after the day she'd had. "Nothing wrong with looking." She faced her momma's lifelong friend, leaned a hip onto the counter and braced one hand on the other. "And lookin' at him is a damn sight better than tryin' to figure out how I'm gonna pull off a major miracle between now and Monday."

Dorothy tucked her order pad inside the pocket of her white apron. Her daddy had named her after Dorothy Dandridge purely because he'd had a crush on the actress when Dorothy had been born, but she'd grown into a woman as beautiful as her namesake. At sixty-eight years old, her skin was wrinkled and her hair a soft gray, but her near-black eyes were still sharp as ever. She eyeballed Evie the way only a mother could. "What kind of miracle are we talking about?"

"The kind where I find a job."

"I thought you were goin' for a supervisor position with the cleaning gig. What happened?"

Evie threw up her hands, then crossed her arms across her chest. "Damned if I know. Something about a security breach and my badge being used to access an attorney's office after hours last weekend. Which is complete crap. Aside from me and Emerson going to the Farmers Market and the church potluck last Saturday, me and my badge were home all weekend. It had to be a mix-up."

"You tell 'em that?"

"'Course I did. But they weren't listening. Said they didn't have a choice but to let me go with their security policy."

Dorothy frowned and ambled behind Evie to the back countertop and the tub of clean silverware waiting to be rolled into napkins. She laid out the first napkin and got to work. "Not sure how that constitutes an emergency. I know you, Evie. You're always bracin' for a storm. Don't tell me you don't have savings."

"All of that's going to Emerson's tuition."

"I thought he was on a wait list. No point in scrimping now if you need it and have time to build it back."

"He's not on a wait list anymore." Evie moved in beside her. She'd been rolling napkins at Dorothy's place for as long as she could remember and had worked through countless crises with the simple task. "The dean called this week and said one of the kids is moving. I can apply for a scholarship, but I have to pony up the tuition to hold the spot while they process it."

"How much is it?"

"$900."

Dorothy's head snapped her direction and her voice rose enough a good amount of the diner's chatter ceased. "$900? Are you insane?"

"Dorothy!" she whisper-scolded with a pointed look in Emerson's direction. "Emerson needs this. All his teachers say he needs this place. Say he's bored to tears in public schools and that a Montessori school is perfect for a kid like him."

"Pshht." Dorothy shook her head. "That much money just to hold a spot, that school better pave him a gold path to heaven and wipe his ass, too." She paused long enough to let a comfortable silence stretch between them, then aimed a sideways look at Evie. "So? What you gonna do?"

"Well, I was hopin' maybe you could let me work for you a little while I look for something else."

Dorothy sighed. A genuine one that said she didn't like sharing the words that came next any more than Evie wanted to hear them. "Can't do that, baby girl. These ladies I got now are quality and if I scrimp on their schedules, they'll go find someplace else to work. Best I can do is give you a call if one of 'em calls in sick, but that ain't gonna happen. They need the money too bad."

Well, shoot.

So much for Plan B.

She placed a perfectly rolled set on top of Dorothy's

growing pile, turned, leaned her butt against the counter and crossed her arms on her chest. "This is such absolute crap." Fear tried to push its way up from her chest, fueled by a healthy dose of long-ignored desperation and frustration. "I can't blow this chance for Emerson. He needs it. He needs…" To smile. To play. To be able to be a kid and just enjoy himself a little while. "He needs *something*. If this school is gonna give it to him, then I'll take up workin' the streets if I have to."

"Not gonna come to that," Dorothy said with all the quiet confidence of a woman who'd already forged her way through raising her own kids. "Lord's gonna give you what you need when you need it. He always does."

"Hmmph." Evie chewed on the inside of her lip to keep from saying what she really wanted to. Namely, that if the Lord was gonna give her what she needed, it'd sure be nice if he'd tell her how he planned to do that sooner rather than later.

Like a magnet, her gaze shifted back to Sergei. The two men she often saw him with at the diner and around town now sat flanked on either end of the round booth. Kir Vasilek was big and intimidating like Sergei, but had beautiful blue eyes and blond hair. He used both to his advantage and had created a heck of a reputation in Mid-City as a supreme playboy. Roman Kozlov, on the other hand, rarely interacted with anyone. Probably because his big, imposing body, menacing features and hard facial structure made people think he was the devil incarnate.

Sergei could eradicate her problems completely.

The thought was a little subtler this time. A murmur uttered with the silken voice of temptation. "What about him?" she said to Dorothy under her breath.

Dorothy twisted and studied Evie's face, then followed her gaze to Sergei. After years keeping a diner open in a rough part of town through every kind of hard time imaginable, not much drew her old friend up short, but in that second, Dorothy showed genuine concern. She covered it almost as quickly as it had come up and went back to her silverware. "Don't think you need protection, doll. I think you need a *job*."

"Well, maybe he knows someone. Could give me a lead or a reference. One look at those clothes he wears and that slick BMW outside, you know he's loaded. That means he's gotta know other rich people."

"He might know 'em. Might even give you a leg up with 'em, but in case you missed it—a man like him does you a favor, you'll end up owing for what you get."

"You did it."

It was a childish response. Something more appropriate for when she'd been sixteen and arguing with her mom and Dorothy about what a girl should and shouldn't wear. Not when she was twenty-eight and figuring out how to pay her bills.

But if Dorothy felt the slight, she didn't show it. Just kept right on rolling. "Lesser of two evils, child. I had thugs taking over my diner. Sergei took care of that and in exchange I give him a place to do business. A small price to pay to keep my place safe, but don't let that handsome face fool you. He's got dark in him. A lot of it. And he's not afraid to let it out." She paused a moment, the look on her face that of a woman searching for the right words to share next. She finally paused and faced Evie, lowering her voice. "Right now, you've got money troubles. You bring him into your life, you'll solve one problem, but might end up with an even bigger one."

"Out of the frying pan into the fryer, huh?"

Her eyes softened, a whole wealth of wisdom Evie couldn't begin to comprehend staring back at her. "Something like that."

Evette sighed and chewed the inside of her lip. The only other option she could think of would have made her momma roll over in her grave, but she threw it out there anyway. "I guess I could ask Uncle Carl for some cash. He was wavin' a big wad of it around here the other day. He's crazy as the day is long, but he's always offering to help me and Emerson."

"No." Dorothy's retort was so hard and fast, Evette felt it like a jolt. While she softened her tone almost as quickly, her hands shook when she picked back up with the napkins. "Your momma had reasons why she kept her distance from Carl. It's best you do the same."

It wasn't the first time Dorothy had expressed her dislike for Carl. *Why* she and her mother didn't like him had never been something they'd been willing to share, but considering Evette didn't like being around him either, she'd never pushed it.

Evette braced her hands on the counter behind her and stared at Sergei.

Sergei turned and caught her gaze.

Trapped it.

Owned the connection so completely Evie would have sworn he'd overhead her entire conversation.

Which was absolute bull-hockey. He couldn't have. He was just an intimidating man with a good sense of intuition.

But he could help her.

Way faster than anyone else in this neighborhood.

She shifted her attention to Emerson, now done with his dinner and staring out the window to the street beyond. "Any chance I can talk you into a hot fudge sundae for Emerson?"

"Any chance I can talk you out of what you're thinkin' about doing?"

"Not unless you can tell me how to get a job by Monday and where I can find another $500 in time to hold that spot for Emerson."

Dorothy kept her silence.

"Come on, Dorothy. You said yourself he's not a complete bad guy. Heck, I remember you actually mentioned you liked him once. You've never even said you liked Father Manny and everyone likes him."

"Yeah, but I *love* you. Same as I loved your mama. You mark my words, you tangle with Sergei Petrovyh, there's no telling what you'll be in for."

"Well, if it makes my boy smile for once, I'm thinking it'd be worth it."

Dorothy shook her head, picked the heavy tub up like it weighed nothing and slid it under the counter. She faced Evie, studied her for long seconds, then nodded and headed for the kitchen. "I'll make two sundaes. Have a feelin' that boy's not the only one who's gonna need a pick-me-up before this day is through."

Don't miss His to Defend *by Rhenna Morgan.*
Available now from Carina Press.
www.CarinaPress.com